THE

THE HAPPY VALLEY

Christopher Nicole

THE SHERIDAN
BOOK COMPANY

This edition published in 1994 by
The Sheridan Book Company

First published by Century Hutchinson Ltd 1989
Random House, 20 Vauxhall Bridge Road, London SW1V 2SA
Legend edition 1991

This is a novel. Except where they can be identified historically, the characters and events are invented, and are not intended to portray real characters or events.

Printed and bound in Great Britain by
Cox & Wyman Ltd, Reading, Berkshire

ISBN 1–85501–657–5

It is, after all, their country.

WINSTON CHURCHILL

CONTENTS

1
MEN AT WAR

1

"If you look through the binoculars, Mr Barclay," Captain Bulwer invited, "you will see Mombasa."

The young man took the glasses and held them to his eyes, leaning against the bridge rail as he did so; although the sea was calm, as indeed it had been ever since they left Aden, the old steamer was inclined to vibrate. He stared to the west. Africa had been a looming shadow on the horizon for some days; now he could make out the lump of the island, a splash of lightness against the dark of the trees on the mainland.

"What does it feel like to be going home?" Bulwer asked.

John Barclay grinned. "I'm still a long way from home, Captain Bulwer."

"Masai land," the captain mused. "Is it as beautiful as they say?"

"Every bit as beautiful," John Barclay agreed. "But it's hardly Masai land any longer, I suppose."

"Of course, they were forced into a reservation after that trouble back in 1906. Were you here then?"

John nodded. "I was ten."

The captain gave him a sidelong glance, as if finding it difficult to believe that this tall, strapping young man could ever have been ten years old. But then, it was no less difficult to accept that in this spring of 1914 he was still only eighteen. "Your dad was mixed up in that, wasn't he?" Bulwer asked.

John Barclay nodded again. "Yes," he said.

But it was clearly not a subject he wished to discuss, the captain realized. "Well," he said. "We'll be in port by this evening."

"That's great," John said. "Thanks for letting me know."

He slid down the ladder to the promenade deck, wondering if the captain had any idea of the true reason for his lack of excitement. Revealed excitement, at any rate. Of course, going home was a thrill – if only he knew for sure what sort of a reception he was going home to. He could thank heavens for Catherine's letter of explanation, tucked away in his wallet – not to mention the funds with which she had supplied him. Even if he knew Ma and Pa did not really approve of Catherine, she was their daughter, and she was thirty-three years old – fifteen years his senior owing to the peculiar circumstances of his parents' lives; sometimes, indeed, he found it difficult to accept that she could be his sister. She was also Lady Portington, and her support would carry some weight. He pushed his lank fair hair from his eyes as he looked down at the white-streaked blue racing away from the ship's side; at least he was returning to face the music.

"Mr Barclay!" Frau Huttingen's voice was guttural but none the less warm. She and her daughter – newcomers to Africa – had found the English boy a most pleasant and informative companion throughout the voyage. "The steward tells me that we should be reaching Mombasa today."

"This evening, Mrs Huttingen," John said, and turned to smile at her and then at Adelheid. He had spent the last five years at an English public school, so girls had played no great part in his life – despite his sister's introductions during the holidays - but he was certainly able to appreciate a pretty face, and Adelheid Huttingen had more than that. Her face, in fact, with clearly delineated jaw and chin, big mouth and straight nose, wide blue eyes and high forehead, the whole framed in waving brown hair which went down to her shoulders, was strongly handsome rather than pretty. It was a face which, as a glance at her mother indicated, would remain attractive throughout her life; the only immediately noticeable differences between them were the pompadour worn by Frau Huttingen, and her somewhat fuller figure. Both ladies were dressed in the skirts and blouses and neat little ties regarded as correct female attire in the tropics – no doubt over the red woollen underwear also prescribed for white women in hot climates. Early as

12

the morning still was, they looked somewhat warm, but excited at the prospect of making land.

"Will we be able to go ashore, do you think?" Adelheid asked. Her English was better than her mother's, and less strongly accented.

"I'm sure the ship will be lying there for at least twenty-four hours," John said. "I should be delighted to show you the sights of Mombasa, such as they are." He wondered, not for the first time on the voyage, how old she was. It was not a question he could ask, and she had never let it slip during their many conversations since leaving Marseilles. She did not look any older than himself, and if her figure, however slim, was already clearly that of a woman, he imagined that might be because German girls were naturally more buxom than their English counterparts. He hoped she was no older. And then wondered why; after tomorrow he would never see her again, as she and her mother were not stopping in Mombasa, but continuing to join Herr Huttingen in German East Africa, away to the south.

"We accept with pleasure," Frau Huttingen said. "I do not suppose you have ever been to Dar es Salaam?"

"I'm afraid not," John admitted. "I have an idea that it is a much bigger place than Mombasa."

"It is German," Frau Huttingen observed. There was not so much pride in her voice as a simple acceptance that her countrymen thought in large terms.

"And how long will it take you to reach your home from Mombasa, Mr Barclay?" Adelheid asked.

"Not long, nowadays," John told her. "There's a train service, you see."

"Oh, how I wish I could see the high country one day," she said.

And how I wish I could show it to you, he suddenly thought, taking himself by surprise. It was slowly penetrating his mind, now that Mombasa was actually in sight, that he really had no idea what he was going to do with his life. Until now, his whole objective had been to get home, but now that he was actually here.... He knew his father wanted

13

him to inherit the farm and, indeed, take over the running of it within a few years – but after Oxford, when he would have returned home a grown man. What *was* Father going to make of an eighteen-year-old who had been expelled from his school? he wondered.

Thus, to appear with Adelheid Huttingen in tow might make them realize he was actually a man. What a heady thought, even if he had no real idea what having a girl like Adelheid in tow could possibly be like – apart from most enjoyable. But Father did not care for Germans. His best friend, and brother-in-law, had been a German – and he had abandoned Aunt Amanda to a terrible death during the troubles of 1906. Father would never be able to forget that. John did not suppose he would be allowed to forget it either.

He excused himself from the ladies and went to his cabin to pack, but was back on the bridge after lunch to watch Captain Bulwer conning his ship through the reef, the local pilot, who had come out on a steam launch, at his side. Now it was possible to smell the island, the strange mixture of stale swamp and fresh forest odours, the overlay of curries – for since the building of the railway some twenty years earlier, the erstwhile coolies, who were mainly Indian, had virtually made Mombasa their own.

He could see the massive walls of Fort Jesus, built on Mvita Island by the Portuguese more than two centuries before. Behind it, on Mombasa Island itself, he could make out the close-packed houses, a mosaic of small buildings, their pastel shades gleaming in the afternoon sunlight, occasionally dominated by the more sober and stately mansion of a European planter or businessman or government official; and, overshadowing them all, were the tall minarets of the Khunzie Mosque and the grandeur of the Holy Ghost Cathedral. The city itself was fronted by the golf course, close to which was the bulk of Government House; away to the north, on the mainland, he could make out the gleam of Nyali Beach, the Europeans' favourite rest and relaxation area when they came down from the highlands.

Behind and beyond, the trees clustered thickly, a portent

14

of the forests, the game, and the people, who were the true owners of this land.

He wondered what his father, almost the first white man ever to penetrate the interior, and certainly the first to live there amongst the Masai, would say to *that* sentiment.

The ship left the golf club and the island to starboard and anchored in Kilindini Harbour, where she was immediately surrounded by lighters and bumboats; her cargo hatches were already open and it was clear that despite the lateness of the hour, work was going to commence immediately.

"What time tomorrow do you reckon to sail?" John asked.

"Dawn," Bulwer said.

"Dawn?" John cried in dismay.

"We're behind schedule," Bulwer explained. "These chaps will have to work all night. So it looks like goodbye, Mr Barclay."

"Yes," John said, and went in search of Adelheid and her mother. "I'm afraid that tour around Mombasa will have to wait," he told them. "Unless you'd care to come ashore this evening."

"No, thank you very much, Mr Barclay," Frau Huttingen decided. "The purser tells me there are mosquitoes and all manner of dreadful bugs in Mombasa at night. He says we'll be much more comfortable here."

"Well," John said, "I'm afraid he is right. So I'll have to say goodbye." His bags had already been transferred to the waiting launch.

"It has been a real pleasure, Mr Barclay," Frau Huttingen said. "If you are even in Tanganyika. . . ."

"I shall certainly call," John agreed, and released her hand to take Adelheid's. "I know you will love Tanganyika, Fräulein," he said. "It is nearly as lovely as British East."

"Nearly," she smiled sadly. "Have a good journey, Mr Barclay. Oh, have a good journey."

He thought she might be close to tears, and certainly she remained standing at the rail to wave him out of sight. He could still smell her perfume on his hand. There were several other passengers disembarking, Englishmen and their wives returning from long leave, but as far as he was

15

concerned they might not have existed – as they themselves were certainly aware. But he was still John Barclay, the son of the most famous of all the white inhabitants of British East Africa. So as the boat pulled in to the dock, Mr Farmer, a lawyer, remarked, "I suppose you'll be taking the train out to Nairobi, Mr Barclay."

"Yes, sir," John agreed politely.

"Which cannot be until tomorrow morning," Farmer pointed out. "You're welcome to spend the night with my wife and me."

"That's very kind of you, sir," John acknowledged. "But I couldn't possibly put you to that inconvenience. I'll stay at the hotel."

"No trouble at all, my dear fellow."

"I'll stay at the hotel," John Barclay repeated, and relieved the firmness of his tone with one of his smiles. "I really would like to."

"Well, you must suit yourself, of course." Farmer recalled that the boy's father also had a reputation for going his own way. With that he resumed his conversation with the other passengers, to John's relief. He knew he had been rude, but he was in no mood for an evening of idle chit-chat or impertinent questions. The story of the life and experiences of his father and mother was imperfectly known for all the popular literature written about them. That was as they wanted it to be; he had no intention of adding anything to the gossip that already surrounded them.

Besides, to stay at the hotel was a necessary part of returning to Africa and becoming assimilated. The hotel was one of the oldest buildings in Mombasa, and when Adrian Barclay had first come here it had been owned and operated by a Somali family. Now the proprietor was a Welshman named Roberts. He had done a great deal of renovating, adding electric light and even chalets at the back for overflowing guests – who were as spasmodic as the electricity. But the essential character of the place was unchanged. To John Barclay it represented Mombasa itself, with its Somali doorman, its Indian waiters, its black yard boys, its spicy odours, its slowly revolving overhead fans, its bar where from sundown the clink of glasses seeped through the rooms, its uncarpeted floors on which heels clicked endlessly and across which the servants shuffled in barefooted whispers, and above all its red-faced, perspiring, walrus-moustached landlord.

"John Barclay, by all that's holy," Roberts remarked. "Your people know you're back?"

"It's a surprise," John told him.

"It'll be that, boyo. Well, I'll put you in the usual room, if that's all right?"

"That will be just fine," John said, because the room, or rather suite – the best in the house – was another essential part of being in Mombasa. Here his mother and father had stayed over thirty years before, and in this room his elder brother had died of malaria. John Barclay the first would have been thirty-one this year, had he survived infancy. Instead he was buried in the cemetery behind the city. John never resented being given the same name as the dead brother he had never known. He understood that it had been a watershed in his mother's life in more ways than one, that had the first John Barclay lived the second would never have been born. He hoped his parents would still feel it was all worthwhile when he got home.

He changed into a white linen suit with a quiet tie, went down for dinner, and afterwards sipped beer in the relative cool of the verandah, looking out at the harbour. The lights of the *Chieftain* were clearly visible, and he could imagine the Huttingens sitting down to dinner in the now almost empty dining saloon. Talking about him? He was just a shipboard acquaintance, soon to be forgotten. As were they. But he thought that to forget Adelheid Huttingen too soon would be his loss. However, Frau Huttingen had certainly been right to fear the mosquitoes, he thought, as he slapped one to leave a bloody splodge on his arm.

"I," said the boy, "am Joseph Kinshasu."

John turned his head; he had no idea there was anyone on the verandah with him. This fellow certainly didn't belong here, and knew it; a tall, slim black youth, with high cheekbones and a prominent nose, he had clearly come up by the yard steps, and now stood in the shadows some six feet away. Yet he was not dressed like a prowler; he wore a western-style suit and a tie. Besides, he had introduced himself.

"Pleased to meet you," John said. "I am John Barclay."

"This I know," the black boy said. "I saw you land from the steamer, and was told your name."

"Yes?" John waited. He was not alarmed or even concerned by the strange appearance of this odd fellow. He possessed the physical confidence that six feet two inches and one hundred and eighty pounds of perfectly distributed bone and muscle engender, and besides, he *was* John Barclay.

"You are going home, to the valley," the boy said.

"That's right."

"You will need a servant," Joseph Kinshasu said.

"A servant?"

"A valet. I will be your valet, Mr Barclay. I will keep your clothes clean and pressed, your boots polished. I will pour your drinks and light your cigarettes. And make your bed," he added as an afterthought.

"My parents already have servants to do these things," John protested.

"But they are your parents' servants," Joseph Kinshasu pointed out. "I will be yours."

"I cannot possibly afford to pay you."

The boy shrugged. "Perhaps you will feed me."

John studied him in the gloom. He was an intriguing fellow. And, as with Adelheid Huttingen, the idea of having someone of his very own was very attractive – he was feeling more lonely at this moment that ever before in his life. "Come over here," he said.

Joseph glanced at the light streaming through the open window, then slowly advanced into it. "I can read and write," he said. "I have been to school, and I have read the books in the library. Some of them," he added.

"Have you now," John said. "How old are you?"

"I am nineteen."

"And what tribe?"

18

"I am Kikuyu."

"And you would go to work in the Masai highlands?"

The Masai and the Kikuyu, who for centuries had lived in too close a proximity for comfort, were hereditary enemies.

"There are no Masai highlands now," Joseph said. "The Masai have been sent to the reservation."

Which was true enough, John reflected.

The door to the salon opened; one of the waiters had seen the black man standing on the verandah in the light and was coming to investigate. "This man bothering you, Mr Barclay? You," he said, pointing at Joseph. "You best be off or I will call the police."

"Man, mind how you speak to me," Joseph Kinshasu replied. "I am Mr Barclay's very own servant."

The Indian looked at John in consternation.

"Why, yes," John said. "I'm afraid he is. I had no idea he would be here. Do you suppose you could find him a room?"

From the first-class railway carriage, Africa could be surveyed rather than experienced. This undoubtedly made for a quick and even a pleasant journey from the coast to Nairobi and beyond, but it was obviously something anyone could do, whereas before the railway was built, the trek had taken weeks. It had been a task for outstanding men, and one or two outstanding women, John Barclay thought, as he peered out of the window. Such as Father and Mother. He had never made it on foot.

The train left at dawn, crossing the Makupa Bridge, which had been built especially to carry the line to the mainland. Joseph had already proved his worth, as John found that he had to do absolutely nothing for himself. The black boy was also in a private heaven of his own, having confessed that the previous night was the first time he had ever slept in an hotel.

"But what are you, a Kikuyu, doing in Mombasa anyway?" John asked him.

"My father decided he would do better on the coast,"

19

Joseph explained. "And took my mother with him. Before I was born."

"Your father must have been an independently minded man," John observed, thinking of the clannishness of African tribal life.

"My father was a fool," Joseph said, without emotion. "He did not do better. He died, leaving my mother with me in her belly."

"Ah," John said.

"She had a hard life," Joseph said. "She worked as a housemaid. Sometimes she was beaten. Do you know this, Mr John?"

"Yes," John said sadly. He was only too aware that many European settlers, and especially the women, took a delight in beating their servants. "But she would not go home to her people?"

"She could not admit such failure," Joseph said. "She was a proud woman."

As you are a proud man, John thought, suddenly.

"She wished at least one of the family to do better," Joseph went on. "So she paid for my education. And then she died."

"When was this?"

"Two months ago."

"Oh, I'm very sorry to hear that."

"She was tired," Joseph explained.

John could believe that. "Do you think she would wish you also to be a servant?" he asked. "Is that bettering yourself?"

"I am not a servant," Joseph said. "I am the servant of John Barclay."

"Ah," John said again.

"There was no other way I could return to the land of the Kikuyu with pride," Joseph told him, somewhat disingenuously.

"I understand," John said, understanding a lot more than that. Here was a young man like himself, wishing to make his way around his people, with pride. And not a lot else.

*

20

From the coast, the railway cut its way through the thickly forested hinterland, before beginning to climb. Soon after that, the trees thinned and then even the grass died, and they were in the Taru desert, still climbing. The railway, John recalled, had taken several years to build and had cost a great number of lives, most from disease. And now, in a couple of hours, he had already travelled as far as it would have taken two days to cross twenty-five years before.

After the desert they reached the Tsavo grassland. This was the home of the fiercest lions in all Africa, a reputation earned at least partly by their wholesale destruction of the Indian labourers, and some of the white overseers, during the laying of the track. Since then it had been virtually open season on the lions, as every white hunter, and every client he could attract, set out to prove his manhood from behind the security of a repeating rifle. Thus there were few lions to be seen, and none at all this day.

Joseph, who was travelling in a train for the first time – although he had clearly read about them because he did not appear nervous – was more interested in the gleaming, snow-covered peak of Mount Kilimanjaro, which could now just be made out to their south. "That must be the highest place in the world," he said.

"Only one of them," John told him. He reflected that Mount Kilimanjaro was actually in German East Africa – the border between the two colonies was only a few miles to the south at this point. Perhaps Adelheid Huttingen would also look at Kilimanjaro, as she and her mother journeyed inland from Dar es Salaam – he had gathered that, like Adrian Barclay, Herr Huttingen was farming some distance from the coast.

Above Tsavo the track entered the rain forest. The jungle had of course been cleared back from the line, and was kept clear by constantly working gangs of labourers, yet it was still possible to imagine the secret damp depths that lay just beyond the tree fringe, the home of monkeys and baboons and snakes and spiders and incredibly beautiful butterflies. And also some of the fiercest of all African peoples.

John glanced at Joseph as the train began to slow for a station. "This is the land of the Kikuyu," he remarked.

"They will not know me, and I will not know them."

"Yet will they know that you are one of them," John pointed out. "Just by looking at you."

"They will not look at me," Joseph assured him. "Africans do not look at those in the first-class carriages.'

Actually he was wrong, but the looks were always quick glances as the people on the platform hurried to and fro, and no one could see into the sudden gloom of the compartment well enough to make out anything of Joseph, who sat well back from the window. But he stared at them. His people, whom he had never seen, in their native habitat.

He was a remarkably strange fellow, John thought. He gave off an aura of enormous confidence, created perhaps by his reading, and yet constantly betrayed himself by his naïvety. He was obviously possessed by a burning desire to return to his own people as somebody, and yet was sneaking in by the back door, as it were. And he was unusually casual for a black man, accepting his place in the first-class carriage as a matter of course, even though the other passengers and the guard had clearly been scandalized. But then, John reflected, he himself had bought the two first-class tickets as a matter of course. Yet Joseph's wish not to be seen by his own people revealed that he was sensitive of his position.

Complex, self-educated, and ambitious, John supposed would sum him up. In terms of an African, that probably meant he was a born trouble-maker. But he was the servant of John Barclay. John thought that, supposing he could persuade Father to accept the black boy, it would be very interesting to see how he turned out.

Still the railway climbed, now passing over huge areas of swampland in which the train seemed to proceed in fits and starts, then descending startling escarpments, but always in the main moving higher, until in the dusk they came to Nairobi.

Nairobi too had once been nothing more than a swamp, and for all its elevation several thousand feet above sea level it retained a dank suggestion of unhealthiness. The town was only fifteen years old, which was sometimes difficult for John to grasp as it had been there ever since he could remember, and yet its newness was evident in the houses, which not only entirely lacked the grace of at least some of those in Mombasa but sprawled everywhere. It had come into existence simply because Sir George Whitehouse, who had supervised the building of the railway, had required an area of reasonably level ground for his marshalling yards, and there had been nowhere else. Around the railway terminus the labourers had first pitched tents and, later, huts; the merchants had soon followed them, to sell them the essentials of life, and a good variety of non-essentials as well; the prostitutes had arrived to relieve them of their pay packets in return for a bit of fun; and the police had followed to maintain some kind of order in the turbulent community.

Then had come the white settlers, encouraged to farm in the limitless highlands that lay only just outside the city. Mostly of very good stock – it was an oddly satisfying thought that Adrian Barclay had been, as a plain ship's officer, considerably lower down the social scale than the lordlings to whom he had shown the way, and was now more famous that any of them – they had brought with them to Africa a mixture of immense wealth, the most snobbish culture in the world, a sixth-form sense of humour and an inordinate concept of their own innate superiority over all the other peoples of the earth, regardless of race, colour or creed.

Their symbol was the Norfolk Hotel, which was some ten years old now, their gathering place when in town. It was also the place to which John Barclay unhesitatingly directed his steps once he left the train, Joseph following behind with the bags.

"Mr Barclay?" asked the clerk doubtfully; like so many of the people John had met on his unpremeditated return home, he was apparently unprepared to believe his own eyes.

"Nobody else," John agreed. "I'd like a room for the night, if you please. And one for my boy."

How grand it seemed.

"Of course," the clerk agreed. "You'll sign for it?"

John scribbled his signature on the sheet of paper thrust at him, and half an hour later was sitting in a tub of hot water.

"It would be better if I slept up here with you," Joseph suggested.

"Can't be done," John told him.

"How am I to protect you while you sleep?"

'Can't be done because this is a white man's hotel," John pointed out. "Besides, what am I going to need protection from, here in the Norfolk?"

A great number of things, he reflected only an hour later, as he sat in the bar drinking a beer and watched as a small, middle-aged red-headed man wearing a dinner jacket but brown boots, untidy hair and bow tie at an angle, made his way towards him.

"John Barclay, as I live and die," the newcomer shouted.

John stood up. "In the flesh, my lord."

Hugh Cholmondeley, third Baron Delamere, shook his hand vigorously. "My dear boy, it is good to see you. God but you're a big chap. Is your dad expecting you?"

"Ah . . . no, sir."

"Ha-ha, you're surprising the old bugger, eh?" Delamere gave a shout of laughter; he and Adrian Barclay, as the first two white men ever to farm in Masai land, were the best of friends. "This calls for a drink. Champagne," he bawled at the barman, who, in anticipation of the command, was already opening a bottle.

"Well, sir . . ." John began.

Delamere had a peculiarly piercing gaze. "You do drink champagne, Jacko?"

"Well, I have," John agreed cautiously, remembering his last night with Catherine, and the headache he had experienced the next morning.

"Heats the blood," Delamere declared. "Now, you must dine with me and tell me why you're back unannounced."

24

"Oh, I . . . I have no dinner jacket."

Delamere raised his glass. "You will be dining with me," he declared, with the simple arrogance of the richest and most powerful man in British East Africa. "I have some guests." He rose to greet them as he spoke. "Baron Blixen. And the Baroness. New arrivals. You won't have met John Barclay, Baron, Baroness. Adrian Barclay's son."

The Baron and his wife, who were apparently Danish, were a large couple who presented an odd contrast, for where the man had somewhat coarse features and a booming laugh, his wife was quiet and watchful, and even, John thought, somewhat suspicious of her new surroundings.

"I have met your father," the Baron told John. "A famous man."

"A man who met the Masai on their own terms and licked them," Delamere declared proudly.

"That's because he was one of them," John suggested.

"Was he really?" asked the Baroness.

"He was taken into their tribe as a boy," John explained. "A long time ago."

"When the world was young," the Baroness murmured, and gave a slight flush as she glanced at her husband. "We are planting coffee, Mr Barclay."

"Father grows coffee," John volunteered.

"Ha-ha," Delamere shouted. "In the valley. Blixen is in the Ngong Hills. Not ten miles from here. It won't work, old man, it won't work."

Blixen went red in the face and drank champagne to hide his anger. His wife turned to John again. "Do you think it could work, Mr Barclay?"

"Anything can work, Baroness," John told her. "If you are determined enough."

'Innocent people," Delamere declared after dinner, when the Blixens had departed. "But Kenya is full of innocent people trying to make money. One worries for the future, indeed one does."

John realized that his lordship was unaware that Adrian

Barclay had told him just how innocent Delamere himself had been when he first came to East Africa, of the number of times he had all but bankrupted himself by his absurd schemes. Of course he had always had the backing of his estates in Cheshire, but he had also possessed the determination to succeed, and had eventually done so in the biggest possible way. The Blixens' fortunes would depend not only on what reserves of capital they possessed, but on their determination, as he had told the Baroness; getting established in East Africa was a rough business.

"Still, it takes all sorts," Delamere said. "Not that I would rate Blixen a snowball's hope in hell of succeeding; he's too interested in the good things of life. Especially the ladies." He sighed. "You know my wife is dead?"

"Oh, good Lord, no," John gasped. "I'm most terribly sorry, sir."

"Happened only a couple of months ago," Delamere said, his voice toneless. "B and G are most terribly upset." Berkeley and Galbraith Cole, sons of the Earl of Enniskillen, were his brothers-in-law. "And she was only thirty-six. Poor child. Hassan, you brown devil, fetch my revolver and another bottle of champagne."

"Your revolver?" John asked in alarm, but the barman was already obeying the command.

"Every so often," Delamere explained, "I feel the urge to shoot something. It relieves the blood pressure. Have a drink."

The liquid welled up the flute and spilled over the top. John had already had several glasses of wine with dinner, on top of the champagne before, and was feeling distinctly uncertain. "I really think I ought to go to bed," he confessed.

"At this hour?"

"What time is it?"

"I have no idea. Ah, Hassan, set up a bottle over there."

"You're not going to shoot in here?" John cried.

"Why not? They'll put any damage on the bill. Besides I never miss," Delamere explained.

He was actually telling the truth, and needed only two

shots to shatter two of the four bottles Hassan had placed on an occasional table – but the bullets still tore great holes in the wall behind.

"Now you have a go," Delamere invited.

John took the gun somewhat gingerly. He had, of course, grown up with guns – everyone in Africa did. And he had been in the OTC at school. But he had never shot when drunk before. He levelled the revolver and fired.

"Missed," Delamere shouted.

But he had not missed the chair standing some feet to the right of the bottles, John realized; half its arm had been blown away.

"Try again," Delamere recommended.

This time he was closer, and with his third shot actually hit one of the remaining bottles. The other guests in the hotel would suppose there was a war starting, he thought; indeed, some of them had gathered in the doorway of the bar to see what was happening. But there was no one in Nairobi who would dare interfere with Lord Delamere's amusement.

"Well done," his lordship commented. "That calls for a celebration. Hassan, another bottle of champagne."

"It is not good to drink so much," Joseph said severely. "You have been sick everywhere."

"You're fired," John mumbled, pulling the pillow over his head. "Go away and leave me alone."

"The train leaves in half an hour," Joseph said, even more severely. "Would you disappoint your parents?"

"Oh, damnation." John rolled out of the bed and allowed himself to be shaved and thrust into his clothes, while the room rotated about him. Only then did he pause to think. "My parents don't know I'm coming."

"They would still be disappointed if you did not arrive," Joseph pointed out, with unanswerable logic.

They just caught the train, having forgone breakfast – which John could not have eaten in any event – and within a few minutes had left Nairobi behind and entered upon the open grassland which stretched for miles on the eastern

27

side of the Rift Valley. The high country, Adrian Barclay had called it, when he first looked on it all but forty years ago, John remembered. The most beautiful place on earth, an endless expanse of rolling grassland - at this moment more brown than green, as the long rains had not yet arrived – studded with thorn trees and acacia, but yet containing hidden streams and copses, patches of glorious fertility amidst the prevailing aridity, only awaiting the coming of the rain to spring into magnificent life.

They reached the valley itself mid-morning, when the train began its sudden, nerve-wrenching descent. Actually the escarpment had been carefully chosen and the descent here was gradual, compared with the abrupt cliff faces which could be found in some places. Even so, John's father had told him how, when the track was first laid, there had been no means of negotiating the escarpments, and the train had had to be winched down by cables – which must have been still more hair-raising.

Even Joseph had to confess his wonderment. "This railway is a marvellous achievement," he remarked. "Do the white men build railways like this wherever they go?"

"Wherever," John agreed.

"And yet, there can have been few more difficult terrains than this," Joseph said.

"I wouldn't say that," John prepared to argue.

"Nor a more beautiful country," Joseph went on, ignoring him. "I had heard this and did not believe it. Those mountains over there, what are they called?"

John looked at the range which lay to the north and east. "The Aberdares," he said.

"This Aberdare . . . he was a Masai chieftain?"

"No," John said. "He was an English politician."

"I have read of politicians," Joseph observed. "They are great men. Will you be a politician, Mr John?"

"No," John Barclay said. "I am going to be a farmer. It is a greater thing to grow the food for men to eat than to tell them how to eat it."

Joseph did not seem entirely convinced. But he was soon again lost in wonderment as the train reached the floor of

28

the valley and the line threaded its way between the extinct volcanoes and the lakes which dotted the Rift. "So much water," he said.

"All salt," John told him, and grinned. 'Except Naivasha."

"Naivasha?"

"That is where I live. You too, now."

They were approaching the lake by noon, and the noise of the train, together with its piercing whistle, caused pelicans and pink flamingoes to rise from the water and flap their lazy way farther from the shore.

"What marvellous creatures," Joseph remarked. He gazed at the now half-collapsed thorn bush fence surrounding the dilapidated kraal. "Masai?"

"Once upon a time," John said, "that was the clan which took my father in as a Morani."

"Famous men," Joseph observed sombrely. "All gone to dust."

"You'd better not let Father hear you say that," John warned.

The train was slowing and the houses were in sight. They were well scattered, for the farm nowadays covered several thousand acres – Adrian Barclay grew not only coffee and corn, but farmed sheep as well as cattle – and employed quite a community, both of white men and black, each with his own area of responsibility, his own house and subordinates clustered around. But the church and the school as well as the meeting hall were close to the station. Joseph looked at them in surprise as the train drew to a stop. "What is the name of this town, Mr John?" he asked.

"This isn't a town," John said. "It is a farm. My father's farm." Now it was time for him to be quietly arrogant. All of this would one day be his.

Joseph Kinshasu scratched his head. He was at last awed into silence.

The train stopped and the people clustered around. The Naivasha stop was mainly to drop mail and supplies; disembarking passengers were rare. Thus the spectators, all black people, were very interested when the door of a first-class compartment opened and a bag was thrown down. Their interest turned to amazement when a black man followed. "But what is this, man?" one of them asked. "Who are you, boy?"

"I am the servant of Mr John Barclay," Joseph explained with patient dignity.

By now John was also climbing down. "But it's Mr John, man," the shout went up. "Mr John." People clustered round to shake his hand. They were mostly Kikuyu. Although Adrian Barclay had obtained permission for certain selected Masai to leave the reservation to work on his farm, he had been unable to find any who would willingly do so. If robbed of their ability to make war as and when they chose, the Morani, the young warriors, still regarded any manual labour as beneath manhood. The people would obviously recognize Joseph as a Kikuyu, John thought. But as they had never seen him before, they ignored him, while their shouts of welcome for the young master raced across the morning. Joseph made no move towards them. Apart from his innate shyness, John realized Joseph was also rather taken aback by the loose African robes they wore, in such strong contrast to his own by now somewhat crushed blue suit.

The stationmaster produced a pony and trap, and one of the black men climbed up to manage the reins. John got into the seat and gestured Joseph to mount beside him.

"I will walk, Mr John," Joseph said.

"Walk? It's damn near a mile to the house."

"It is right for a servant to walk while his master rides," Joseph asserted.

It was John's turn to scratch his head. But he was not going to beg the idiot. "Well, you'd better give me the bags," he said.

"I will carry the bags, Mr John," Joseph said, and immediately set off.

He was such a strange fellow, John thought. Almost arrogant before, he was now being a sort of backwards arrogant by deliberately debasing himself in front of his own people. But the driver was looking over his shoulder at him. "So let's go," John said. They passed a perspiring Joseph a moment later. "It's the big house," John told him.

"I knew that, Mr John," Joseph said.

It was time to stop worrying about his strange acquisition and start worrying about himself, John knew. The roadway from the station sloped down towards the lake, but long before it got there they were on the house property itself, passing well-watered green fields and a tennis court, and proceeding down an avenue of royal palms, with the kitchen gardens and staff quarters away to the right. Adrian Barclay had built the first house on this site back in the 1880s, and a lot had happened since then. Soon they were passing the garages in which the two motor cars waited, and then the dogs – Rhodesian ridgebacks – were barking and the pony was sidestepping nervously.

"It'd be an idea to drop me here," John said. "And thanks for the ride . . . Moyono, isn't it?"

"That's me, Mr John," the driver said, delighted to have been remembered.

John got down, gave him a wave, and then, heart pounding, walked along the side of the house to come out next to the verandah. The house was three storeys high, and on each floor there was a verandah looking down the sloping lawn to the water itself. And there was the lake, low at the moment because of the lateness of the rains – there were years when it almost dwindled to nothing more than a large swamp – with the stumps of long dead trees, indicating that once upon a time even here must have been tropical rain forest, protruding through the shallow water to make a perfect roost for the pelicans.

But however low, the lake was immense in its vastness. If the farther side, at this point, could just be made out, the northern reaches were lost in the noonday haze. The waters were incredibly still. Yet when a wind sprang up they could have all the superficial roughness of shallow seas.

His attention was caught by the dogs, who came bounding down the wide front steps to charge at him with raised hackles, changing their demeanour as they got close enough to recognize him, and then frisking around him like puppies.

31

He patted their heads and looked past them to the tall, white-clad figure on the verandah. "Mr John?" Safah-ben-Ali asked. "It cannot be."

"It can and it is, old man," John shouted, running up to greet his father's butler, the dogs at his heels. "And it is good to see you."

They clasped hands. Safah-ben-Ali was ten years older than Father, John knew, and was therefore sixty-seven. He was the guide who had first brought Adrian Barclay to this land, and he had remained his faithful servant ever since. As a Somali, he had found himself in an even more uneasy environment than the white man, since his people were known to, and hated by, the Masai, whereas the strange beings with white skins and explosive devices had appeared almost as gods. Yet, like his master, he had made himself accepted and respected by the Morani. Indeed, he had gone farther than Adrian Barclay in taking Masai women as his wives and fathering by them a clan of sons – although amongst the rumours surrounding Adrian Barclay's adventurous youth were those about his own Masai women. Obviously before he had met Mother, John supposed. It was not something he had ever chosen to investigate. But he had been married to Mother at a very early age . . .

Safah was releasing his hand and turning to look at the double doors which led into the front hall of the house, and the two people who had just left the drawing room in which they had been enjoying their before-luncheon aperitifs.

"John?" Joanna Barclay asked. She was fifty-four, a small woman who still retained traces of her American accent – she was born in Boston, and had eloped from there to marry her English sailor and be carried off to the wilds of Africa, when they had indeed been wilds. A pertly pretty woman, she had kept her figure under control and there were only faint traces of grey in her red-brown hair – she could still draw a second glance from any man on the street, even in her 'plantation gear' of divided skirt and loose blouse, knee-length stockings and thick shoes. "John," she said again. "But . . ."

"What the devil?" asked the man at her shoulder. Adrian

Barclay was six feet four inches tall, and was built even more solidly than when, as a boy of eighteen, he had amazed and frightened the Masai with his feats of strength. Now he was fifty-seven, but there was no stoop to his shoulder, and if his belly bulged, it was the paunch of prosperous confidence; he had made his way through enough dangers and deterrents to destroy most men.

"Oh, Johnnie," Joanna Barclay cried, and ran forward to take John in her arms. He swept her from the floor, then looked past her at his father.

"What's happened?" Adrian Barclay asked, also coming forward. He reached for John's hand and squeezed it. "Welcome, anyway . . . but, what's happened?"

John drew a long breath and looked at his mother.

"Maybe we should all go inside," she suggested. "Safah, you'd better tell cook there'll be three for lunch."

"Heard the racket from the station," Adrian Barclay said as he escorted his son into the drawing room, where the chintzes and the ornaments, the carpets and the occasional tables, the photographs and the paintings, might have meant they were actually in Surrey . . . were it not for the sun blinds and the fans, and indeed the sun itself, throwing its shadows in every direction. "Had no idea it was you. A drink?"

"Well . . . I wouldn't say no to a beer. I had dinner with Lord Delamere last night."

"Did you? Oh, dear." Joanna pulled him down to the settee beside her.

"I had no idea about his wife. But he seemed to be taking it quite well. It was great fun, actually. If a little destructive. And it left me with a king-sized head."

"Then you'd better have a hair of the dog," Adrian decided, opening a bottle of champagne. "And tell us what has happened."

He filled a glass and held it out, and John drank gratefully before drawing a long breath. "I've been expelled from school."

There was a moment's silence while his father and mother stared at him.

33

'Expelled?" Joanna asked at last. "What did you do?"

"I punched a master on the nose."

"You what?" Adrian Barclay shouted.

"Oh, Johnnie," Joanna said.

"Well, he was disgustingly rude. About you, Father. He called you a white nigger."

Adrian gazed at him with raised eyebrows. "One of your masters said that?"

"No. None of them would ever do that. But that was the trouble. We had been to Cranbourne for the big rugger game, you know, and walloped them. I got three tries. Well, maybe that put them in a bad mood, but afterwards, when we were about to board the coach to return home, this fellow, their games master, said to his team, 'We can't really expect to lick a school which plays the son of a white nigger.'"

"Of all the darned cheek," Joanna cried.

"Who was this man?" Adrian demanded.

"Some fellow named Woodman. He'd been out to Mombasa, apparently, and travelled up as far as Nairobi. Maybe you've met him."

"Can't say I remember anyone by that name," Adrian confessed.

"Well, you wouldn't," Joanna pointed out. "Not a man like that. So you punched him on the nose. Good for you."

"And got sacked," Adrian pointed out. "What did Haskins have to say?"

"Well, he was very sorry about the whole thing. But apparently boys can't go around punching masters on the nose. He said, if I was prepared to write a letter of apology, and deliver it myself at Cranbourne . . ."

"You didn't," Joanna snapped.

"I refused," John agreed.

"Good for you," Joanna said again. "I always thought this English public school lark was a waste of money."

"That's all very well," Adrian growled. "But what chance has he got of going to Oxford now? They're not going to accept a chap who's been expelled. And what about your final exams?"

"Well . . . I suppose I've skipped those," John said.

"Damn," Adrian said. "You've just about torn up your life."

"But how did you get back here?" Joanna asked.

"I touched Cathy. She was an absolute brick. Produced my fare, had me up to stay with them until the ship was due to sail, even came down to Southampton to see me off." He grinned; things were going much better than he had dared to hope. "I had the devil of a job keeping her from going down to Cranbourne herself and hitting this Woodman over the head with her umbrella."

"And what does Portington think about it?" Adrian asked.

"He seemed very sympathetic. He really does support Cathy in everything."

"Yes." Adrian said grimly. He had not taken to his son-in-law, the more so because he knew that Portington's family felt their son and heir had been led astray by the untamed half-American girl from darkest Africa – and because he also knew their suspicions were very accurate, even if Catherine Barclay had not lived in Africa for some time.

"I'm so glad you went to Catherine," Joanna said wistfully. "Is she . . . well, all right? She writes so seldom."

"She's in great form."

"Did she say when next she's coming out for a visit?"

"Well, no. She seems awfully busy."

"Drinking and smoking and throwing parties," Adrian grumbled.

"That's all to do with being a liberated woman," Joanna reminded him.

"The hell it is. You were as liberated a woman as any of these suffragettes or whatever they call themselves, without having to ruin your health to prove it."

"That's maybe because you carried me off to Africa before I ever had a chance to sample anything interesting," Joanna said, with a flash of that roguishness which must have made her so attractive as a girl. "I don't suppose Catherine is . . . well, I don't suppose you know about things like that."

35

John had no idea what she was talking about.

"Catherine has never had the time to get pregnant, any more than she has the time to write or to visit Africa," Adrian remarked. "And we're getting off the subject. What the devil are we to do with this young prize-fighter?"

But there was no anger in his tone; he was proud of what his son had done, John knew.

"Put him to work," Joanna said. "The hell with Oxford."

"And a Rugby blue? He was pretty sure of that."

"And a Rugby blue," she said firmly. "It'll be just great having him home at last. If that's what you want to do?" she added anxiously, looking at John.

"More than anything else in the world," he told her.

"Excuse me, Mr Adrian," Safah said, standing in the doorway. "But there is a strange African at the door, saying he belongs to Mr John."

Once again his parents looked at John.

"Oh, that will be Joseph," he said casually. "My boy."

"Kinshasu," Adrian Barclay mused. "You're not related to old Chief Kinshasu, are you?"

"He was my grandfather, sir," Joseph explained.

"Why, you sly devil," John shouted. "You never told me you were the grandson of a chief."

"Was it relevant, Mr John? I am not a chief."

Joanna stared at her son with her mouth open.

"And your father was expelled from the kraal," Adrian went on.

"My father left the kraal after a quarrel with his father," Joseph said carefully. "He wished to become a Christian."

"Well, hooray for him," Joanna commented.

"It was not for religious purposes, Mrs Barclay. It was because he thought that would help him to make his way in the white man's world."

Once again Joanna was left speechless.

"He did not succeed," Joseph added.

"But you intend to," Adrian suggested.

"No, sir. I have no desire to make my way in the white man's world. If I have a way to make, it will be in the black

36

man's world. But right now I have no desire other than to be Mr John's servant."

"Yes," Adrian said, rendered as uncertain as his wife by the young man's aplomb. "Well, Safah, you had better show Joseph where to put Mr John's bags, and then find him some quarters. And tell him what he has to do."

"You come with me, eh?" Safah said belligerently.

Joseph looked at John.

"Safah will show you where to go, Joseph," John said.

Joseph gave a brief bow, and followed the Somali from the room.

"You mean I can keep him?" John said

"If you wish to. He seems a very odd fish."

"Very odd," Joanna agreed. "You don't think there could be trouble?"

"I don't see why there should be," Adrian answered. "Kinshasu's kraal is a long way from Naivasha. And anyway, even if Joseph's father had remained, he would never have been in line for the chieftainship; he had a dozen older brothers, and there must be three times that number of senior cousins knocking about. But where on earth did you pick him up, Johnnie?"

"Well, I suppose you could say that he picked me up," John confessed, and told them of Joseph's appearance in Mombasa. He was tempted also to tell them about Adelheid and her mother, but decided against it; he had come out of the Cranbourne affair one hundred per cent better than he had anticipated – it would be stupid to upset Father now, especially when the Huttingens had no relevance whatever any more.

"Well, maybe he'll turn out to be the perfect Man Friday for you," Joanna said when he had finished. "As Safah was to your father." She put her arm round John again, and kissed him some more. "It is so good to have you back."

It was so good to be back, John thought, as he rode his horse out into the fields the next morning. Joseph had wanted to accompany him, and had been bitterly disappointed to be told by Safah that was not part of a servant's duties, and there was more than enough to be done at the house. Safah, being married to Masai women, had always regarded the Kikuyu with suspicion, and a renegade Kikuyu was worst of all, as far as he was concerned.

But it was impossible to find fault with Joseph, who went about his daily tasks with tremendous energy and enthusiasm. If he had disavowed any intention of seeking success in the white man's world, he was certainly interested in learning all he could about that world, and he surprised Adrian and Joanna yet again when he asked their permission to read some of the books in the library. They gave it, but Adrian was doubtful. "I'm not sure God intended the Africans to read," he said at dinner.

"You're becoming prejudiced in your old age," Joanna told him. "Now *that* I never expected to see."

"It's not prejudice," Adrian protested. "It's common sense. What can he read about, except things he can never know and certainly never have? It'd be different if there was an African literature."

"Do you suppose that will ever happen?"

"Maybe Joseph will create one," John put in.

He was delighted with his strange servant, not least because, as Joseph had stressed from the beginning, the Kikuyu was his servant and no one else's, and he left no one in any doubt of that fact. His first retainer!

But he was even more delighted to be back, to enjoy the chill nights and brisk dawns, so odd when so close to the equator – the lake was some six thousand feet above sea level – to be amidst the familiar people, white and black, who all gave him such a rousing welcome, and now to be able to play his part in the running of the farm. Not that there was much running to be done immediately. The fields had already been cleared and burned, after the Masai way of cultivation, in readiness for the coming of the long rains, and indeed these arrived only a few weeks after John.

Then it was a matter of waiting for them to end. The rain was not unceasing; there were even days when the sun shone for hours on end, but the lowering clouds were never very far away, and the often fearsomely heavy downpours

38

discouraged a great deal of outdoor activity. Yet the cattle still had to be tended and the cows to be milked, and there was repair work which always needed doing and which was usually carried out in the wet season, however soggy and uncomfortable it was for everyone.

There were pleasures in the wet season as well, principally those of having time to spare, to sit on the verandah and get to know his parents again, to discuss various abstractions with Joseph, who in many ways, John was coming to realize, was fast developing into a surrogate for the brother he had never had and always wanted. Best of all was the pleasure of watching the lake slowly rising, and the parched earth turning from brown to green, the multi-coloured flowers suddenly sprouting where it had seemed almost desert, and the arrival of huge flocks of birds – cranes and herons to explore the lake, plovers to wheel above the developing earth.

"It's a rebirth," Joanna said. "I can understand why they used to sacrifice a virgin every year to make it happen."

There was more social activity in the wet season as well, as the European population found itself with time on its hands. At least once a fortnight, Adrian, Joanna and John would get into the Daimler and follow whirring windscreen wipers over very uneven roads to Lake Elmenteita, where Lord Delamere had an even larger spread, and a house crammed with the family silver and crystal, and where he entertained on a lavish scale, making up with his food and wine for his weakness for foolish after-dinner games – John observed that his lordship did no shooting inside his own home.

The Delameres had not always lived on this scale, in Africa; during the hard early years they had possessed nothing better than a mud hut, but all had come right in the end. That made Lady Delamere's sudden death the more tragic – but her husband had been brought up to conceal his personal emotions, and was attempting to continue as if nothing had happened, although the Barclays all knew how much he was suffering.

The Barclays had their own dinner and luncheon parties,

to which not only the Delameres came, but farmers from all around, often, if the weather was really bad, to spend the night. Amongst those invited were the Blixens, together with, when he was around, their great friend Denys Finch-Hatton, who, for all his public school education, had opted to earn a living as a white hunter, and was apparently very successful at it too. Adrian Barclay did not approve of hunting for sport rather than food, but even he warmed to the spontaneous charm of the young Englishman, and both he and Joanna liked Baroness Blixen, even if there were few in the highlands could see much that was good in her husband.

The rains ended in June, and then the farm became a hive of activity, as the crop was planted, the cattle were re-pastured and the coffee was harvested. John himself had been very much on the fringes of social activity, being by far the youngest person present at most of the gatherings. The offspring of the farmers were all where he should have been: at school or university in England. Only Monica Belfield, daughter of the Governor, was remotely his own age, and even she, the most eligible young woman in Kenya, was somewhat older. He was more interested in watching his parents' contemporaries at their ease, something he could not remember having done before, but could not help being occasionally bored, and from time to time disturbed at the points of view they held, their conviction that the African could never be anything more than an uneducated savage, who was at best lazy and incompetent and at worst bestial and dangerous. Then he had a tremendous urge to trot out Joseph to talk to them – only to reflect that he had no idea of Adrian and Joanna Barclay's actual thoughts on the black people whom they employed and amongst whom they had lived for so long. Although they appeared to get on well with them, and their labour force was a happy one, he knew that they had seen a great deal of both the bestial and dangerous side of the black people – who in turn had seen, and still occasionally saw, equal examples of the bestial and dangerous aspects of white people. So he said nothing, and spent more and more time with Joseph, usually fishing on the lake in one of the flat-bottomed punts which lay on the shore.

He realized that he actually knew very little about what Joseph thought of the white people, or even if he was happy. Nor did he know if he had the right to intrude into the black boy's private world, to go in search of answers which might embarrass him or, worse, estrange them.

Joseph's conversation was certainly always concerned with the white man's world. He was not only apparently learning all he could about British politics, and seemed to know more about the various prime ministers than John himself, he was also very interested in world events, and devoured the newspapers which usually arrived several weeks late. John never read newspapers in the summer, and in the winter it was only to see the rugby scores. Thus he was quite taken aback one glorious evening as they sat in the punt waiting for the fish to bite, and Joseph asked, "Do you think there is going to be a war?"

"A war? Between whom?"

"Well, Austria and Russia, over Serbia."

"Austria and Russia? Over Serbia?" John was incredulous.

"Did you not know, Mr John, that the Serbians have murdered an Austrian archduke?"

Joseph could have done well as a schoolmaster, John reflected; he had the ability to make one feel a total fool. "I heard my parents saying something about it," he muttered.

"Well, the Austrians are determined to destroy Serbia, I have read. And Russia will not let them. And Germany is determined to support Austria. And France will then have to support Russia. I have read that even Great Britain may become involved."

"Holy smoke!" John shouted. And he wouldn't be there. He hurried back to the house to ask Father what he thought.

"Don't be a chump," Adrian Barclay told him. "England doesn't get involved in continental wars. Where did you get such a silly idea."

"Well . . ." John decided against involving Joseph. "I read it in the papers."

"Journalistic claptrap," Adrian declared. "They have to find something terrifying to put in their columns or nobody would buy their rags."

But only a week later Lord Delamere came bumping down the drive in his Rolls-Royce, hooting the horn with one hand and firing his revolver into the air with the other. "Haven't you heard?" he shouted when the Barclays emerged to find out what was happening. "We're at war with Germany. By God, we're at war!"

2

"I don't believe it," Adrian Barclay declared. "England, at war with Germany?"

"Well, you'd better, because it's true." Delamere took the whisky and soda Safah had hurriedly poured and drank deeply. "The whole damned shooting match has gone up. England, France, and Russia on one side, with Serbia of course, and Belgium. . . ."

"Belgium?" Adrian shouted.

"Don't you read your newspaper, old man? It's Belgium started the whole damned thing. Well, by being invaded. Against us are Germany and Austria. There's talk about Italy coming in, but no one seems to know for sure."

"And I'm not there," John grumbled.

"Thank God for that," Joanna said.

"Your mother's right," Delamere said. "We need you here."

"To do what?" Adrian demanded. "There aren't any Germans in British East. Not any more," he added grimly, thinking of Kurt von Schlieben, his dead sister's husband.

"There's one whole hell of a lot over there," Delamere said, throwing out his arm to point dramatically to the south. "A whole German colony, in fact."

"They're not likely to trouble us," Adrian said.

"I wouldn't care to bet on that. Anyway, we're surely going to trouble them."

"Whatever for?" Joanna inquired.

"There's a war on," Delamere explained with, for him, considerable patience. "Oh, Safah, bring me another Scotch. There is a war on, my darling Joanna, a war which we have to win. And we can only do that by defeating the Germans, everywhere and anywhere they happen to be. Taking their colonies, sinking their ships, destroying their farms. . . ."

Good God, John thought, I'm at war with Herr Huttingen. And therefore with Adelheid. Only women aren't involved in wars, as a rule.

"I think that's as ridiculous as it's unchristian," Joanna was declaring. "Okay, so they want to have a war in Europe. They're always having wars in Europe. I don't see any reason at all why we should become involved. The Germans in Tanganyika and we up here have lived in perfect peace for years."

"They are absolute Huns," Delamere insisted. "It says so in the papers. Some of the things they have done in Belgium . . . my God, they are unrepeatable. I assure you, Joanna, if we do not conquer German East, they are in time going to think about conquering up here, and if they do that it is not going to be very nice. Especially if they come up with native levies."

So maybe women are involved after all, John thought, with a most peculiar sensation. He could remember the feeling of terror in 1906 when the Masai had gone to war against the white men. Of course he had only been ten years old then.

"So what are you proposing to do?" Father was asking. "Raise a force and invade Tanganyika?"

"That's up to Henry Belfield," Delamere declared, referring to the Governor of the protectorate. "I certainly intend to offer my services in any capacity he requires. I imagine there'll be quite a few of the younger planters who will volunteer."

"Well, you can count me out," Adrian Barclay said. "I've had my share of campaigning."

"My dear fellow, no one would suggest you should come along. I mean to say, you're all of sixty." Delamere was forty-four.

"Not quite," Adrian corrected him. "But I'm old enough to have some sense."

"Younger fellows," Delamere repeated, and looked at John.

"Oh, you can count me in, my lord," John said enthusiastically. If only to rescue Adelheid Huttingen, he thought.

44

"Oh no you don't," Joanna cried.

"Oh, let him go," Adrian growled. "He's had it too soft around here for too long. Maybe it'll do him good."

John accompanied Lord Delamere into Nairobi to see the Governor.

Sir Henry Belfield was one of those massively calm men, in strong contrast to the excitable Delamere, but he was taking the situation seriously enough. "Yes, indeed," he agreed, "It is my intention to launch an invasion of German East Africa just as soon as sufficient forces can be accumulated. Sufficient regular forces. They have to be regular forces," he hurried on as Delamere began to show signs of exploding, "because there are regular German forces in Tanganyika – at least, down on the coast. And it is on the coast that we intend to launch our campaign. However, that does not mean we shall not need considerable volunteer forces to back the regulars up, and replace them in their guard duties against German action."

"But, if we are invading Tanganyika, sir," John asked, "who is going to invade us?"

"My dear boy, there are Germans everywhere. Our latest information is that the battlecruiser *Koenigsburg* is in the Indian Ocean and approaching the East African coast. We have no ships with which to oppose her at the moment."

And are our volunteer rifles going to work against naval guns? John wondered. In any event, Nairobi was a couple of hundred miles from the coast; the German warship was hardly going to trouble them here.

"That's all very well," Delamere said. "But my chaps will want to do more than stand sentry."

"Your chaps?"

"The volunteer cavalry I am proposing to raise."

The Governor stroked his chin. But he knew from experience that Delamere could not be opposed, only diverted. "I tell you what, old man, if you really are determined to do something . . . this is in the strictest confidence, of course, but our people are also talking of launching a raid over the Tanganyika border up here, to distract Lettow-Vorbeck's

45

people. He's the German commander in Dar es Salaam, you know. Well, it will be a difficult campaign, because of the terrain. The regulars will need considerable support for their baggage and things like that. Now, Hugh, if you were to recruit a baggage column for us from amongst the Kikuyu. . . ."

"Waste of time," Delamere declared. "Cowardly rogues, the Kikuyu. And ill-disciplined. If I'm going to recuit any native force it'll be from the Masai."

"The Masai?" Belfield was distinctly alarmed. "I couldn't possibly allow that."

"Stuff and nonsense. Of course you can. They're the best fighting men in Africa."

"But you are not recruiting a fighting force. You are recruiting bearers." The Governor's calm was beginning to disappear like water from a holed bucket.

"Whoever I recruit will be going to war," Delamere announced grandly. "And therefore must understand what war is all about. The Masai understand that. They are splendid people. And besides, they will follow me anywhere. And John, here. Adrian is too old, more's the pity, but John is a Barclay. The Masai worship the name of Barclay."

The Governor was shaking his head, but more in despair than refusal. "I have no idea what the Colonial Office will say."

"They can say what they like. Tell them they have given you a war to win, and that you intend to win it." Delamere got up, and John hastily followed his example. "I will have my men ready to march in a fortnight. You'll let me have my orders by then."

"Hugh," the Governor begged, "you are not to arm them. Please promise me that."

"Recruit the Masai," Adrian Barclay said, with a gleam in his eye. "Damn it, I think I will come with you, after all."

"You will do no such thing, Adrian Barclay," Joanna declared. "You are far too old to go traipsing through the bush and being shot at. As you say, you've done all that. As for you. . . ." She looked at John.

46

"He will be perfectly safe," Delamere assured her. "He will be serving under me. Now, Jacko, you must equip yourself with a revolver and sixty rounds of ammunition, a rifle and sixty rounds of ammunition . . . I don't suppose you have a sword?"

"No, sir." John looked at his father.

"And neither do I," Adrian said. "Do you have any idea how much all of that is going to weigh?"

"That's why we are recruiting bearers," Delamere pointed out. "You will also need some good bush clothes . . . I don't suppose we'll have uniforms for the first few weeks, more's the pity. And iron rations. Dried beef and that sort of thing. Tinned stuff."

"Just how long are you going to be away?" Joanna demanded.

"Who knows, dear lady. Who knows?"

"You have to have a servant, Mr John," Joseph insisted. "How can a white man go to war without a servant?"

"Lord Delamere didn't say anything about a servant," John protested.

"That's because he took that for granted. Do you think he is going without a servant?"

Adrian realized that he could not envisage Lord Delamere going anywhere without several servants. But would they be Kikuyu? On the other hand, he must be his own man, and besides, he really did want to have Joseph along.

The following day they assembled on the front lawn at Naivasha. As John had suspected, Delamere was accompanied by seven of his personal Masai tribesmen, beside whom Joseph, for all his height and his considerable physique, suggested a lamb surrounded by wolves. His lordship had told his men they were going to war, and had allowed them to dress the part: they were naked, save for their headdresses, which were composed of huge, drooping ostrich feathers, and a leather belt, from which hung their small clubs and their hunting knives, but their bodies were daubed in red earth, and each man carried a spear.

"His excellency said they were not to be armed," John whispered.

"Oh, he was referring to rifles, my dear fellow." Delamere was more interested in Joseph, who was dressed very much as his master. "Are you sure you can trust that fellow not to run a mile at the sight of a German soldier?"

"Of course I'm sure," John protested, and hoped he was right – then reflected that they were not going to see any German soldiers, at least on this safari.

He, Delamere, and Joseph rode off; the Masai preferred to lope along beside them – and John knew that they could probably keep that up as long as most horses. But Joseph was not impressed. "It is not right," he commented, fortunately out of earshot of his lordship, "for grown men to run around revealing their genitals. And in front of your mother, too."

"Mother has seen the Masai going off to war before," John told him, and wondered if he should say more. He had not, in fact, related any of the family history to Joseph, because he had not wanted to boast. No doubt the Kikuyu had picked up enough of it from Safah.

Even Joseph became somewhat pensive the next day when, after they had left the Rift Valley for the higher ground – for the Masai had been entirely expelled from their traditional lands – they saw a lone warrior standing on a crag perhaps a mile away, gazing at them. If he was already surrounded by wolves, they were tamed wolves; now he was about to encounter their fellows in their natural state.

"They know we are coming," Delamere said with satisfaction. "They'll have a welcome for us."

Late that afternoon they saw the thorn fence surrounding the kraal, and beyond, the tragically small herd of cattle which was all this clan of the tribe, or any other, for that matter, now possessed: their once vast stock had been virtually destroyed by rinderpest.

Delamere halted them perhaps a hundred yards from the kraal. Thus far they had seen no people, but after they had stood still for some time they became aware that they were, in fact, surrounded. The Morani had been hidden in the rocks and brush outside the kraal, and now they advanced slowly, a trifle jerkily, and even John, who knew these people revered his father and anyone named Barclay, felt the hair on his neck begin to prickle. Joseph's horse moved restlessly, undoubtedly disturbed by its rider's reaction.

The Morani had observed their fellows with the white men, and that they were dressed for war, so they had hastily done the same. Now they stood, staring at the intruders, resting on their spears. But it was neither the weapons nor the naked bodies nor the headdresses which made them fearsome, nor even their reputations; the most awesome thing about a Moran was his face. Here was the epitome of the handsome African, the high cheek-bones, prominent nose and thrusting lips, but in the case of a Masai Moran, encased in the smoothest black skin it was possible to imagine, a flawless complexion born from a lifetime of drinking milk in which animal blood had been mixed. Add to this the utter arrogance of their expressions, as they gazed at the white men from beneath half-lowered eyelids, each face, each body, immobile, but indicative of such suppressed energy waiting to be released, and John could understand the terror they had created for so long in East Africa.

Delamere dismounted, and John and Joseph followed his example. Joseph took the bridles of the three horses while Delamere and John stepped away from them, surrounded by Delamere's escort.

In return, one of the Masai moved clear of the warriors. This was an older man, his rank evident in the splendour of his headdress, which was an entire lion's head, the huge white teeth lying on his own forehead. "My lord," he said, speaking Swahili, the lingua franca of East Africa.

Delamere held out his hand, and the chieftain shook it. "Umtalo," he said, in the same language. "You have met young Barclay?"

"Young Bar-clay," Umtalo said, and shook hands in turn. "You are like your father. But not so big." He inspected John's shoulders and arms. "But the same strength. That is good." Then he looked at Joseph. "Kikuyu," he remarked.

"My servant, Chief Umtalo," John said.

49

The chieftain gazed at him for a moment, then turned away. "We will dine," he said. "It is all prepared."

The clan had slaughtered a cow for the occasion, a very special honour in their straitened circumstances; it had already been spitted and roasted over an open fire, and now the chieftain and his guests sat down to enjoy the meat, together with the other elders of the tribes. The Morani drank the blood, and Joseph was left watching from where he continued to hold the horses.

"My man must eat," John told Delamere.

"They will not have him sitting down with us," his lordship said. "But you may take him something."

John took a hunk of meat and went back to the Kikuyu. Joseph was staring at the Masai with interest, and beyond the men at the women, who had left the kraal to inspect the newcomers. If the matrons wore skirts, the unmarried girls were quite naked, save for various bead necklaces, which they regarded as the most valuable things in the world. Tall and straight like their menfolk, they made a most attractive sight. But not, apparently, to Joseph. "These people are savages," he commented. "And you would take them to war?"

Delamere was in fact explaining to Chief Umtalo what he wanted, and the chief was looking extremely pleased. "We go to fight," he said.

"Oh, quite," Delamere agreed.

"Ahem," John remarked.

"But you will fight alongside the white soldiers," Delamere told the chief. "And you will be required to carry their food and ammunition."

"My Morani are not bearers for the white men," Umtalo declared proudly, and looked at Joseph. "Not like the Kikuyu."

"Your men are great warriors," Delamere agreed. "But if you would go to war, you must fight the white man's way."

Umtalo considered this for some time. Then he said, "We will leave the reservation to fight this war?"

"Certainly. With the blessing of the Governor."

50

Further consideration. "There will be pay?" he asked at last.

How are the mighty fallen, John reflected; a Masai, wishing to be paid to fight.

"Of course," Delamere promised.

Umtalo considered this also for some time. His decision had already been taken, but it was not his way to show any haste. It was perhaps an hour later when he said, in the midst of a conversation about something else, "My people will go to war with the white soldiers."

"HE is going to be hopping mad," John remarked, as they made their way home the next day, having secured a promised mobilization of the Masai.

"He worries too much," Delamere replied. "Do you suppose I would have got them to volunteer if I'd told them they were going simply as bearers? We can sort out who does the fighting when the time comes."

John was distinctly doubtful about that but, as it turned out, the Governor raised no objections, because the whole situation soon changed dramatically. The regular forces in British East Africa were somewhat small, consisting of two battalions of the King's African Rifles, composed of black men although officered by whites, and a handful of English troops, and although reinforcements were known to be on their way from India, the general officer commanding was of the opinion that he could use all the volunteer help he could get. He was not, of course, thinking of the Masai, but was anxious for Delamere to implement his original idea and raise a force of irregular cavalry.

This was very easy to do, from the farmers and the Englishmen in Nairobi. Indeed, several troops of light horse were raised, under various commanders, while a good number of Europeans also volunteered to return to England to fight. To his lordship's delight they were issued with uniforms, of a sort, or at least told to dress alike in clothes which nearly every white man in Africa possessed: a slouch hat, pinned up on one side, a bush jacket, matching khaki trousers tucked into brown leggings, and brown ankle boots.

Each man wore a bandolier across his chest and over his left shoulder, and was armed with a new Lee-Enfield .303 rifle, revolver and sword, all government issue, and each man was required to equip himself with two horses, and a servant, similarly dressed and equipped – to the enormous delight of Joseph – but unarmed save for a machete. When they paraded in Nairobi an enormous crowd turned out to cheer them, and they were ceremonially presented with their colours – a Union Jack with a lion embroidered in the canton – by Lady Belfield.

"Delamere's horse," his lordship said proudly at the cocktail party after the parade. "Seventy-seven of the finest troops in the world. I only wish there were more."

"You are quite unutterably handsome," Joanna told her son, who, having been in the OTC at school, had, for all his youth, been given a sergeant's stripes by the commander. "You're not actually going to do any fighting, are you?"

"Well, I hope so," he replied.

"The Germans aren't fighting anybody," she pointed out.

Perhaps not in Africa. But they were certainly fighting in Europe; news arrived of how they had nearly taken Paris, while in Poland they had won a tremendous victory over the Russians. "Doesn't look too good," Delamere confessed. "But we'll win in the end. We always do. If only they'd let us get on with taking German East."

Plans were certainly afoot, but his lordship was not pleased when he discovered that his regiment, as he called them, was to receive a regular officer as captain. "You've no military experience, you see," the Governor explained. "Those fellows who raised their own regiments to fight in South Africa during the Boer War were all ex-Army officers. But you're welcome to volunteer to serve under Captain Pullar. You'll be given the rank of lieutenant."

"Ha," Delamere remarked. "No military experience, eh? I'll bet I could shoot his ears off and he wouldn't even know they were gone until he put his hand up to scratch."

He, and his men, were even more dashed when Captain Pullar turned out to be accompanied by a drill sergeant, who began to teach them to look and act like soldiers. "We got together to fight the Hun, not gallop around a parade ground," his lordship grumbled. But his enthusiasm returned when a squadron of dragoons arrived by train, together with an overall commander for the Nairobi Garrison, as it was now being called.

"The situation is as follows," Colonel Bush explained at a conference of officers he asembled in the newly built Muthaiga Club just outside the city, which was fast replacing the Norfolk as the place to go. John certainly went. He was only an NCO, and therefore not invited, but he was a member of the club, so no one could keep him out; nor did the officers' conference appear particularly private.

"The Navy chaps have really done something rather splendid," the colonel went on, "in that they have forced the cruiser *Koenigsburg* to take shelter in the Rufiji River, which is" – he looked down at the large map which lay on the table, while his audience clustered round – "here." He indicated the river, some sixty miles south of Dar es Salaam.

"Cruiser?" someone asked. "We were told she was a battlecruiser."

"Cruiser," Colonel Bush said firmly. "A light cruiser, as a matter of fact. But none the less dangerous for that. I can now reveal that in addition to several merchantmen, she engaged and sank *HMS Pegasus* just off Mombasa."

That silenced his audience.

"Now," he continued, "she has, as I say, been forced to take refuge up the Rufiji River, and is being blockaded there. Obviously it would be a great thing to capture her or destroy her. Thus a campaign in German East becomes more than ever necessary. So here is what General Aitken proposes to do. With the main part of his army, as well as the KAR, and supported by such naval units as are available, he intends to launch a seaborne assault on the port of Tanga, here." Once again he indicated the map. "You will observe that Tanga is only about sixty miles south of Mombasa, just across the border, in fact, which greatly assists the logistical situation. It is also less well defended than Dar es Salaam itself. Now, once Tanga is in our hands, he proposes to wheel his forces down along the coast to take Dar es Salaam from the rear. The enemy have only a few hundred men in German East, and although the blighters have actually raised a force of black soldiers of their own, we don't suppose they are up to much, so the whole operation should not take very long to complete. Once Dar es Salaam is in our hands, and this fellow Lettow-Vorbeck safely locked up, why, then we shall move south and take the *Koenigsburg*.

"Now, chaps, our task is to move south from Nairobi, cross the border and cut the railway line that leads from the coast into the interior; that will prevent the German garrisons from reinforcing the coast. Once that is done, we ride east to join the main force. I'm afraid you must prepare for a campaign of at least two months, if we are going to achieve all our objectives. But at least you'll be home for Christmas, eh, with the satisfaction of having done a good job well. Are your Masai bearers ready to move, Lord Delamere?"

"My Masai bearers have been ready to move for six weeks," Delamere told him. "Sir."

"Then the column will move out at dawn the day after tomorrow. Dismissed, gentlemen."

"Two months?" Joanna cried. "Two months in the bush, being shot at?"

"Oh, come now, Mother," John protested. "Didn't you go into the bush, to be shot at, when you first came out here?"

"With bows and arrows," she said reminiscently, and then smiled. "You're right. I'm being an old mother hen. But mind you come back in one piece. Your father always did."

"Nothing can happen to me," John insisted. "I have Joseph to look after me."

It was odd how reassuring that thought was.

The excitement was enormous as the little army assembled for its campaign, and as the Masai Morani, some forty of them, loped into town. The stares of the populace were matched by those of the Morani. If to the good people of Nairobi these fearsome warriors had hitherto only been legends, none of the Morani had ever seen a city before – since 1906 Nairobi had been strictly out of bounds, and they had never had any reason for going there.

"A fine body of men," the Governor commented, glancing anxiously at his wife, who was holding her hat in front of her eyes. Unlike her daughter. "Don't they ever wear any clothes?"

"Why should they?" Delamere asked.

"I think you should move them out as quickly as possible," his excellency recommended. "My dear fellow, the bishop is here. And you'd better take away those nasty-looking spears."

"They need them," Delamere insisted. "To kill game."

But John suspected that he, and everyone else, was relieved when the order to march was given, and the brigade, as Colonel Bush proudly described his three hundred men – including the Masai – moved out in a column of twos. The dragoons were leading and the volunteers behind, although Bush allowed the volunteers, who knew this country better than any of his men, to send up the advance guard.

Their route lay roughly due south, along the northern edge of the Nyeri desert, to the border with German East Africa, which took them three days.

"Can there really be a higher mountain than that, Mr John?" Joseph asked as they camped on the third night under the shadow of Kilimanjaro.

"There is one right here in British East," John told him. "Only eighty-odd miles north of Nairobi. They call it Mount Kenya."

"That I would like to see."

"Well, maybe we'll make a safari up there next year. Just you and me. Would you like that?"

"I would like that very much, Mr John," Joseph said.

At noon next day they rode into the little village of Namanga, but there were no Germans to be seen, and the dusty track stretched on to the south.

"They were here, but they left when they heard you were coming," the headman explained.

"How many?" Delamere inquired.

The headman held up both hands, spread, then one hand.

"Maybe a dozen," Delamere decided.

"Who the hell told them we were coming?" Colonel Bush demanded.

"It was brought by the birds," the headman assured him solemnly.

"These people are all related to the blacks on the other side," Delamere explained. "They've known we were coming for days."

"Hm," Bush commented. "Well, how far is it from here to the railway?"

"Thirty miles."

"Right. We'll camp here for the night, and move on tomorrow. But, my lord, put a picket of your men a quarter of a mile south of the village." He grinned. "May as well take possession of our first German soil, eh?"

John rode with the picket down the road for a quarter of a mile, and there found a suitable clump of trees beneath which they could make their camp. "You'll have a guard up all night," he told the corporal. "And at the first sign of trouble, start shooting and we'll be with you in a jiffy."

"What kind of trouble do you expect, Sergeant?" the corporal asked, looking around him at the empty countryside.

"There does happen to be a war on," John pointed out.

"But the Germans have gone."

"Yes, but we don't know how far. So keep your eyes open."

"If you ask me, the whole damned business is a load of codswallop," grumbled one of the troopers, "meant to keep us from the ngong."

"Who said anything about a ngong?" John asked.

"The headman," the trooper replied. "He's set on having one."

"Oh, lord," John muttered, and trotted back to the camp. But the headman was indeed set on holding a dance to entertain his guests, and could not be dissuaded by either Colonel Bush or Lord Delamere. John suspected his intention was both to prove his patriotism – he had probably held one for the Germans as well – and to placate the Morani, of whom his people were plainly terrified. So instead of getting to their beds, the brigade sat around and watched the young men and their women performing the stately foot-stamping movements, to the accompaniment of surging drumbeats. As both males and females were naked, and part of the dance consisted of bringing their bodies against each other and doing some squirming, with inevitable results, the troopers clearly didn't want to go to bed at all.

"I've a nasty feeling there could be trouble," John muttered to Delamere.

"My dear boy, these are English soldiers," Delamere said, which was not entirely reassuring.

The dancing did not end until well after midnight, by which time John was feeling pretty aroused himself. Watching all those breasts and buttocks and erected penises and bristling pubes made him think of Adelheid Huttingen, and feel quite ashamed of himself. But tomorrow he was going to cross into her land, and seek to capture it. And her? That was an unbearably romantic fantasy to set on top of the sexual one.

Certainly he did not feel like bed, and so he decided to take a walk down to the picket and see if they were awake. He left the glare of the fire and the now very sleepy soldiers and dancers, and strolled down the track, his boots making little noise on the grass-bound earth. He calculated he must have walked about three hundred yards, and even in the darkness – it was a moonless night - he could make out the copse where the picket had been stationed. Suddenly he heard a distinct click. He looked left and right, and realized he was between two men; each wore a uniform not unlike his own, although instead of a bush hat they had conical white topees on their heads.

57

And they both carried rifles, which were pointing at him. "Oh, hell," he said.

"Do not make a noise, Englander," the first German said, in English, "or we will shoot you. Now, raise your arms."

John hesitated only a moment. He had left his rifle at the camp, and although he still wore his revolver, he knew he would never have the time to draw it. But to be taken prisoner, just like that. . . . He sighed, and raised his hands.

The first German said something to his companion, who stepped forward and unclipped John's holster, taking out the gun and throwing it to the ground. "You are our prisoner," the spokesman said. "Now walk to those trees."

"What have you done with my men?" John asked.

"They are also our prisoners. They gave us no trouble. They were all fast asleep."

"Damnation," John said. But then, he had been wide awake and no more successful. He was taking his first step towards the copse when a very familiar voice shouted, "All right, chaps, open fire!"

Instantly what seemed like a burst of riflefire came from fairly close to his right. Neither of the Germans was hit, but they were certainly alarmed and took to their heels, while John hurled himself back along the track to regain his revolver, which he did after a moment's scrabbling. Meanwhile several shots came from the copse, indicating that the Germans were not alone. The British fire had ceased for the moment, although there was great activity from the village, with a bugle blowing and men shouting and horses neighing. John faced the copse, still lying down, the revolver thrust forward, and listened to pounding footsteps. A moment later Joseph hurled himself to the ground beside him. "We must get back," he said.

"You?" John shouted, and realized Joseph was carrying his rifle. "Where are the others?"

"There are no others, Mr John," the Kikuyu explained.

"You came alone?"

"I could not let you walk into the darkness all by yourself.

But you have never shown me how to reload this rifle," he said reproachfully.

"Well, I'll be. . . ." John listened to hoofbeats, from both in front and behind him. A few minutes later Delamere and a dozen of the volunteers arrived, closely followed by Bush and several of the dragoons.

"They should not know I fired the rifle," Joseph whispered urgently, as he and John scrambled to their feet.

"What the devil is going on?" Delamere demanded. "Jacko, are you all right?"

"Yes, my lord. It was a German ambush, into which my man and I stumbled."

"Well, it's a damned good thing you did," Bush declared, "or they might have surprised the camp. What about your picket?"

"I'm afraid they were taken prisoner, sir," John explained.

"Without firing a shot?"

"Poor devils were surprised," Delamere growled.

They went forward to the copse, and by the light of matches saw that there must have been a considerable number of Germans, who had apparently walked their horses up to the copse and there surprised the sleeping volunteers.

By now the entire camp had turned out, together with the Masai, and the leader of the warriors, a relative of Umtalo named Mbango, began talking to Delamere.

"What's he saying?" Bush wanted to know.

"He wants to go and get my men back," Delamere said.

"Get your men back? Him?"

"And his Morani. I'm inclined to let him do it, Colonel. There's none of us up to tracking like these fellows, and besides, the Huns will see us coming for miles. The Masai will be upon them before they know it. It'll put the fear of God into them as well, which will be no bad thing."

"Really, my lord," Bush protested, "I am surprised at you. You'd turn these savages loose on civilized men?"

"The Germans use native soldiers. So do we."

"Trained men. Disciplined," Bush pointed out. "These savages . . . good Lord, we'd be reported to the Geneva

Convention. I'm sorry, my lord, but the answer has to be No."

Delamere looked as if he would have liked to argue, but decided against it and took Mbango off for a chat. Meanwhile Colonel Bush stood the force down and told them to get what sleep they could.

"Mr John," Joseph asked, as they returned to their tent, "how could those men surrender without fighting?"

"They were taken by surprise," John said. "Oh, it was their own fault, I know. They obviously didn't put out a guard, as I told them to."

"But just to give up . . . would it not have been better to die?"

"Well, I suppose that's a point of view."

"How can there be any choice? Will they not be tortured before they are killed?"

"Tortured? Killed? Good lord, Joseph, they're not going to be killed."

Joseph was clearly puzzled. "Then what will be done to them?"

"Why, nothing. I suppose they'll be sent to Dar es Salaam, where we will set them free when we take the place."

Joseph scratched his head, clearly bewildered. "Then what was the point in taking them prisoner at all?"

"Well . . . the rules of war, I suppose."

"We do not fight wars like that in Africa."

"I know you don't. But we're trying to teach you to."

"There is no logic in what you do," Joseph pointed out. "You go out and fight a man and try to kill him, but if he decides he has had enough and throws down his gun you treat him as a friend. Having perhaps just killed his friend. That is frivolous, Mr John. Killing is a serious business, and if you set out to kill people, you must kill them all."

It was John's turn to scratch his head as Joseph blew out the candle. He had never thought of it like that before. Nor did he wish to think of it like that now. Joseph could be a confoundedly annoying fellow. But also a very brave one, to whom he owed his freedom. "I'd like to thank you," he said into the darkness.

"Thank me, Mr John?"

"For coming to my rescue." He grinned. "Even if you damn near got me killed."

"It is my business to protect you, Mr John," Joseph said severely.

John closed his eyes. But he did not suppose he was going to do much sleeping. He was too excited by what had happened, and if he was certainly disappointed in the showing of the volunteers he was not going to let Joseph know it.

But he was more pleased with himself. While Joseph had shown remarkable courage and ability in the way he had bluffed the Germans into thinking they were being attacked by a sizeable force, he had himself also revealed quite a lot of courage, he decided. The only emotion he could recall during the fracas was one of annoyance at walking into the arms of the Germans. Certainly he had not felt any fear when the bullets were whizzing about his head.

Thinking that, he fell asleep. It seemed only five minutes later that he awoke to find it was dawn, and Lord Delamere was standing in the doorway of his tent. Never had John seen his lordship looking so downcast. But then, John could not recall ever having seen Delamere downcast at all.

"Whatever is the matter, my lord?" he asked, scrambling to his feet.

"The Masai," Delamere said in stricken tones. "Mbango has taken the buggers home."

3

John ran outside, to find the rest of the officers also gathered, together with the troopers and the volunteers, staring at the neatly piled boxes and knapsacks left by the Morani. Apparently nothing had been stolen, but the warriors had taken their departure. Only Lord Delamere's personal servants remained, to tell what had happened.

"Mbango says that you have insulted his people," they explained. "He does not believe that you will let them fight at all. He does not believe you intend to fight at all. He will not take his Morani merely to be bearers for a white man's safari."

"Well, I'll be damned," Colonel Bush remarked. He looked at Delamere. "You know these people, my lord. Can they be brought back?"

"I doubt it."

"I'd be grateful if you could try, my lord. Without bearers we are going to have problems – unless we can recruit from these people here."

"I am quite sure you can do that, Colonel," Delamere said. "But I would strongly advise against it. These people will throw your goods away and take to their heels the moment you see a German, if they do not actually betray you."

"Well, then, I must ask you to follow the Masai and endeavour to bring them back," Bush said again.

Delamere hesitated, and glanced at John. But he could not take the troop sergeant – and he had made the appointment himself. He had his men gather his gear.

"Are we going to remain here, sir, until the bearers return?" Captain Pullar asked.

"I don't see how we can do that. We were sent to cut the railway. We'll have to proceed with what we can. You'd better leave a detachment of the volunteers here to guard the rest of our gear, until either his lordship returns with the Masai, or we can send for them. The remainder of the brigade moves out the moment they've breakfasted."

John said goodbye to a thoroughly disgusted Delamere, but he was more concerned not to be one of those left behind. In this he was fortunate, and his spirits were again high as they rode out of the village in mid-morning, the volunteers forming an advance screen, every man now anxious to retrieve the troop's reputation by locating and despatching as many Germans as possible. Like the dragoons, they carried only their rifles and ammunition, and four days' rations — no tents or changes of clothing.

Alas for their hopes of a fight, the country was absolutely empty. They camped for that night some ten miles north of the railway, forming a sort of zareba within which they felt safe from German assaults, although Bush was now taking the situation much more seriously and had sentries on guard all night. The next day, just on noon, after another leisurely start, they sighted the track running like a huge iron snake across the bush. But still no Germans.

"I imagine they've worked out that they can't oppose us with a dozen men," Bush decided. "Well, we'll tear up these tracks. Do a good job of it now."

The troopers fell to work with a will, digging up the sleepers to burn them, and piling the rails. Obviously the rails could not be destroyed, but without sleepers the track could not be relaid in a hurry. Meanwhile the volunteers were sent out on patrol, split into two groups, one under Captain Pullar and the other under John, who found himself given the rank of brevet lieutenant in Lord Delamere's absence, not only because he had already been their sergeant, but because of his coolness at Namanga.

He was appointed to ride west for several miles and ascertain that there were no Germans in the vicinity. It was suggested he spend the night out and return next morning, by which time the troopers would have finished the job of destruction. He had thirty men, but not Joseph, as servants were forbidden to accompany their masters on an actual campaign. He threw out an advance guard and flankers, and proceeded up the track for some distance. The ground was as undulating as all the high country on either side of the border, and contained the usual number of secret hollows and copses, large boulders and small hills, but still appeared to be quite empty of humanity. There was quite a variety of game, and the volunteers were with difficulty restrained from opening up with their new magazine rifles, quite the most destructive weapons most of them had ever owned.

"We're here to kill Germans, not antelope," John pointed out, but he allowed Corporal Smithson and Trooper Brown, the two best shots he had, to bring down a buck apiece for their evening meal. A halt was then called, and the dead animals were skinned and carved, while the flankers rode in to report all was quiet.

"We'll camp here for the night," John decided. They were situated in a small hollow, about three hundred yards to the right of the track, where there was a spring of water, nearly dry but still sufficient for thirty men and their horses. A fire was soon blazing, and the men were roasting their antelope steaks and drinking their water laced with the brandy almost every man carried in his knapsack. John walked up to the top of the surrounding escarpment, accompanied by Smithson, to look out over the country as the sun began to sink into the west.

"Who said war is terrible," Smithson remarked. "Those lads are having the time of their lives, Mr Barclay. Just one long safari. Of course it's a pity about Withers and the boys being taken prisoner."

"Damned carelessness," John grumbled.

"I wonder where they are now," Smithson ventured.

"Miles away, poor buggers. Well, I'm for some steak, Corporal. But we'll have men on guard all night up here."

"You reckon that's really necessary, sir?" Smithson asked, and then said, "Holy smoke!"

John turned to look in the direction in which the corporal was pointing, and saw several horsemen walking their mounts along the track. "Down," he snapped, half pushing Smithson to the ground.

"Those must be the buggers who took Withers," Smithson said. "We could nab them in turn, Mr Barclay."

"They're only scouts," John told him. He had already seen the dust about a mile behind the advance guard, and a few minutes later they could make out a large body of mounted men, perhaps a hundred strong, followed by an even larger body of men on foot, also marching next to the railway line. The mounted men wore uniforms very similar to those he had encountered at Namanga; the men on foot were in lighter gear and, although it was now getting dark, he had no doubt they were askaris, native soldiers - they were loping along at nearly the pace of the horses.

"Do you think they spotted us?" Smithson gasped.

"If they knew we were here, we'd all be dead by now, or prisoners," John said. That the Germans had not heard the rifle shots or seen the smoke of the fire was certainly mainly because the light wind was from the north, but it was reassuring to realize their scouting was no more efficient than the British had hitherto been. "They're off to attack the colonel and the brigade." He peered at the column, which was certainly a strong one; if they also obtained the advantage of surprise, the result could be a British disaster. "They'll be in position by dawn."

"Hell's bells," Smithson muttered. "Then we'll be cut off."

"Like hell we will." John slid back down the slope, the corporal beside him. "Douse that fire," he commanded. "Quickly."

The men stared at him.

"Germans," Smithson said briefly. "All about."

There was no further hesitation.

"And prepare to move out," John said.

"If they're all around us," someone said, "wouldn't we be better off staying right here as they haven't spotted us yet?"

"They're not interested in us," John told him. "They're off to attack the brigade, probably at dawn tomorrow. But they have foot soldiers with them, and although they're moving pretty fast, we can move faster. We'll ride round them."

"Back to brigade?" asked someone else. "Right into a battle?"

"For God's sake," John snapped. "Isn't that what we're here for, to fight a battle?"

"We'll never make it, Mr Barclay," Smithson objected. "As soon as we start to canter, even, they'll hear us. Those askaris have sharp ears."

"Then they'll either have to catch us or kill us," John said. "Either way there'll be a lot of noise, and that will alert brigade. Anyway, if only one of us gets through, that'll stop the surprise."

The men looked at him, and then at each other. They hadn't really come out here to sacrifice themselves. But no one had the courage to declare himself a coward.

"What about all this grub?" someone asked.

"Take as much of it as you want in your saddlebags," John said. "But there won't be any cooking until this show is over. Now, prepare to mount."

For a moment he thought no one was going to obey him, in which case he had no idea what he was going to do, but then first one, and then another, and then the rest began packing up the meat and picking up their gear. John returned to the top of the rise and studied the Germans. The column was just about past them by now, and he reckoned that within fifteen minutes it was going to be utterly dark. He went back to his men. "We'll walk our horses out, to the south, as soon as it's dark," he said. "Then, when we've covered about two miles, we'll mount, turn east and ride like hell. Understood? We'll keep together as a body and be prepared to return fire if we have to, but the important thing is to regain brigade."

"One of us," someone said dolefully.

"One will do," John said again, looking from face to face.

Fifteen minutes later, as he had estimated, it was dark enough to move out. He led the way, with Smithson at the rear to make sure there were no stragglers; he had formed a column of ones, each man and his horse immediately behind the other, taking his direction as best he could from the stars. It was a heavenly night, as so often on the high ground, and although the temperature was already beginning to drop quite sharply, as they were moving he did not suppose it was going to be desperately uncomfortable.

There was hardly any wind, but they could still hear the movement of the Germans, over to the north of them, although obviously the Germans could not hear them making the same noise but on a much smaller scale, and down wind. Yet his heart pounded and he was aware of sweating despite the chill – if they *were* to be discovered, they would be wiped out in a moment. Nor was it reassuring to know that the men behind him were in an even more nervous state.

He walked for an hour, by his watch, before he gave the command to halt and went back down the line, making sure everyone had kept up and that every man knew what he had to do. Then he gave the order to mount. Still he kept south-east, for another hour, until he reckoned they were about parallel with the German force; all sounds to the north had died as the gap between the two groups opened up. This was actually more eerie than before; it was like playing blind man's buff, only with loaded rifles.

Now he gave the word to canter due east, and the little column increased speed, while he brought them into twos. They moved rapidly across the arid bush, with only the occasional stumble in the darkness; one man was thrown but regained his horse quickly enough – neither was hurt. John knew that he commanded, at the least, a body of superb horsemen.

He looked at his watch; it was ten o'clock. They had been on the march for three hours. He called a halt to give the horses a breather, and to listen. "Hear anything?" he asked Smithson.

"I think I can," the corporal replied. "Difficult to be sure, though."

After a ten-minute break, they remounted and rode on, now at a brisk trot. He estimated they could not be more than a couple of miles from the British camp when there was a sudden challenge from in front of him. He had no idea what was said, but he knew it wasn't English – and that was good enough. "Ride through them," he shouted. "Charge! Oh, and draw swords."

The volunteers responded with a will. Steel rasped, and they gave a cheer as they rushed at the German patrol, which was taken by surprise by the impetuosity and size of the charge. Rifles cracked, and John heard a shout of pain from someone close by. Then he saw dark shapes in front of him, perhaps a dozen men on horseback. He pointed his sword at them, struck one man with his horse's shoulder, throwing him aside, cannoned into another, and then was through; he had not actually touched anyone with his sword.

About fifty yards farther on he drew rein to look back and see how many of his men he still had, and was pleased to discover most of them. But the Germans were recovering from their discomfort and opening fire again. Immediately another volunteer was hit, and tumbled from his saddle, while more shots came from the north to indicate that the main German body was now aware of their presence.

"We can't help him," John shouted. "Ride. Ride like hell."

They galloped into the night, followed by rifle shots and a great deal of noise, and listened to a bugle call from in front of them: the racket had awakened the British camp.

"Don't shoot," John bellowed. "It's us. But there are Germans behind."

Colonel Bush had formed another miniature fortress with railway track and bush, and over this the fleeing volunteers vaulted their mounts, to fall from their saddles into the arms of their servants and comrades, while Colonel Bush and Captain Pullar and the other officers hurried up to discover what had happened. Everyone had his tale to tell, of how Jimmy had stopped one, and George had cut down that German, and Harry had a bullet in the arm, and Peter was coughing blood – Bush had to take John aside to discover the truth. "Do you think they'll still attack?" he asked, for the noise from the west had died.

"Well, they know we're waiting for them," John said.

"That was good work, Barclay," the colonel said. "Good work. It will not go unrewarded, I promise you. Now go and have something to eat and a rest."

Joseph was waiting for him. "I should have been with you," he remarked. "You could have got yourself killed, Mr John."

The Germans decided against attacking, having no doubt been shaken by the appearance of a troop of British horsemen in their very midst. Although the dragoons and the volunteers stood to their arms the whole day, nothing happened, and a cautious patrol that evening ascertained that the enemy had retired. "I wonder where," Bush remarked. "I'm inclined to go and find out."

"We need food and water," Pullar reminded him.

Bush nodded. "We'll send a patrol back to the village to see if Lord Delamere has got the Masai back yet, and to return with rations," he decided.

So it was a matter of spending another day in the sun, waiting for something to happen. The volunteers were in a mood of mixed elation at their success, and gloom at the loss of five more of their comrades. Of these, only one had been definitely established as dead; the others were probably prisoners. But they were also certainly wounded, and no one knew how they were being treated. There were also half a dozen wounded amongst those who had returned, and these were sent off to Namanga with the ration patrol, with orders to return to Nairobi and the hospital there.

"Still, I think we can say that we have accomplished the first part of our mission and given the Huns a bloody nose," Bush said with some satisfaction.

John was not inclined to agree with him, as so far as he knew none of the Germans had been killed; and they had not been defeated, they had only retired up the line to await a better opportunity for an attack. He hoped it would come soon. Sitting around an empty plain with no change of clothing, no water to wash in much less shave, and only two days' rations left, was not a pleasant business.

That afternoon the patrol returned, bringing some food, and also devastating news. Not only had Delamere not yet returned with the Masai, but they had encountered a despatch rider from Nairobi, who accompanied them back to the brigade to inform Colonel Bush that the attack on Tanga had been utterly defeated by the Germans and the British force had retired to Mombasa. The orders from General Aitken were therefore for all units to pull back to the border for the time being, until further reinforcements were received.

"For heaven's sake," Captain Pullar remarked.

John felt the same way. They had 'invaded' German East Africa, suffered twelve casualties and antagonized the Masai – to absolutely no purpose.

"That's war," Colonel Bush said wisely. He had served in South Africa against the Boers and had no doubt encountered this sort of thing before.

But there was even worse in the despatch wallet: orders for them to remain in Namanga and defend it against an expected German counter-attack. So they made their way back to the village and there set up camp. This time they were not quite so welcome; the headman was not pleased by the idea of some two hundred and fifty white men permanently encamped on his doorstep, making his village a fortress and eventually, perhaps, a battlefield.

Colonel Bush certainly turned it into a fortress, having his men throw up earthworks, dig trenches and, of course, latrines, mounting sentries, and generally making a thorough nuisance of themselves to the villagers. Except for the girls, who found the presence of so many stalwart and bored white men most stimulating. "Next thing, we'll have a rash of VD," Pullar grumbled.

So there they were, and there they stayed; the idea of that triumphant return to spend Christmas with their families was quickly forgotten. For the troopers it was no more disappointing than any other aspect of army life. They were manning an outpost which the enemy showed not the slightest inclination to attack, they had food and water, and even women, and they knew that one day they would either

70

be relieved or recalled. The volunteers were not so sanguine. Most of them had left their farms in the firm conviction that this was going to be a short campaign. Now they began to suspect it might last a very long time. Nor were they reassured when some entrepreneur organized a safari from Nairobi to bring their wives and sweethearts to them, as they could not go home. The white ladies did not like the look of the naked black girls any more than the black girls liked the look of the memsahibs.

Adrian Barclay himself came up to the frontier to have a look and see how John was getting on. He also brought news of Lord Delamere and the Masai, none of it good. The Morani had flatly refused to return to the army merely as bearers, and his lordship, entirely agreeing with them, had put the matter before the Governor. But Belfield was by now in the hands of the military men, who had decided that the Masai were actually guilty of mutiny and desertion, and had determined that they should be punished. The result had been a military expedition not against the Germans, but against the Morani, which the Masai had enjoyed more than the British soldiers. The fiasco had thus resulted in, as usual, unnecessary casualties, further antagonism and the total fury of Delamere at seeing his beloved people so mistreated; his lordship had resigned from the army forthwith and taken himself back to his farm, wishing perdition on the whole war effort. "He suggests you do the same," Adrian told John.

"Do you want me to?"

"No. A man should always finish what he begins. And all wars are colossal mistakes, in every sense, from beginning to end. Besides, you're quite a hero, you know."

John wasn't quite sure why – he was still terribly aware of the men he had had to leave behind during that dash through the German ranks – but apparently he was.

The resignation of Delamere had disturbed the military. As they hadn't felt able to refuse his lordship's determination to go home, they were aware that this precedent might turn out most unfortunately if other volunteers decided to follow his example. So John found himself recalled temporarily to Nairobi, where he was entertained to dinner by the Governor, along with Adrian and Joanna, and then, at a public ceremony, invested with the Military Cross. Lord Delamere refused to attend the ceremony. "But he is actually very proud of you," Adrian told him.

John was also confirmed in his rank as lieutenant, and after a night on the town with Monica, suitably chaperoned by their respective fathers, returned to Namanga to encourage his men.

But John was not at all sure how long he would be able to hold the volunteers. Fortunately, early in the new year things began to improve. Thousands of troops began to land at Mombasa, mainly from India, and with them they brought a new general, Aitken having been fired for his incompetence at Tanga. His replacement, General Tighe, immediately sent off stirring messages to all the men of his command and announced that he intended to clear the enemy out of German East Africa in one decisive campaign.

Unfortunately, there were already rumours. "Oh, he'll do it all right," said the officer who brought the despatch to Namanga, "if he stays sober long enough."

Tighe did not lack energy, however. He reorganized the situation in British East, and started his columns moving across the border. General Lettow-Vorbeck – *he* had been promoted following his brilliant defence of Tanga – realized that he could not hope to fight a pitched battle when he was so desperately outnumbered. He commanded only about two thousand German soldiers, and a somewhat larger force of askaris, whereas Tighe had close to a hundred thousand men at his disposal, so he fell back to defend Dar es Salaam. But his men indulged in guerilla tactics, launching sudden attacks upon any isolated British force and defending river crossings with great tenacity before melting away into the jungle. The British advance was therefore slow and uncertain – no one could any longer doubt that they were in for a long war.

Yet it was a great relief to be able to abandon Namanga, which was by now something of a cesspool, and advance once more into northern Tanganyika. Now they were in every way the hunters rather than the hunted, and the squadron's strength had been considerably augmented by new recuits. Their months on the border had not been entirely wasted, as they had been drilled until they could now give a passable imitation of regular soldiers.

Their mission was to seek and destroy any of the enemy they encountered, and also anywhere the enemy might shelter or had possibly stored supplies.

John had spent much of his spare time at Namanga thinking about Adelheid – and grimly resisting the temptation to have a go at one of the local girls – and it was with a considerable feeling of alarm that, chasing what they suspected was a German patrol, he and his men came upon an isolated farm, some hundred miles within the Tanganyika border. The place was surrounded, but was obviously not concealing any soldiers. On the other hand, no one could doubt that they had been there, despite the protests of the farmer.

John – who had definite orders as to what to do in these circumstances – was very relieved to discover that the man was alone save for two black hands; he had sent his women to the south for safety. He hoped other farmers had done the same. While he would have loved to come across Adelheid in one of these remote outposts, he doubted she would ever wish to speak to him again after he had destroyed her father's livelihood. The farmer burst into tears as he watched the volunteers piling dried grass inside and around his building, then striking matches, while his herds were driven off to augment the ever increasing meat requirements of the army.

"The fortunes of war," John tried to explain, but he doubted he had much success as he watched the tears rolling down the unhappy man's cheeks.

Joseph approved. "War is war," he reminded his master. "And must be carried to a successful conclusion, whoever gets hurt." John had a feeling that had he been in command of the British army, instead of Tighe, Tanganyika would have been conquered in a couple of months, even if it had by

73

then been reduced to a smoking ruin. Yet it was enormously reassuring to have Joseph at his back and, being in command of a troop, he could issue his own orders and make sure that the Kikuyu always *was* there. His combination of determination to protect his master, personal courage and total ruthlessness made him the perfect warrior – John wondered if Lord Delamere would ever recognize the worth of the Kikuyu, when given their opportunity.

Meanwhile, they campaigned, while the huge British army, never opposed by more than a twentieth of its size, slowly moved across the vast expanses of Tanganyika to invest Dar es Salaam. John enjoyed campaigning: it was the most purposeful thing he had ever done in his life to this time. It had the spice of danger – he had now been under fire at least a dozen times – and the spice of adventure; he had been living with men he had come to respect and who, more importantly, had come to respect him; and he had had both his courage and his ability pronounced to the world – he was now a captain. No one would ever be able to take these achievements away from him.

While Joseph . . . ? "Will you be glad to get home, when the Germans have been beaten?" John asked.

Joseph considered the question. He had the typical African's way of thinking deeply before replying to any important matter. "I will be happy where you are happy," he said at last.

He still retained the power to be terribly irritating. "Have you no wish to live a life of your own?" John demanded.

Another consideration. A conversation between him and Chief Umtalo, John thought, could well take a week to cover a single subject. "I will live my own life, Mr John," Joseph said at last, "when it is so willed."

John knew he was not speaking of any African witchcraft sign; he had been brought up a Christian and was a devout one – at Naivasha he had attended service every Sunday, as he did at the camp meetings in the army. And yet his view of warfare was so implacably unchristian.

"How will you know when it is willed?" John asked.

74

"I will know, Mr John," Joseph said, with total confidence.

Under Tighe's direction, the cavalry eventually succeeded in dislodging the Germans although Lettow-Vorbeck once again evaded destruction by performing a brilliant march to the south-west through the bush, actually cutting across behind the British horsemen. He had been defeated, certainly; it was estimated that his total force had been reduced to little over five thousand men, of whom hardly more than a third were German – but he was still in the field.

The cavalry were utterly chagrined, but General Tighe reassured them that the fault was not theirs. "We must just continue the pursuit," he told them. "We'll get him, one of these days. And at least we have cleared the path to the south."

Tighe now decided on another cavalry raid while the main army settled down to take Dar es Salaam. Only sixty odd miles to the south there was an immense prize waiting to be seized. Orders were given for a strong force of cavalry to ride for the Rufiji River, where the *Koenigsburg* was still holed up, and cooperate with the Navy in taking the ship. Every man was keen to be involved, but to his delight John's troop was one of those chosen, as it was deemed that the volunteer cavalry, with their knowledge of African conditions, would be able to travel faster across the bush than the regulars, and it was a case of getting to the ship before anyone suspected what they were about.

"You'll split into three columns," Brigadier Maitland told them, "each of three hundred men. The first will proceed by way of the coast and make contact with the Navy. The second will go by way of Morogoro and head straight for the ship. The third will swing round by Kilosa and come down the river from the west. The task of this column will be to prevent Lettow-Vorbeck from getting any reinforcements to the cruiser, should he discover what we intend."

The inland sweep was given to the main body of the volunteers, three squadrons commanded by Colonel Pullar, who had been promoted. Colonel Pullar in turn split his command into three, allowing each squadron to operate independently for logistical purposes – they were as usual travelling light and would have to live off the country – and setting the rendezvous on the river itself, just below the Ruaha Rapids, some forty miles above the warship's reported position.

It was the first time since the farm-burning days that John had been given an entirely independent command, and he rode off with his band of veterans, as they were now, Lieutenants Brown and Smithson at his shoulder, Joseph and the bugler behind them, and the rest of the volunteers trotting in a column of twos. Their rapid advance took most of the natives by surprise, as well as the Germans. In one village they found all the white people hastily packing up. John had no idea what to do with them, so he told them to get on with it and surrender to the nearest British force behind him. Then they rode on again, approaching another village. Beyond the village, they had been told, were several farms. This certainly promised some more fresh food, which was badly needed, as well as drinking water. But the scouts came hurrying back with the news that they had been fired on from a fortification on the outskirts of the village.

"Soldiers?" John asked.

"I don't think so," the corporal replied grimly. "They shot too straight. Poor Clamp bought it. There was also a lack of cohesion about their movements. But they were white men all right."

"Hm," John remarked. Thus far the German farmers had left the fighting to the soldiers, although he did not doubt they had also raised volunteer forces to defend their colony. If in uniform, they had to take their chances, just as his men did; he did not like the idea of fighting civilians. But he could not allow himself to be checked at this stage; however much he would have liked to bypass the resistance, his men needed that food and water, as did his horses.

"Well," he said, "we'll have to move them. Smithson, you'll take forty men and make a sweep to the west to get

76

behind them. Two miles should do it; I'll give you half an hour. Brown, you'll bring the rest behind me."

He led the advance down the track and soon came in sight of the village. There old-fashioned barricade-type defences had been thrown up, and as the British column came in sight there was a burst of firing which sent the volunteers to shelter. There were several casualties, none of them serious.

"They're a determined lot of bastards," Brown commented.

"They don't know what they're up against," John said. "This could be a bloody massacre. Make me up a white flag."

He himself took the flag of truce forward, with only Joseph at his elbow. He walked his horse slowly down the beaten-earth road until, about a hundred yards from the barricade, he was halted by a shot in the air. "That's far enough, Englander," someone shouted.

"You are outnumbered and outgunned," John said. "I am calling upon you to surrender."

"We will surrender when we are ready, Englander," came the reply.

"Now, what the devil does he mean by that?" John muttered.

"I would say they are endeavouring to give their families time to get away," Joseph suggested.

"Of course." He raised his voice again. "Your people cannot escape," he called. "My men have already ridden round behind you."

"Then we must sell our lives dearly," the German called, and fired again. This time the bullet kicked up dust in front of them. "Next time I will shoot straighter. You have one minute to get out of range."

John hesitated, then wheeled his horse and trotted back up the road, Joseph at his heels.

"You must destroy them now, Mr John," Joseph said.

Brown was of the same opinion. "I'd say he asked for whatever he gets, Captain Barclay."

John sighed, but he knew they were right. "Very well,"

he agreed. "Mount the machine gun. Spread your men to either side, and have them advance through the bush as the gun starts firing. Tell them to take their time; we want Lieutenant Smithson's command to come in from the rear."

The machine gun was emplaced directly in front of the barricade, at just inside maximum range, and a few minutes later began its deadly chatter. They could see pieces of wood from the piled tree trunks flying into the air; that a good number of the bullets got through could not be doubted. The Germans replied as best they could, but they were distracted by the riflefire coming from the bush to either side as Brown's men advanced, while now there was a burst of firing from behind them.

"Lieutenant Smithson has encountered the fleeing people," Joseph observed with quiet satisfaction.

John wished he could share his elation; he had no doubt at all that a considerable amount of murder was being done this day. But it had been the Germans' choice. "Keep firing," he said, but only a few minutes later a white flag was again raised, this time over the remains of the barricade. "Bugler," he called. "Sound cease fire."

The noise slowly died behind the notes of the trumpet, and John remounted and walked his horse forward, Joseph as usual immediately behind him, while Brown's men rose out of the grass to follow him up to the barricade. The sight there was sickening. There had been perhaps forty white men and a few Africans defending the village. Of these more than half were on the ground; several were dead, but most badly wounded by the flying bullets.

"Have you a doctor?" John asked the most senior-looking of the surviving white men, in the scanty German he had managed to pick up during the campaign.

"We sent the doctor with the women," the German replied, in good English.

"Then we must get him back. Lieutenant Brown, send a rider to Lieutenant Smithson requesting him to return here with all despatch, with his prisoners. Meanwhile, mein Herr, we must do what we can with our field dressings."

His men fell to, while he and Brown inspected the village.

78

"You are all from here?" he asked the spokesman, who turned out to be an engineer named Hoffman.

"From the farms. There are several only a mile or two to the south. This was a good community."

"It will be again, under British rule," John promised him. "But it was very foolish of you to take on regular soldiers."

"It was the decision of Herr Huttingen. He is the senior planter, and he hates all Englanders."

John frowned at him for a moment, as the name slowly registered through his preoccupation. "Did you say Huttingen?"

"Why, yes, that is his name."

"Where is he?"

"He was hit by your machine-gun bullets early on."

John ran up the street, followed by the lieutenant, Hoffman and Joseph, not one of whom had any idea of the reason for his agitation. He reached the area behind the barricade which had been turned into a temporary dressing station. The volunteers were giving water laced with brandy, and cigarettes to the wounded Germans, several of whom were in a very serious condition, judging by the amount of blood coagulating in the dust. With the flies already gathering, and the men moaning and crying out, and with the black population of the village having emerged from their various hiding places now that the firing had stopped, to stare at their erstwhile masters – and their new ones - the scene was even more repulsive than half an hour before.

"This is Mr Huttingen," Hoffman said, and knelt beside a man who had clearly been very well dressed before two bullets smashed into his chest, leaving the black coat and waistcoat a bloody mess in which his gold watch chain had become embedded. His eyes were closed, but he was still breathing, if stertorously.

John also knelt. "Does he know any English?" he asked.

"Oh, yes," Hoffman said. "It was he answered your flag of truce."

So arrogantly, John thought. But so bravely, too. And Adelheid's father! "Herr Huttingen," he said.

The dying man's eyes flopped open and slowly focused through a haze of pain.

"I wish you to know how sorry I am that this happened," John said. "There is a doctor, your own doctor, coming to help you. But I also wish you to know that your wife and daughter will be safe and well taken care of."

The tortured brow slowly gathered into a frown. "My wife and daughter?" Huttingen muttered. "You know of them?"

"It was my great pleasure to sail with them from Marseilles to Mombasa at the beginning of last year," John explained.

"Der Englander," Huttingen said. "They spoke of you."

"I will make their care my personal responsibility, sir," John promised. "Until you are well again."

The eyes had half closed. Now they opened again, and blazed almost fiercely. "My wife and daughter will want no help from you, Englander," he said. "They will hate you, as I hate you. They will spit on you, as I will do." The lips tried to gather saliva, then relaxed as his eyes closed again.

4

Slowly John got to his feet.

"I told you that he hated Englanders," Hoffman observed. "And now he is dead. You must not bear a grudge, Herr Captain."

John turned away.

"You are too kind to these people," Joseph told him. "They are civilians who took up arms against you. I have read that men who do that are treated as guerillas and executed. All of these men should be executed. It is what the Germans themselves did to French guerillas when they had their war forty-five years ago."

"Let's hope things have improved since then," John said wearily. "They were, as you said, only trying to give their families time to get away."

His heart was pounding quite painfully, for now he could hear the creaking of wheels and the shouts of the Africans as well as the thud of hooves, and a moment later the captured caravan came into view, surrounded by Smithson's men. There were some German men in the wagons, now disarmed, and a considerable number of women and children. They had been momentarily stunned by their capture, but now they saw with horror what had happened to the men who stayed behind to cover their retreat. With screams and wails they climbed down to hurry to their loved ones. In their midst, John was relieved to observe, was the doctor. But also in their midst were Frau Huttingen . . . and Adelheid.

He stood on the edge of the throng, gazing at her. She had not changed in the year and more since he had last seen her, save perhaps that her complexion had become a trifle sunburned. But the strong face, shaded beneath a wide-brimmed straw hat tied under her chin, was still the same, as was the tall, full figure. She might even be wearing the same white blouse and dark blue skirt; but now she had removed the tie, and her sleeves were rolled up to the elbow.

She did not see him, as she and her mother pushed their way forward and knelt beside the dead man.

"Those are the women you knew?" Joseph asked.

John nodded, and wisely Joseph made none of his belligerent comments about the fate of women in war.

The hubbub became general. Several of the Germans had died, or were clearly about to do so, and the lamentations filled the air. The volunteers stood around, thoroughly embarrassed by the whole thing, holding their weapons as if they wished to conceal them – and thus their part in what had been close to a massacre.

John realized he had to pull himself together and take charge. "Lieutenant Brown," he said. "We'll make camp outside the village for tonight and move on tomorrow. Lieutenant Smithson, you'll post sentries."

The lieutenants saluted, but Smithson asked, "What are we going to do with these people?"

"There is nothing we can do with them, Mr Smithson," John told him. "We have no facilities for taking prisoners, and these people, in any event, are civilians. That they chose to oppose us was an act of madness on their part. Arrange a burial party for poor Clamp; it should be done immediately. Herr Hoffman," he said, "I am putting you in charge of your people. We shall not trouble you further. I would advise you to bury your dead as soon as possible." Desperately he made himself look away from the German women and pretend they weren't there.

"And then?" Hoffman asked.

"That is up to you. My men and I have a mission to carry out, and will proceed on our way tomorrow morning. You may either remain here, or take yourselves off, but I have no idea where you can go."

Hoffman considered. "Are there other Englanders behind you?"

"A great number. But they are still some distance away. However, when they get here, if you are not so foolish as to fire upon them and kill some of them, they will not harm you."

"Your men have taken our weapons," Hoffman observed. "My own choice would be to remain here. But we cannot exist in the midst of all these blacks without guns."

'Do they hate you that much?" John asked.

Hoffman returned his gaze. "Do they not hate you, Herr Captain?"

John had never really thought about that. "Without guns you would find it even more difficult to go through the forest," he remarked.

"Our position will be impossible, without guns."

"Your guns will be returned to you, Herr Hoffman, when we leave tomorrow. But I must warn you that any man who again fires upon a British soldier will be tried by court martial and hanged. Make no mistake about that."

Hoffman's smile was bitter. "I think we have learned our lesson, Herr Captain," he said. "But I am grateful for your forbearance."

"Herr Captain Barclay," said a soft voice from behind John.

For a moment he felt quite paralysed. Then he slowly turned to look at her. There was blood on her hands and staining the front of her blouse where she had held her father against her. Her hair was beginning to drift down from beneath her hat, and her face had grown paler in seconds, while her eyes seemed to glow at him.

"Fräulein," he said.

"You are responsible for this . . . this massacre?"

"I command these soldiers," he replied.

"Then you are a murderer," she cried, and swung her hand. He could have checked the blow easily enough, but he made no move to do so and allowed her hand to slash into his cheek with a force that all but knocked him over.

Instantly Brown, who had followed her, grasped Adelheid's arms and twisted them behind her back. She gave a little gasp but refused to cry out, although pink spots now flared in the sunburn and the bodice of the blouse suddenly became filled with heaving flesh.

"Let her go," John said.

Somewhat reluctantly, Brown released her, and her arms fell to her side. Still she panted.

John rubbed his cheek. "I am sorry for the death of your father, Fräulein. Believe me, I did not know he was behind that barricade."

"Would it have made any difference if you had?" she spat at him.

He considered as carefully as Joseph might have done. Then he said, "No, Fräulein. This is war. My men needed what this village has to offer. Your father was a civilian. He committed a military crime by opposing us with a gun in his hand. He, and all of his men, could have been hanged."

"And you expect me to be grateful," she said, but less vehemently, "that he was shot instead."

"I expect you to understand, Fräulein," John said, and stepped past her.

Trooper Clamp was duly buried, with full military honours.

By then the camp had been pitched some quarter of a mile from the village. Joseph erected his tent and brewed a pot of tea. "Why do you not take her?" he asked. "As you say, this is war, and in war a woman is the spoil of the victor. Besides, she attacked you."

"She was distraught," John said. "And in our wars, women are respected."

"Not always."

"I know," John said. "You have read about it. Go away and read some more, and leave me alone."

Carefully Joseph poured the tea into the mug and stirred it, then stood up. "I think that you are very fond of this woman," he said. "If you do not take her while you have the chance, you will regret it for the rest of your life."

He walked away before John could reply, and John was left to sip his tea and brood at the trees, and listen to the dull thuds of the spades biting into the earth, and the mournful singing which accompanied the burial of the dead

Germans. There had been no singing over the grave of Trooper Clamp, just half a dozen shots fired into the air.

Would Adelheid be singing? He supposed so. She would regard that as an important part of giving her father a proper burial.

He lay down with his hands beneath his head and looked up at the sky. "I think you are fond of this woman," Joseph had said. Well, he could hardly argue with that assessment. He had not really thought of another woman, either romantically or sexually, since returning to Africa, and he had never done so before then either. Romantically and sexually – a powerful combination, out here in the bush, beneath an African sky, with the sounds of battle still ringing in his ears, the lust of battle still coursing through his veins. He probably wanted a woman more now than ever before . . . and he was in absolute command of everyone here. The thought made him sweat, then he sat up and shook his head – and gazed at her standing in front of him.

"Go away," he said.

"I . . . I have come to apologize." Her voice was low.

He raised his head to look at her; she had not changed her clothes, but she had discarded the hat, and the splendid brown hair flowed past her shoulders. "Apology accepted, Fräulein," he said.

"But now you hate me."

"No," he said. "Do you not hate me?"

She sighed. "I know that you did what you felt you had to," she said. "I . . . I behaved stupidly. You should have had me flogged for striking the commanding officer."

"Is that what a German captain would have done?"

"Oh, yes," she said.

"Then consider it done."

She dropped to her knees. "It is strange to meet like this after so long, in such horrid circumstances. To be enemies. Do you ever remember that voyage?"

"Do I ever forget it?"

Her flush was back. It made her look quite beautiful as it spread all the way down to her exposed throat. "That was a happy time for me, too. The happiest I have ever known."

85

He frowned. "Have you not been happy here?"

She hesitated, then gave a quick shake of the head. "Ours was not a happy home."

"And yet. . . ."

"I can feel grief, and anger, for my father's death, Mr Barclay, even if I was not happy when he was alive. We were separated for too long. Mother also. He came here to set up his farm seven years ago, and only two years ago did he feel sufficiently established to send for us. We were happy then. Perhaps we had forgotten what a stern man he was. And he had grown sterner. While we . . . we had become frivolous. At least in his eyes."

"He ill-treated you?"

Her gaze drooped. "He exercised the rights of a husband and father, Mr Barclay, yes." She stood up. "I did not mean to say these things. I meant to say that I had been happy to know you, once. And to apologize."

She turned, and he got to his own feet. "Wait."

She hesitated.

"What will you and your mother do now?"

She faced him. "What will you let us do now, Mr Barclay?"

"Whatever you wish. I have told Herr Hoffman that you are all free. My men and I are on a mission; we are not capturing farms and villages."

"Then we must be grateful to you. I do not know what we will do. I do not think we can manage the farm on our own. And for what purpose? Will your government not confiscate it when the war is over?"

He could not resist a smile. "Are you so certain we will win the war?"

"Here in East Africa," she said, "yes."

"I suspect your General Lettow-Vorbeck may have something to say about that. Fräulein Huttingen . . . Adelheid . . . may I call you Adelheid?"

Her breathing had quickened just a shade. "You may call me anything you wish, Captain Barclay."

"Because you are my prisoner?"

"Because I would like you to."

They looked at each other. He could not touch her, because they were within sight of the entire volunteer camp. "Then I would like to ask your permission to come and find you, as soon as the war is over."

Her head moved backwards slightly, as though she had been given a light tap on the chin. Or perhaps she wanted to look at him more directly. "Find me?" she asked.

"I . . . I would like to marry you," he said.

"Marry me?" she asked, her voice little more than a whisper.

"Is the idea so repugnant to you?"

"Because of my father, you wish to marry me?"

"Because I love you. I fell in love with you on the ship, and have thought of you ever since."

She continued to gaze at him for several seconds, then she turned away again, but instead of walking directly towards the village, she went round the back of the tent, where she was hidden from the troopers.

John hesitated only a moment, then followed her. "Are you out of your mind?"

She faced him. "Aren't you? Isn't everyone who goes to war?"

She was in his arms, and he was kissing her mouth with all the pent-up excitement of a man who has only known this was possible, never sampled it to the full. And she was responding. Their mutual innocence led to a clash of teeth, then their tongues were together, and his hands were closing on her shoulder-blades and sliding down to her buttocks before being hastily recalled, and then stroking under her arms to touch the softness of her breasts. Instantly she moved her body to and fro, allowing him to feel her nipples beneath his palm, while she sighed with mounting desire.

He held her away from him, and her eyes, which had been shut, opened. "I shall come for you," he said. "When the war is over. And I shall marry you. If you will have me."

"Now," she said. "Now."

He shook his head. "When the war is over."

"I shall never see you again."

"You will. You will be my wife. I swear this. But you must promise to wait for me."

"I will promise. Oh, I will promise, Captain Barclay. . . ."

"The name is John."

"John. Oh, John. How that name has been in my mind! I will wait . . . but I would rather be sure, now. Be yours." Her voice was breathless, her body still against his, throbbing with anticipation. She had utterly surrendered. But to him, or to the god of war, death and destruction?

To take her now would be more than a crime; it would be a sacrilege. Besides, he wanted her as his wife, not a woman lying on the ground. He knew now he had wanted her almost since the day they had first met, on board the *Chieftain*. He shook his head again. "That would be wrong, and it would be twice as wrong were I to be killed."

"John! Oh, John!" She put her arms round him again and held him closer than ever, certainly feeling his responding desire. "Touch me again, as you did just now."

"Adelheid . . . listen!" He pulled himself free and took the signet ring given him by his mother from his little finger. "Wear this. It makes you mine, as long as I live. Wear it until I come back for you, or until you hear that I am dead. Will you do that?"

"Of course. I will do anything. Anything!" She was against him again, and sliding down his front to his knees. In another moment she *would* be lying at his feet, and that would be irresistible. He could hardly believe that this magnificent woman had actually felt the same about him as he had felt about her for all these months. If only they had both known.

He held her shoulders and raised her again. "You must go now. Please. I will come back. You have my word."

She was against him for a last, long, lingering kiss, then she stepped away of her own accord. "You are too honourable, John Barclay," she said. "But I love you, and I will always love you." Carefully she fitted the golden band over the third finger of her left hand.

"You cannot wear it there," John protested.

"I will," she declared. "And I will wait for you, right here. This I swear. Now go and win your war."

She turned and walked away. She did not look back. Only when she was almost at the village did he remember that he still did not know her age.

"That is good," Joseph observed. "To have taken the woman. A man needs a woman. A commander more than anyone."

"You have read that too, have you?" John asked. He was too elated to be annoyed, although it was obvious everyone in his command knew he had taken the German girl behind his tent, and everyone put his own interpretation on it.

"Of course. To him who has the most responsibility should go the greatest rewards," Joseph said.

"Well, it may interest you to know that I did not 'take' the woman, Joseph. I asked her to marry me."

Joseph stared at him.

"And she said Yes," John went on.

"You are very young," Joseph remarked.

John supposed Joseph was right in that judgement. He was not yet twenty. And he was in love for the first time in his life. It was the most heavenly feeling, compounded by Adelheid's response. He had never allowed "feelings" to women before. Of course Mother must have felt something pretty strong for Father to go rushing off to Africa with him against the wishes of her family. And Catherine . . . it was difficult to decide whether or not Catherine had feelings. She certainly had emotions, to which she gave great licence. And even lusts, if all the stories about her were true. Lust was something else he had never allowed in a woman, save for his sister. But Adèle – he would call her that, always, he determined – had certainly lusted for a moment or two behind the tent. Just as strongly as he had, he thought. The idea that they could experience such a mutual passion, that she might want physical love as much as he did, was quite heady. Did that make her less of a woman than she should be? Or more of one?

For the first time in his life he wished he had been more

intimate with either his mother or his sister; then perhaps he might know more about women.

But she loved him. And he loved her. And the world was a wonderful place. "Well," he told Joseph, "I may be very young, but when the war is over, Miss Huttingen is going to be your mistress. I should bear that in mind, if I were you."

Joseph did not seem impressed.

Whereas only a few days before he would not have minded if the war lasted forever, now he wanted it to be finished tomorrow. He convinced himself that perhaps the destruction of the *Koenigsburg* might help that to happen, and urged his men onwards. They had ridden away from the village the next morning, and looking back, he had seen Adèle standing alone from the rest of the Germans and watching them, and allowing a handkerchief to flutter from her hand. He wondered if she had told her mother what had happened. It was something he should have done himself. But he had not been able to bring himself to do so within a few hours of killing Huttingen; he had only Adèle's word for it that Frau Huttingen had hated her husband.

They hurried south and soon reached the river. They bivouacked there for one more night, then proceeded along the northern bank to the rendezvous with Pullar.

That morning they heard a tremendous outbreak of what sounded like thunder coming from the east. "Naval guns," Smithson said. "They're going at her."

They increased speed even more and reached the rendezvous that afternoon. Colonel Pullar was there, but Captain Wharton did not arrive till next morning, having also had a brush with a German militia force and found them more difficult to push aside. Now at last the regiment proceeded, once again towards the sound of big guns firing, now following the river as it plunged over a series of rapids to sea level, and forced to dismount and walk their horses through the dense bush.

When they pitched camp for the night, huddling the tents close together on the banks of the river, John was uneasy and restless. He couldn't sleep, and spent the night prowling around the sentries to make sure they were all awake. Slowly as the night progressed he became aware of a noise coming through the forest towards him, the oddest sound he had ever heard: a creaking, groaning, slithering, accompanied by shouts and curses, and the cracks of whips – as if some huge, prehistoric swamp monster was being driven upriver by its captors.

"Shall I sound the alarm, sir?" asked the corporal in command of the guard.

"Let me call the colonel," John told him, and hurried off to awake Pullar, who was not very amused to have his night's sleep interrupted – and even less amused when he heard the sound.

"Good God!" he commented. "What can it be?"

"I should like your permission to take a patrol and investigate, sir," John said.

Pullar hesitated. "Well, I suppose someone should. But make it quick, Barclay. Meanwhile we'll put the camp in a state of defence."

"Without too much noise, sir," John requested. "They don't know we're here."

By this time the entire encampment was awake. He summoned Smithson and a dozen men and set off on foot in the direction of the noise. It was the first time he had ever attempted to move through thick bush in the dark, and it was slow going. His men carried machetes, but he could not allow them to hack indiscriminately in case they were heard, so it was a matter of pushing trailing branches and vines from their faces, dragging their boots and leggings from unsuspected soft patches, tripping over fallen tree trunks, and trying to convince themselves it was true that snakes were at their most torpid during the hours of darkness.

But the noise in front of them grew steadily louder. John was sure they were quite close to whatever it was, as they could now hear quite clearly the words of command, the constant exhortations and the cracking of the whips. Even so, he was taken totally by surprise when the bush suddenly ended and he found himself standing on the edge of a quite broad track cut through the forest. Advancing along the track towards him was a group of men; there was no moon, but the sky was clear and the early morning was quite bright now he was out of the tree canopy, and he had no difficulty in recognizing the men as German sailors, or that they were armed with Mauser rifles.

For their part, they were equally taken aback, and their commanding officer shouted a brusque challenge.

"Back into the bush," John snapped. "On the double."

His men hurried back into the trees, and the Germans opened fire. The bullets ricocheted to and fro, but no one was hurt. The sounds of movement further down the road ceased, but there was a great deal of excited chatter.

"Keep going," John urged his men, driving them as fast as possible some hundred yards into the now protective jungle, regardless of the thorns and branches which were ripping their uniforms to shreds. Then they were out of breath, and he called a halt. "Down," he gasped, for the bullets were still whistling through the trees, and now they could hear the crashing sounds of the Germans advancing into the bush.

"We're hellishly outnumbered," Smithson whispered. "What'll we do?"

"You'll take the men back to the regiment," John told him. "With all the haste you can. Tell Colonel Pullar the sailors from the *Koenigsburg* are ashore and moving west, presumably to join Lettow-Vorbeck. Tell him they have some heavy equipment with them, and I intend to find out what it is. I'll be back as soon as I can, but he should be prepared to move out."

"Yes, sir," Smithson said doubtfully. "You sure you'll be all right?" Like most of his men, he had become very fond of his youthful captain.

"If you get going now, yes," John told him.

The Germans were closer, but moving more slowly now, hampered as they were by the bush. The volunteers turned and stole into the gloom, and John swung himself into the branches of a tree he had already selected. He had climbed enough trees around Naivasha as a boy, and had no difficulty in making his way several feet from the ground, where he was not only safe from the Germans but could overlook a part of the roadway. It was disturbing to think that the regiment had been forcing its way through the bush for the last twenty-four hours when hardly more than a mile from them had been this good, open surface – but that was typical of the maps they had been given, and of the lack of adequate reconnaissance which seemed to dog this army.

But the Germans certainly had known the road was there, and what to use it for. As he peered into the slowly lightening dawn, he saw a very large force of sailors and marines, surrounding and driving an even larger force of Africans. The Africans were harnessed to stout cables and moved slowly forward, uttering a doleful chant which filled the forest, dragging an immense wooden platform mounted on wheels – and on the platform there was a huge naval gun.

The very scale of the operation took his breath away. The crew of the *Koenigsburg* might have lost their ship, but they had obviously anticipated that eventuality – the gun must have taken some time to dismount and carry ashore – and were prepared to continue fighting as soldiers.

The men who had chased his patrol into the trees had now given up the pursuit and returned to the road, where in the growing daylight John watched them conversing with several officers. But as no fire had been returned, he doubted they were aware they had actually encountered a patrol of British soldiers. Certainly there was no slackening in the onward march of the juggernaut. But additional flankers were thrown out to either side, tramping through the forest fringe, and it was more than an hour before the Germans had marched by and John felt he could come down from his tree. Then it was a matter of hurrying back to the river just as fast as he could, regardless of scratches and bruises, arriving with his clothes torn and his face and arms bloody, to find the volunteers standing to behind hastily constructed abattis, rifles and machine guns at the ready.

"Just about given you up for lost," Pullar remarked. "And

I must say, my dear fellow, that you are in a terrible condition. Really, officers should endeavour to be properly dressed at all times."

"I was hurrying, sir," John pointed out. "There are several hundred sailors over there, marching an African labour force to the west and carrying with them what could be a four-point-one-inch gun, sir."

"Good God! Several hundred, you said?"

"At least five hundred, sir."

"That's damn near the entire complement of the ship, as I understand it," Pullar remarked.

"Yes, sir. But they don't know we're here."

"Thank God for that. Pass the word for every man to keep absolutely quiet. No smoking, and no chatter."

John gazed at him in disbelief. "I meant, sir, that if we were to move through the forest, we could take them by surprise."

It was Pullar's turn to stare in disbelief. "Are you out of your mind, Captain Barclay? You've just said that they outnumber us by two to one."

"But we'll have the advantage of surprise," John repeated, with a sudden sense of desperation.

"At two to one that won't matter. No, no, we were sent here to stop any reinforcements reaching the sailors from Lettow-Vorbeck, and we have done that. I can't have my men shot up to no purpose."

"What about reinforcements reaching Lettow-Vorbeck from the ship?" John almost shouted.

"Five hundred men? That's not going to make a lot of difference."

"Five hundred top-class fighting men, sir? He's kept us on the run for over a year with just two thousand. And what about the gun? That's a bigger piece than our army possesses. Surely we have no choice but to attempt to capture it, even if we get shot up doing so."

"My dear fellow," Pullar said, with admirable restraint, "I very much fear all of this campaigning is getting you down. Of course I understand that you amateur soldiers don't really understand the ins and outs of warfare. Now,

94

if you'd been to staff college, as I have, you would understand that war is the art of the possible, and even more important, of realizing what is impossible. There is no possibility of two hundred and fifty men attacking five hundred with any chance of success. We would get ourselves killed or captured to no purpose, and that would not help the war effort one little bit, now would it? One should never be afraid to give praise, and in this instance, one simply has to hand it to Jerry for a marvellous piece of work. Quite marvellous. I take off my hat to him. But I am not going to let him do even better. No, indeed. What we shall do is remain here, lying doggo until he is well away, and then we will make all haste downriver to link up with General Maitland and inform him what the cunning rogues are up to. Now then, Barclay, you go and have a shave and a change of clothing. You look perfectly dreadful."

Joseph was waiting with a cup of tea. "You are all cut up," he remarked.

"Don't you start," John warned him, "or I am going to break your bloody neck."

"I do not understand it at all," Joseph said. "I have read of how the British Army defeated Napoleon Bonaparte and many other great soldiers. Were they commanded, in those days, by men like Colonel Pullar and Colonel Bush?"

"God knows," John said.

"It is very puzzling," Joseph said, and began applying salve to John's cuts. "It really does not seem possible."

John was inclined to agree with Joseph, although he would not have admitted it.

The Germans having passed, the regiment continued on its way to join the rest of the brigade, when Colonel Pullar was actually congratulated on having learned what the enemy was about. The colonel magnanimously gave full credit to John's feat in having overseen the Germans from up a tree, which entirely caught the imagination of the senior officers and earned him another mention in despatches.

That Lettow-Vorbeck had now gained a tremendous accretion of strength did not seem of any great importance;

the Army and the Navy were more elated at the destruction of the German cruiser by the two monitors, and the volunteers were taken to see the abandoned hulk of the warship on her side in the shallows. Apparently there had been the most tremendous gun duel between the monitors and the larger vessel, as John could believe, remembering the noise. The British had been assisted by a spotter plane, but just how inaccurate the shooting had been was proved not only by the large numbers of Germans who had got ashore, but by the even larger number of dead fish and dismembered crocodiles which had floated up on the banks of the river.

Still, the last German ship at large on the high seas was now sunk, and the Royal Navy could go home feeling that they had accomplished their task. The East African Army could not, as General Lettow-Vorbeck had not yet been sunk, and the weary business of attempting to bring him to book began all over again. Letters arriving from Naivasha were no more encouraging, as they told of terribly costly and unsuccessful battles in Flanders, and gave no hope of an early end to the war anywhere.

"We can't help feeling happy that you are in Tanganyika instead of France," Adrian Barclay wrote. "Catherine is of course in France, serving with the nurses. She is apparently having the time of her life. Portington is with the Guards, naturally. Nothing much happens here. Oh, Blixen has gone home. I'm not quite sure if it's to Denmark or to fight for Germany. And it has been decided not to ask the German members of the Mombasa Club to resign, as long as they continue to pay their subscriptions – the club needs the money."

John wondered what Joseph would make of that way of fighting a war, and decided not to reveal the contents of the letter, however sorry he felt for the Kikuyu, who naturally received no letters at all and might have been existing in a total vacuum, apart from his "Mr John". He also debated writing to tell his parents about Adèle, but finally decided against that too. They might well be distressed, and if he were to stop a bullet it would be entirely for naught –

besides, sometimes, as dreary day succeeded dreary day, he wondered if the whole thing had not been a dream.

But in the new year of 1916, there was a sudden turn for the better. The war in Europe was going from bad to worse, and the British Government realized that the large forces tied up in East Africa could be used on the Western Front. So yet another new general was despatched to Mombasa; he was one of those civilians so despised by the staff officers. But he was a civilian with a military background: his name was Jan Smuts, and during the Boer War he had been one of the most daring of the enemy commanders. Now firmly attached to the British side, as he, and all the other Afrikaaners, reckoned they had more to gain from a British victory than a German one, Smuts arrived, together with a large contingent of South African troops, and the East African Army very rapidly felt a firmer hand controlling its affairs.

Dar es Salaam fell, and the pursuit of General Lettow-Vorbeck became inexorable – but unsuccessful. Tall, erect, red goatee beard crisply trimmed, Smuts might look the epitome of a soldier and possess the drive lacking in so many of the earlier generals; but Lettow-Vorbeck was a genius. Smuts drove him out of German East Africa, so he invaded Portuguese East – Mozambique – still with hardly a handful of men, but using that naval Long Tom to deadly effect. The British naturally had to go to the aid of their allies, Portugal having entered the war on their side, and the weary soldiers trekked south.

John realized he had now been a soldier, and away from home, for two years, with no end in sight. What had indeed begun as a grand safari was now turning very sour indeed, as the volunteers heard stories about the deliberate humiliation of British soldiers taken prisoner by the Germans – such as being forced to perform menial labour before the black people – with particular attention being paid to those who had made their homes in Africa. There was even a rumour that a South African had been flogged to death by Africans, on German orders. This was regarded as a deliberate attempt to denigrate British rule over the blacks, and naturally affected the volunteers more than the regulars. Even the news, early in 1917, that the United States was entering the war on the Allied side, a matter of some importance to John because of his half-American ancestry, did not immediately lift their spirits.

From John's point of view, the most upsetting thing of all was the continuing absence of any news from Adèle. He had hoped that his campaigning might take him back to her village, but it had not, and although he wrote letters addressed to her he never received a reply, so that he did not know if any of them reached their destination. He could not even discover if she was alive or dead, had been taken off to some internment camp or was still trying to manage her father's farm – or had fallen in love with someone else and thrown away his signet ring. If her unexpected passion had been pure delight, he could not help but feel that a girl who *could* feel like that would not be able to exist for very long without revealing her passion to someone else.

But there was nothing he could do about it. Even discreet attempts to inquire brought official disapproval; she was, after all, an enemy. There were times when he was almost tempted to follow Lord Delamere's example and resign, but he knew he would never do that. So it was a matter of wearily campaigning, week after week, month after month, and even year after year. They followed Lettow-Vorbeck into Mozambique, and drove him out of there. But he merely withdrew into some more British territory, Northern Rhodesia, and the whole chase began again.

"You know what I think, Mr John," Joseph remarked. "I think that we are going to follow this man right round Africa."

That was certainly a possibility, John was willing to concede: thanks to the great land grab in the last century, the German could keep going forever without ever leaving territory which belonged to either Britain, France or Portugal, all his country's enemies, and therefore made to support his forces without payment.

"Would you like to go home, Joseph?" he asked.

98

"Home, Mr John? My home is where you are."

John felt quite embarrassed. But Joseph, for all his strictures, obviously had become very fond of him indeed, and more than that, very proud. Colonel Pullar had fallen by the wayside – his total unfitness for command having been noted by Smuts, he had been sent to a desk job in Nairobi – and John had been promoted major and placed in charge of what was left of Delamere's Horse, now a somewhat attenuated body. It was not bad going for a twenty-two-year-old. Quite apart from his medal.

Certainly he would have been lost without Joseph, who looked after him like a mother hen and, he was sure, kept him in a state of health equalled by few of his command. But Joseph was interested in other aspects of his health as well. He had more than once hinted that John, however much he might be in love with some entirely ethereal female, was doing himself no good by remaining a military monk. Obviously he guessed, if he had never actually been certain, that his employer was still a virgin, and found this distressing as well, in a war hero.

John agreed with him, but quite apart from Adèle, as commanding officer, first of a troop, then a squadron, and now a regiment, he had seen such constant evidence of the venereal infection which resulted whenever his men got together with native girls that the whole idea repelled him. In addition, there was his upbringing, in which his mother had played the major part; he had been taught that the blacks were an inferior species, and that miscegenation was almost bestial. It was an ingrained prejudice which, however much he had learned to respect and value Joseph, he was not able to shrug off.

But with every passing day the temptation grew, especially as Joseph promised him that the girl he would bring to his master would be clean in every way. Just how he would find that out John preferred not to discover, but after a particularly vicious little rearguard action, in which several men were hit and the adrenalin was forced to flow somewhat more freely than usual, he knew he had either to get drunk or have a woman – and he had no liquor. They were bivouacked close to the small river they had just forced their way across, the Germans having as usual withdrawn into the bush, and only a short distance away was a native village. Into this Joseph disappeared, while the wounded were being attended to and the dead buried, and returned much later that evening, well after dark, with a small blanket-shrouded figure in tow. John was having an after-supper pipe, by now devoutly hoping his servant had been unable to discover a suitable bedmate. Thus he looked up in alarm.

"This one is good, Mr John," Joseph said. "She speaks English, but I have told her not to speak. She is a virgin, so she must be pure, yet she knows what must be done."

John was aghast. "You have secured a virgin? How in the name of God did you do that?"

"It was a matter of money," Joseph explained. "These people would sell their souls for the right price." He spoke with considerable contempt, but of course he was not talking about the Kikuyu – although John recalled that he had been fairly contemptuous of his own people as well.

"I don't really think I can accept that," he said. "I mean, I can't take her with me. What happens afterwards?"

"She, and her father, accept the situation," Joseph explained. "I have told them how great a man you are, and they look upon it as an honour. Mtala."

The girl dropped the blanket, and John could not help but put down his pipe. He doubted she was more than sixteen, perhaps less. Her figure was straight and slender, her breasts small but high and pointed, her legs good.

"I have made her bathe," Joseph added.

There was going to be no resisting her, John knew. Not after so many years, and so many thoughts, and so little news of Adèle. But accepting that, he wanted it done as quickly as possible, without knowing what was involved. He took her into the tent, and then did not know whether to kiss her or not; he did not really want to, and she did not seem to expect it. She was more interested in his penis, and for the first time he experienced the pleasure of being handled by a woman. As he knew nothing of what she might expect or require, he did no more than fondle her breasts

100

and buttocks, and was then inside her, without any awareness that she *was* a virgin, and spent only seconds later, a
tremendous outpouring of what might have been the
accumulated semen of four years.

She would have stayed in case he wished her again, but
he wanted only to be rid of her. Joseph escorted her back
to the village, and returned some time later; John had no
doubt at all that he had also sampled her charms. But the
Kikuyu was well pleased. "Now you are a man, Mr John,"
he said.

John had never felt so ashamed of himself in his life.

John felt even more ashamed a week later, when a despatch
rider rode into their next bivouac, yelling and screaming
and blowing his trumpet. "In the name of God," John
shouted at him. "You'll have every German in Africa
knowing where we are."

"That's what we want to do, Major," the man said
happily. "We want them to know the war's over."

The troopers crowded round incredulously.

"Fact," the rider insisted. "Germany, Austria, Turkey,
the whole damned shooting match, have surrendered. Just
like that."

"Well, I'll be damned," John said. "Does Lettow-
Vorbeck know about this?"

"Not yet," the rider said. "But it's the job of the first
British unit to make contact with him to let him know."

This took another week; they were constantly probing
forward under flags of truce now. These were regarded
with suspicion by the Germans and several times fired upon,
but at last John got an under-officer to listen to him, and a
promise that the message would be carried to the general.
John hurriedly contacted brigade headquarters, and on 23
November 1918, General Lettow-Vorbeck came into the
British camp under his own flag of truce. For the first time
the British soldiers looked upon the thin, emaciated figure
who had resisted them for more than four years, at odds of
sometimes twenty to one.

But the war was over, and they could go home. "You will have a hero's welcome," Joseph told John.

"I should think you deserve one as well," John suggested.

"Of course," Joseph agreed. "But the servant of a hero is always a hero as well, Mr John."

2
THE HAPPY VALLEY

5

John had no desire to go home immediately. Much as he wished to see Naivasha and his parents again, he wanted to find Adèle more. But the ending of the war did not mean the instant ending of his military career. It was necessary to remain with the regiment, first of all on guard duty over the surrendered Germans. The regiment was eventually slowly returned to British East Africa in the spring of 1919, and ceremonially disbanded, after a victory march through the streets of Nairobi, which was also a passing-out parade.

Their welcome was tumultuous. Wives, sweethearts and children lined the streets, and the new Governor, Sir Robert Coryndon, shook each man by the hand. "On men like you," he said in his speech, "battle-hardened but with the soil of British East Africa in your veins, does the future of this protectorate depend."

Adrian and Joanna Barclay were there, of course, to hug their long-lost son again and again. "To have you back, with hardly a scratch," Joanna sobbed.

Adrian squeezed his hand. "Portington bought it, you know. At Cambrai."

"Oh, my God," John said. "I had no idea. Cathy . . . ?"

"She's still with the nurses. Seems to be bearing up very well. We've invited her to come back out here, of course, but we haven't had a reply yet."

"Poor old Cathy," John thought. A widow, at thirty-eight. He supposed she would have been left fairly well off, but still, thirty-eight seemed such an awkward age for a woman. Then he recalled himself. "I had Joseph with me throughout the campaign," he said.

Adrian and Joanna shook hands with the black man. "We felt happier knowing you were with our son," Joanna said, as if he had been a stranger. But then, John thought, he *is* a stranger to them.

Lord Delamere was also there, to shake his hand and embrace him. "Under you, my boy," he said, "my regiment has become famous. I don't know how you stuck those military nincompoops for as long as you did, but I'm proud that you did. I'm even prouder that you've come back to Nairobi. We are going to need men like you."

He was repeating what the Governor had said, and John found it difficult to understand why. But he could see that both his parents and their oldest friend were looking much older than when last he had seen them. Of course, getting on for five years was a long time, but he thought that they were older than they should have been, as if they had a great deal on their minds.

In the circumstances, he felt obliged to return with them to Naivasha for at least one night, and in fact he was glad he did so. To stand in his own bedroom, and even more, to lie on his own bed, to eat good food and drink good wine, to look down the slope at the lake . . . these were essential to make him realize that he was no longer a soldier.

Joseph clearly felt the same way, if perhaps in a different context. He laid out John's clean clothes for dinner and stood regarding them with a quizzical expression. Then he said, "When you go into the fields tomorrow, Mr John, I can come with you?"

For three years, ever since John had been promoted captain and was able to make his own rules about servants, they had gone everywhere together.

"You're damned right," John told him. "From here on, where I go, you go."

Joseph grinned. "Then I am truly glad to be home."

"But we're not going into the fields tomorrow," John reminded him. "We're catching the train to Nairobi, and then Mombasa, and the first available ship to Dar es Salaam."

Joseph looked concerned. "You really mean to go after that girl, Mr John?"

"I do. Tomorrow."

"Then maybe you should tell your mother and father," Joseph suggested.

*
106

Of course that had to be done. John fortified himself with two whiskies and broached the subject after dinner. Adrian Barclay actually gave him his cue. "Your mother and I have been thinking," he said, somewhat diffidently; five years before he had said goodbye to an eighteen-year-old boy who had been something of a delinquent, and now he was faced with a twenty-three-year-old man, at once nearly as tall as he was, certainly as powerfully built, and something of a hero into the bargain, "That the time has come for you formally to take over the farm."

"If you feel that you want to," Joanna added hastily.

"The fact is that I'm sixty-two," Adrian went on, "and frankly more than a couple of hours in the saddle makes my back ache." He paused, and they both anxiously watched John's unchanging expression. "I'd still be here, in a consultant capacity, of course," Adrian continued. "But only if you need me. And naturally we'd work out some totally equitable financial arrangement. How about half the profits?"

"That's far too generous," John protested. "I'll be quite happy with a salary. And of course I'll manage the farm for you, Dad. There's just one thing. . . ." It was his turn to pause and draw a long breath. "I sort of think I should get married as soon as possible, and really make this my home."

"Why, Johnnie," Joanna cried. "I think that's a marvellous idea."

"Bit young to be getting married, aren't you?" Adrian remarked.

"Oh, really, Adrian," Joanna protested. "You were no older."

"Well. . . ." Adrian Barclay flushed. "Circumstances were a little different then."

"Circumstances are always the same, when a man wants to get married," Joanna declared. "Or a woman. There simply isn't any time to lose! I only wish there were some really eligible girls in Nairobi, but really, they have become a terribly fast set, all smoking and drinking spirits in public, if you please. As for what else they get up to. . . . I know: Catherine must surely have some nice friends."

"Ha," Adrian remarked.

"I already know the girl I wish to marry," John said quietly.

They stared at him.

"In fact, I have already proposed and been accepted," he said.

Now they looked at each other. They knew he had not had the time to meet any prospective wife since returning from the campaign. "I suppose some of the nurses were awfully nice," Joanna ventured.

"This is a German girl," John said.

This time the silence was longer. "A German girl?" Adrian asked at last. "You mean . . . someone you met during the war?"

"Oh, Johnnie," Joanna said. "You didn't, well . . . oh lord."

"I didn't rape her, Mother, and she isn't pregnant," John said. "As a matter of fact, we met on the ship coming out here, back in '14. I think I fell for her then, but I didn't say or do anything about it, because there seemed no chance that we could ever see each other again. But we bumped into each other, oh, four years ago, now."

"You've been seeing this girl for four years?" Adrian Barclay demanded. The word "seeing" was clearly a euphemism.

"No," John said. "That's just it. I haven't seen her since."

"Four years?" Joanna cried. "My God, she could be dead, or anything."

"She could," John agreed. "That's why I have to go out there and find her, just as rapidly as possible, don't you see?"

"Is she expecting you to do that?" Adrian asked.

"Yes. Yes, she is."

"Why?"

"Because I asked her to marry me. I gave her my signet ring."

"You mean she said Yes?"

"Of course she said Yes," John told him, with an effort stopping himself from shouting. "We love each other."

108

"Oh, dear," Joanna muttered.

"You do realize that people can change quite a lot in four years," Adrian pointed out. "Especially in wartime."

"I do realize that," John said. "I quite understand what you are trying to say, Father. I understand that it is entirely possible that Adèle may have had to do some fairly unpleasant things just to keep alive. She may even have had to prostitute herself. But I asked her to marry me, and I intend to find her and see if she still wants to go through with it, no matter what."

"Adèle," Joanna said. "At least it's a pretty name."

John and Joseph left next morning. John was well aware that he did not have his parents' blessing, and that although they would not attempt to stand in his way, they were both praying fervently that Adèle was indeed dead, or married to someone else.

Or ruined beyond repair? He did not know for certain his feelings about that. The previous evening he had spoken with a good deal of bravado, spurred on by the unaccustomed whiskies. But suppose he did discover that she had prostituted herself? Or what he felt would be worse from his point of view, that she might have given herself, from an excess of desire? Then he reminded himself that he was the last person on earth to cast that particular stone. And with that came the memory of the feel of her in his arms, of the magnificence of her hair and her scent and her flesh, of the pulsing womanhood which had been pressed against him, and of that strong, handsome face.

He would find her, and he would make her his, no matter what had happened during the four years of their separation. The only thing that would stop him was if she was dead. O God, he prayed, let her not be dead.

Joseph understood his master's mood, and was less searching in his remarks than usual. He had offered no opinion on the proposed quest, save to point out that John's parents would not approve, and he had certainly been right there. But Joseph also had a lot on his mind, John knew. Of the forty-odd black servants who had ridden off to war in 1914, only seven had returned. One or two had been shot by the Germans. One or two had deserted. Most of the casualties had been through fever and general debility.

But the servants had been only a fraction of the total. Joseph had spent his time since getting back to Nairobi devouring everything he could find to read about the war, and the war in East Africa more than anywhere else, and he had unearthed some horrifying facts. No less than fifty thousand British East Africans had become casualties during the conflict, for one reason or another – a quite staggering figure, especially when set against the much smaller losses suffered by the white soldiers, who had actually been doing the main part of the fighting. A brain like Joseph's, filled with facts and figures of other campaigns, had to arrive at a very unpleasant answer to those figures: that the British, and the volunteers from British East – as long as their skin was white – had received preferential treatment when either wounded or sick, and more, that the King's African Rifles had been forced to take on the brunt of the actual fighting as well.

John could not be certain whether his black friend was relieved to be leaving the protectorate once again, at least for a while, so as not to be reminded of what had happened to his people, or whether he would have preferred to stay and communicate his deductions to other thoughtful Africans. John rather suspected the latter, and did not know what to do about it, because the Joseph who had gone away a boy, like himself, had also very much returned a man.

But Joseph had a problem, as John had discovered during the long intimacy of the war years, which prevented him from being a man, at least in the eyes of his people – and, indeed, prevented him from ever being one of his people. Because his father and mother had been baptized as Christians, before he had been born, he had never been circumcised, and he was now well past the age at which a Kikuyu youth was ritually placed under the knife, as a sign of burgeoning manhood. Were Joseph to attempt to regain his place amongst his people, he would suffer untold humiliation.

That explained a great many of his attitudes, but made him, John thought, that much more faithful a servant.

Getting back to German East at all, much less finding Adèle, was a far more difficult business than John had suspected. The two territories were still in complete chaos. Shipping out of Mombasa was spasmodic, and all the berths were booked for months in advance. After waiting for several days and trying to bribe officials to find room for Joseph and himself, John solved that problem by chartering an Arab dhow which traded along the coast.

The monsoon was due any day, and Joseph was distinctly apprehensive as they passed through the reef and into the huge swell rising out of the Indian Ocean.

"Drowning is the least thing you have to worry about," John told him, watching the somewhat villainous-looking crew at work on the lateen sail. "We'll probably have our throats cut."

"Oh, there is no chance of that, Mr John," Joseph said. "I took the liberty of packing this." And from their communal knapsack he produced John's Smith and Wesson service revolver. "I have two boxes of cartridges, too," he said.

"You are just brilliant," John shouted, and Joseph smiled for the first time since the evening of their return to Naivasha. John left the revolver very ostentatiously on top of the knapsack, where the Arabs could not fail to notice it. How odd it would be, he thought, if after having fought in a war for five years with no certainty as to whether or not I ever actually killed anybody, I have to shoot an Arab sailor.

But he didn't, although it took them six very uncomfortable days to work their way down the coast. Indeed, by the time they made Dar es Salaam Joseph and himself and the crew were very good friends. However, as they had been forced to spend the entire six days on deck, with no facility for either washing or shaving, much less changing their clothes, and as the Arabs had a bad reputation, they were promptly arrested as smugglers by the still very twitchy British garrison of the captured seaport. Fortunately the commanding officer knew all about Adrian and Joanna

Barclay, and John had a passport with which to identify himself.

But then began the tedious business of securing transport into the interior. There were trains running, but they were invariably full and very slow. John wouldn't have minded either of those inconveniences, but it was even slower obtaining a permit for him to travel through the captured land, which was still in a state of turmoil, with the black people not at all sure who were their masters. The port captain issued a permit readily enough, but at each stop there was a new official to be persuaded or browbeaten into doing likewise, so that they proceeded in fits and starts, their discomfort increased by the sudden arrival of the wet season, which reduced the ground to a quagmire and made everyone uncomfortable, short-tempered and un-cooperative.

It was far more distressing, however, to observe the pitiful condition of the German settlers. All had had their farms either destroyed by the actual campaigning or ruined through their inability to ship any crops; all had inevitably seen their erstwhile authority over the blacks thrust aside. Even if their soldiers had humiliated British prisoners during the struggle – supposing that were true – the British were the victors, it was they to whom everyone, white or black, had to go to for permission to do anything, and it was they who doled out food and punishments. The Africans had always had to live under white people, and they could understand that when one side was on top, only that side mattered. But some of the Germans were virtually starving, too proud to accept British handouts, or too antag-onistic to cooperate in any way.

John became more and more depressed, and oppressed, at the thought of what he was going to find, and more and more impatient with every delay. Meanwhile Joseph watched, and listened, and undoubtedly remembered. He said little, which was unusual for him, save for a single very telling comment, on about their fourth day after leaving Dar es Salaam, when he observed, "How are the mighty fallen.

112

Do you suppose, Mr John, that *any* of these white people ever imagined such a fate could befall them?'

Obviously he was thinking that if such an upheaval in status and authority could overtake the Germans, it might also one day overtake the British. It was not a point John cared to argue. As a first generation white East African, he could conceive of no other place to live than Naivasha, nor of any other way to live save in complete command of the black people. In any event he was too excited, and fearful; they were nearing the end of their quest.

The railway did not actually go to the village of Dagaba, but from the station at Mgata it was apparently only a day's ride, and they were told that it would be possible to hire horses. So at Mgata they left the train, stepping down into the rain.

The coming of the long rains, so important an event in the yearly growing cycle of Africa, was a period of more than usual misery for Adelheid Huttingen. It meant that instead of being parched dry for day after day, she was soaking wet; it also meant that she worked longer hours, as drying the clothes was a much more time-consuming business when they had to be taken in at the first sign of a dark cloud, and then laboriously pegged out again the moment the sun returned. But then, she would remind herself, what else did she have to do but launder clothes? Quite apart from it being necessary to keep herself from starving, were she not constantly occupied, and so exhausted at the end of every day that she dropped into her cot and went fast asleep, she would long ago have gone mad.

But then, was she not mad in any event?

How exuberantly she had claimed to be mad that afternoon when she offered herself to John Barclay, because then the whole world had been mad. Since then, she had an awful feeling that the world had returned to sanity, leaving her on the outside. Except that she, too, had been forced to become at least partly sane. Only the memory of his so surprising proposal remained. But that had been four years ago, when he had also been mad. Now he too was no doubt sane. Too sane to wish to remember his madness.

That he might not be coming back for her was a growing cloud far larger than any rain squall. In the beginning she had been totally confident. He could have taken her there and then; she had reached a moment in her life when the unending discomfort and banality of her existence had made essential the total surrender of her body and her mind to someone, as essential as sleep to an over-exhausted explorer. But he had chosen not to accept her surrender, although he had wanted to, she knew. He would come back. It had been very important to be sure of that, even before the British soldiers left. She had known her visit to their camp would not go undetected, but no one had said anything – Mama had in any event been prostrated, if not with grief, with the overwhelming catastrophe which had come upon them.

Herr Hoffman had decided that, with Papa dead, he was the chief man in the community, and had lost no time in asserting that authority; besides, he had been given it by John Barclay himself. So he had held her arm that evening, and said in a low voice, "Was it wise, to visit the English camp? That is fraternizing with our enemies."

"They are our conquerors," she had replied.

"Temporarily. And then, to go behind the tent with that Englander . . . and your father hardly cold."

She had not lowered her gaze, although she had wanted him to release her; his fingers were like talons. "He is an old acquaintance, and I wanted to apologize for having slapped his face. Is it a part of your duties to eavesdrop?"

"It is certainly part of my duty to look after the morals of this community. You took him behind his tent. For what purpose?" His eyes gleamed at her. "And what is this?" He had raised her hand to look at the ring.

"It is a keepsake. He has asked me to marry him."

"And you have agreed? To marry an Englander? An enemy of your country who is also the murderer of your father? Do you realize that I could have you arrested for treason? Or hand you over to those women who have also

114

lost husbands and fathers? Do you know what they would do to you?" His eyes had gleamed ever more brightly as he thought of it. "They would shave your head, for a start. And your body as well."

Still she had refused to be afraid. "And what would you tell Captain Barclay when he comes back for me? Because he is going to."

That had been her first and, she suspected, her only victory. Hoffman had released her arm, and the subject had been dropped. For some time. For even if John Barclay had not come back for her as soon as she hoped, other British soldiers passed through the village from time to time; certainly it had only occasionally been visited by German troops, and then they had always been on the run from one place to another, so obviously being chased that it had not been worth Hoffman's time to denounce her.

Hoffman by then had been discovering other roads to Rome. As she had told John Barclay, it was not a practical proposition for her mother and herself to manage the farm by themselves. It would not have been practical in any event, in a society where white people were not supposed to undertake physical labour and which had been ruled by men and the whip – there was little of the friendship she had observed between John and his black servant, between black and white in the German colony. But to compound their misfortune, Mama had never recovered from Papa's death. This was a mystery to Adelheid, who had more than once lain awake and listened to her mother screaming as he hit her again and again. Once she had made the mistake of going into her parents' bedroom to protest, and had been seized and thrown across the bed, her nightdress bundled around her shoulders, while Papa had lashed her buttocks raw. Having grown to womanhood in his absence, or indeed the absence of any men close to hand, it had been a shattering experience, like being raped. She had not interfered again. And she had not shed a tear to see him lying in the roadway with his life bled away; from the moment he had looked upon her naked body, much less struck it, she had hated him.

But Mama had wept, and moaned, and wailed, and lost interest in living. And thus they had faced starvation, especially when the last of their cattle were requisitioned by Herr Hoffman to form a pool on which the entire community could draw. Times were hard for them all, he had explained, since they could neither send goods out nor get them in while the British and German armies raged back and forth across the country.

"It is a sad situation," Herr Hoffman had observed, coming to call, taking in the peeling paint and the leaking roof, the absence of servants . . . and Mama lying in her bed, sniffling, "I doubt your mother will survive."

Adelheid had not replied to that. She doubted it too.

"That is sad," Hoffman had repeated. "But it is even sadder to see a beautiful girl like yourself growing thin and pale. I doubt your Englander would like to see you looking like this. Do you still believe he is coming back for you?"

"Yes."

"You are a great optimist. It has been more than a year, now. Has he written to you?"

"Of course," she had lied.

"But you have not received the letters, eh? That is sad, too. I would help you, if you would let me."

She had waited, knowing what was coming next.

"I have money, and authority, and much to offer a woman." Hoffman had been holding her hand again, but gently, his finger sliding up and down her wrist, while he gazed at the tight bodice of her gown; then his hand had moved to her upper arm, and two fingers had reached across to move lightly across the material. Her entire body had stiffened; only John Barclay had ever touched her there before – and she had wanted that. "I cannot offer you marriage, because I have a wife in Germany. But I can offer you a home, and creature comforts, and a man's body. I am sure you miss these things."

"I cannot miss what I have never had, Herr Hoffman."

"You expect me to believe that you are a virgin, after you went behind the tent with that Englander?"

"Yes," she had said.

116

"Then he was a fool. But that is obvious. And you are even more of a fool for believing such a man still remembers what you look like. As for being a virgin, a woman in your position cannot afford such luxuries. But I will be gentle with you." He had squeezed her hand with those powerful, claw-like fingers of his. "I know how to make a woman very happy."

"And also how to disgust her."

He had glared at her, then released her and stood up. "You will starve, Fräulein, and end up lying in the dust. And when you are there, I am going to come along and step on you."

That night she had cried herself to sleep, but from more than just despair. The touch of his fingers, however repugnant the man, had yet awakened the powerfully sensuous desires of her nature, and if she had sinned as a girl she had resolved never to do so again since John Barclay's proposal.

Next morning she had known that Hoffman would be proved right, and might even possess her, if she did not bestir herself. So she had gone to all the neighbouring farms and the white houses in the town, and asked the women if she could do their laundry. They had nearly all said yes, as they were all having trouble in keeping their black servants, who were eager to go off and find some British to work for. Those who remained were both amused and angry at this unexpected competition. If she ever left the clothes and sheets on the line without being there to keep an eye on them, she would find them daubed with mud. Thus she spent almost fifteen hours a day on the verandah, watching. She forgot about the appearance of the house — there was nothing she could do about it anyway. She had erected several lines on what was once the front lawn, and she filled her iron herself with burning embers from the wood fire — built from trees she had cut down herself — and did her pressing on the front porch.

She had even attacked one or two of the bolder black women who tried to disrupt her washing in daylight. With her father's sjambok, the thick leather whip with which he had flogged her and Mama, she had driven them away; she was a big, strong young woman, for all her lack of proper food, and her skin was white. That still counted for something, when used aggressively.

Thus she had survived. To what purpose she no longer knew.

Mama had died at the end of 1917, and then she had considered leaving Dagaba. Hoffman had by then left too, and with the British now in virtually total command of the whole of German East Africa there was some movement in trade, and her trade in particular, for a British camp had been set up on the outskirts of the village, and she extended her business to include them. The Tommies were delighted to have such a handsome laundress, and paid well. They wanted more than laundry in return, of course, but she refused them all.

One evening three of them had decided not to accept her refusal, and had waylaid her on her way back from the camp, throwing her to the ground and ripping her skirt and blouse as they tore them off, snarling over her like the mad dogs their sexual urge had made them become. She had fought them with a tigerish antagonism, leaving one man almost sightless and another clutching his genitals in agony after she had kicked him. The racket had been heard by an officer, with the result that, battered and bruised as they were, all three were sent to the stockade. Since then she had been inviolate.

The commanding major had been terribly apologetic. She had informed him right off that she was engaged to Captain Barclay, and he had been impressed, if sceptical. But he had been able to tell her that John was alive and well, so far as he knew, and now a major, but also that he was far away down in Portuguese East, still pursuing General Lettow-Vorbeck.

Still, that was the best news she had heard in years. Yet it had intensified her desire to leave Dagaba. She even had a little money put aside now, from her unceasing labour over several years, and although she had promised to wait for him here, she was obsessed with the thought that she

118

could perhaps find him. The major had pointed out it was not practical. Even had it been possible for a young woman to travel around war torn Tanganyika and Mozambique by herself, he was under orders to keep the civilian population where it was until, as he put it, "things could be sorted out".

So she had stayed, in hateful Dagaba, for month after weary month. When news came of the armistice, she had been overjoyed. She had opened one of her father's last remaining bottles of wine and got herself quietly and independently drunk. Her life had become so lonely, so lacking in human company save in strictly business terms, that she felt more at home by herself, where she could neither be sneered at nor patronized nor propositioned – nor assaulted. Again, the officers at the camp would have rectified that willingly, and no doubt honourably; they all knew she was engaged to one of theirs – or at least she thought she was. But she had no use for them either. She had no use for anyone, until John came to fetch her.

But he had not come. The armistice had been signed five months ago now. She had reasoned that it would of course take time. One did not cease being a soldier merely because the shooting had stopped. She had decided on a certain date when he should appear. That date had now passed, and the long rains were back again, and her body ached in every muscle and every joint. She was perpetually hungry, and for more than food, and the feeling of despair was growing upon her. The new major was less friendly than the old, and had flatly refused to make any attempt to discover where John might be or what he was doing, and had informed her that there was no hope of a travelling permit for at least another six months.

So she wept as she did her pressing, still keeping a watchful eye on the drying sheets, even if the black women had given up trying to harm her, and wondered how it was possible that a young woman who had led an utterly blameless life – save for those sweetly secret moments of midnight self communion – could find herself in such a pit of the

119

most utter misery. Then she heard feet on the path outside the house, and looked up, and saw him staring at her.

For a moment she could not believe her eyes, was certain that having dreamed about him for so long, she was seeing a vision. But then she saw the black servant, who always dressed like a white man, in the same bush clothes and the same slouch hat, at his shoulder, and knew that it was real – she had never dreamed of Joseph.

Slowly she stood up, suddenly aware, for the first time in years, that her hair was unbrushed and her clothes torn and very imperfectly darned – it had hardly seemed important before – and that her feet were bare because all her shoes had worn out, apart from a single pair of boots she was saving. And that one wing of the house had collapsed, the wood rotted away and eaten by termites.

He stopped at the foot of the steps. "Adèle?" he asked.

She made no reply. She could not speak. And after a moment he came up the steps. "Adèle! My God, Adèle! What have they done to you?"

"I. . . ." she licked her lips. "They have done nothing to me, John. I – I have been waiting for you."

He looked past her, into the house, left and right, at the washing he had brushed aside as he had come up the path, then at the ironing board and the heaped clothes.

"I had to earn a living," she explained.

"Oh, my God, Adèle," he said. "What you must have endured. Your mother . . . ?"

"Mama died two years ago. But I think she really died the day Papa was killed. I . . . I must apologize for my appearance. These are my working clothes."

He still had not kissed her, not touched her. To have waited so long, for so little. But now he turned. "Oh, my dearest Adèle," he said. "I have dreamed of you every night. But this. . . ."

"I am alive," she said. "And waiting for you. If you still want me."

"Want you?" She was in his arms, and he was kissing her face, while she felt him against her as she had on that

120

afternoon so long ago. She looked past him and saw that Joseph had carefully turned his back, and then felt herself being lifted from the floor and carried inside the house, where the rotting furniture smelt of damp and mildew. While he still kissed her. She dared not believe this was actually happening, that her years of waiting were over, that she was going to be carried away into a land of milk and honey, where Tanganyika would only be a scar across her memory.

He set her down and held her away to look at her. "Oh, my darling girl," he said. "There is so much we have to do. So much time to make up for."

"Would you like something to eat?" she asked. "Something to drink? There is some of Papa's wine left. And I have some bread, and some corn porridge. . . ."

"Is there no food in the town?"

"Yes, but. . . ." She bit her lip.

"Joseph," he shouted. "Joseph."

"Yes, Mr John." The black man appeared on the verandah; the floor creaked beneath his weight. "Miss," he said, raising his hat. It was the first time he had ever addressed her.

"This is the future Mrs Barclay, Joseph," John said. "Your future mistress."

"I know that, Mr John," Joseph said.

"Well, I want you to go into the town and buy some meat. Chicken would be best. And bread and vegetables. And butter."

"Butter is terribly expensive here," Adèle told him. "So is meat."

"You will never have to worry about expense again," John promised her, and she felt colour flaring into her cheeks. She wanted to weep.

Joseph left, and they were alone. "Have you anything to wear?" John asked.

"I . . . I have some clothes," she said cautiously. "Where are we going?"

"To the camp, first of all, to find the padre and arrange our marriage."

121

"Our . . . now?"

"Right away. Oh, there'll be another ceremony in Nairobi. A big one with everybody at the cathedral. Mother and Father will want that. But I want to marry you now." His grin was shy. "I don't ever want to let you out of my sight again for a moment."

"My dear fellow," said the Reverend Captain Ponsonby. "I can't just marry you like that. There have to be banns, and God knows what else."

"Don't be a chump," John said gently. He had met Ponsonby before, during the war. "This is urgent. Miss Huttingen and I have been waiting for four years to get married. And I intend to leave with her for Dar es Salaam tomorrow morning. Now are you asking me to escort an unmarried woman all by herself across Tanganyika? Think of the moral implications."

"Well, as to that. . . ." Ponsonby gave Adèle an anxious glance. She was indeed attracting some attention, for she was wearing the white linen dress with its matching hat that, with the boots – which she also had on – she had been saving for this occasion, and no one in the camp had ever seen her so well dressed before. "I wonder if I could have a word with you in private, Barclay."

"I am sure you can say anything you wish to in front of Miss Huttingen."

"Well, really, old man. . . ."

"He feels that he should tell you how I have lived alone for the past two years," Adèle said. "And that he does not really know how I maintained myself for that time."

"Hm. Well, I would keep your thoughts to yourself, old man," John said. "Or I might just wring your neck. Now, are you going to marry us or not?"

"Absolutely not," Ponsonby said. "As for taking the, ah, lady out of here, you will have to obtain permission from Major Rawlinson, and I can tell you that won't be easy."

"What are we going to do?" Adèle asked as they went outside, her spirits beginning to sink again.

"Well, if that's their attitude I'm going to have to ask you to come away with me, unmarried."

"I would leave with you this minute, John. But I meant about the permission."

"I'm not putting up with any rubbish from Rawlinson," John said, for he had also known the major, as a lieutenant, when he himself had already been a major.

"There can be no movement of German civilians except for essential purposes," Rawlinson declared. "Fräulein Huttingen knows this. She has applied for a permit already, and been refused. I cannot have unattached females wandering all over Tanganyika Territory."

"Horace, my boy," John said, ignoring the fact that Rawlinson was several years older than himself, "I wish you to listen to me very carefully. I am taking Miss Huttingen out of here tomorrow morning for the purpose of marrying her. I am doing that simply because that stuffed-shirt oaf Ponsonby won't marry us here. Now, the only way you are going to stop me is to place me under arrest, and if you do that, I promise you, I am going to have that crown off your shoulder so damned quickly it'll make your eyes blink. So be a good chap and sign that permit and I'll get out of your life and you can pretend I never existed."

Rawlinson blinked at him. But he knew all about the Barclays, and not only the wartime exploits of the big man in front of him. He knew about their friendship with Lord Delamere and their power in the counsels of the Governor of British East, who was by way of being also temporarily in charge of German East. And thus he knew that John Barclay might very well be able to carry out his threat.

"Well," he remarked, "if you are so damned determined to make a total fool of yourself, Barclay, with —" his gaze took in an awestruck Adèle, who had become, like everyone else, used to regarding the occupying army as arbiters of life and death — "this young woman —" loading his voice with all the innuendo he could manage — "then I have no desire to stop you." He scribbled on an official form. "There's your permit."

John took it, glanced at it, folded it and put it in his

123

pocket. "Thanks, old man," he said. "Now, I am going to try to forget what you have just said, but I know I won't succeed, so just stay away from Nairobi for the next few hundred years, will you. I might just not want to see you."

"Those men were your comrades," Adèle reminded him, as they returned to the farm.

"My comrades were the volunteers. I never got on too well with the regulars." He held her hand as they walked to where they had tethered the horses, assisted her to mount, staring to left and right as she swung her leg over – there were no side saddles available – well aware that soldiers and civilians were watching them. "This time tomorrow, my darling girl, you will have brushed the dust of this lousy place off your feet forever."

"I can hardly wait. But John . . . all those remarks . . . there will be people like Rawlinson and Reverend Ponsonby in Nairobi, too."

"There are people like that everywhere," he said. "But we don't let them matter, if we have any sense. Now tell me where you'd like Joseph and me to sleep tonight." He had already seen that there was only one habitable bedroom in the house.

She gazed in front of her as their horses clip-clopped up the road towards the farm. Joseph was there, cooking their dinner. She could already smell the delicious odour of frying chicken. She was in the best hands she had ever known. There was no need to be afraid, ever again.

"I would like you to sleep with me," she said.

His head turned.

"It'll make people talk," she said. "But people we are going to leave behind. Besides, they all think that . . . I am no better than I should be. Is that not how you English put it?"

"I suppose it is. And I don't give a damn about what people say. If I didn't that day . . . well, I knew we were going to be separated for some time. And I didn't want to tie you. . . ."

"I understand that," she said.

124

"I only wish. . . ." He changed his mind about what he might have said.

"I have waited for you," she told him. "That is the truth."

They were at the broken gate, and he was holding up his hands to lift her down. "I know," he said. "And I am very humble."

"You?" She turned her face up to him, and smiled, and he kissed her, and suddenly they were both in a great haste. They almost ran up the garden path. Joseph came on to the porch, and John waved at him. "Tether the horses, there's a good fellow. And what time is dinner?"

"It can't be ready for maybe an hour, Mr John," he protested.

John slapped him on the shoulder. "Joseph, you are a genius."

Adèle had already gone into the bedroom and was leaning against the wall. She had spent part of that afternoon cleaning and tidying, and the place looked almost neat – but there had been nothing she could do about the smell of rot and decay, even with the windows wide open. "I'm afraid it's not very nice."

"Anywhere you are, is very nice."

She licked her lips. While she wanted him so very desperately to make love to her, because she wanted so very desperately to belong, she was suddenly so afraid that she wished it had already happened and were done. All the unpleasant sexual images she had accumulated seemed to rise up in front of her eyes: her father stretching her across this very bed, Herr Hoffman stroking her arm and touching her nipple, the English soldiers holding her arms and legs and making lewd comments as they tore off her drawers. Each event had made her turn more inward on herself, more resolved never to share any part of herself – save with this one man. But supposing he was as brutal as all those others?

He stood in front of her. He could see her uncertainty. "You're sure you want this to happen, now?" he asked.

She gazed into his eyes. "Yes," she said. "But . . . you will have to show me."

He held her shoulders, then slipped his hands up her neck to hold her face and stroke her hair.

She gave a little shiver, suddenly aware of how dirty her hair was, how dirty she was all over. "John. . . ."

Instantly his stroking stopped.

"Do you think we could have a bath?"

"Do you have a bath?"

"I have a tub."

"Then I will fill it for you."

He left the room. They were sparring, she knew, in the most adorable fashion, both knowing what they wanted to happen, both hesitating to take the decisive step. She rather thought a bath might flatten a lot of hurdles – if he would do what she wanted. It had been one of her favourite midnight fantasies, that of being bathed by a man: this man. The sex urge was taking control of her mind as much as her body, as it had done that day behind the tent. Besides, she knew she must bind this man to her for ever now. Before the enormity of what he was doing dawned on him.

She undressed, carefully hanging up her dress; it was the only good one she still possessed. Boots and stockings and underclothes she left on a chair, and then she pulled on her best remaining dressing gown and stood in the doorway to watch him coming back carrying the tub, which was already half filled with water – his strength, both of mind and body, was a constant revelation to her, and a delight.

Joseph followed, hefting two more filled buckets, which he emptied into the tub as John placed it on the floor. "It's only lukewarm, I'm afraid."

"That's all I wanted," she said.

"Well . . . we'll leave you to it."

Joseph had already left the room. "I do not wish you to," she said.

He hesitated.

"If . . . if we are to be together always," she said, losing some of her own confidence, "then . . . should it not be

126

always?" She attempted a smile. "You could scrub my back."

Still he gazed at her, and she untied the dressing gown and let it slide from her shoulders to the floor, then stepped into the tub and slowly sat down. She had admired her body enough times to know that it was worth looking at, that it cried out to be possessed. Above average height for a woman, and well boned, her long-enforced diet might have done her a good turn, for she had always known that a little careless living could make her fat. Instead she was as hard as an athlete, with muscles rippling in her arms and legs and in her belly too, after long weeks of lifting washing tubs and hefting her own water. The muscles had kept those big, round breasts which had so fascinated Herr Hoffman high and firm, as the constant exercise had kept the hips narrow and girl-like, their beauty enhanced by the luxuriant pubes.

She bowed her head to throw her hair forward, and soaked it as well, waiting, no longer able to see him . . . and heard the gentle thump as he knelt beside her. "If I were to touch you, Adèle," he said, "I wouldn't know where to stop."

She tossed her head and the wet hair flew back over her shoulders. "Then why stop?" she asked. "I am yours, my dearest John. I have waited for this moment for four years. Why stop?" She gave him the soap.

It was the most glorious sensation she had ever known, to feel his slippery hands sliding over her shoulders and down her back, then stroking her breasts. She had been waiting, and dreaming, and preparing herself for such a moment for so long, and it was every bit as marvellous as she had hoped.

He worked his way down to her belly, and would have returned the soap, but she shook her head and put her legs out of the bath, one on each side of the tub, to let him continue, while the wild wantonness of her behaviour, the knowledge that he was making her his, filled her senses.

They gazed at each other as he washed her toes. He had taken off his shirt and she could admire his quite magnifi-

127

cent torso, his physique enhanced by his four years of campaigning. She wanted the rest of him. "Will you draw another?" she asked.

He shook his head. "I'll use yours."

She put her hands on his shoulders to stand, uncoiling her long body before his eyes. "I don't think it's very clean."

"If it's your dirt, I want to share it," he said, and finished undressing.

Adèle had never seen a naked white man before, and she had never been able to bring herself to look closely at a black man's body. She had seen an erect penis because one of the soldiers who attacked her had dropped his pants before she kicked him, and had been repelled by it. But John's penis, which was no less demanding at this moment, was the most wonderful thing she had ever seen.

He wanted her to bath him in turn, but she was at once too afraid and too impatient, and gave him no more than a quick wash before handing him her still damp towel. Then she waited for him to stand up and take her in his arms, two wet bodies pressed together, demanding each other. There was no holding back now. She had not expected the pain, and that diminished her growing ecstasy. Yet she did not want him to stop. Then it was over.

"Oh, my darling, darling girl," he said. "I adore you."

Adèle sighed, and closed her eyes. Heaven had been in the right place, after all.

"Nervous?" John asked, as the train pulled into the little station.

"Of course," Adèle replied.

She did not look nervous. Indeed, one of her most attractive facets was her self-possession, John thought. No doubt her character, which he had found positive enough on board the old *Chieftain*, had been toughened by her years of tribulation. But he was constantly delighted by the manner in which she took everything in her stride: the long wait for the train at Mtala, then the even longer journey back to Dar es Salaam. It had taken them three days, and there had been no opportunity for sharing a bed. Yet they had shared each other, nestling beneath a blanket, soothing each other to sleep, while Joseph had carefully turned his back on them.

In Dar es Salaam they had been fortunate enough to secure passages on a ship bound to the north which called at Mombasa on the way. That was another tremendous experience, because they were able to recall their month together on the *Chieftain*, when they had both wanted the intimacy they now shared, without realizing that it could ever be attained. On the three-day voyage they hardly left the confines of their tiny cabin. "And at last you'll be able to show me Mombasa," she had said.

Briefly. He wanted to get her up to Naivasha before any bush telegraph informed his parents that he was on his way. But they had to spend a night in the hotel before catching the train, to the great interest of Mr Roberts, and of everybody else. It was at the hotel that Adèle gained her first glimpse of just what being the wife of John Barclay involved; his arrogance towards the major and the Reverend Ponsonby might just have been arrogance. Now she realized that she would indeed be marrying an East African aristocrat, even if he had no handle to his name.

Again, she had taken her sudden elevation in her stride, had appeared to enjoy it, but without any false dignity. Mombasa had nothing very much to recommend it, but she had been in raptures over the train ride up to Nairobi, where it had again been necessary to spend the night. How proud he was as he took her into the Muthaiga Club on the outskirts of the town. There were people there he knew, and to whom he nodded, without wasting his time introducing Adèle . . . time enough for that.

"Is your father really the most famous man in East Africa?" she had asked, wonderingly.

"Indeed he is." He had reached across to squeeze her hand. "He's not at all formidable, believe me. Neither is Mother."

But now they were here.

The trap took them down the slope to the house. Joseph

was now relaxed enough to place the bags in the trap itself and ride a mule behind them. Adèle gazed at her future home. "It is quite beautiful," she said. "And all of this is yours?"

"Well, Father's, actually."

"Including the lake?" she asked.

"I'm afraid not."

"That would be too much," she agreed. He could tell that she was impressed, which was what he wanted more than anything, to make up for her terrible hardship since her father's death. Besides, he estimated that although Herr Huttingen had achieved solid comfort, he had never been rich. Really rich, like his parents. Even if they lived unostentatiously, the very land that they owned, the immense acreage of the farm, meant they were millionaires.

The trap came to a halt, and the lawn and downstairs verandah were suddenly filled with people. Safah was there, with his wives, and the house servants were there . . . and Mother and Father were standing at the top of the steps. They knew it was their son returning, and they also knew that he would not have come empty-handed.

John stepped down, and gave Adèle his hand. She held it tightly as she endeavoured to smile at all the strange faces, wishing to greet them all, yet afraid to take her eyes off the couple at the top of the stairs. There had been no time for any shopping expeditions, such had been John's haste to get home, but last night the staff of the Muthaiga had exerted themselves, and her white dress was washed and pressed, and looked almost clean, if it would never again look new. They had been able to buy a new hat in Mombasa, and beneath it she had carefully put her hair up this morning, leaving her face unusually exposed – it was a very long time since she had put her hair up. But she knew that her looks benefited. It was a strong face, made stronger by her experiences; it concealed the butterflies which were roaming her stomach.

John shook hands with Safah and escorted Adèle to the foot of the steps. "This is Adèle," he said formally. "Adèle, Adrian and Joanna Barclay."

Adele wasn't sure whether or not to curtsey. Instead she took a step up, and Joanna took several down. "Adèle," she said. "But you are quite beautiful." There was no surprise in her voice, just satisfaction, Adèle realized; she had not expected that her son would return with less than beauty, and was happy to have been proved right. Standing on the step above her, Joanna embraced her, hugging her close, while Safah nodded his approval and the servants shuffled and stamped their feet.

Joanna released her and embraced John instead. "Johnnie," she said, her tone covering both congratulations and possessiveness. Adèle faced Adrian Barclay. Despite having come to know John so well, she was yet unprepared for the size of the man, the giant aura he threw off. She prayed that it would embrace her as well, as he took her hands and then gently drew her forward for a kiss on the forehead, which surprised her. "Welcome, Mrs Barclay," he said quietly.

"Oh," she gasped, and looked at John.

"We'd better go inside," he suggested.

They went up the stairs, Joanna still holding John's hand, Adrian walking at Adèle's shoulder. She felt she had to say something. "This place," she said. "It is quite wonderful. The air, the . . ." She paused, helplessly, as they reached the verandah.

"It takes getting used to," Adrian Barclay agreed, and ushered her inside. Safah had already opened the champagne and laid out the glasses. Adrian handed Adèle a glass, then gave Joanna one, and John. "I didn't suppose you had had the time to get married," he said. "But welcome to Naivasha, Mrs Barclay."

She drank, and felt tears spring to her eyes.

"There'll be talk," Joanna said. "But there is always talk, about the Barclays." She gave a bright smile. "Quite a lot of it entirely true." She had obviously discussed their attitude with her husband, and was now determined to implement it as quickly as possible. She held out her hand, and when Adèle, after a brief hesitation, went forward and took it, led her to one of the settees and sat her down,

131

sitting beside her. "Now," she said, "we must plan. John told us that your father was killed, poor man. But your mother . . . ?"

"My mother is also dead," Adèle said.

"Oh. Oh, you poor thing. Then I shall be your mother, from this moment," Joanna declared, and glanced at John and Adrian. "Oh, do stop standing around like lost sheep. We have a wedding to plan."

It was the event of the year, celebrated in the cathedral in Nairobi, and attended by everyone from the Governor down. The story of how John Barclay had delved into darkest Tanganyika and returned with a beautiful German bride rapidly became well known; that they had spent considerable time together before regaining British East Africa, and that the wedding could not take place until she had been a resident at Naivasha for some three months, merely spiced the tale, with wagers being laid as to whether or not they shared a bedroom at the Barclay house – which they did, John having been quite firm on the matter. This meant that by the time he led her up the aisle, Adèle was six weeks pregnant, but even if they didn't know it yet, if she hadn't been going to produce a somewhat premature baby everyone in the protectorate would have been disappointed.

Lord Delamere insisted on giving the bride away, having quite fallen for her when he met her, and he had naturally been the first of the Barclay friends to have that honour. The Baroness Blixen, who was gallantly attempting to keep her farm going in the continued absence of her husband, composed a poem in their honour and Ewart Grogan organized John's stag party, which was rather terrifying.

Grogan was one of those larger-than-life characters, very like Adrian Barclay himself, who for a bet had actually walked from Cape Town to Cairo shortly before the war, and had now decided to settle in the best country he had passed through on his epic adventure. He could be a charming man, as well as a most aggressive one, and he was always charm itself to John Barclay, as he was a close friend of both John's father and Delamere, although he did not appear to have much in common with either. The friendship made John slightly uneasy. He seemed to feel undercurrents swirling around him; he heard half-finished sentences and caught knowing looks between these old African hands. Whatever the secret they shared, he knew it had nothing to do with him or Adèle as people ... but he also suspected he was going to be let into this inner circle at some time in the near future – and he was a little tremulous about what he was going to find.

At any rate, the stag party raged at the Muthaiga Club all night, and ended with most of the glasses and at least half of the furniture in the place smashed.

John was lying across his bed, feeling as if a good part of him had been smashed as well, next morning when Joseph brought him a hair of the dog, a brandy egg-nog. With a tremendous effort he sat up. "Are you sure that is not going to kill me?" he muttered.

"It is going to make you feel one hundred per cent again, Mr John."

John drank cautiously, and did indeed feel better. Then he discovered that Joseph was still standing immediately in front of him, and still holding the silver tray on which he had brought the egg-nog. On the tray there was an envelope. "What's that?" he asked.

"It is for you, Mr John," Joseph said.

John frowned, picked it up and slit it with his thumb. It was addressed to *Mr John Barclay*, in a somewhat careful hand he had never seen before. Inside was a single sheet of paper, on which was written:

Dear Mr John,

It is with great sadness that I must this day ask you to accept my resignation. I take this step with many regrets but am afraid it is unavoidable. I know that I am leaving you in more capable hands than those of my own, and hope that you will understand and believe that I shall always be grateful for having been granted the privilege of riding at your side during the war.

Yours very sincerely,
Joseph Kinshasu

Slowly John raised his head. "What in the name of God are you doing?"

"I am resigning, sir."

"Buy why, for heaven's sake."

"There are things I must do with my life, Mr John, as I know there are things you wish to do with yours."

John frowned at him. "It's not to do with Miss Adèle, is it?"

Joseph looked uncomfortable. "I would find it more difficult to leave your service, Mr John, were I not certain that you will enjoy the care and comfort of a very good woman," he said carefully.

John scratched his head; that had been a lot to absorb in his mental state. "I know she would like you to stay," he said.

"I would willingly do so, had I not other things to do."

"What other things? What are you going to do?" John demanded.

"They are private matters," Joseph said.

John's frown deepened. "You're not planning to make some kind of challenge for the leadership of your clan, I hope? That way is only trouble. You'll wind up in gaol."

"I am not considering becoming a leader of my clan, Mr John," Joseph said, again speaking very carefully, and laying some stress on the word "clan" which escaped John.

"Well, that's a relief," he said. "Not off to get married, are you?" he asked, attempting to be jocular.

"No, Mr John, my time for marriage is not yet come. Now, sir, if you will excuse me . . ."

"You're not leaving now?" John cried. "For God's sake, man, I'm getting married this morning."

"I will assist you to prepare for the wedding, Mr John. But with your permission, I should like to leave tonight."

"Well, of course, if you must." John's frown was back. "Joseph . . . you do have a job to go to, I hope?"

"Yes, Mr John. I have a job to go to."

John nodded. "Nevertheless, I must give you a bonus."

"I could not accept that, Mr John. It is I who owe you money, for leaving at such short notice."

134

"Stuff and nonsense," John said, and got up to slap him on the shoulder. "We campaigned together, didn't we? And you saved my life, at least once." He looked into the dark eyes. "Damn it all, I'm going to miss you, you old bugger."

"Silly chump," Adrian Barclay commented. "These people never know when they're well off. And it's plain jealousy. You can see that. He has a typical valet's attitude towards a wife moving in."

John was quite sure that was not the real reason for Joseph's going, but he did not have the time to think about it in the excitement of the wedding and the afternoon and night-long reception at the Muthaiga afterwards. The party overflowed into Nairobi itself, taking in the Norfolk and several other establishments, not all of them very salubrious, with Adèle in her white satin gown dancing a polka just on dawn.

Adèle had set out to enjoy herself, to prove that she could, literally, let her hair down as much as any of the madcap English men and women who were to be her future friends, and that she was not abashed by her equivocal position. But John knew she was acting, however successfully. Her eyes were constantly looking at him to make sure of his approval and, for all the glasses of champagne she accepted, very little actually passed her lips. He estimated she was perfectly sober when they finally crawled into bed and she lay on her stomach beside him.

"You're upset about Joseph," she said.

"Well . . . it came as a bit of a shock."

"And on your wedding day," she said. "I'll never forgive him for that."

"Well, I would like you to. He acted as he thought best."

She looked into his eyes. "You were very fond of him."

"Yes."

"Very close."

"What is it they say, that a man can be a hero to all the world excepting his valet?"

She smiled, and kissed his chin. "I am going to be your

valet from now on, John Barclay. I am going to look after you in every way. And you are still going to be my hero."

In many ways, he supposed that Joseph had indeed become redundant with the appearance of Adèle. It would, in any event, have meant the end of their intimacy. Adèle had no desire to change his ways; she happily came fishing with him on the lake – but there was only really room in the boat for two. Just as there was only room in his heart for one, he realized. He wanted to be with her all the time and felt really lonely when her condition stopped her riding the acreage with him after the third month. He preferred to spend his time with her on the verandah, basking in the sun of her personality, to going into Nairobi.

Joseph would not have fitted into any of that, and had clearly realized it from the beginning, whereas he had not. Good old Joseph. He wished him well and was distressed that he could learn nothing of where he had gone or what he was doing.

He was delighted at the way in which Adèle was accepted by his parents. They had been separated for such long periods from Catherine, who seemed to have entirely turned her back on Africa, where she was born and spent her early years – perhaps they had been too traumatic? John wondered – and had not seen her since they were last in England, in the summer of 1912. In being pregnant, Adèle was fulfilling the duties of a daughter in a way Cathy had never considered, apparently, and they warmed to her for that reason.

There were others. In the strongest contrast to the flamboyant excesses of their natural daughter, Adèle wished only to remain on Naivasha, inhaling the crisp mountain air, sitting in a deckchair on the banks of the lake, driving in the car across to Delamere's or one of the other farms for lunch, but always anxious to be home by evening. Nairobi had no attractions whatsoever for her; the Barclays could not help remembering how the last time Catherine was out to visit she had been in Nairobi just about every night. That was a long time ago, but from all accounts she had not changed. It warmed John's heart to watch Adèle and Adrian and Joanna sitting together playing auction bridge, or discussing the flower garden, or Joanna and Adèle knitting away at baby's booties. He thought he had never been happier, and hoped that the same could be said for Adèle, that here in the peace of Naivasha the dreadful memories of her existence during the war would finally be laid to rest.

He wanted nothing to interfere with the idyll they had created for themselves, and felt a pang almost of anguish the day there was a great commotion at the station when the train arrived, and he went on to the verandah to discover who the new arrival could be, to find himself gazing at his sister.

"Well, hello there," Catherine, Lady Portington, said. "I've come home."

6

Catherine Barclay had always taken after her mother rather than her father – fortunately, as she was a woman. Thus she was of no more than average height, and had red-brown hair, which should have been a glorious splash of colour surrounding her pale cheeks, but which she had cut absurdly short – to John's eyes – so that it was not visible at all beneath the solar topee she was wearing. She had also managed to conceal her attributes as a woman beneath a khaki blouse and trousers; she had always had a good, if slender, figure, but he got the impression that she was thinner than when last he had seen her, in 1914.

Her green eyes had not changed, however; they were at once warm and brittle, a most disturbing combination whenever they fixed on an object, the position he found himself in at that moment. "Aren't you even going to say Hello?" she inquired.

"My God, Cathy!" He ran down the steps to take her in his arms, aware of a good deal of movement behind him.

"Cathy!" Joanna screamed, dragging her daughter away for a tearful embrace. "Oh, Cathy!"

Catherine looked past her mother at Adrian Barclay. "Hello, Dad," she said.

"My dear girl." He held her shoulders and kissed her on each cheek, and then gave her a bear-hug which made her gasp. "If you'd told us you were coming we'd have met you in Mombasa."

"I'm quite used to travelling alone, Dad," she pointed out. "I'm a big girl now, remember?"

"We were very sorry to hear about Portington."

"I know. You wrote and told me so."

"Then you did get our letters?"

She laughed, and kissed him again. "I always got your letters. I'm sorry I'm such a bad correspondent." But she

138

was looking past him in turn. "And this is the famous Fräulein."

"Adèle," John said, hurrying up the steps to take her hand. "My sister Catherine."

Adèle held out her hand. "I have heard so much about you, my lady."

"And I have imagined so much about you," Catherine told her, mounting the steps to kiss her cheek and then gaze into her eyes. "But you really mustn't call me 'my lady'. Those days are done, thank God." She stepped back. "You really are rather delicious, even carrying all before you."

Adèle was just beginning to show. Now she flushed, and glanced at John, who threw a protective arm round her shoulders to give her a squeeze.

"I'm afraid my sister says what she thinks – when she thinks it," he told her.

"But Cathy" – Joanna had her arm and was propelling her into the house – "we've so much to talk about. There's so much for you to tell us. . . ."

"Like how long you're here for," Adrian said from her other side.

Catherine paused to smile at Safah. "Remember me, old man?" she asked.

"I could never forget you, Miss Catherine," the Somali said, with a stately bow.

Catherine wrinkled her nose. "I'm not sure that's a compliment." She went into the drawing room. "How long, dear Papa? I rather thought I'd give the place a whirl. As a home, I mean. If there's room."

"You mean . . . you'll live here?" Joanna cried. "Oh, Cathy, that would be marvellous . . . but what about the Earl, and . . . ?"

"The Earl, bless his heart, will be the most relieved person on this earth to know that I have decided to settle several thousand miles from England." Catherine sat down, crossing one trousered knee daintily over the other. "I would love a drink."

"Champagne," Adrian said. "Safah, we'll have a bottle of the — "

"I'd rather have a pink, if it can be arranged," Catherine said.

"A pink?"

"Gin," she explained. "I'll show you how it's made, Safah, and then you'll know." She accompanied the butler into the bar, struck a match to warm the glass, and used it to light a cigarette. Through the opened door her father, mother and brother watched her, rather like three rabbits keeping an eye on a cobra, Adèle thought. Which was no doubt unfair, but she could not help the feeling than an alien presence had entered the magnificent peace of Naivasha.

"Well," Adrian said, "perhaps we should all have one."

"There we are." Lady Portington threw the bitters into the sink and measured the gin. "Add water to taste. Just a little for me. I'm trying to get several layers of dust from my throat. Oh, Daddy, I left my bags at the station."

"Someone will bring them up. Well. . . ." Adrian Barclay raised his glass. "To a reunited family!"

"Oh, indeed." Catherine consumed half her drink at a gulp, watching the other faces as they sipped the almost neat gin.

"You haven't quarrelled with the Earl?" Joanna pressed.

"Oh, good Lord, Mumsy, I don't quarrel with people. The Earl and I have never seen eye to eye. He thinks the most fortunate thing that has ever happened to him was that I married his youngest instead of his eldest son. They all thought poor Porty was an idiot, anyway. Well, I suppose they were right. But he was awfully nice to me."

The family continued to gaze at her, at once spellbound and apprehensive.

"Anyway," she want on, "England is a dreadful place right this minute. Drab, dreary, mutinous, everyone expecting to be top dog . . . ugh! So. . . ." She looked from face to face. "Here I am."

"And here you will stay," Joanna announced. "Just as long as you wish to." With a great effort she finished her pink gin, gave a little shiver and stood up. "Now, come

140

along and I'll show you to your room. Safah, if someone could fetch Miss Catherine's bags I'd be most grateful."

"Right away, Miss Joanna," Safah said.

Catherine found herself being propelled towards the door. "But before you do that, Safah," she called. "Mix me up another pinkers, there's a dear."

"Well," John said, as Adrian hurried after his wife and daughter, "what do you think of her?"

Adèle placed her drink on the table; she had only allowed the alcohol to brush her lips. "I think she is as exciting as you always said she was," she said carefully.

"So when are you expecting the baby to arrive?" Catherine asked, sitting down beside Adèle on one of the cane settees on the verandah. It was early morning, and the men had already gone out, while Joanna was discussing the day's menu with Safah.

"I think it will be just after Christmas," Adèle said.

"That'll be a bore for you," Catherine said. "But it's still four months away, and you don't look too bad. Coming into town?"

"Town?"

"Nairobi. Dad said I could take one of the cars."

"But whatever do you want to go into Nairobi for?"

Catherine gazed at her for a moment. "Whatever do you want to stay here for?"

Adèle was not going to be put down. "Because it is my home," she said. "And I like it."

"And you intend to remain here for the rest of your life, day in, and day out?"

"Perhaps," Adèle said.

Catherine offered her tin of cigarettes, and when Adèle shook her head, lit one for herself. "I suppose you had a fairly traumatic war," she remarked. "Down in the jungle, with the various armies trampling over you."

"I am sure my war was hardly to be compared with that of a nurse," Adèle countered.

"Oh, mine was great. It was so very interesting. You know, I've always thought I knew a lot about men. But they

141

were always acting. I didn't know it at the time, of course. Men are always acting. Either they've been given a role to play, or they've created one for themselves."

"Do you think your father and brother are always acting?"

"Of course. The great white chiefs. Empire-builders. Codes of honour. That's all pure shit, if you'll pardon the expression."

Adèle wasn't sure she wanted to; she knew what the word meant, but it had never been used in her presence before.

"But when you're a nurse," Catherine went on, her voice becoming almost dreamy as her head was wreathed in cigarette smoke, "you see the other side. It's difficult to act when bits of you have been shot away. God, some of those boys were in a bad way. You'd see them looking down at themselves, at the blood and what was left of an arm or a leg, and just watch them dissolve. But really."

"That must have been quite terrible," Adèle said.

"Oh, no. It was heavenly."

"I don't think you really like men," Adèle ventured.

Catherine gave her a quick glance; perhaps she had not expected her sister-in-law to be quite so perceptive so quickly.

"Well," she said, "would you, after being exposed to Porty and his dreadful family? And his dreadful friends. It was all so romantic, you know, this lord coming out here and sweeping me off my feet. Well, actually, he swept me off my feet in England, but then I had this thing that the man I married must be able to stand shoulder to shoulder with Dad. So I brought him out here, and he didn't do at all badly. So I said Yes. He was the biggest actor of them all. But I suppose he had a heart of gold; he let me get on with living my own life, and then left me everything he possessed when he stopped a German bullet. Oh, I do apologize. But I really don't bear your people any grudge. Best thing that could have happened. Porty at thirty was amusing. Porty at forty was a drag. I just cannot consider what Porty would have been like at fifty. Imagination simply boggles. But I was telling you about those poor kids. They lived in a kind of dream, half delirious, half terrified, remembering things, anticipating things . . . we used to have to sit with them and try to stop them going out of their minds with pain and fear. Do you know, often there was only one way to do that. Men! Would you believe that I have sat for over half an hour with a dying man's hand between my legs? He didn't know he was dying, poor kid."

"You . . . ?" Adèle could only stare at her.

"Well, it was keeping him happy," Catherine said. And smiled. "Actually, it was keeping me happy too. There's something awfully stimulating about a dying man's fingers. Where are you off to?"

Adèle had got up. "I'm really not feeling very well," she said.

"Now that's odd," Catherine Portington remarked. "I always thought morning sickness was over by the fifth month. Tell me, Adèle, have you ever had a man's hand between your legs?"

"Safah, you old Muslim devil," Lord Delamere remarked as he stamped up the front steps of the Naivasha house. "I want a good stiff whisky and soda."

"Of course, your lordship. But would you not care to try a pinkers?"

"A what?"

"Gin, and bitters, and water," Safah explained.

"Sounds dreadful. I'll stick to Scotch. Anyone in?"

"Miss Joanna is in the kitchen, and Miss Adèle is on the verandah. Miss Catherine is in Nairobi. I will send for Mr Adrian."

"There's a good fellow." Armed with his whisky, Delamere headed for the verandah; Adèle had rapidly become one of his favourite people. "My dear girl, all alone?"

Adèle, now very large indeed, patted her stomach. "I am never all alone, Uncle Hugh." That was the name he had asked her to call him.

"Ha-ha. Don't know how you women stand it. Still, won't be long now, eh?" He sat beside her and kissed her on the cheek. "How are you getting on with Cathy?"

"We don't see very much of each other," Adèle explained. "She considers me something of a . . . drag?"

"Yes, that sounds like the right word, in her language. Exciting girl, what?"

"Ah . . . oh, indeed."

"But I suppose, being so much older. . . ." Delamere checked himself before he could get into deep waters. "You going to be able to have much of a Christmas?"

"I don't see how I am going to avoid it. I believe Cathy is planning a vast party."

"Yes. Ah!" He looked up as Adrian and John rode their horses into the yard and dismounted.

"Hugh!" Adrian came up the steps. "What's the news?"

"Much as we expected," Delamere said. "As from next year we're going to be a Crown Colony."

"Damn," Adrian commented. "Aren't they giving Rhodesia virtual independence?"

"Virtual," Delamere agreed. "So it's not good. But there's even worse."

"What are we to be called?" John asked, giving Adèle a squeeze of the hand and a kiss on the mouth.

"Ah, well, there they've come up with something rather bright. Kenya."

"Kenya? But that's the name of the mountain."

"So it's to be the name of the colony as well," Delamere explained. "It has a ring to it. Oh, yes, I like that."

"But not a lot else." Adrian snapped his fingers, and Safah hurried forward with two pink gins, which had become the standard morning drink of the household.

"Not a lot. As you know, being a Crown Colony means that we are going to be governed by a lot of nincompoops from Westminster who won't be able to tell a Masai from a Kikuyu. I've told HE that we simply have to have a considerable stake in the Executive Council, otherwise there could be a disaster. I also told him that we took a dim view of this Indian nonsense."

"What Indian nonsense?" John asked.

Delamere glanced at him. "Simply that they are also demanding to have a say in how the colony is to be run."

144

"The Indians?" John asked in amazement.

"There happen to be over twenty thousand of them, and less than ten thousand whites, at the last count," Adrian reminded him.

"Yes, but. . . ."

"So we brought them here in the first place," Delamere agreed. "That was our mistake. Or, rather, the mistake of that idiot Whitehouse. Now they are claiming that the economy of Kenya . . . I do like that name, one whole hell of a lot better than Tanganyika . . . that the whole economy will collapse without their support."

"They could have a point," Adrian remarked.

"Nonsense," Delamere declared. "They are also claiming that as they spent the past five years fighting for king and country they are entitled to a say in how it is governed."

"The Indians?" John asked, in greater amazement than ever.

"Well, again they have a point," Adrian commented. "I think well over two million Indians were mobilized, and a good proportion of them fought on the Western Front."

"I am talking about the Indians here in Kenya," Delamere announced. "We all know what their contribution to the war effort was. So far as I am aware they did not suffer a single casualty here in East Africa – but five of the buggers were shot for conspiring with the enemy." He glanced at a spellbound Adèle. "With respect, my dear girl."

"I am quite sure the Colonial Office is well aware of what the Indians did, and didn't do, during the war," Adrian said placatingly.

Delamere snorted. "Don't you believe it. This fellow Winston Churchill . . . do you know, I quite took to the beggar when he was out here in 1910. Thought he had brains. But now he's at the Colonial Office he seems to have gone round the bend. He apparently thinks the Indians may be justified."

"Well, if the Indians are justified, what about the Africans?" John asked. "Heck, if the Indians outnumber us by two to one, how much do the blacks outnumber us by, for God's sake?"

145

"And they were here first," Adrian murmured.

Delamere gave him an impatient glance. "They're not politically minded, thank God. Although they're getting their oar in as well. This fellow Harry Thuku . . . do you know him, Jacko?"

"Thuko? Can't say I do. Should I?"

"Well, your friend Kinshasu has got mixed up with him."

"Joseph? Mixed up? What exactly do you mean?" John had not heard anything of, or from, Joseph since his wedding day.

"Who is this Thuku?" Adrian asked.

"Well, he's self-appointed head of the YKA. That mean anything to you?"

"Not a thing."

"It stands for Young Kikuyu Association. And they are grumbling about a whole lot of things. Mainly that they were swindled of a lot of their land when we all first came here. . . ."

"This was Masai land," Adrian snapped hotly.

"Oh, quite, quite. So was mine. But those fellows who have settled near Nairobi took Kikuyu land. For God's sake, Nairobi itself is built on Kikuyu land. And then they're throwing in a lot about how they fought during the war and how wages have been reduced over the past year."

"Well, so have profits."

"Of course, my dear fellow. But these savages don't understand about profits. They're also agitated about this pass law that's just been introduced."

"Quite unnecessary, in my opinion," Adrian said. "We managed without anything like that before."

"Well, HE seems to think it's necessary to keep an eye on them, and he could be right. But the blacks naturally feel they're being made third-class citizens. This fellow Thuku is talking about refusing to accept them. Now, that is going to cause trouble. HE is rushing a law through the Legislative Council to make it a felony for an African to refuse to carry his identity card and produce it when required, a felony."

"And you say Joseph is mixed up in all this?" John asked wonderingly. "*Joseph?*"

Then he wondered why he was so surprised. Joseph *would* become mixed up in something like that. But to think that was why he had resigned . . . he had said he was going to a job.

"Thuku's right-hand man, according to the police. Oh, they have an eye on him, I can tell you. As a matter of fact, I told Coryndon that he should be locked up. I always had my doubts about that fellow. Oh, and Thuku too, of course. But he wouldn't do it. Craven coward. Afraid of what the papers in England might say."

"So what is going to happen?" Adrian asked.

"Well, I outlined our points of view," Delamere said. "I told him that we hadn't come here and sunk our roots into this soil – and what is more, made it pay for the first time in history – to be taxed by a bunch of giddy coolies. Nor did we intend to have any coolies setting up house next door to us. For heaven's sake, the next thing the whole valley would be riddled with syphilis. Everyone knows all those coolie bints are riddled with it . . . oh, I do beg your pardon, my dear girl."

"Perhaps I should go inside," Adèle ventured.

"Not on my account. I'm talking about the future of your child, you know."

"And what did HE say?" Adrian asked patiently.

"Nothing. That's the problem. He seems to be entirely at the mercy of those dunderheads in London."

"They do employ him."

"That's not the point. It's up to him to put our views to them, not blindly follow their instructions when everyone knows they have no idea what they're doing."

"So what happens next?"

"According to him, we just have to wait and see. So I went along to have a word with Grogan."

"Ah," Adrian said.

John looked from one to the other. "Perhaps someone would care to tell me just what is going on?"

Delamere looked at Adrian. "He doesn't know?"

"Well . . . I haven't told him, no."

"Then I think you should."

Adrian looked at Adèle.

This time she stood up. "Now I think I must go."

"Sit down, girl," Delamere commanded. "You're not going to betray your husband."

"Betray?" she asked in consternation, and sat down again.

"There is a determination," Adrian said, speaking in a low voice but very clearly, "amongst the white farmers and settlers, that, as Lord Delamere has said, we did not sink our roots in this soil to be governed by any other than our own. There may be only nine thousand of us, but I think I can safely say that seventy-five per cent of those nine thousand are capable frontiersmen. Most of them are war veterans, and then there are people like Hugh and myself, who, if I dare say it, came here when there was no one at all to back us up in our dealings with the natives, and succeeded."

"I have an idea you are about to talk treason," John said quietly.

"Treason?" Delamere demanded. "Stuff and nonsense. We have already chosen our motto: *King and Kenya*. Nothing treasonable about that. What we are talking is common sense," he declared. "If it comes to a fight, which pray God it won't, no one is going to doubt our allegiance to the King, God bless him. But there is absolutely no reason for us to declare allegiance to any British government which knows nothing about the place."

"Not even if they are the legally elected government of Great Britain?"

"Did you vote for them, Jacko?"

"Well . . . no. I don't have the British vote."

"Quite. Yet they are going to put a lot of wogs in to govern you. For heaven's sake, man, you're half-American. What did your ancestors do when they found themselves in a similar situation?"

John looked from one man to the other once again. "I'd say things were a little different, then."

"Things are never different," Delamere told him.

John tried to decide whether the volunteers were better or worse than Washington's Continental Army. Probably not worse, at the beginning. The point was whether they had the basic determination of the Americans. "So what do we fight with?" he asked.

"Now here's the crux of the matter. Of course we all hope it'll never come to fighting. But we must be prepared. Grogan is organizing things. What he wants is every farmer steadily to accumulate a stock of weapons. Good weapons, mind. And ammunition, and that sort of thing. There are plenty of good reasons for doing so. Lions, these black agitators. . . ."

"Those are good reasons for buying machine guns?"

"Leave that end of things to Grogan."

"Um," John commented.

"Then there's the matter of HE."

"What about HE?"

"Well, my dear fellow, he is bound to object if we have to take over the colony. He'd be violating his oath otherwise. He'll have to be arrested."

"You can't be serious."

"Never more serious in my life, Jacko. We don't mean to harm the fellow, of course. We've already decided where we'll hold him. Excellent trout fishing. But the important thing is that we all pull together. I'd like to hear you say that you are with us to the end."

John glanced at his father.

"It's something we may have to do, Johnnie," Adrian Barclay said.

John hesitated, then nodded. "So I'm with you, to the end."

"Good boy." Delamere shook his hand. "Now I really must get across to Galbraith and bring him up to date." He went down the steps, accompanied by Adrian, and there paused; they were out of earshot of John and Adèle. "What are you going to do about Cathy?" he asked in a low voice.

Adrian frowned at him. "Do about her?"

"Of course, you never get into Nairobi, do you?"

149

"And Cathy spends a lot of time there. I am aware of that."

"You know she . . . ah . . . drinks?"

"It hasn't escaped me. Doesn't everyone? Especially when they're in Nairobi."

"Oh, quite. And I don't want you to think I'm pushing my nose in where I shouldn't, but the fact is, there's talk."

"About her drinking?"

"Well . . . about what she does when she's had a skinful. You know she spends nights in town?"

"Of course I do, Hugh. She's living here, remember? Do you really expect me to play the heavy father and forbid that? She's a grown woman, and a widow."

"Hm. Just how old is she, old man? If I'm not being indelicate."

Adrian grinned. "In this case, you are. She's pushing forty."

"Good heavens. I would never have believed it. Don't woman have the change when they're forty?"

"A little later, I think."

"But I mean, they should go off the boil, shouldn't they?"

"Don't you believe it. Some only come on the boil around that time."

"Ah. Yes. Well . . . I must be off."

"Hugh," Adrian said, "you have either said one hell of a lot too much, or one hell of a lot too little. I think we have known each other long enough to be able to stand some plain speaking."

"Yes," Delamere agreed unhappily. "Well . . . there's talk at the Norfolk that one night last month Catherine did a strip on the bar and danced some rather, well, obscene knees-up thing."

"A strip?" Adrian asked. "You mean . . . ?"

"Everything," Delamere told him. "Every damned thing."

"Oh, Christ. Who was there?"

"Quite a few. All men. She'd been buying them drinks. Do you give her an allowance?"

"God, no. Portington left her a wealthy woman." Adrian looked as if he had been sandbagged.

150

As Delamere could see. "Only a rumour, old man. That bartender is a born liar."

"But he claims to have been there?"

"Well . . . really, I promised Galbraith I'd be over for lunch."

"There's more."

"Well . . . she has this habit of taking a double room . . . and in the morning both beds have been slept in."

"Damn," Adrian said. "We haven't heard a word of this."

"You don't think Joanna knows?"

"I'm damned sure Joanna doesn't know. And you are not going to tell her. She'd have a fit."

"My dear fellow, I wouldn't dream of it. But . . . I really think something needs to be done. At a time like this it is very necessary for the British community . . . well, to demonstrate its superiority to the world. At least in public."

"Yes," Adrian said grimly. "Leave it with me. I'll have a word with Cathy."

"I am quite terrified," Adèle confessed to John. "All this talk about armed rebellion. . . ."

"It'll never come to that," John told her. "It's actually the biggest load of *Boy's Own Paper* codswallop I have ever heard."

"Do you really believe that?"

"I do. I don't say there may not be a crisis. We may even have to declare our independence . . . but there is no way any British government is going to send troops to East Africa to kill their own kith and kin on behalf of the Indians. Or even the Africans."

"So what would they do?"

"God knows."

"They couldn't just accept it."

"No. I suppose they couldn't." He grinned. "They'd probably take away our passports."

"You mean, you'd stop being British?"

"Well, we'd become Kenyan. Issue our own passports."

"And never see England again."

"Never is a long time. It'll work itself out, believe me."

151

He held her close for several moments, stroking her hair as he knew she liked, and kissed her cheek. "Now I have to go into Nairobi."

She pulled away. "Nairobi? Now?"

"Right this minute. I imagine I'll have to stay overnight. Don't worry, I'll grab a bed at the club and be back tomorrow morning."

She held his arm. "But why? What's the matter?"

"The matter is that idiot Joseph. I have to have a word with him."

"Joseph," she said contemptuously. "Judging by what Uncle Hugh has been telling us, he deserves to be locked up."

"That's what I'd like to prevent, Dela. I'll be back tomorrow."

It was the time of the short rains, and a steady drizzle fell as he drove the Austin Seven – Cathy was out in the other car – up the twisting road from the valley towards the city. The road was empty – it was always empty, even in fine weather – and he had the time to think as he peered past his windscreen wipers at the unchanging, ever vibrant landscape, the termite hills, the trees, the absence of life. There was still a good deal of game in the highlands, even after so much of the land had been appropriated for farming, but for the most part animals had the sense to stay away from the roads over which, they had come to know, iron animals were wont to charge at great speeds.

He was aware of feeling resentful. Not just at Joseph: at Delamere, and Grogan, and even Father; at Churchill and Thuku and everyone who was conspiring to take away the quality of dreamy peace and contentment which had always been the most valuable aspect of Naivasha. He felt that he had had enough crises in his life. What was particularly annoying was that he did not recall anything like this before the war. Undoubtedly there had been crises. The Masai uprising was one, when all their lives had been at risk. Father had sorted that out, dominating events by his immense strength of mind and body. Now he was getting set to dominate this crisis as well. But things were different, no matter how they might argue that nothing ever changed. The most obvious change had been in Father; he was all but sixty-three years old, even if he didn't seem to realize it.

As for Joseph . . . the utter idiot. He watched the roofs of Nairobi come into view, and discovered that his irritation had grown into a positive anger. He drew up outside the Muthaiga Club, stamped into the bar and demanded a telephone book. Rifling the pages, he soon came across the address of the YKA; it was, as might have been expected, in one of the less salubrious areas of the city.

"Put me down for a room for tonight," he told the barman; it was already four thirty in the afternoon.

"Of course, Mr Barclay."

"Why, Johnnie!"

He raised his head and looked at his sister, who had clearly just awakened from her siesta. She wore trousers, as she invariably did during the day, but slippers rather than boots, no socks or stockings; the top three buttons of her shirt were open, revealing rather a lot of white flesh, and even her short hair managed to look tousled. In fact, she was dressed as she might have been after rising from her nap at Naivasha, as if the Muthaiga Club was her own home. He glanced at the barman, but the Indian did not seem concerned.

"I thought I saw the car from my window," Catherine told him. "What brings an old fuddy-duddy like you to town?"

"Business. I have to rush. Don't you think you should dress yourself properly? This is a public place."

"Relatively speaking." She lit a cigarette. "So hurry about your business, baby brother. You going home tonight?"

"I had meant to stay here."

"Why, that's great. We must have dinner together. Just you and I. Just as we did at Portington, that night in '14 before you came back here. Won't that be nice?"

"Yes," he said doubtfully. "If you're properly dressed. I'll see you later."

He got back into the car and drove into the city proper, leaving the wide, tree-lined avenues of the suburbs for a growing sense of concrete and steel, of people hurrying to and fro beneath raised umbrellas and wrapped in mackintoshes which would leave them as sweat-wet within as they were rain-wet outside. His wheels splashed through puddles as he turned off the main streets onto unsurfaced roads, where the prevailing aspect to either side was wood and corrugated iron. He drew to a halt at crossroads, and looked left and right, seeking a street name and not finding it.

"I can help you?" The girl was hardly more than a child, wearing only a skirt and blouse, her feet and head bare; she was an Indian, and possessed the exquisitely delicate features of so many of her countrywomen.

"I'm looking for the office of the Young Kikuyu Association," he said, rolling down his window.

"Oh, they down there." She pointed. "Turn left and then right. You want to come inside?"

"Eh?"

"I living right here." She pointed at the house which formed the corner. "You come inside, and I will let you dry me. My mummy will let you dry her, too. Only five rupees."

He stared at her. Perhaps because of the stress which had accompanied his drive, the additional annoyance of seeing Cathy looking like a slut in the Muthaiga Club of all places, the rain, and more than anything else, the fact that he had had no sex now for some weeks after being used to a very regular ration until Adèle reached the sixth month of her pregnancy, he found himself thinking what a pleasant thing it would be, to rub this girl's back . . . and her front. And her mother's, if the mother looked anything like the daughter. Even if, according to Lord Delamere, the odds were they would both have syphilis. He had never been with a whore in his life . . . unless that girl Joseph produced in Rhodesia could be so described.

But that memory made him feel total revulsion for the idea, as well as reminding him why he was here. "Some other time," he told the girl, and drove off. In his rear-view mirror he could see her standing there in the rain, no doubt waiting for some other potential victim to come by – on instructions from her mother.

The Young Kikuyu Association office was as much a corrugated-iron-roofed shack as any of its immediate neighbours, but it did have several bicycles leaning against it, which indicated some activity. He banged on the door, and then opened it and stepped inside, flicking water from his hair; the noise of the rain pounding immediately above his head made him feel as if he had entered a base drum.

A black girl seated behind a table gazed at him. Her face was passive but her eyes hostile as she took in his colour. He looked around. Two men sat on straight chairs on the other side of the room, also staring at him. There were some posters on the wall, several in Kikuyu but three in English. One had a picture of Karl Marx, another of the Russian revolutionary Vladimir Lenin. The third, remarkably enough, was King George V.

"I can help you, mister?" asked the girl. Her voice lacked the liquidity of the Indian.

"I'm looking for Joseph Kinshasu."

"You got an appointment?"

"An appointment? Good God! You tell him Mr John wants to see him."

"Mr Kinshasu is a busy man," the girl said. "I going see if he is free."

She got up and went through the door behind her. John gazed at the two black men, and they gazed back at him.

"Mr John." Joseph came through the door with both arms outstretched. "But it is good to see you."

John studied him. In place of the white man's bush clothes which Joseph always wore on the farm, he had reverted to the blue suit in which he had first appeared – a different blue suit, obviously, but none the less of shoddy material and tailoring. He had also lost some weight, John estimated; he wondered how often his old friend had a square meal.

"It's good to see you too, Joseph," he said. "Can we have a word?"

"Of course, man. Come inside." Joseph held the door

155

for him, while the black girl sat down behind her table again. Her eyes still smouldered.

Beyond the door was a narrow corridor, off which opened three doors. The rain pounding on the corrugated-iron roof was even louder in here. Joseph opened the first door on the left and showed John into a tiny office, which contained a table, two chairs and a filing cabinet. The table was bare, save for an inkwell and a pen. Joseph sat down and gestured John to the other chair.

"Is this what you left me to do?" John asked.

Joseph looked somewhat embarrassed. "It was necessary, Mr John."

"Necessary to stir up your people? No good can come of it."

"Necessary to remind my people that they *are* people. They fought for this land just as much as you or I, Mr John."

"Agreed. And they will get their reward."

"When?"

"They won't get anything at all while they are being encouraged to accuse the white people of stealing their land," John said. "Who dreamed up this idea, anyway? Harry Thuku?"

"My people have always known their land was stolen, Mr John," Joseph said quietly.

"But it's taken them two generations to say so."

"As I said, it has been necessary to remind them that even men with black skins have rights."

"And do you suppose antagonizing the white men will gain you those rights?"

"We will certainly not attain them by lying down to be trampled on, Mr John. Or by tamely accepting that we must have passports to move about inside our own country."

John frowned. "My father always said that reading could never do any African any good. The pass books are going to become law whether you like it or not. And no white farmer is going to give up any land because of some imagined grievance which took place forty-odd years ago."

"There are some laws which have to be changed, Mr John."

"And you reckon you can change these? Joseph, you are sticking your neck out, and unless you are very careful, someone is going to come along and chop it off. And that of your friend Thuku. Now look here, the best thing you can do is quit this nonsense and come back to Naivasha. Naivasha is your home. Come back, and I promise I'll do what I can about this land business."

Joseph's eyes had grown cold. "You are very generous, Mr John. But I do not wish to work for you, or for any white man, ever again."

John met his gaze, and then tried a different approach. "You're not even a member of the tribe."

"How can you say that, Mr John?"

"I can say that, Joseph."

Joseph's eyes became colder yet. "They know nothing of me, save that I am a war hero. Just like you, Mr John. That makes them very happy to have me working with them."

"You mean you never take your trousers off in front of anyone."

"That is right, Mr John. I am trying to help my people, and I think if you were to betray me, that would be a sad reward for my years of service."

John stood up. "You are going to wind up in gaol. You do realize that? And you are not going to find it at all pleasant."

Joseph remained seated. "Not all life is pleasant, Mr John. But it still has to be lived."

"Damn it," John exploded. "You make me want to punch you on the nose."

Still Joseph did not move. "I would not do that, Mr John. Because I might punch you back."

They stared at each other for a moment, then John turned and left the office.

John returned to the club in an even worse mood than he had left it. He had entirely wasted his time, he thought, as he showered and changed into a dinner jacket, and had been insulted into the bargain. He had not expected that. Joseph had always had a stubborn, almost mulish streak – and he had certainly never doubted that he was always right and everyone else was always wrong. But the idea that Joseph would ever raise his fist to him, or to any white man. . . . He had been very tempted to teach him a lesson there and then, save that a brawl would probably have meant them both being arrested, and that wouldn't have helped the reputation of the white population. But Joseph had it coming. When he got his come-uppance it would do him a world of good.

He went downstairs, and found Catherine already in the bar. For a moment he wondered if she had been there ever since he left, and then realized that she couldn't have, because she had indeed changed her clothes. Now she wore an off-the-shoulder gold lamé evening gown which left her pale flesh glowing and revealed a more spectacular décolletage than anyone would have supposed she possessed, looking at her dressed normally. Her hair had been brushed, she wore a lipstick and, if he doubted she could ever be described as beautiful, she was by far and away the most attractive woman in the room – and there were several others, with their escorts, mostly clustered round the dowager Lady Portington: obviously she was buying. He thus found himself in the centre of a small cocktail party, talking to people he didn't know very well and at that moment had no desire to know at all.

"You said just you and me," he muttered at his sister.

"Of course I did." Catherine stood up. "That's all, folks. I'm off to eat."

There was a chorus of protests and some goodbyes, and John escorted her into the dining room. "What on earth do you find in their company?" he asked.

"Not a lot. But it's better than reading a book."

"Is it?"

"I think so," she said quietly.

"Cathy. . . ." He leaned across and held her hand. "Does it ever occur to you that you're just wasting your life away?"

"Aren't we all?"

"No. We're not."

"Of course. We're busy growing coffee and maize and thumping ourselves on the chests and declaring that we are great white men, while our wives are busily producing more of us to carry on the charade. Does it ever occur to you that a hundred years from now no one will know, or care, that you once lived at all? Not even your grandchildren."

"Is that why you never had any children?"

She made a moue. "I nearly had one, once. Then I miscarried. Six months! It was dreadful."

He frowned. "Does Mother know about this?"

Catherine shook her head. "I never told her. Anyway, that once was enough."

He squeezed her hand. "Poor old Cathy. I'm most dreadfully sorry."

"So go ahead and cry, if you like."

"Did you?"

Her chin came up, then she smiled. "Yes. For a while. Then I thought I'd get on with living."

They ate in silence for several minutes. Then he asked, "You going to marry again?"

"Good God, no."

"Why on earth not? You really are a most attractive woman, you know."

"Words of praise from my baby brother. Have you ever considered why a woman gets married at all?"

"Well . . . I suppose not. Security?"

"Oh, indeed. That's important to most of the poor bastards. And they want kids, and to get out of their parents' home. And it's the thing to do. And most important of all, it's the only way they can make sure of being regularly screwed, the way you men have the world set up."

"Cathy," he protested. She had a penetrating voice.

"Don't you think girls want to be screwed as much as boys?" she asked.

"Well, I. . . ."

"Don't tell me. Your German cow lies there like a dummy and lets you get on with it."

159

"She is not a cow," he snapped. "And. . . ." He changed his mind, and drank some wine.

"Aha. So she's a passionate wench, is she?"

"I am not going to discuss Adèle and myself with you."

"You'd never believe it," she remarked. "Girls with big boobs never reckon they have to be passionate. God, you must have fun with those tits."

"If you don't shut up, I am going to walk out on you."

"On your sister? Whatever would the neighbours say?" Her brittle eyes mocked him. "Anyway, you asked me a question. So there it is. I don't need security. I don't need anything, except regular screwing. And a long time ago I discovered something: when you have both the money and the mind, a girl can get just as much regular screwing outside marriage as in it. So why bother?"

"You are impossible."

"Nonsense. I merely refuse to behave as other people do, just for the sake of it." She leaned back in her chair to finish her wine, and looked around the dining room. "Do you know, I think I've slept with at least a quarter of the men in here? And I've only been back four months."

"Cathy!"

"It's quite true. I'll get the rest after dinner."

"Jesus Christ! And you can just sit there, with them on either side. . . . I think the sooner you get out of Nairobi – out of Kenya – the better."

She leaned forward again, and presented her décolletage. "Are you expelling me, brother dear? I've come back here to live. For the rest of my life."

He didn't know what to do. Certainly he had no desire to spend the rest of the evening in her company, amongst her various partners. Or would victims be the better word? he wondered. On the other hand, he didn't want to abandon her just in case she did start hunting seriously for a companion for the night. And in the Muthaiga Club, of all places. Obviously all the barmen and stewards would know about it, as well as the housemaids. That probably meant all of Nairobi. Thank God Mother and Father had no

160

idea . . . but they would. And what would happen then he did not care to think.

In any event, there was nothing he could do about it tonight. They returned to the bar after dinner, and she was immediately surrounded by men. John now realized that it was less her lavishness in buying drinks that mattered, than that they all knew she was easy game. The idea made him so angry he wanted to punch them all, but that sort of thing just didn't happen in the Muthaiga Club, so he went to bed instead, resolved to take her back out to Naivasha the following day, if he had to carry her over his shoulder.

He lay down and was asleep in seconds; it had been a long and tiring day, both physically and emotionally. He slept heavily and had a succession of erotic dreams, because of the dinner conversation and the Indian girl. But not only had he grown up in Africa, he had also spent four years campaigning, and he was instantly awake when he heard the doorknob turn.

He remained absolutely still as it swung in. It was impossible to suppose anyone would attempt to commit burglary inside the Muthaiga Club; besides, he instantly knew who it was, from the scent of her perfume. And now he could make out the flutter of her dressing gown as she was for a moment caught in the corridor light. Then the door closed, and the room was again dark.

John sat up, the sheet carefully folded across his thighs; he slept naked, and the dream had given him an erection. "Do you have any idea what time it is?"

"Three o'clock. The witching hour, when all the world sleeps. Except those who have somewhere to go."

"And you have somewhere to go? Or are you on your way back." He switched on the light.

"Oh, turn that off," she said.

He obeyed, having caught just a glimpse of blue dressing gown and red hair.

"I came to apologize," she said.

"Accepted. But I'd like you to come back to Naivasha with me in the morning."

"I was going to, anyway. These people are all creeps. They all hate my guts, really. Certainly the women."

"Can you blame them?"

"Jealous cows." The bed creaked slightly as she sat down; he was bathed in the scent of her perfume. "I don't think you and I should ever quarrel."

"I'll agree with that."

"Because you're all I have," she said. "Really and truly."

"Oh, come now."

"Really and truly," she repeated.

He listened to a slithering sound, but could not decide what it was. Then something was happening to his sheet, and a hand passed over his penis. The enormity of what she was doing was too great for him properly to grasp it for a moment, then he discovered that she was sitting astride his thighs, and that she was as naked as he was. "Cathy . . ." he gasped.

Catherine leaned forward. "I've wanted to fuck you ever since you came to me after being kicked out of school," she whispered. "And who's ever to know?"

He felt her breasts touching his chest, and a moment later she was kissing him with an opened mouth, while a slight adjustment of her hips had him inside her, caught in the contraction of her vagina. With an effort he threw her off and switched on the light. She had sprawled across the bed, on her back, gazing at him with arched eyebrows. Now she sat up. "Are you really such a creep too?" she asked.

John swung his hand and slapped her across the face.

7

"Maybe you'd like to tell me exactly what happened," Adrian Barclay suggested.

"No, I don't think I would like to do that," John replied.

"Your sister returns here with a face the size of a coconut and one of her teeth loose, and says you hit her, and you don't think you owe us an explanation?"

"I'm sure I owe you one, Father," John said. "Has Cathy said anything?"

"No. I don't think you're her favourite person at this minute, though."

"The feeling is mutual. But as she hasn't, then I won't either, if you don't mind. If you want me to pack up and get out of Naivasha, I'll do so. Now."

"Don't be a chump." Adrian slowly filled his pipe, looking out of the study window at the lawn and the lake. "Something to do with a man, I imagine?"

John frowned at him. "You know about that?"

"It seems everyone knows about that. Care to talk about it?"

"It was a man," John said. "I don't like to see my sister prostituting herself."

"Come now, isn't that pitching it a little strong?"

"Maybe she's the one doing the paying, but it's the same thing in my book."

Adrian sighed.

"Does Mother know about it?" John asked.

"No. And I wasn't going to tell her. Now I suppose I'll have to, if she's ever going to speak to you again."

"Would you like me to do it?"

"No. Better if I handle it. What I would like you to do is make it up with Cathy."

John hesitated, then nodded. "I'll have a word with her," he promised.

*

But he would not make it up with her. When he knocked on her door and she said, "Come in", and then saw who it was, she drew up her knees – she was in bed with an icepack on her face – and stared at him as if he were a snake. "If you touch me," she said.

"I wouldn't touch you with a ten-foot pole," he told her. "But I gather you have at least had the sense not to tell Dad the truth."

Her lip curled. "You mean *you* haven't?"

"I've told him something he can accept."

"And he believed you?"

"Yes. He seems to know more about your goings-on than you suspect. So you're not going to be very popular around here." He advanced across the room, and she seemed to tighten herself into a ball. "I just want you to know that if you ever tell the truth, to anyone, much less Father and Mother, I am personally going to break your neck."

Her eyes flared at him. "One day," she said.

"One day," he agreed. "I suggest you make that a long time off."

"I am so terribly sorry," Adèle said.

"About what?" he asked.

"About you and Cathy quarrelling."

"I haven't noticed that you and she are great friends."

"That's not the point. But . . . brother and sister. . . ."

"One of those things," he said.

She looked into his eyes. "It was nothing to do with me, was it?"

"No. Nothing to do with you."

"And it's nothing you want to discuss?"

"No," he said.

She accepted his decision. But he could tell she was troubled. Men don't go about nearly breaking their sister's jaws without very good cause, and although she had heard some of the rumours surrounding Catherine, she couldn't find anything in them properly to explain what he had done.

His mother felt the same way, he could tell, even if she was shocked to learn just how her daughter had been

164

spending her time in Nairobi. She was tearful when Catherine, four days later, announced she was moving out.

"Not back to England?" she protested.

"Good lord, no," Catherine said. "I like it here, Ma. But Naivasha is a little remote for me. I think I'll get a house in town."

"Cathy. . . ." Joanna held her hands. "You. . . ." She didn't know how to say it.

Catherine kissed her on the cheek. "I have to live my own life, Mumsy. I never tried to dictate yours to you, now did I?"

Joanna sighed. "But you will come to visit?"

"Of course I will. You wait."

John understood his mother's feelings, but he was glad to see his sister go. There was something more important to worry about: the birth of his child. It was a simple matter; Adèle was made for child-bearing. It was a girl, whom they named Elizabeth, after Adèle's mother.

Adèle fed Lizzie for six months, but then a nanny was installed; as her African name was unpronounceable, she became Nanny. John could tell that Adèle wasn't altogether happy with the idea of having her child looked after by a black woman; her innate dislike of the Africans – which he blamed on the essentially more tyrannical rule practised by the Germans in Tanganyika before the British conquest – was the only aspect of her character that disturbed him. But Nanny was very efficient and loving, and Adèle was able to spend more time with her husband. Indeed this was a new experience for them, because whereas Adèle had wanted only to remain in the peace of Naivasha when she first came to Kenya, happy to be away from the traumas of Tanganyika and her ghastly existence during the war, she was now beginning to feel that she belonged in Kenya, and was prepared to act the part of a Barclay wife. Naivasha became again the centre of huge luncheon parties, and she began to accept invitations to visit other houses, especially Elmenteita, where she remained a firm favourite with Lord Delamere.

This was a happy time. Just to have Dela back again as a lover was heaven for John; it helped him to combat the memory of that night at the Muthaiga Club, which haunted him. Because he had wanted what Cathy offered? That was unthinkable. Even the spreading rumours of what went on at the other Barclay residence, just outside Nairobi, where Catherine, Lady Portington had bought herself a vast six-bedroomed mansion, and where, it was murmured, there were all kinds of scandalous goings-on, did not impinge on the mood at Naivasha. Joanna simply refused to believe the rumours, or even to discuss them with Catherine when she came over once a week for Sunday lunch.

John refused ever to be alone with his sister, and made sure that Adèle wasn't alone with her either. He had no doubt at all that both Adèle and Joanna still felt he had been far too forceful in his handling of whatever had happened at the Muthaiga, and were waiting for the opportunity to effect a reconciliation. He had no desire for his wife to be so swamped by that powerful, evil personality that she might accept an invitation for *them* to attend one of Lady Portington's soirées.

In any event, their happiness resulted in another pregnancy, and Malcolm Barclay was born in April 1921. Both John and Adèle would have liked to name him after his grandfather, but Adrian talked them out of it. "One three-syllable name in the family is enough," he said.

Again Adèle fed the babe for six months, and it was October 1921 before John again had her all to himself. But this was better than before, because now they had a complete family. And they were a complete couple, lost in a personal intimacy from which the rest of the world was excluded. Even the tensions of the colonial situation began to abate, as the British Government showed a willingness to talk rather than insist.

Now that they could spare more time to be together, they would sometimes take a weekend all by themselves, Joanna promising to keep Nanny under a watchful eye at all times. John tried taking Adèle on safari to shoot lion, but he could tell she was uncomfortable in the bush, surrounded just by black bearers, and the sight of one of the jungle monarchs, so noble even in death, reduced her to tears. More often they would go into town, for shopping and a cinema show, perhaps. They never stayed at the Muthaiga. John said this was because he could never tell when Catherine might be throwing one of her parties there, but actually it was because he had come to hate the memory of the place, the thought that there he had, however inadvertently, committed incest.

Instead they took a room at the old Norfolk, which was still the centre of Nairobi social life, and was also far more convenient for the shops. They were there in the third week of March 1922, and were having an after-luncheon port when they saw the waiters putting up barricades over the windows.

"Expecting a storm?" John asked the barman.

"Plenty trouble," the Indian replied.

"What kind of trouble?"

"Man, Mr Barclay, that Young Kikuyu Association, they are bad men."

"Young Kikuyu?" John sat up. "What are they doing now?"

"Man, Mr Barclay, they are saying that Harry Thuku and that Joseph Kinshasu are telling their people that today they must all come to Nairobi and fill a truck with their identity cards and dump the whole lot in front of Government House, as a protest."

"Oh, Jesus," John remarked, and finished his drink.

"Just what do you think you're doing?" Adèle asked.

"Well. . . ."

"There is nothing you can do by going down there," she said.

"Joseph is going to find himself behind bars if he isn't careful."

"Maybe that's where he deserves to go," she said. "You're not responsible for Joseph Kinshasu, Johnnie. He quit your service because he felt he had other things to do. You can't chase around for the rest of his life trying to get him out of trouble."

167

He sighed. "I suppose you're right, Dela. It's just that he's so intelligent, and yet at the same time so stupid."

"Which must mean he's not so intelligent after all," she pointed out. "Let's have our siesta."

They were sleeping in each other's arms, their naked bodies cemented in their mutual sweat despite the whirring overhead fan, when they were awakened by the noise of trucks and the murmur of people. John knew immediately what it was; the Norfolk was only just down the street from police headquarters. He got out of bed and stood at the window. Looking through the lowered blind, he saw the police vehicles drawing up and several armed policemen ringing the back of the Black Maria as six men were virtually flung down. Their hands were handcuffed behind their backs, and although they must have been quite smartly dressed when they began the day, their suits were covered in dust where they had been rolled on the ground, and even from a distance he could see that they had bruises on their faces and heads. There was more to come – the policemen were kicking them as they tried to get up. And one of them was Joseph Kinshasu.

He began to dress.

Adèle sat up. "Where are you going?"

"I won't be long. I'm just going to nip next door and make sure everything is on the up-and-up."

"Johnnie," she protested. "It's none of your business."

He sat on the bed and took her in his arms. "Joseph saved me from being taken prisoner once. Maybe he even saved my life. Now he's in the hands of a bunch of men who loathe the Kikuyu. I can't just let him be beaten up for doing something he believes in. Can I, Dela?"

She gazed at him, then kissed him on the mouth. "Then hurry back."

When he looked from the window, John had seen people already gathering on the side of the street opposite the police station. When he reached the street itself, he discovered that the crowd was several hundred strong, nearly all Kikuyu.

The people appeared perfectly peaceful in intent. They stood or squatted on the pavement and spilled over into the road, but the only problem they were presenting was to traffic, and there wasn't much of that. A police sergeant was talking to them, but he didn't seem to be getting very far.

Then one of the Kikuyu saw John, and pointed. "Is Mr Barclay."

The shout was taken up. "Mr Barclay!"

"You going get those boys out of there, Mr Barclay?" someone asked.

John grinned at them. "Well, that depends on what they've done," he said, and went inside.

He found a great many more policemen, all equipping themselves with rifles and bandoliers, as he made his way to the inspector's office. "Expecting a battle, Curtis?" he asked pleasantly.

"With those devils you can never tell, Mr Barclay," the Englishman replied. "Don't tell me, you've come to see Kinshasu."

"I just wanted to make sure he'd been able to call his lawyer."

"Men like Thuku and Kinshasu don't have lawyers," Curtis said contemptuously.

"Then perhaps it's time they did. I would like to see Joseph, yes."

Curtis pointed a pencil. "You have no right, you know. Your name may be Barclay, but I am entitled to hold those men incommunicado for twenty-four hours."

"Curtis," John said, still speaking pleasantly, "don't be a bloody fool and get on my wick. Let me see Joseph."

Curtis glared at him for a moment, obviously dreaming of a day when even John Barclay might be found to have transgressed the law sufficiently to be arrested, then jerked his head. "You know where the cells are."

"Thank you," John said.

A sergeant waiting in the corridor would have checked him, but looked past him and obviously received some kind of a signal from his superior, because he stepped aside.

169

John made his way past the usual collection of drunks and prostitutes, and came to the cell where the six Kikuyu were incarcerated. They looked even more roughed-up at close quarters; none of the police constables were Kikuyu, of course, and there had undoubtedly been inter-tribal animosity involved.

The men raised their heads at his approach and looked at him unsmilingly. He recognized the short and thickset Harry Thuku from his photograph in the newspaper some weeks before, but the other men he did not know. Save of course for Joseph, who rose to his feet with a look of relief on his face. But then Thuku said something, and his expression changed again. John had quite a few words of Kikuyu, but Thuku spoke both very quickly and very quietly, and he was not able to understand.

Joseph had certainly borne the brunt of the police aggression. What had once been a smart grey suit was ruined, one of the sleeves pulled right out of the shoulder, the jacket split up the back, the knee of one of the trouser legs torn. His tie had been forced up against his throat so that he was breathing with difficulty, and as he was still handcuffed he had been unable to do anything about it. John reached through the bars and released it. "You have trouble," he remarked.

Joseph inhaled gladly. "They are bastards," he said. "They have been waiting for this opportunity."

"And you gave it to them, you chump," John said. "But they may have overstepped the mark. Now, I am going to get you a lawyer."

Joseph's eyes smouldered. "Me, Mr John?"

"All of you."

"Why are you going to do that, Mr John? I don't work for you any more."

"Do you know, that's exactly what my wife pointed out." John shrugged. "Let's say . . . for old time's sake?"

"We don't want no white man's lawyer," Harry Thuku growled.

John looked at Joseph; his face seemed to have closed.

"Joseph," he said, "refusing to carry an identity card carries a possible sentence of two years at hard labour."

"You have an identity card, Mr John?"

"Well . . . no." John flushed.

"You are outside the law," Joseph said. "Like the lawyer you're going to get us. We don't want a lawyer."

"You'd rather spend two years in the Chalbi Desert, breaking stones?"

"We don't want a white lawyer," Joseph said again.

John sighed. He could tell that Joseph was secretly crying out for help, but that he dared not go against his companions. And in that case there was nothing he could do for him. "Pity," he said, and walked back along the corridor.

By now the entire station was crammed with policemen, summoned from their time off, and every man was armed. There were at least a hundred and fifty of them, and Curtis had also buckled on a revolver.

"You know," John said, "you could start a war."

"It's my business to prevent one," Curtis snapped. "When you are finished stirring things up, Mr Barclay."

"I'm finished, Curtis," John told him, and walked back to the hotel. The mob, which had now grown to over a thousand strong, gave him a cheer, and he waved at them again.

Upstairs, he found Adèle fully dressed and watching through the slats of the blinds.

"God, I was scared," she said when he entered the room.

"I think you had every reason to be, if not for me," he agreed. "Pack your bag and get out of here."

"Eh?"

"There could be trouble," he explained.

"But you're not coming?"

"I think I should hang about, just in case."

"Then I'm staying too."

"Adèle." He held her shoulders. "I know how to deal with these situations, believe me. Now listen. Pack your bag, go downstairs, get into the car, drive out of the back gate and go home. I'll come down by train tomorrow."

"No," she said, her face assuming a more determined expression than he had ever seen on it before. "No. I—"

A shot rang out, and then another, and then a whole volley. John hurled her across the room, sending her sprawling beside the bed and gasping for breath. "Stay there," he snapped, and flattened himself against the wall, while he sidled to the window.

"Johnnie! For God's sake be careful," she begged.

"I intend to be," he promised her, and cautiously parted the slats, to see people fleeing in every direction, while the policemen gathered outside the door of the station fired again and again, and ominous dark heaps accumulated on the road. But the mob was dissolving rather than attacking, racing down side streets, some even trying to get into the locked foyer of the hotel itself, screaming their fear.

The firing stopped, as if the policemen had suddenly realized what they were doing. After the repeated explosions, the silence was almost breathtaking. Then it was broken again, by the moans of the dying.

Slowly Adèle pushed herself up and came to the window. This time John did not stop her. She stood at his side and peered with him through the blind at the street. "Oh, my God," she said, gazing at the bodies, and the blood. "Oh, my God! Did they attack the station?"

"No," John said. His voice was thick.

"But. . . ."

"They were standing there," he said. "And some damned fool of a policeman fired his rifle." His face was bitter as he looked down at her. "Those people aren't going to forget today. And when they decide to avenge it, God help us all."

"Twenty-five killed," Adrian Barclay said. "Including several women and a teenage boy. Jesus Christ!"

"Couldn't have happened at a worse time," Delamere agreed. "The lunatic who fired the first shot should be strung up by the balls."

"I'd be inclined to do that to the officer in charge," John growled. "For not keeping his men in hand, and for not stopping the shooting sooner. Arrogant bastard."

172

"Well, it's done," Delamere said. "No use crying over spilt milk. And no use hanging our heads in shame, either. We can't let a tragedy like that turn into a disaster for us all. We have to face it out. If necessary, we have to prove to the world that it was unavoidable."

"You must be joking," John said.

"Listen, Jacko," Delamere said, "there comes a time in a man's life when he has to make certain decisions. Those decisions cannot always be on the basis of right and wrong; they sometimes have to be based on simple survival. If we let the papers and the politicians take us apart on this one, we are going to wind up second-class citizens of this country, or any country. Believe me, I am as sorry about what happened as you, but we have to think of ourselves, and our loved ones." He paused to smile at Adèle, and then to look at the lawn where Lizzie and Mal were playing. "Thuku and Kinshasu did commit a crime. We have to make sure the possible consequences of that crime are understood by everyone, that their defiance of the pass laws was the signal for a revolution which could have swept white rule out of Kenya."

"For God's sake, Uncle Hugh. . . ."

"It's that, Jacko, or you may as well go upstairs and pack your bags, right now."

John looked at his father.

Adrian sighed. "I'm afraid Hugh is right, Johnnie. However sad it is, we can only make things worse by wearing a hair shirt over it. We simply have to prove our point now."

"More than that," Delamere said. "We have to prove it in London. I intend to write immediately to Churchill and ask him to receive a delegation of Kenya settlers to discuss our problems. And I intend to send a copy to *The Times* just in case he isn't interested."

"A delegation?" Adrian asked. "Composed of whom?"

"Everyone I can raise," Delamere said. "And I intend to have a Barclay with me."

They both looked at John.

"I know Uncle Hugh is right," Adèle said.

"He's not planning to take any wives or children," John pointed out.

"Well, I have no great desire to visit England right now," she said. "When the children are older, perhaps. But you cannot let other men's stupidity take this away from you."

"From us," he reminded her.

"From Malcolm."

He couldn"t argue with that; he couldn't argue with any of them. The Nairobi massacre had to be justified, and absorbed. It was a feeling which gripped the entire white community. If the colony, and from all reports, the world, was horrified by what had happened, public opinion in Kenya – which meant white opinion, because there was no other that was articulate save for the Indians, and they tended to side with the whites against the Africans – was that the police would not have opened fire without some very good cause connected with the machinations of Thuku and his dastardly gang; machinations of which the world at large was ignorant.

This left the defence lawyers, appointed by the court, a very difficult task, especially as they got no cooperation whatsoever from their clients. One of them, Billy Adams, drove out to Naivasha to see John. "It would be an enormous help if someone of influence would stand up in court and point out what a storm in a teacup this is. Introduce some sanity into all this hysteria," he said.

"Wouldn't that be contempt of court?" John asked.

"Not if it were done skilfully enough," Adams argued. "If you were to agree to appear as a character witness for Kinshasu, who, after all, used to work for you, then I could lead you into answering certain questions which could put the whole thing into a different light. Otherwise those fellows don't have a hope in hell. The police are already dropping all manner of dark hints about the subversive material they found when they raided the YKA offices. I don't think they found a damned thing which should stand up in a court of law, but the jury is going to be composed of white men who have been frightened by the affair, and frankly, the whole business stinks."

174

John agreed. "I'll appear as a character witness for Kinshasu," he promised.

But both Adrian Barclay and Lord Delamere vetoed the idea. "That is quite ridiculous, Jacko," Delamere protested. "Think of it: a member of my delegation, soon to put before the Colonial Office our certainty that we are the only people capable of governing this colony without revolution, standing up in court and declaring that any talk of revolution is absurd? It wouldn't do. We'd be laughed out of town."

John looked at his father.

"I'm afraid Hugh is right," Adrian said. "I know you and Kinshasu were by way of being friends, but he has opted to go out on his own and defy us, and he must accept the consequences. I'm sure he knows that too," he added. "He always struck me as being quite a sensible chap."

John supposed they were as right as Adams had been. He realized that however unimportant the defiance of the pass laws had been in itself, it could well have been the opening shot in a struggle to decide who was going to control Kenya. In such a situation no man could sit in the middle. And there was only one way he could jump: his skin was white, and he hoped to inherit the farm – and leave it to his son.

He wrote Adams a letter, informing him that in the circumstances he felt he could not appear as a defence witness, but enclosing a character testimonial for Joseph, which could be read to the jury, from a former employer who had always found him honest, reliable and essentially peaceful by nature.

The trial took some time to come to court, as the prosecution was determined to round up some kind of evidence that the Kikuyu had indeed plotted a revolution, and throwing away their pass books was to be the starting signal. John didn't attend, but he read the reports, and it was obvious that the prosecution could not prove its contention. On the other hand, there was equally no question that the six men *had* thrown away their pass books and incited others to do the same, and they did not help their cause by defying the authority of the court. Predictably, they were all sentenced to what was euphemistically called 'internal exile' in the north of the colony.

"So that is that," Adèle said. "I am sure it will do Joseph a lot of good. Maybe we can all enjoy Christmas now."

The delegation was due to leave for England soon afterwards; she was far more concerned about this than the fate of some angry African, because it would be the first time she and John would not have slept in the same bed for almost four years. Yet she was also relieved, and indeed delighted, to discover that the prospect of a lengthy separation was not quite as horrifying as it would once have been. She was finding her feet. She had come here as a penniless refugee and an orphan, aware that her only hope of survival lay in the big, strong man who had so marvellously fallen in love with her. Then, even the fact of his love had been terribly uncertain to her. She had been over-conscious of the presence of the black servant, of the mental intimacy between the two men, of their shared experiences which left her the outsider, in her mind.

She had loathed Joseph Kinshasu from that moment, as he had been such a barrier to her achieving an equal intimacy with Johnnie. She had never been so relieved as when he resigned on their wedding day; that had been the best of all the presents given her. To have him suddenly appear again, summoning his Mr John to his aid, had been like a slap in the face. Especially when John had responded so quickly and eagerly. Two years in the desert would indeed do the rascal a lot of good.

But her new-found confidence was based on a lot more than the departure of Joseph Kinshasu. In four years she had made a very real home. She adored Adrian and Joanna, and felt they were at least fond of her. She actually admired Catherine, as a woman who would go her own way regardless of adverse comment – and even more, as a woman who had the wherewithal to do so. She bitterly regretted that the pair of them had got off on the wrong foot, and looked forward to a real reconciliation, which might well be possible in John's absence.

She was beginning to enjoy the rest of Kenya society, the knowledge, which had spread slowly through her system like a warm drink, that she was now a member of the most important family in the colony, that no one could ever again be rude to her or humiliate her. That she mattered!

She had even taken to going to places by herself, and these explorations, sometimes accompanied by the children, increased when the settlers' delegation finally left for England at the beginning of March. She would often drive over to the Baroness Blixen's coffee plantation in the Ngong Hills just outside Nairobi, for lunch and a chat. For a variety of reasons she found the Baroness a fascinating companion. She, being Danish, was, like Adèle, essentially an alien in this very English society. She was also in a difficult position, for she had no John Barclay on whom to lean. Her husband had deserted her, and yet kept returning to Kenya to go on safari, shooting big game with various wealthy or famous people. East Africa, indeed, had become the mecca of all those bored or frustrated men who felt the necessity to prove themselves by hanging a lion's head or a pair of buffalo horns over their mantelpieces in England, with a photograph underneath which was supposed to prove they had actually fired the fatal shot. The decimation of the once teeming wildlife in the high country so concerned Adrian Barclay that he had insisted a discussion on some way of preserving the colony's most important heritage – in his opinion, anyway – be included on the agenda for the London conference.

The constant round of shooting parties was sad for the Baroness in another way, in that her friend Denys Finch-Hatton, the best of the "white hunters", was in constant employment, and therefore she saw little of him. Few people in Nairobi doubted that they were lovers – but then, few people in Nairobi were in any position to cast stones on that account, if all the rumours were true.

There was another aspect to the Baroness's personality which attracted Adèle: her feeling for the black people. She lived alone amongst them and relied on them entirely, especially for everything to do with the running of her plantation, which was an increasingly difficult business. She even seemed to be friends with them. This was something Adèle wanted to achieve, if it could be done. She knew her prejudices were entirely a result of her upbringing by her father, who had regarded the blacks as dangerous beasts, only to be kept in their place at the end of a whip. That background had been an important inspiration for the immediate hostility she felt for Joseph Kinshasu, quite apart from his relationship with Johnnie. And she would always loathe and fear Joseph, she knew. But he was only one man, and she was equally aware that she was committed to spending the rest of her life in this country, surrounded by Africans.

Yet the Baroness's easy intimacy with what she called "her" people was something she simply could not bring herself to emulate, nor could she raise much sympathy when her friend declaimed angrily about how the Africans were ill-treated by the British. Adèle thought she should have tried living in Tanganyika under German rule for a year.

But her principal aim during John's absence was to achieve that reconciliation with Catherine. Her sister-in-law still came to lunch most Sundays, on occasion somewhat the worse for wear, as if she had had very little sleep. And her parties, or those she attended, still attracted rumour and innuendo. No one knew for sure what went on, of course; the Portington crowd, as it was known, kept to itself. Although it apparently embraced all branches of society, its core came from the recent arrivals from England, mostly moneyed or even titled people who had decided to turn their back on strikes and financial crises and disillusioned workers in favour of the best climate in the world, perpetual sunshine – and the right to do exactly as they pleased. Adèle, who had done her share of reading, supposed that they were re-creating a seventeenth century squirearchy, complete with Restoration morals – as in many cases they were direct descendants from those happy-go-lucky Cavaliers.

She wasn't sure what to make of it. Her own upbringing had been so strict that she did not really understand what "immorality" involved. She did not regard herself as having been desperately immoral in surrendering to John, or indeed, seducing him, before they were married. He was her man, and had been ever since 1915. Catherine was a widow, and therefore was betraying nobody by having a lover. That she smoked and drank too much was again her choice. The other rumours, that these parties included wife-swapping and other truly immoral activities, Adèle dismissed as pure sour grapes on the part of those who were never invited. And while she knew that Johnnie would not approve, she was determined to get herself into that magically exciting circle - after all, if she could effect a reconciliation between her husband and his sister, everyone would surely be overjoyed. Joanna most of all.

Being accepted by Catherine was not an easy task, after everything that had happened. Cathy regarded her as John's appendage, and obviously did not consider they could ever now be friends. It was Joanna who discerned Adèle's anxiety to reach some kind of rapport with her sister-in-law, and, as Adèle had expected, was delighted. Joanna must have had a word with her daughter, because Adèle was taken by surprise one June Sunday after lunch, when she went upstairs to watch Nanny putting the children down for their siesta and Catherine accompanied her.

"Such lovely children," she said.

"It's sad you never had any," Adèle commented.

"Never wanted any of my own," Catherine said. "But I can admire other people's. Especially my own nephew and niece. I suppose you're finding life pretty dull with Johnnie away?"

Adèle felt a sudden rush of excitement; she knew what was coming. So she lied. "Pretty."

"I was wondering if you'd care to come over and spend the night with me, sometime."

"Why, that would be lovely," Adèle agreed. "If you're sure I won't be putting you out."

"Good Lord, no. Why not come for next weekend? Come on Saturday afternoon. I'm having a little supper party that night, and I know my friends would enjoy meeting you."

179

"That would be quite lovely," Adèle said again.

Adèle's excitement grew. So what if Johnnie might disapprove? She was an adult human being, and Cathy was her sister-in-law. Besides, if she could disprove some of the rumours. . . .

But she was in no doubt that she was going to have to compete not only with Cathy, but with a lot of other women who would be waiting to show up the German country bumpkin. So she decided on a new gown for the occasion, and hurried into Nairobi – and to her delight found exactly what she wanted: being both tall and strongly built, she had not the easiest figure to fit. Yet here was a pale blue crêpe, with a high bodice secured by a halter neck. The back was exposed, save for a single panel which connected the halter with the skirt at the base of her spine. The effect, as she looked at herself in the mirror, was to display magnificently a large area of broad, strong white flesh, and yet keep her perfectly decent. As accessories she chose a silver lamé handbag, and silver kid shoes. The whole outfit cost a fortune, in her opinion, but she reminded herself that she was a Barclay now, and money hardly mattered.

Joanna as usual promised to keep an eye on Nanny, and after lunch on Saturday Adèle took the Austin Seven – John had insisted she learn to drive, and she was grateful for that – put her maid Lucy in the back and went into town.

She was more excited than she could ever remember. She had to go back to her very first formal dance in 1913, when she was sixteen years old, to recapture a similar feeling. Then she had worn her first ball gown, and she had been allowed to put her hair up for the first time – Papa was already in Africa and Mama perhaps knew that things like balls would be gone forever once they set sail. Mama of course accompanied her as a chaperon, but that had not prevented her from being the belle of the ball; her card had been filled within minutes, and she had not missed a dance. She adored dancing, and the only tiny regret she felt about her marriage was that it apparently did not interest Johnnie.

She wondered if there would be dancing tonight.

Cathy was apparently busy when she reached the house, and she was shown to a large and airy bedroom by Murgatroyd, the black butler. As Cathy had once jokingly remarked at lunch at Naivasha, "His name isn't really Murgatroyd, of course. But I've always wanted to have a butler called Murgatroyd." He was quite a young black man, presumably a Kikuyu, Adèle thought, who was flawlessly dressed in cutaway coat and striped trousers. She wondered if he resented his elevation to being a kind of toy poodle for his mistress, but if he did, he showed no sign of it.

The room contained a double bed, but she had become used to sleeping by herself in a double bed, and enjoyed being able to spread her legs. There was a room in the servants' quarters for Lucy, but she hardly had time to get settled in before assisting her mistress to dress for dinner. Adèle had decided to leave her hair loose – pompadours were out of fashion, anyway, and for all the daring of the gown, she felt she needed the protection of flowing brown tresses.

When she went down the stairs, she felt like a queen, but she paused before she got to the bottom, because Cathy was waiting for her, and she realized that there was no hope of her, or anyone else, being the belle of the ball in Cathy's house. As befitted her status as a widow, even of several years' standing, the Dowager Lady Portington wore a black lace dinner gown over a crêpe-de-chine lining. But the entire outfit only stretched from just below her knees to just above her nipples. Her shoes were silver, and she wore a black velvet choker, on which was pinned a large sapphire brooch which went with the sapphire on her finger. The contrast between black dress, white skin, auburn hair and the glowing blue of the jewels was breathtaking.

She was smoking a cigarette from a silver holder, but this she now took from her mouth. "My dear," she said. "You look divine."

"So do you," Adèle said, wishing she had been able to think of something a little more original.

181

"Oh, this old thing," Cathy said. "I really must get something new one of these days. Now come along and meet everybody. They are just dying to meet you."

Feeling somewhat like a Christian about to be thrown to the lions, Adèle followed her sister-in-law into the drawing room. She had not been in there before, and again her breath was taken away. It was a large room, opening on to a mosquito-screened verandah with steps leading down to a secluded croquet lawn at the far end of which there was a swimming pool. To the right, an arch gave into an equally spacious dining room, where the table was laden with silver and crystal. The drawing room itself presented a vast expanse of polished wood, across which were thrown a variety of rugs and animal skins, kept in place by occasional tables topped by brass trays heavy with brass ornaments in the shapes of various animals. The chairs were of comfortable cane, although there were a couple of divans and one leather-upholstered settee against the wall by the fireplace; the winters in Nairobi could be quite cool enough to require a log fire.

The room somehow managed to look elegant and yet lived in at the same time, and obviously the Pekingese who had barked shrilly on her arrival that afternoon, but who were apparently now locked up, normally had the run of it.

Cathy's "small supper party" turned out to consist of eighteen people apart from themselves, eight women and ten men. One or two of them Adèle had met before, briefly, and one or two of the others were vaguely familiar to her, but for the most part their names swirled about her head, as Catherine could appreciate. "Never mind, my dear," she said. "You'll know everybody much better before the evening is out. But this is Jimmy."

Adèle was not impressed by the man, who was an inch shorter than herself and wore a fashionable toothbrush moustache to go with his slicked-back dark hair. She gathered he was her escort for the evening, however, and reflected that he could have been worse.

Murgatroyd was circulating with glasses of champagne cocktails, made with more than the usual amount of brandy, and everyone was already fairly tight, but that they were pleased to see Adèle could not be doubted; she was a new face, a new experience, she supposed, in their tight circle. They crowded round her to talk and ask questions about Tanganyika and Germany, and of course about the Barclays and Naivasha. She gathered that only one or two of them had ever been to the farm, and then only briefly.

She actually had no desire to talk about her in-laws, especially in front of Cathy, but to her surprise her sister-in-law seemed more than willing to reminisce about her famous family. "Do you know what my earliest memory is?" Cathy said. "Of being carried on my father's back, in some kind of harness, through the forest below where we are now. Ma was there too, carrying little Johnnie . . . that was just before he died. There were no porters, because none would venture into the Kikuyu country at that time; they had a fearsome reputation. But we had to get from the farm to the coast – I don't remember why – and so we walked. Just the four of us."

"You mean your mother and father walked," one of the men corrected her. "You were carried. Haw, haw, haw."

"But weren't you terrified?" cried one of the women.

Cathy appeared to consider. "I don't think so," she said. "Not even when the arrows started to fly. I was with Pa."

"You mean they *shot* at you?"

"Oh, they were always shooting at people."

"My *God*!" shrieked one of the other women, who seemed to be an American. "What did you do?"

"Pa sorted them out," Cathy explained. "He was good at that."

"He must have been awfully brave," said another woman. "I've read somewhere how the Kikuyu once captured a white man and they murdered him, oh . . . in a most dreadful fashion."

"Oh, yes," Cathy said. "I remember. They staked him out and then every member of the clan – men, women and children – urinated on his face until he drowned."

"Ugh!" Adèle exclaimed. "That cannot be true."

"Cross my heart and hope to die," Cathy said. "It was

only twenty-odd years ago, too. But that's nothing. Let me tell you how they circumcise their girls when they reach puberty."

"You are going to put us off our dinner," Jimmy said.

"Oh. Then I'll keep it until afterwards."

"But *why* do they circumcise their women?" one of the men wanted to know.

"For a very good reason: to keep them faithful. Once the clitoris and the lips of the labia have been removed, it's very difficult for a girl to have an orgasm. So she loses interest in sex and just submits to her lord and master."

"I think that's just awful," the American woman said. "I should hate that."

"Snap." Cathy looked at where Murgatroyd was standing in the dining room archway. "I think supper's ready."

"Supper" was a five-course meal, beautifully cooked, and flawlessly served by Murgatroyd and two assistants. Now they were on to claret, and the evening grew more animated. Unused to so much drinking, Adèle found herself yawning by the time the dessert was reached, and wondered how late these soirées lasted. She was very relieved when the ladies excused themselves and trooped upstairs to Cathy's bathroom, which, in blush pink, was as elegant as the rest of the house.

Here the conversation became more risqué than ever. "You know what I want to know?" the American woman asked. "Have any of you girls ever slept with a *black* man?"

"Good lord, what an idea," someone remarked.

"I have," Cathy said dreamily.

"You haven't!" Adèle snapped.

Cathy glanced at her. "Are you calling me a liar, darling?"

"But . . . that's impossible. I don't see how you could."

"Easiest thing in the world. And the best."

"Who was he, Cathy?" the others asked. "Who was he?"

"Not a chance," Cathy said. "That's one secret I am going to keep." She smiled at them. "Else you'd all be wanting a turn."

Adèle was more shocked than she had ever been before. She almost wished she hadn't come. Because if that were true, then Cathy was everything John suggested she was. But of course it couldn't be true. Cathy was just inventing it to make the others ooh and aah, as she must have invented that frightful story about the man being killed by the Kikuyu. Why, there were Kikuyu all about them. All the servants in this house were Kikuyu. And if it had happened only twenty-odd years ago . . . It had to be an invention.

She wanted only to go to bed, but to do so now would be the height of bad manners. She would have to sit out at least another hour of these pointless, obscene stories. They returned downstairs, where the men had moved into the drawing room with their cigars and port, and where Murgatroyd had the coffee brewing. "You'll have a liqueur, Dela," Cathy invited.

Adèle had always wanted her to use that pet name. Cathy really was a lovely person, she thought. Of course she had been making it all up. "I don't think so, really," she said. "I've had a skinful. Cathy, would it be awfully rude if I sidled off just now? I can hardly keep my eyes open."

"It would be awfully rude," Cathy said. "Anyway, we'll soon wake you up. We're about to play a game."

"Oh." She watched Murgatroyd placing a roulette wheel in the centre of the cleared dining table. He had also arranged several freshly opened champagne bottles on the sideboard, so that the guests could go on drinking for some time to come. Oh, Lord, Adèle thought. Quite apart from wanting to stretch out, she had always been afraid of gambling. Then she reminded herself that she was Mrs John Barclay: she could afford to lose.

Murgatroyd was standing in the archway again, waiting, and Cathy caught his eye. "Okay, folks," she cried, assuming a nasal accent to match that of her friend, which she could do quite easily as she was half-American herself, "let's play balls."

They hurried forward to stand on both sides of the table, getting as close to their hostess as they could. She was in front of the wheel, and Murgatroyd had withdrawn. "The high spot of the evening," Jimmy murmured, putting his arm round Adèle's waist. "It's all a con, of course. Cathy

185

knows exactly what is going to happen, who is going to get whom."

Adèle had no idea what he was talking about, while she was puzzled at the absence of an odds mat, or indeed a ball for the wheel. But she was too tight to work it out.

"Now then," Cathy said. "Most of you know the rules of this game, but for those who haven't played it before –" she looked from Adèle to another couple who were also clearly new to the circle and the house, from the way they had exclaimed about it – "I can tell you that there are six bedrooms upstairs, the doors of which are now firmly locked. Access can only be gained by means of one of these keys." She held up a canvas bag which jingled when she shook it. "There are ten keys, as there are ten couples, and that means there is going to have to be a certain amount of sharing. But that only adds to the fun."

They gazed at her, faces shining with anticipation, while Adèle tried to think. Was she being told she had to share her bedroom? She didn't like the idea of that, not only because neither Lucy nor herself was particularly tidy but because there was only the one bed.

"All right," Cathy said. "Who'll have first go? You, Claude," and she held out the bag towards the other newcomers.

"Oh, I say," Claude murmured, glancing at the woman with him, who was obviously his wife, and then plunging his hand into the bag. "Number three."

"That's my room," Adèle said, without thinking.

"That's one with a double bed," Cathy announced. "Lucky you, Claude, if you have to share. Now let's see. . . ." She took the key back from Claude, placed it on the zero and then spun the wheel. "Whee!"

Adèle felt as if she had suddenly been kicked in the stomach, as she at last understood what was going to happen. And that Jimmy, whose arm was now tight round her waist, was right: Cathy could select exactly when to stop the wheel – it was obvious from the way she glanced at the eager faces before the key arrived pointing at the American woman.

"Well, hey!" she cried.

"Oh, I say," Claude repeated, again glancing at his wife, this time apprehensively: the American was a very pretty woman. But Mrs Claude merely gave a little shrug of acceptance of the situation.

"Off you go," Cathy said.

"She's right-sided," commented one of the men, who appeared to be the American's husband.

"Oh, I say," Claude said again. He had apparently lost the power of coherent speech.

As she had lost the power of coherent thought, Adèle realized. She could only think that she had to get out of here. "Cathy," she said urgently. "I really am not feeling very well. I think I should go and lie down . . ."

"Who's got cold feet?" Cathy asked, and everyone laughed. "I told you she'd want to sidle off," she announced. "But you are going to lie down, darling. Very soon."

"I meant. . . ."

"Oh, stop being so bloody prissy," Catherine snapped, her voice suddenly as brittle as her eyes. "All right, you can have next go, Jimmy."

"Aha," Jimmy said, and thrust his hand into the bag. "Golly! Another three."

"Lucky you. Hear that, Claude?" Cathy called.

Claude and the American stopped at the foot of the stairs to discover who they were going to be sharing the bed with.

But that too had been previously determined, and before Adèle could decide what she was going to do, the wheel had been spun and come to rest pointing at her.

"Yummy," Jimmy said.

"I think you could let Claude have a go after you," Cathy suggested.

"Oh, I say," Claude commented.

Adèle drew a long breath. If they wanted her to be rude, then she would damned well have to be rude. "If you think," she said, speaking as clearly as she could, "that I am going to share my bed with either of these . . . these creeps, you have another think coming. I don't share my bed with anyone except my husband."

187

"Well, really," remarked one of the women, as if she had just uttered an obscene word.

"So I'll say goodnight." Adèle turned and faced Jimmy.

"You are being an awfully poor sport," Jimmy commented.

"Get out of my way, little man," Adèle commmanded.

"I agree," Cathy said. "I think you are being a complete shit."

Adèle paused in surprise and turned her head.

"You virtually ask to be invited to my party," Cathy told her, "and you sit around like a damned prune all evening, then you insult my guests, and now you want to spoil our fun. Well, I'm fucked if I am going to let that happen, you jumped-up little German arsehole."

Adèle stared at her with her mouth open. She had never been addressed like that in her life.

"So you get the hell upstairs with Jimmy and give him a good time," Cathy ordered.

Adèle got her breath back. "You . . . you dare to suggest such a thing to me? You . . . horror!" She turned back to face Jimmy. "Get out of my way."

"She's going to have to learn the facts of life," Catherine announced. "Bring her over here." She swept the roulette wheel from the table with a crash. "Put her here, in front of me."

Adèle glared at Jimmy. "If you lay one filthy hand on me, you. . . ."

Jimmy lowered his head and ran forward. She was taken utterly by surprise, and his shoulder butted into her stomach, driving all the breath from her lungs, while her head and torso flopped over his back. She immediately pounded him with her clenched fists.

"Help me," he shouted, as he tried to straighten, carrying her across his shoulders, and found he couldn't; instead he sank to his knees.

Adèle began to get her breath back. "Put me down, you bastard," she shouted, continuing to hit him as hard as she could.

"I think he needs help," Cathy said: "Claude. George. Peter. Give him a hand."

"Oh, I say," Claude remarked, but he came forward; Jimmy was holding her tightly across the bottom, digging his fingers in, and she couldn't straighten. She swung her fist at him, and missed; he caught her wrist. Then she felt hands on her legs; and realized they must have thrown her skirt up – in the heat of an African June she was not wearing stockings, and indeed wore no underclothes at all except for her knickers.

"You bastards!" she screamed at them. "Somebody help me."

But nobody was going to. With two men lifting her legs, and two more holding her arms, Jimmy was able to straighten, still holding her buttocks, and she was carried across the room, gasping and fighting, and dumped on the table with a force that again drove all her breath from her lungs.

She had landed on her side, but was immediately rolled on to her back. She tried to sit up, and was forced down again; everyone seemed to have hold of a piece of her. She gazed up at their drunken, grinning faces – she no longer felt the least drunk herself. She could not believe this was happening. Nor could she believe that they hadn't even started to amuse themselves yet.

Cathy's face was there too, her eyes glittering with a mixture of arousal and anger and contempt, and anticipation. "Now," she said. "Strip the bitch."

"Oh, I say," Claude protested.

"That's going it a bit, Cathy," the man called George murmured.

"It'll ruin her gown," remarked the American woman, who had rejoined the group round the table, as Claude was obviously not going to perform while this entertainment was at hand.

"So I'll buy her a new dress," Cathy said. "Oh, you are a lot of cowards!" She seized the halter neck of Adèle's gown and burst the catch.

189

"Cathy!" Adèle begged. "For God's sake, Cathy! Please!"

"Whee!" Cathy laughed, and pulled the bodice down to Adèle's waist. "Oh, look at those tits. Aren't they quite out of this world! Forty if they're an inch. Come along, everybody, have a feel."

Adèle screamed her anger and outrage as everybody felt her, including Cathy. She gasped and panted, and bared her teeth, and they laughed.

"Now for the rest of her," Cathy announced.

Material ripped, and her gown was pulled apart. They cheered as they waved her knickers above her head; she had long lost her shoes in trying to kick.

By now she was too exhausted to fight them any more, and could only lie and pant.

"I think she's ready," Cathy said. "She's all yours, Jimmy. You'll have to do it here. We'll hold her down for you."

"Jesus," Jimmy commented, staring at Adèle's face. "She'll have me for rape."

"Oh, you are the most dreadful little man," Cathy pronounced. "Are you going to mount her or not?"

"Ah . . . I don't think . . ."

"Oh, drop dead. Larry?" She looked across the table.

"Count me out of this one, Cathy," Larry said. "I don't think she's keen."

"You lousy bastards," Cathy commented, but as she looked around the male faces she could see not one of her guests was going to risk actually raping John Barclay's wife.

"We've had our fun, Cathy," the American said. "Let's get on with the game. If Adèle doesn't want to play, well . . . I guess one of us girls will have to cope with two men." She giggled. "I'll have a go."

"No," Cathy said. "She had this coming. If you won't mount the bitch, then we'll –" she hesitated, looking down at her sister-in-law. "We'll shave her crotch."

"Oh, I say," Claude commented.

"Come along now," Cathy said. "It'll be tremendous fun. One of you must have some shaving cream in your gear."

"Well," Jimmy confessed.

"Go and fetch it. And your razor." She looked down into Adèle's face. "We're going to leave you all *bare*."

Adèle screamed.

She didn't know if she had fainted, or if she had passed out from sheer exhaustion. She felt bruised in every way, from her head to her toes, where she had been banged and bumped as she had fought them, where her flesh had been the subject of restraining hands as they had held her from moving, and from the pit of her stomach to the last recess of her brain, where she had been humiliated and tormented. But now she was alone; there was actually no one holding her on to the table, no one standing above her, grinning at her. Presumably they had abandoned their game and just paired off.

She moved, slowly, cautiously. She did not want to look down; she could still smell the sweet-scented soap with which she had been smothered, still feel the fingers stretching her skin taut as the razor had been passed over it, still hear the laughter and the comments. The three British soldiers who had assaulted her outside Dagaba had been no worse than these . . . aristocrats.

She rolled on her side and fell off the table. She landed on her feet, then looked left and right. The lights still blazed, and she could see her gown lying in a crumpled mess on the floor. It was ruined, but she could wear it to go home. And when she got there! As she picked it up she heard a movement. She straightened, holding the gown in front of herself protectively, and watched Cathy rising from the sofa, where she had been lying on top of Jimmy. Both were naked.

"Well, see who's woken up," Cathy commented. "You look as if you need a drink."

"If you come near me," Adèle said as Catherine stepped forward. She looked left and right, and seized a forgotten steak knife from the sideboard. "I am going to cut your filthy heart out."

Catherine paused, eyebrows arched. "Who's a poor sport, then?"

191

"You. . . ."

"Look," Cathy explained. "We were drunk, and we had a bit of fun. So forget it."

"Forget it?" Adèle shouted. "You must be out of your tiny mind. Forget it? I am going home to Naivasha now. There I am going to tell Mother and Father exactly what happened here tonight. And then I am going into Nairobi to make a statement to the police. I am going to have you locked up. All of you."

"Cathy," Jimmy said uneasily, from the sofa.

"Oh, shut up," Cathy recommended.

"But I think she means it."

"You're damned right I mean it," Adèle told him.

"Cathy. . . ." This time it was almost a wail.

"Oh, get out," Cathy told him. "Go and bang on one of the upstairs doors."

"But. . . ."

"Out," she said again. "My sister-in-law and I need to have a little chat."

He grabbed his trousers and sidled towards the stairs, and nearly fell up them.

"You have nothing to say to me," Adèle said. "Not now, not ever."

"Don't you think so? We're related, darling. What do you think Johnnie will say when he learns you have laid criminal charges against his very own sister."

"I think Johnnie knows criminal charges should have been laid against you years ago."

"Do you?" Cathy sat down and crossed her legs. "You are a naïve little bitch, aren't you? Don't you suppose Johnnie knows what sort of parties I have? Don't you suppose he's been to them?"

"That's a lie!"

"Is it? You should remember that I have known him longer than you, my darling. He won't come any longer, of course; he gets so insanely jealous when he sees me carted off by another man. But, do you know, I would rate Johnnie as my very best lover."

192

"You . . . you are unspeakable. Do you expect me to believe that? Your own brother?"

"And your husband," Cathy said thoughtfully, and stroked one finger down the side of her face reminiscently. "Why do you think he hit me, that evening at the Muthaiga?"

"Because. . . ." Adèle hesitated. She didn't actually know. Nobody did. Except Cathy. And Johnnie!

Cathy smiled. "Exactly, my dear. We had a date. That never crossed your mind, did it? Well, I don't suppose it crossed anybody else's mind, either. But we had been dying to get together again. It had been such a long time. A whole war since we had last been alone together. And then he went out on some kind of business, and I got tight, and randy . . . silly me. He came back up to my room – and there I was, in bed with someone else."

"I don't believe you," Adèle whispered. But her belly had filled with lead. She had known all along that Johnnie would never hit his sister merely because he had discovered she was playing around. It had to be something far more serious, far more personal.

Cathy continued to smile. "Think about it," she recommended. "And then think: do you really want to force Johnnie to make a choice between you and me? You might get a very nasty shock. You could even wind up where you started, as a penniless German orphan. What would you do then, my darling?"

Adèle stared at her, hardly breathing.

Cathy uncoiled her legs and stood up. She went to the sideboard and poured two glasses of champagne. "I think it is absolutely essential, for the good of us both, that we remain the best of friends. The *closest* of friends. Don't you?" She held out one of the glasses, and Adèle took it as if in a dream. Then Cathy raised her own. "To us," she said.

8

Adrian Barclay himself drove the Daimler down to the Naivasha station to meet the incoming train. Lord Delamere's Somali chauffeur was there with the Rolls from Elmenteita, but Adrian ushered both Delamere and John to his car; the Rolls could follow on.

"Tell me how you got on," he said. "Your cable was a little enigmatic."

"Well," John began.

"We got on damned well," Delamere announced. "Although we're not going to admit that to anyone. To begin with, Churchill was out and Devonshire in. Sensible fellow, Devonshire. Quite capable of appreciating our point of view."

"So he fobbed you off with promises and assurances," Adrian commented.

"Like hell he did. He fobbed us off with cast-iron guarantees."

"Such as?"

Delamere held up his hand and ticked off his fingers. "One, that we will have a permanent majority on the Legislative Council. Two, that all Indian immigration into Kenya will be stopped forthwith."

"Good God!" Adrian remarked.

"And three," Delamere said triumphantly, "that the high country is as of now reserved for white settlement only, for nine hundred and ninety-nine years. That means forever. You can now start calling this the white highlands."

"Well, I'll be damned." Adrian braked in the yard. "You must have felt pretty good about that. Congratulations."

"Oh, we haven't actually accepted his offer yet."

"Eh?"

"Well, we were only a delegation. And we didn't want to

appear too eager. I told him we'd have to bring his proposals back here and put it to a settlers' meeting."

"But you are going to recommend acceptance?"

"Of course."

"And there is no one not going to take your recommendation. But what do the Indians think of all this?"

"They can think what they like. That is the Government's proposal."

"And nothing about the blacks? The massacre?"

"Ah, well, that turned out rather well, actually. Everyone understands that the blacks are quite incapable of running anything, much less a colony. And now everyone over there has it firmly fixed in their minds that the buggers are on the verge of rebellion. Oh, yes, Thuku and Kinshasu did us a world of good with their little upheaval."

Adrian glanced at his son.

"All quite true," John confirmed.

"Well, this certainly calls for a celebration." Adrian opened his door, and then paused. "What about the animals?"

"For God's sake," Delamere declared in disgust. "I bring you the best news any white man in this colony has ever had and all you want to know about is animals."

"They're more important than men," Adrian pointed out.

"We've good news there too," John told him. "The Government is going to set up a commission with the idea of delegating parts of Kenya and Tanganyika as national parks, where no one will be allowed to shoot game, except with a camera."

"Waste of time," Delamere snorted.

"I think it'll work," John argued. "These are going to be huge areas, in which a whole lot of animals will be safe."

"And more and more will accumulate as they realize it," Adrian said. "That's great."

"And the Kikuyu and the Masai will claim once again that they've been robbed of their land," Delamere added.

"I still think it's a step in the right direction. Safah," Adrian called. "Champagne!"

They had walked round the front of the house, and John

195

now hurried ahead of them to be the first up the steps. He was disappointed that Adèle and the children hadn't been at the station to greet him, but assumed, as his father had made no comment, that they were all well. And there they were. Three-year-old Lizzie was already half-way down. "Daddy," she shouted. "Daddy!"

He scooped her from the ground for a hug and a kiss, and then did the same for Mal, who couldn't stand properly yet. With a child in each arm he approached the women. The women? He stared at his sister, but was being embraced by his mother. "Oh, Johnnie! Is it really good news?"

"The best." He kissed her, set the children down and faced Adèle.

"Welcome home," she said.

She was as beautiful as he remembered her. But there had been a change, and for a moment he was not quite sure where, although he knew she had put on a little weight. "My darling girl," he said, and took her in his arms. He almost hesitated because although it was quite early in the morning, there was alcohol on her breath, and it wasn't champagne.

But she had hesitated too, and their embrace was reluctant on each side. He looked past her at Catherine, who smiled. "Haven't you a kiss for me, Johnnie?"

He brushed her cheek with his lips, and was then caught up in the congratulations and welcomings and the champagne and the chat. From time to time he looked at his wife, and found her as often as not looking at his sister.

Joanna noticed his preoccupation, and found an opportunity to take him aside. "We're all friends again now, Johnnie," she said. "Do let's keep it that way."

He gave her a hug, and waited. But it was not until after lunch that he was able to take Adèle upstairs, and even then Cathy came with them, almost like a chaperone, to the landing, before saying, "Have fun," and going off to the room she occupied when at Naivasha.

John closed the door behind them, and leaned against it. Adèle sat on the bed. She had consumed a great deal more alcohol with her lunch, and he could see that she could hardly keep her eyes open. But he was determined she should. "How did the great reconciliation come about?" he asked.

Adèle seemed to wake up. "I suppose ... it just happened. She is your sister."

"And now you're the best of friends?"

"Well ... shouldn't we be?"

"I had got the impression you didn't like her."

Adèle shrugged. "I suppose I didn't approve of her. Perhaps because I felt you didn't approve of her."

"But now you do approve of her?"

Adèle tilted her head, almost defiantly. "Shouldn't I?" she asked.

He didn't seem to be getting anywhere, and it didn't seem to matter at this moment. After six months, there were other things he wanted to do more than discuss Cathy. He began to undress. "I'd hate you to get into the habit of drinking as much as she does."

"What's a little drink now and then?" Adèle asked. Her eyes were closed, and now she gave a sigh and fell back across the bed.

John stood above her, naked. "Aren't you going to undress?"

Her eyes opened, and she made a moue as she looked at him.

"Oh, I'd forgotten you'd want your oats. Won't be a moment."

She rolled off the bed and began to remove her clothes, while he lay down to watch her. She had never used an expression like that before. But that was also irrelevant as he gazed at her unveiling body. For six months he had dreamed only of that body, that smile, that hair, that personality. And now it was his again. Thinking of Cathy, and her possible influence on Adèle, was a waste of time, once he was here ... and yet, there was something slightly different about the body too, which he couldn't quite place until it occurred to him that her pubic hair had slightly changed both shape and colour. But that was ridiculous.

She was in his arms, and when he began kissing her she

197

kissed him back with as much passion as ever. He didn't want to hurry; he lay with her on his chest, her hair falling into his face, gazing at her.

"I love you," he said.

"Do you?" she asked.

"Do you doubt it?"

She looked into his eyes. Then she said, "Is it true that the Kikuyu circumcise their women?"

"Why, yes. Lots of African tribes practise female circumcision. It's a way of keeping them faithful to their husbands. A circumcised female is less likely to roam, they say."

"Because she finds it harder to have an orgasm."

"I suppose so. The areas removed are the most sensitive. Dela . . ." It was an odd conversation to be having when about to make love.

"And is it true the Kikuyu once murdered a white man by having every member of the tribe, man, woman and child, urinate on his face?"

"Good Lord, Dela . . ."

"Is it true?" she asked, moving on him.

"Well, yes it is. Where in the name of God have you picked up all of that stuff? Cathy! It must be Cathy."

"What makes you say that?"

"Because she is a mine of useless erotica and downright beastliness, that's why."

"But those stories *are* true?" Adèle persisted.

"Oh, yes. One thing about Cathy, she never lies. She doesn't have to, with the life she's led." He rolled her on her back and entered her, and climaxed seconds later. Then he raised himself to look down on her; she certainly hadn't. "I think I owe you one," he said.

"Forget it," she told him. "I suppose you needed it more than me." He didn't actually take in the remark; he was more concerned with the tear which suddenly trickled out of her eye, and soaked the pillow.

"If you knew what a weight it is off my mind to have this political business sewn up, at least for the time being," Adrian Barclay said. He and his son walked their horses

*

over one of the lanes between the maize fields; the short rains had come and gone, and it would soon be Christmas. The valley was still green, and the birds were singing. It was a simply glorious day.

"You mean, to feel that all of this is ours for the rest of time," John agreed.

"The rest of time is a very long stretch of the imagination," Adrian commented. "Let's say, to feel that Jo and I won't have to fight for our land. Assuming we don't live to be a hundred."

John glanced at him. "That's a pessimistic point of view. Both that you won't live to be a hundred and that I, or someone, will be fighting for this land in thirty years."

Adrian gazed ahead of him at the seemingly endless fields of corn; in the distance they could just make out the shade trees – bananas – of the coffee plantation. "Not with guns, I hope. But I don't feel I'm leaving you all that much of an inheritance."

"All of this isn't enough?"

"Things change," Adrian said sombrely. "The blacks are going to become more numerous and more articulate as time passes. The Indians are already resentful at being designated second-class citizens."

"We have a guarantee from the British Government, Dad. If there was real trouble here, we'd have British troops to defend us."

Adrian sighed. "If they didn't have anything better to do," he said. Then grinned. "I'm being pessimistic. Perhaps sometimes I wonder why we should be so fortunate as to have enjoyed this country, this land, for our lifetimes. Of course there are problems ahead. But none you won't be able to solve, with a little bit of guts, intelligence and, occasionally, ruthlessness." He glanced at his son.

"Is that how you would suggest I solve my current problem?" John asked.

Adrian looked ahead again. "That's a tricky one,"

"But you know what it is." It was the first time he had raised the subject between them.

"I would say that any man whose wife takes to the bottle

has a problem. Did you know that Jo left me once? Or wanted to. If circumstances hadn't stopped her going, we would have split up. And you would never have been born. Life certainly moves in a mysterious way."

John was not in the mood to be sidetracked. "You think Adèle has left me?"

"Mentally. At this moment."

"Why?"

"Now that I wouldn't know. But it mightn't be a bad idea to find out."

"How do I do that?"

"You could try asking her."

"Asking her? I hardly ever seem to get her alone. At night she just collapses into bed and is fast asleep before I can say knife. During the day, as often as not she's up at Cathy's. She's there now, stormed off this morning because I wouldn't accept Cathy's invitation to dinner on Christmas Eve. Do you know what she said? 'You're just jealous.' That was an odd thing to say, wasn't it?"

Adrian made no reply, and after riding a few more yards in silence, John went on, "I blame Cathy."

"How can you do that?"

"Because this odd behaviour began while I was away. Did Dela see much of Cathy during that time?"

"Why, of course she did. They became friends. I have to say that your mother and I are glad about that."

"Did she go to any of Cathy's parties?"

"Several. Why shouldn't she?"

"And . . . nothing happened?"

Adrian frowned. "You mean all those rumours? For God's sake. I am sure if anything had happened, Joanna would have known. As for those rumours . . . they're put about by those sick barflies at the Muthaiga Club who have nothing better to do, and who're jealous of Cathy's money and position and joie de vivre. Hell, I know she drinks too much and she smokes too much, and I'm sufficiently old-fashioned not to approve of a woman doing those things, but I hope I'm also sufficiently intelligent enough to know that times change. Cathy is a woman of the world. The modern world. Maybe Adèle is trying to become one too, and just can't carry it off as well." He glanced at his son. "Maybe all that's wrong is that she wants you to become a modern man, instead of an African pioneer." He gave another grin. "Don't ask me to understand women. I gave that up long ago."

John said nothing, and they rode on in silence. Father knew nothing of the real Cathy, that was obvious. Or if he did know, he had entirely rejected the knowledge, because she was his only daughter. And of course he could know nothing of just how far she would go when she wanted something . . . or how far her desires could go, either. It was the thought that she might be corrupting Adèle which was so distressing. And she *was* corrupting Dela, if only in teaching her to drink – although Dela, thank God, had resisted the temptation to smoke. But he had no doubt that Dela would resist all other temptations as well, certainly with him here. Nor could he fault her as a wife. She was as enthusiastic a lover as she had ever been. Sometimes he even thought he was seeing shadows where there was only bright sunlight, entirely because of Cathy. So Adèle was right: he was jealous of her friendship with his sister. But there was more, he knew. The forest nymph he had so romantically carried off from her drudgery had disappeared while he was in England. Perhaps, as Father had hinted, she had just grown up. But in doing so, a portion of her mind had been closed to him, and that had not happened before. He resented that, but he did not know how to unlock such a secret place.

He sighed. Women, he thought. He adored his wife, but over these past couple of months he had found himself thinking back to the war, to the uncomplicated life of those days, uncomplicated in more than just the absence of women. There had been no racial tensions, no problems in the distant future, just the business of staying alive from day to day, Joseph and himself. He smiled. Joseph had had his huffs, but they hadn't mattered, and huffs or no, he had always been there, making the bed, preparing the tea, cooking the lunch, greasing the revolver, making provocative remarks. Joseph was the best friend he had ever had.

He wondered how the poor old bugger was faring now, breaking rocks up in the Chalbi Desert.

By Christmas 1923, Joseph Kinshasu knew he was going to die.

The fact had been made plain to him many months ago, even before the trial, but being human he had refused to accept the evidence of his own senses.

He had always kept his secret with great care. This meant that he had not been able to have a normal sex life. He had fancied Betty, the girl at the office, and he suspected that she had fancied him, but he had pretended total disinterest, and found sex, when it became necessary, with one of the Indian whores just round the corner.

And now Betty was dead. She was one of the women killed by the flying bullets of the nervous policemen, that terrible March afternoon.

Then his hate and anger had overflowed, and that had brought his destruction. Although he had been roughed up more than anyone when they were arrested, the attitude of the police changed after Mr John came to see that he was all right. That was before the shooting, and he had wanted to accept the offered help – he never doubted that Mr John would bail him out if the going got *too* rough. Harry Thuku had forbidden it. Harry had wanted them to be brought to trial. Harry had wanted them to be martyrs. And he had blindly followed Harry, while still putting his trust in Mr John: Mr John would never let him down, however they might have differed in the past. And the knowledge that John Barclay was interested in him made the police treat him with kid gloves, no matter how rude or arrogant he was towards them; and that led him to be even more rude and arrogant.

But then Mr Adams came to see him, and explained that Mr John, while willing to write a letter in support of his character, was not willing to appear in court on his behalf, and that he was soon to leave for England. Joseph was shattered by that withdrawal of his shield, at least partly because there was naturally, a policeman in the interview room while he spoke to Mr Adams, and the policeman heard everything that was said.

The evidence of this came that very afternoon, during exercise. The six of them were walking slowly round the compound, each watched by a guard, when suddenly a booted foot was thrust between Joseph's legs, and he tripped and fell.

"Man, you can't stand up?" the policeman asked. "Let me help you." And he kicked Joseph in the groin.

Joseph screamed in agony and anger, and the policeman looked more concerned than ever. "Man," he said, "you hurting. You give me a hand here, eh?" he called.

Two more policemen came, one to hold Joseph's wrists and the other his ankles while the first took down his pants to twist his genitals. Those policemen were intent only on a bit of fun, of hitting back at the most difficult of their prisoners . . . and they destroyed him.

"Man," the first policeman said. "But what is this?" Then he laughed, and called the other prisoners to look at what he had uncovered. "Man," he said, "but you fellows been playing with a boy."

He had pronounced a death sentence. But there would be no execution. Thuku was not basically a man of violence, and if Joseph suspected some of the others were, such as Tom Ngolo or Harry Kinkardu, they followed Thuku's lead. Thuku's lead was in the direction of ostracism. It was not merely a personal rejection of a liar and a cheat, a man who had wormed his way into their affections as well as their counsels without the right to do so; Thuku knew that if his right-hand man and closest associate was discovered by the Kikuyu at large to be an alien, his authority amongst them might suffer. From that moment Joseph had been cast out.

All the while they were sharing the same cell, night after night, then the same dock in court, day after day . . . and then the same sentence, of two years exile in the Chalbi Desert. To stand up to that constant emotional buffeting a man needed friends. Thuku had the other four. Joseph

Kinshasu had no one; Mr John had never even come to court.

But that was nothing compared with what lay ahead. Then a man would need friends more than ever. Harry Thuku was unlucky here too. As the leader, he was separated from the others and sent to a different camp. The remaining five were herded together into the same truck and driven north. On that journey the dying began.

They travelled with their hands cuffed behind their backs, in the company of six policemen. They sat in the hot sun on a narrow bench along one side of the truck, and when they fell off after a particularly severe pot-hole they were kicked by the police until they painfully regained their seats. When the truck stopped, they were thrown out and forced to squat like gigantic, armless birds, until the police were ready to move on. Such food and water as they had been given was thrown at their mouths. And the local people gathered round to stare and jeer.

It was a journey to turn a man's heart either to stone or to water. As he watched Ngolo and Kinkardu and the others gazing at each other, he knew that they were drawing strength from each other. He squatted alone, in his misery.

The journey was miserable in other ways than loneliness and maltreatment. The road over which they drove passed between the Aberdares on the left, and Mount Kenya on the right. He wept as he looked at the twin peaks. If the Aberdares, named after a successful politician, were a measure of his own failure, the twin peaks of Mount Kenya were a measure of how far he had descended in the scale of life. He and Mr John had been going to climb those peaks in 1919. That would have been a happy safari, the two of them braving the unknown, as they had done during the war. But instead Mr John had gone off to look for his woman, and *he* had gone off to look for his destiny. And wound up in this sun-scorched truck with his hands bound behind his back, an aching void in his head and his belly, and an aching void in his heart.

After two days they came to Lake Turkana. Joseph had heard of Lake Turkana, but had never expected to see it.

Even in his depair he understood he was looking at one of the great natural wonders of the world, where the various minerals in the sandy soil had combined to create a marvellous turquoise colour in the water. Lake Turkana was known as the Jade Sea, and he could understand why.

Not the least part of its beauty was that this splash of colour emerged suddenly from a brown wilderness; the Chalbi was close at hand. The water stretched out of sight into the distance, and looked the more inviting because of their long and uncomfortable journey. "You thirsty?" the sergeant in charge of their escort asked. "Well, drink, nuh? And wash yourselves. You smelling worse than a whore with diarrhoea."

They could not believe their good fortune as the handcuffs were taken off and they were allowed to dash down the beach and into the water – while the policemen stood and watched. And laughed. The water was so salty and bitter it had made them vomit, and the lake was the home of huge Nile crocodiles, hardly less than fifteen feet long, one of which had been hovering by the shore, only his eyes visible. He lunged at the foolish men who would invade his kingdom, and they fled, shouting their terror. While the police laughed.

They camped on the shore of Lake Turkana, and the next day a new escort arrived, for here they were saying goodbye to the truck. And if they had thought the journey from Nairobi to Turkana bad, the journey from Turkana to the camp was indescribable. It led them out into the true desert, where the camp was. And now they were in the care of prison warders, not policemen. Their handcuffs were taken off but their wrists were then bound together in front of them and secured to a rope, which formed a halter around the neck of the next man in line; thus yoked, the five of them walked behind a camel on which rode the first guard. There was only one other, who rode his camel behind; they knew the five prisoners weren't going anywhere.

Joseph brought up the rear as they stumbled over the

stony ground and gasped beneath the heat of the sun. He listened to the others comforting each other.

The camp was some fifteen miles east of the lake, and the guards were in a hurry to get home. By the time they arrived there, the following morning, the five prisoners were nearly dead with exhaustion, but then they had to stand to attention before the commandant, a red-faced white man.

"Welcome," the commandant said. "You are here for two years, so you may as well try to make the best of it. We shall feed you and try to keep you busy. What else you do is up to you. But do not try to escape. There is nowhere to go." He pointed east. "Out there is just desert and no water." He pointed south. "Down there is just desert and no water." He pointed north. "Up there is just desert and no water until you reach the Ethiopian border. The Ethiopians do not like strangers crossing their border. And back there – " he pointed west – "is Lake Turkana. The Turkana tribesmen like strangers even less than the Ethiopians. So do not be stupid. Stay here, and work. Two years is not an eternity."

But it was, for those who had to break rocks in the boiling sun. The high spot of their week was the arrival of the truck from Turkana to load the stones and take them back, their ultimate destination Nairobi, where they would help to create some white man's mansion. But it was possible to learn what was happening in the outside world from the truck driver, and even receive letters and messages from family and loved ones. There were never any messages for Joseph Kinshasu.

But even those with friends in the camp, and loved ones waiting for them, found the conditions intolerable. The other thirty odd prisoners were of different tribes and stayed together in little groups. The Kikuyu wished to do the same, but one of them broke for it one night. No one went after him. They knew that if he did not return he would be dead. In fact he did return, dragged, his head bumping, at the tail of a Turkana camel, his ankles secured to a rope from the tribesman's saddle. He was alive, but died the next day – nobody had troubled to feed him water for that time.

Joseph had had some faint hopes that Ngolo and Kinkardu and Bolomo, the three surviving Kikuyu, might welcome him back after the death of their friend. But they did not. And survival for him then became a very uncertain matter. He was the only prisoner who did not have the support of at least one friend. Thus he was the victim of them all; whenever they felt like an extra ration of food they stole his, and whenever their misery got too much for them they beat him up. The guards never interfered. What the exiles did while not breaking rocks was entirely up to them.

It was then he knew that he would never leave the Chalbi alive.

But having accepted that he must die, his brain began to fill with ideas. If death was to be his lot, then surely he could choose the time, the place and the method. Having arrived at that conclusion, other ideas, other thoughts, which before had been too horrible to contemplate, began to flood his mind. If he died, it would be in a memorable fashion. But if by any chance he were *not* to die, then he would live in the most memorable fashion as well.

He planned, with the careful cunning, the immense patience, of a man who has nothing to lose. It took him three weeks to find what he wanted. Then one day at the rockface he uncovered a stone which might almost have been carved to make a primitive cutting edge. In fact, as he had read that there were scientists who considered that Kenya might be the cradle of mankind, he wondered if it was not actually a neolithic artefact. Certainly it would serve his purpose.

The following night he left the camp, He knew no one would come after him, and in any event, he wasn't going very far: he had to come back. He walked for about two miles, due east, until he found some thorn bushes sprouting out of the dry earth, and there he squatted. He had to wait for daylight, and he felt that the bushes might provide some shelter from the sun.

It was the longest night he had ever spent, sitting alone in the desert, and during it he thought of a great many things. Of Mr John, and the way he had turned his back

207

on him. Of the woman, big-breasted and sexually desirable – through the window he had watched her and Mr John playing with each other in the bath at the house at Dagaba, that very first day . . . and had known then there could be no place for him in their future. He thought of the Barclays, rich and powerful, and of their daughter, whom he had seen often enough on the streets of Nairobi, her breasts, if not so large as those of her sister-in-law, bobbing up and down beneath her thin shirt; she was apparently even richer and more powerful than her parents.

And he thought of Betty, lying on the pavement, blood streaming away from *her* breasts.

As he thought of Betty he watched the sun rising out of the desert to the east. It was time to act. Slowly he stood up and removed his tattered trousers. These he laid on the ground beside him. Then he sat down again and looked down at himself. He had only the vaguest idea of what he had to do and knew that he could easily make a terrible mistake – but in that case he would simply die. He was prepared for that. Yet he felt that success would depend on his having as large an area as possible to work on, and besides, it might be for the last time. So he handled himself to an erection, picked up the stone knife, uttered a prayer to the great Ngai, god of all things Kikuyu – he could not feel this was a Christian labour he was about to perform – and cut into the foreskin.

The pain whipped his breath away and replaced it with hot tears. Yet he held the skin and continued cutting, until the morning rotated before his eyes and he collapsed on the sand. It could only have been for a few seconds, because then the pain woke him up again, and he saw that the blood dripping down his leg was still wet. Beside the blood, the strip of skin drooped from his now shrunken penis.

There was no hope of another erection. He seized the flesh and continued cutting, creating a great circle round the shaft, sobbing and moaning, his breath coming in huge gasps, until the torn skin came away in his hand. Then perhaps he fainted again. He was not sure. He knew he writhed on the ground, desperate to stay on his back to prevent any soil from entering the wound. As he was alone he needed to exercise no restraint, and he screamed and yelled at the sun, and begged Lord Ngai for assistance – and Lord Ngai came to his aid, in the form of visions which ripped across his consciousness.

In time the torment passed. At least, it was surpassed by a greater awareness of his thirst and his hunger, and his general discomfort. It was time to go back, to victory or death.

He struggled to his feet, his thighs stained with blood, afraid to look at the misshapen lump between his legs. He put the Stone Age knife in the pocket of his trousers, but the trousers themselves he slung over his shoulder. Then he began to walk, carefully placing one foot in front of the other, stumbling over the pebbles, trying to forget the pain. From time to time he fell down and lay, unable to get up, while he moaned and wailed. In time it grew dark, and he struggled on beneath the light of the moon. And all the time he saw the hideous, obscene visions, welling out of the pain in his groin, surging through his mind. He became aware of hatred, of the black policemen who had shot down Betty and many others, of the white women who lorded it over their servants and had the power to separate a man from his master . . . and most of all, of the master who would allow these things to happen, and turn his back on one who had served him faithfully and well.

It was long after dawn the next morning when he came in sight of the camp, and the convicts were just being led out to the rockface. He topped a shallow rise and looked down on the huts, and the commandant's house, and the men assembled there with their guards. For a moment no one saw him, then someone looked up and pointed.

Two of the guards, Somalis, came towards him. "Man," the first one said, "You are one stupid black-faced nigger. You know this is the lash?"

Then he stopped and stared. His companion did the same, and they turned and hurried back to call the commandant.

209

Joseph went on walking. If he stopped walking now he would fall down and die.

The commandant came out to see. "Man, sir," the guard said, "I think he done castrate himself."

The commandant came closer. "Jesus Christ," he said. "What did you do that for, you stupid bastard."

Joseph gazed at him. "I am a man," he said. "I am a man!" he shouted. He looked at the watching prisoners. "A man," he shrieked.

The commandant scratched his head. "It's the sun," he said. "You'd better put some antiseptic on that prick. Then twenty lashes will do. He did leave the camp without permission."

The pain of the antiseptic was worse than the pain of the circumcision. But then the pain of the flogging came on top of all. That was a blessing in disguise, because parched as he was, the whip yet made his muscles so collapse with agony that he passed water; he knew the greatest risk had been that the swelling would be so intense he would be unable to urinate. Then, within a few days, he was almost well again, even if his member was an ugly, horrible thing, even to his eyes.

But he found himself surrounded by people. Tom Ngolo was there, and Harry Kinkardu, and Rupert Bolomo. "Man," Ngolo said, "Harry Thuku will be proud to know what you have done."

Joseph had no thoughts for Harry Thuku now. Harry was a man of peace. Harry was a man of the past. Joseph knew now that his vision would come true, that he would become the leader of his people, after all. "Harry Thuku is nothing," he told them. "Harry Thuku believed we could deal with the white people. Do you believe we can deal with the white people?"

"No," Tom Ngolo agreed. "Or with the black people, either, unless they are Kikuyu. But how can we fight the white people, with their armies and their guns — and their ships of war? I have been to Mombasa," he said proudly.

"I have seen the British warships in the harbour. How can we fight the British warships?"

"Do you not think I have been to Mombasa?" Joseph said scornfully. "I campaigned in Tanganyika with the British Army. I know their strengths. And their weaknesses. We will defeat them."

"We?" Rupert Bolomo asked.

"Us four?" Harry Kinkardu asked. "And Harry Thuku?"

"Us four," Joseph told them. He wanted no more part of Harry Thuku. "And those who will follow us."

"Where are they?" Tom Ngolo asked.

"They are there," Joseph told them. "Waiting to be led. Waiting to be shown the way. We will show them the way." He spoke with absolute confidence, because he had learned the way. The way lay through pain and suffering, and an appeal to man's most basic instinct; those of sex and violence.

"How will we do these things?" Harry Kinkardu asked.

"We will form a society," Joseph told them. "A society which will be dedicated to ending the white man's rule here in Kenya. We will be the nucleus, we four here tonight. But we will hurry slowly, and make our plans well, and increase our numbers carefully. We will be model citizens when we are released from here. We will carry our pass books . . ."

"Harry Thuku won't like that," Tom Ngolo said.

"Harry Thuku is no longer important," Joseph said. "We are important. We will form the nucleus. If Harry wishes to join us, then he may. If he does not, then we shall do without him. The nucleus is what matters. Because we will enrol others, while we work for the white man and reassure him, all the while planning his destruction. Until the night, across all of Kenya, when we will strike!"

"That is too slow," Rupert Bolomo objected. "If we take too much time, we will be betrayed. There is always a traitor who will go to the white people."

"Not if we bind them to us," Joseph insisted. "This will be a secret society. We will bind them to us. We will bind the entire Kikuyu nation to us."

211

"How?" Tom Ngolo asked.

"We will make them swear a sacred oath."

"What sort of oath?"

"I will devise the oath," Joseph told them.

Because he had no doubt he could do that too. He had no doubt he could do anything now. The proof lay in what he had done, and in the respect shown to him by everyone else in the camp. All had known his disability, all had felt contempt for him. Then he had walked away into the desert and made himself a man. No matter that he had made himself repulsive to any woman who might ever look upon him. He was a man. No one had any doubt about that.

And he was a natural leader of men. He had no doubt about *that* either. He knew the way to men's hearts, and minds, and bellies. He had known the urges, and he knew how to make them into matters of great import.

Nonetheless, he studied the concept of a binding oath with great care. When he was ready, he secured from the camp cook the thorax of a recently slaughtered kid – the camp maintained its own herd of goats. This he took with him to a meeting of the four. With his Stone Age knife, which he still kept in the pocket of his trousers, he cut a hole in the thorax, about one inch in diameter, and then he cut a short stick, about four inches long. These things, he knew, a European would consider the purest mumbo-jumbo. But he also knew that the Europeans had allowed themselves to become divorced from the things that mattered, the gut desires which they were afraid of and rejected, however much they dreamed. That was their weakness. And that was his strength.

Then he wrote the oath.

Tom Ngolo volunteered to be first. Joseph commanded him to take off his trousers, and push his penis through the hole in the kid's thorax. Then he told him to hold the shaft of his penis in his left hand, while with the short stick he stirred the thorax and sought what meat was still to be found. While he did this, Joseph read the words of the oath, which Tom repeated after him:

'I speak the truth and vow before our God
That if I am called upon to fight the enemy
Or to kill the enemy – I shall go
Even if the enemy be my father or my mother, my brother or
    sister
And if I refuse
May this oath kill me,
May this he-goat kill me,
May my friends kill me,
May this meat kill me.'

Then Ngolo ate the meat he had scraped from the thorax.

The others took the oath in turn. Kinkardu was pessimistic. "Is one oath sufficient?" he asked.

"I will devise other oaths," Joseph promised. "One oath
is sufficient for us, because we are the nucleus. On us will
our people build."

"We must have a name," Tom Ngolo said. "We four."

"And those who will join us afterwards," Rupert Bolomo
said.

"A name," Harry Kinkardu said. "A name."

They looked at Joseph. He was their acknowledged leader
now, far more than Harry Thuku had ever been. He picked
a name out of nowhere, something which might catch the
imagination and was easy to say. "We shall call ourselves –
Mau Mau," he told them.

9

From the train, Joseph looked out at Lake Naivasha as the station approached. He was conscious of curiously mixed emotions. On the one hand it was difficult to accept that his prison sentence was actually at an end, that there would be no more floggings and no more exposure to the sun and the glare off the desert, no more bad food – in the fortnight since his release he had occasionally had to pinch himself to believe it. And he could hardly believe that he had been given a suit of clothes to wear and enough money to tide him over until he could find a job. As he did not understand the point of view which dictated that a man who had "paid his debt to society" should immediately be treated with the utmost kindness, he had not been softened by it because he had recognized it as charity, white man's charity, the contempt of the great for the weak and beaten.

He was neither weak nor beaten. But the fools did not know that.

The four had devised their strategy at great length before leaving the desert. They were ex-convicts, and they knew their activities would be carefully monitored by the police for some time to come, thus it was necessary for them to live exemplary lives for that period, but also to take up positions which could later on be used to the maximum effect. For him the way had been obvious: return to John Barclay, beg his forgiveness, abase himself and become again the valet of the person who would soon be the most powerful white man in Kenya.

Such a prospect added to the ambivalence of his feelings. The thought of returning to the peace and comfort and prosperity of Naivasha was heady. The thought that he was going there with the deliberate intention of one day destroying Mr John, and the woman, and all of his children, was more heady still. It gave his life more purpose than it had ever possessed before.

The train stopped, and he stepped down. He had no suitcase, and carried his few possessions in a brown paper parcel under his arm. He was recognized, of course. The people stared at him and muttered to one another, and he drove them back with the cold anger of his stare. Then he remembered that that would not do at all. He had to act the role of the returned convict, a man shattered in body and mind, anxious only never to transgress again. So he bowed his head and shuffled from the station, and walked down the hill towards the lake.

Dogs barked and bared their teeth, but they too remembered him, and a few moments later he stood on the lawn and looked up at Safah. Safah was now a very old man indeed, approaching his eightieth year, and yet he stood as erect as any Somali ever had, peering at the black man from beneath shaggy eyebrows. "You have business here?" he demanded.

"Do you not remember me, old man?" Joseph asked.

"I remember you. You are a criminal who has besmirched my master's name," Safah said.

"I have been to the desert for two years," Joseph said. "I have paid my debt to society." He was repeating what the camp commandant had said to him a fortnight before. "I have learned my lesson. I wish to apologize to Mr John, and return to serve him to the end of his days." Which, he reminded himself, was no lie.

Safah continued to stare at him. Then he said, "You had best speak with him yourself."

Joseph had also heard the sound of hooves, and turned to face John Barclay as he rode on to the lawn, dismounted and threw the reins to the black groom who hurried forward. "Joseph?" he asked incredulously.

Joseph in fact was no more surprised at the sight of his erstwhile master. John Barclay, he knew, could not be more than twenty-nine years old. But he looked forty. Not in any physical way, for there was no grey in his hair and very little paunch to his body – there he was as hard and strong as

215

he had ever been. But his expression was tired, and his mouth turned down. It was difficult to imagine this man ever smiling, and once he had perhaps smiled too readily.

A Barclay, unhappy?

Joseph bowed. "It is I, Mr John," he said.

"What are you doing here?" John inquired.

"I have come to see you, Mr John. I was released from prison a few days ago, and I came here as quickly as I could."

"Why?"

"I wish to ask for my position back, Mr John."

"You want to come back to work for me?"

"If you will have me, Mr John," Joseph said. "I have learned the error of my ways." Another phrase the camp commandant had used. "I know how wrong I was. I wish only to atone for my crime."

"Well, I'll be damned." John Barclay went up the steps, taking off his topee as he did so. "You hear that, Safah?"

"I heard that, Mr John," Safah agreed.

John turned and looked down the steps, and actually smiled. "I can't say I'm sorry to see you, you great oaf. Had a hard time in the desert, eh?"

"It was hard in the desert," Joseph agreed.

"Well, come on in," John Barclay said. "Safah will show you where to go. Or perhaps you remember. Adèle," he said as his wife emerged on to the verandah. "You won't believe this, but here's Joseph wanting to come back to work for me."

Joseph watched the white man with a slight frown. There was nothing of the old total love in his voice as he addressed the woman. Rather had his smile faded and the weariness returned.

"No," Adèle said.

Joseph's head turned. She had not changed at all, he thought, except that she might have put on a little weight and that there was more colour in her cheeks than he remembered. Certainly she was still a very lovely woman . . . but staring at him as if he had been a snake.

"No?" John asked.

"I don't want him here," Adèle said, her voice low and vehement. "I don't want him working for you. Get him off the farm. Get him off."

Joseph stood absolutely still. His plans had not taken in a reaction like this.

"I'm not with you," John Barclay said.

"I do not want him on Naivasha," Adèle said, speaking in a low, vehement voice. "He is evil. Make him go away."

John Barclay gazed at her for several seconds, then he turned back to Joseph. "I'm sorry, Joseph," he said. "But you cannot have your old job back. Nor can you remain on Naivasha. I am sorry."

Joseph stared at him in utter dismay. It had simply never crossed his mind that he would not be able to implement his plan from beginning to end. All because of the woman who had always hated him. He stared at her in turn, then he walked out of the yard.

John left Safah standing on the verandah, also no doubt bemused by the unexpected turn of events, and followed his wife into the drawing room. Adèle went straight to the bar and started mixing herself a pink gin. He stood beside her, took the glass from her hand and threw the contents into the sink. She gazed at him, eyes wide and cheeks flushed.

"I think a drink can wait," he said, and wondered why he had not done that over a year ago. "Now tell me what all that was about."

"I . . . I do not like that man."

"That was apparent. I suspect he doesn't like you, now."

"He never did. And does it matter?"

"Probably not." But her reaction to Joseph was the most positive mood she had revealed to him since his return from England very nearly two years ago. Her aloofness, the refuge she seemed to have taken in that secret recess of her mind, had in that time slowly driven them apart, because however hard he tried to take his father's advice and become more "modern" in his outlook, he did not succeed, at least in penetrating Adèle's personality. He had even tried attending

217

Cathy's parties from time to time. They had been unutterably boring, and at the same time distasteful, even if he had seen nothing at them to justify the rumours. He had felt as if he were a very old man at a gathering of teenagers who were merely waiting for him to leave before starting to play party games. While Cathy had, with great deliberateness, he knew, teased him with oblique references to that night at the Muthaiga Club, revelling in the terrible secret they shared, often looking at Adèle as she spoke, as if to say, "If you only knew". He had tried privately to warn her to stop it, in case she went too far, and she merely laughed. "What are you going to do, brother dear? Hit me again?"

And after every party, Adèle had withdrawn further. Because she knew there was something between brother and sister? He could not accept that. But certainly because she felt excluded from their apparent rapport.

But here she was, suddenly taking a stance. He could not let such an opportunity pass, and however sorry he was for Joseph, he was pleased the situation had arisen.

With great patience, she was reaching again for the gin bottle.

"I said, let it wait," he reminded her.

She gazed at him, eyebrows arched, face suddenly watchful.

"I had supposed," he said, "that you no longer cared what I did, or who I employed."

"That is strange," she replied, "as I am your wife."

"Sometimes I wonder about that too," he said.

"Because I am not your sister?" The words slipped out perhaps before she had intended; she bit her lip and took a step backwards.

He frowned at her. "Just what do you mean by that?"

"I meant nothing." She turned away, and he caught her arm. "Please," she said. "You're hurting me."

"I think we had better go upstairs," he said. She hesitated, then went in front of him. He closed and locked the bedroom door. Safah had watched them, and no doubt there would be some gossip in the pantry, but he no longer cared about that.

Adèle sat on the bed. "Do you want sex?" she asked.

"Is that all you think about?"

Her head came up. "It is what I am here for."

"Do you really believe that? I love you."

"Can I really believe *that*?"

"For God's sake! I came for you, didn't I? I loved you. I brought you back here. I made you my wife. You are the mother of my children ... What has Cathy been telling you?"

She stared at him.

"I must know," he said, while a terrible suspicion entered his brain.

Adèle sighed, and her shoulders slumped. "That you love her," she muttered.

"Cathy? Good lord."

"Don't you?"

"Well, she is my sister. I don't approve of her. But ... well, I suppose I do love her. But ... you can't be jealous of my own sister, Dela."

"Not even when she is your lover?"

"My ... Jesus Christ!"

"Isn't it true?" Adèle spat at him. "Isn't it true that the reason you don't like her parties and carryings on is pure jealousy, of other men getting their hands on her?"

"She told you this?"

"If you knew ..." Adèle started to weep. "But she doesn't lie. You told me so yourself, when you first came back. I asked you," she sobbed. "And you said she doesn't lie."

John sat beside her, keeping his raging fury under control with an effort. "So she told you about that night at the Muthaiga Club."

Adèle raised her head; tears were dribbling down her cheeks. "Amongst others."

"There weren't any others. And what happened then was an accident. She took me by surprise. I'm ashamed of it. But more of her. That's why I hit her."

"Because of the other man."

219

He scratched his head. "I think you had better tell me everything Cathy said to you," he said.

Adèle cried, and told him. For how long, he wondered, had she wanted to tell him. Why, for very nearly two years. But she hadn't dared. "Why?" he asked her.

"Because . . . because she said if I did you would throw me out rather than lose her."

"Good God!"

"It was the night . . ." She sighed. "The night they shaved me. God, it was the night they shaved me."

"They did *what?*"

"It was the party," she said, her voice toneless. "They wanted me to go to bed with Jimmy Wildman, and when I refused, they . . . Oh, God, Johnnie, they stripped me naked, and held me down on the dining table, and shaved me."

"Catherine allowed that?"

"She made them do it," Adèle said, her voice hardening. "And when I threatened to go to the police, afterwards, she told me about you and her. That's when she said you would throw me out if I caused a scandal. She said I had to be her best friend, or you would hate me."

"And you believed her."

"I had to. I – I have nothing. Nothing," she repeated. "Nothing at all."

He took her in his arms, held her against him and smoothed her hair. "You poor, poor darling. She is about the vilest woman on the face of the earth. She must be. How many people were present when she told you all this?"

"Nobody," Adèle said. "Just her and me. In her living room. Both naked. It was like something out of Dante."

"Yes," John agreed. "That's one blessing, at any rate. Well, everything is going to change now. I suggest you just get undressed and go to bed for the rest of the day. Just lie down and relax. I'll be back this evening."

Her head jerked up as she looked at him. "What are you going to do?"

"Have a word with my sister."

She caught his hand as he stood up. "But, Johnnie, Mother and Father . . ."

"Don't tell me they know too."

"No. No. But she's their daughter. Johnnie – "

"You leave Mother and Father to me," John said. "And Cathy too. Just get one thing through your head. I love you. And this is your home. No one, but no one on the face of this earth, is ever going to drive you away from Naivasha. You have the word of John Barclay."

He thanked heaven that Mother and Father were over at Elmenteita for the day; Father had now definitely retired, as he was sixty-eight years old, and spent more and more time with his great friend, no doubt reminiscing about the past, the adventures they had shared . . . when Cathy was a little girl. Perhaps Father had never properly appreciated that she had grown up. Mother even less so.

He took the small car and drove up the hill to Nairobi. He was missing lunch, but he did not feel like eating, anyway. It was half past two by the time he reached the house, which was locked up and shrouded in silence. But he knew she was in: her Armstrong Siddeley was in the garage.

He banged on the front door, and again, then heard shuffling footsteps. An elderly black woman peered at him from the window beside the door.

"Open up," he told her. "I've come to see the mistress."

She blinked at him, undoubtedly recognizing him. "Ow, me Gawd," she remarked. "Mr Murgatroyd," she shouted. "Mr Murgatroyd, you best come out here."

Obviously Catherine was entertaining, John waited with some impatience for several minutes until the butler himself appeared hastily tucking his shirt into his pants and looking as if he had just got out of bed. "Man, Mr John," he said. "The mistress ain't expecting you."

"No, she isn't," John agreed. "You going to open this door? Or am I going to knock it down?"

The bolts rasped and the door swung in. "She don't like to be interrupted in her siesta," Murgatroyd warned.

"Is that a fact," John said, crossing the drawing room to the stairs, and looking up at Cathy, who was standing at the top, wrapped in a dressing gown.

"Why, darling," she said. "What brings you out in the afternoon sun? Nothing wrong at the farm, I hope?"

"Not now," he said. "Have you got company?"

"Me? At three o'clock in the afternoon?"

"Then I was wrong." He climbed the stairs towards her. "You and I have got to have a little chat."

She gazed at him. "Downstairs," she said.

"Upstairs," he corrected. "Where we can be alone. Murgatroyd," he called. "Push off, there's a good fellow, and don't make yourself a nuisance."

Murgatroyd, who had advanced to the foot of the steps, looked up at his mistress.

"If he doesn't," John said pleasantly, "I am going to break his bloody neck."

"Before you break mine?" she asked.

"Yes."

She made a moue. "Go back to bed, Murgatroyd," she said. She walked in front of her brother into her bedroom; she had certainly been in bed – the covers were tousled. "Do you mind if I take off my robe?"

"I would prefer you to keep it on."

She shrugged, went to the dressing table, lit a cigarette and sat on the bed, knees crossed; the dressing gown fell back to reveal her legs. "Something tells me you have not actually come here to make love to me, Johnnie boy. So . . . die Hausfrau has been talking."

"Did you really think you could get away with it forever?"

"Get away with what?"

He stood above her, and she fell back across the bed. The dressing gown opened further. She wore nothing underneath. "I did some thinking on the drive up here," he said. "I was coming here to beat you senseless. I was also going to get a list of everyone who was at the party, when you had your little game with Dela . . ."

"And beat them senseless, too?" she laughed. "You'd go to gaol."

"It'd be worth it, just to stand up in court and tell the world the kind of people you and your friends are. However, I reflected that Ma and Pa are fairly old, and it would be rough on them. So I am not even going to hit you. I am going to give you one week to leave Kenya . . . forever."

"You seriously think you can come here and order me out of the colony?" She sat up again. "Just who the hell do you think you are?"

"I am John Barclay, in case you've forgotten," he said. "And don't make any mistake about it, Cathy. If you try to fight me, I am going to plaster the story of you and your parties over every newspaper in the world, and Adèle is going to bring charges of assault, battery and attempted rape against every man at that party."

"And you'd kill Ma and Pa," she said.

"No," he told her. "You would have done that."

They stared at each other. "You are a poisonous little rat," she said.

"And you are a filthy little bitch," he replied.

Another stare. Then she laughed again. "Keep your lousy colony," she said. "And your German goody-goody. And your blacks and your Indians and your whole damned happy little valley."

"One week," he said. "You can decide what you tell the parents."

"Oh, mistress," Murgatroyd wailed. "What I going to do without you?"

"You'll look after the house," Catherine told him.

"But you ain't going to be here, mistress."

"For a while. I'm not selling up. I wouldn't do that to you, Murgatroyd. I'm just going home for a spell. Business matters. I'll be back. And until I am, you'll be in charge."

"I going to be too lonesome, mistress."

Catherine smiled. "Dear Murgatroyd." She kissed him on the cheek. "Just wait for me. And, Murgatroyd, if you ever talk . . . you're out. Remember that."

"Oh, I don't talk, mistress. I don't ever talk."

"I didn't think you would. That's why I'm trusting you.

223

I will write to you every month, and I will send you money every month, and you will keep the house exactly as it is now, so that when I come back, I can walk right in that door and know that I am home. Will you promise to do that for me?"

"Oh, yes, mistress, I will do that for you."

Catherine nodded. For all his faults, and some of them were distressing, he really was a dear man, she thought, perhaps as much of a husband as she had ever had. And he thought of himself like that. Perhaps for that very reason she was not unhappy to be getting away from him for a while. She would miss him though, because he was the best poke she had ever had. He was so good she had even from time to time considered broadening her field, as it were. But she had only once done so, because she had not expected his reaction: immorality with white people was fun and games; immorality with black people was betrayal. Yes, she would be glad to be away from him for a while.

But she dared not let him know that. She waved away the girl who had just entered the drawing room with her Pekingese, who were of course accompanying her.

"Come upstairs," she said to Murgatroyd. "We have half an hour before it's time to go to the station."

It seemed that all Kenya uttered a sigh of relief when Catherine, Lady Portington, sailed away for Suez and England. Even her intimates had found her a bit of a strain over the preceding couple of years as she reached for new sensations, and those intimates who had all been at the party on the night Adèle was humiliated lived in mortal fear of John Barclay fnding out. With Cathy gone, they felt they could breathe again.

In fact, John did not press Adèle on the matter. Perhaps it *had* all been fun and games, he thought, to which she had over-reacted. More important, seeking the culprits out could only lead to scandal and embarrassment for Adèle herself. Besides, there was only one truly guilty party, and she was now gone.

Even Adrian and Joanna felt a sense of relief, John

guessed. If they loved their daughter and were sorry to see her go, fearful that they would never see her again, they were not so blind as to be unaware that she had been a distruptive element in the family as well as the colony. With Cathy gone, Naivasha again became a happy, peaceful place. The farm prospered, all of Kenya seemed to be prospering. Adèle became pregnant again, and Adrian Barclay the second joined Lizzie and Mal. John's happiness was complete. Even the fears for the future felt by Adrian Barclay appeared as an old man's pessimism. The white-controlled Legislative Council was proving highly successful – the Indians had accepted their place as second-class citizens, and Harry Thuku seemed to have learned his lesson and was no longer agitating. Joseph Kinshasu had quite disappeared. They were all aspects of a Kenya which had also disappeared and been replaced by a Kenya bound for the perpetual uplands of prosperity and pleasant living, in which a man could bring up his family in total comfort and security, trusting them to smiling black faces, while he turned the rich earth into gold; a world of dinner parties and cocktail parties, of tennis parties and croquet parties, of swimming parties – John installed a swimming pool at Naivasha, because the lake was regarded as unsafe, due to the presence of bilharzia-inducing organisms in the stagnant water – and breakfast parties, of safaris and expeditions to Mombasa to lie on the beach.

Even the sad news of the stock-market crash in New York did not have any immediate impact. People surely still had to eat, and drink coffee, even while going bankrupt.

But in 1931 Lord Delamere died. He was only sixty-one, and the catastrophe was unexpected. He was buried on a knoll overlooking Lake Elmenteita, his coffin surrounded by his friends and admirers, and overlooked by a body of Masai Morani given special permission to leave their reservation in full war dress to say farewell to the man they had worshipped almost as a god. The Legislative Council immediately put forward plans to have a statue erected to him in Nairobi. He, more than any man, even perhaps Adrian Barclay, had made the colony what it was.

225

And it was as if, without Delamere to charge at every problem and brush it aside, the happy days had suddenly come to an end. Now the great depression at last began to bite. Coffee was the first casualty. It cost just over seventy pounds to get a ton of coffee from the farm to the London sale rooms, where it had been fetching one hundred and twenty pounds a couple of years before. With enough acreage, that represented a tidy living. Now the sale room price fell to seventy; it became cheaper to use coffee beans as fuel than to send them home.

The following year the locusts came. John had only heard about the locusts, because the last invasion had been when he was just a child. He knew it was a serious matter, but still could not understand the concern shown by his father and Safah, both of whom had experienced the last plague, when locusts were first reported in the north of the colony, having come down from Ethiopia. Adrian Barclay, seventy-five years old now, looked out at his fields, his still massive shoulders hunched. "What a waste," he said. "What a waste. We'd better set them alight."

"What, all that corn? All that coffee?" John was horrified.

"It's the only way to make them pass through in a reasonable time," Adrian told him.

But John would not hear of it, and he was in charge now. So they waited, and watched the sky, while he refused to believe that they were talking about a holocaust, until one evening a locust landed on the front verandah. Safah killed it immediately, with a repugnance he had never shown towards the most virulent snake or spider.

"It is a horrible-looking thing," Adèle commented.

And Lizzie gave one of her tremendous shudders; at twelve she was just beginning to look like her mother, and would undoubtedly be a beautiful woman. "Are there going to be lots of them, Safah?" she asked.

"There will be very many," Safah said. "They will cover the sky."

"Oh, really, Safah," Adèle laughed. She was first up next morning, as she often was, standing at the window to look out at the lake and beyond. "Now that's odd," she said.

226

"What?" John asked sleepily.

"Well, the rains aren't due for another couple of months, are they?"

"No." He got out of bed.

"Then what's that huge storm cloud up there?"

He went to her side and looked at the enormous grey-brown blanket, shutting out the sky. "Jesus Christ," he muttered.

"But what is it?"

"Those are locusts," he told her.

He roused the servants, and they shut up the house as if expecting a siege. But that is what they *were* expecting. He went outside to make sure the horses and dogs were properly protected, and was overtaken by the swarm before he got back to the house. Several of the yard boys were with him, and they found themselves enveloped in a whirring, seething, sticky, loathsome mess, so thick it might have been fog, but a living fog, which seemed to whip their breaths from their nostrils and left them struggling to regain the shelter of the house. When the doors were opened to let them in, the locusts came in too. "Aaagh!" Lizzie screamed, flailing the air with her arms.

Mal swung at them with his cricket bat, and broke a lamp. Little Adrian clung to his mother and screamed. Adèle looked as if she would like to scream too, but she just stared at him, and at Adrian senior and Joanna. "What's going to happen?" she gasped.

"They will eat everything," Adrian Barclay told her. "Then they will move on."

Those inside the house were soon disposed of, but all day and the following night the farm was assaulted by the horrible creatures; it sounded as if they were surrounded by a giant sea, lapping at the very roof. When the noise finally died away, after dawn, John and Adèle went out on to the verandah; neither had slept, although the children had finally dropped off.

Their feet crunched on dead locusts. The lawn, stripped bare of grass, was covered in them. The farm stank of death

227

and decay. And the once green fields were nothing but ravaged empty corn-stalks.

Surprisingly, the coffee trees had survived almost intact. "I remember that from the last time," Adrian said. "I think they are too tough for the little buggers." He stood with his hands on his hips and looked around him. "Well, one lost year."

There was money in the bank, and the Barclays would survive the locusts. Others were not so fortunate. Karen Blixen came over to lunch, and told them she had sold.

"You're leaving Kenya?" Adèle was aghast.

"There is nothing left," the Baroness told her.

She would have been bankrupted anyway by the depression; the locusts were merely the last straw. As John had realized when he first met her and her husband at the Norfolk Hotel back in 1914, their success would not only hinge on their determination, but their resources. She had had all the determination in the world, as evidenced by the way she had kept going for nearly twenty years, but her husband had not, and alone she had lacked the resources to cope with the collapse of the coffee prices.

She also, now, lacked the determination. She was unwell – there were whispers that she had syphilis, contracted from which source no one could say, although the finger of guilt was naturally pointed at the Baron – and to cap her woes, her friend Finch-Hatton had been killed in a plane accident; he was his own pilot.

The Baroness had become such a fixture in the Kenya landscape that her departure caused something of an upheaval. But there was change, death and decay in every direction. John persuaded his mother and father to take a holiday while he put the farm back together; they had not left Africa for far too long, with the war, John's marriage and Cathy coming back to Kenya. Now they would have the opportunity to visit her in England, and even to cross the Atlantic and renew their acquaintance with Joanna's family. As they were both over seventy, they were aware that it was probably the last such trip they would ever make, but they were both fit enough, and John told them to stay away as long as they wanted. Even with Cathy. Several years' absence had made her seem less of a menace, and if he knew Adèle would never forget that night, and the misery that followed it, they had again learned how to love too well to waste time in looking over their shoulders. So long as his sister never returned to disturb the peace of Naivasha, John was content.

Adèle went with Adrian and Joanna. Not to stay with Cathy, of course. That she would have to see her was inevitable, but she was past the stage when she would ever allow herself to be influenced by her sister-in-law.

The purpose of her trip was ostensibly to place Lizzie and Mal in English boarding schools, but she took little Adrian as well. It was also to allow her to visit England for the first time in her life, and she would be a travelling companion for the old folks.

The true reason for her trip, as she understood well enough, was that John wanted them all out of Kenya. He had the farm to replant, and he knew how depressed they all were by the wholesale destruction the locusts had caused. But there was an even more pressing reason, again attributable to the locust invasion: with their crops destroyed as much as any white man's, trouble was again looming with the Kikuyu.

The question was, as before, land. Since the arrest of Harry Thuku and Joseph Kinshasu and the others, the Kikuyu had accepted the white man's rule with a passivity which had surprised a great many people, and had some old Africa hands muttering that it was not good, that Africans who did not openly make trouble were obviously planning trouble in secret. John was inclined to subscribe to this viewpoint, which was why he was anxious to have Adèle and the children, as well as his parents, out of the way until it was resolved.

But the new agitation over land was raised openly and in a perfectly statesmanlike manner by the chieftains, and thus taken seriously by the Colonial Office. They, as usual, sought compromise and, with Delamere no longer there to bully them, managed to push through a scheme whereby the Kikuyu were given quite a large area of land which was not actually being used by any of the white settlers. Like all compromises, it pleased neither party. The settlers considered that it was a breach of their nine-hundred-and-ninety-nine-year agreement with the British Government; the Kikuyu reflected that it was obviously useless land – and their land, anyway – which had been so magnanimously presented to them.

John preferred to play no part in the legislative battles. He knew that many settlers felt that he was letting the side down, as he was their obvious leader now that men like Delamere and Grogan were dead, and Adrian Barclay was past his allotted span. But he had always felt that the Kikuyu had had a raw deal, and he still from time to time found himself wondering where Joseph had got to, whether he was prospering, or whether, indeed, he was still alive. He would certainly have expected Joseph to be involved in any fresh land agitation. But although he made private inquiries from time to time, he could find out nothing about his friend. Joseph seemed to have vanished off the face of the earth.

He finally swallowed his pride and went to his old enemy, Inspector Curtis, now Detective Inspector Curtis, who gave his sour grin and said, "Your old pal, Mr Barclay? Oh, yes, we've kept an eye on him. But he's left Kenya."

"Left Kenya?" John was incredulous.

"Took ship for England; back in '29."

"Good God!"

"Not so strange, really. All these black trouble-makers think they'll find people to listen to them in England. The problem is, they so often do. Poor downtrodden black people! They get socialist politicians to listen to them, and sponsor them, and they get taken up by rich bitches who reckon it's the thing to have a black face at their cocktail parties. We have quite a list of them. Kinshasu, a fellow named Ngolo, another named Kenyatta . . . all soaking up British culture so they can find out the best way to murder us in our beds."

*

John was rather pleased Joseph had made the decision to leave Kenya; not only would it show the fellow how the other half lived, but it would keep him away from the risks of another spell in the Chalbi Desert, which he reckoned could do no one any good.

With the land crisis officially resolved, at least for another few years, and after he had replanted the farm, John could devote himself to his principal pleasure; playing his part in the creation of the game parks which had been mooted some ten years before, and which were at last coming to fruition. He agreed with his father that the once teeming wildlife of the Kenya and Tanganyika uplands was a far more important heritage to be passed on to posterity than the ambitions of a few money-hungry farmers; and the parks very rapidly began to pay off, as those wealthy Europeans and Americans who had once come to shoot, now brought their families to stare and photograph – and spend a great deal of money, which helped the colony's ailing economy.

He was also able to bring his family home, at least his parents and Adèle and little Adrian. Lizzie and Mal were both settled at boarding school and, according to Adèle, enjoying it thoroughly. He was delighted at how well they all were. Adèle had even accompanied Adrian and Joanna across the Atlantic to the States, there to meet in-laws of whom she had never previously heard. The holiday had broadened her outlook and made her, he thought and hoped, slightly less rigid in her attitudes.

Certainly she had seen Cathy, but only briefly. Cathy was now living mostly on the Riviera, where she had a house, and had come to England mainly to see her parents. She had tried to persuade them all to return with her to Cap d'Antibes, but Adèle had refused, and Adrian and Joanna also decided against it. It was nice to suppose, John thought, that they now considered Adèle more of their daughter than their own flesh and blood.

She had, Adèle told him, been the same Cathy, brittle and sarcastic, cold and yet erotic – there could be no doubt that she was living the way she always had, down in her Mediterranean villa.

"I hope you don't mind," Adèle said, "but I have given the strictest instructions at each school that under no circumstances are either of the children ever to be allowed to visit her, or receive visits from her."

"I would have minded if you hadn't done that," he told her.

The most important thing was that she was back, and they could renew their love. For as she entered her middle thirties Adèle grew more desirable than ever, at least to him. It was incredible that she should have been, and remained, the only woman he had ever loved or wanted to love, the only woman with whom he had ever shared a bed – save for those two occasions which he wanted to forget more than anything else in the world. No wonder Cathy considered him the biggest fuddy-duddy in the world.

So once again, he thought, we are entering upon a happy time. In 1935, when the farm prices began to pick up again, he was thirty-nine years old. Adèle was a year younger. And they loved each other as much as ever. The children were happy at school in England, and came out for the summer holidays to bask in the delight that was Kenya; at Easter and Christmas they necessarily had to go to other families, but seemed to enjoy that too; they knew Naivasha was waiting for them. Lizzie was fifteen, and fast becoming as much of a beauty as her mother; fourteen-year-old Mal was already nearly six feet tall and played a good game of rugby; Adrian junior, being so much of an afterthought – he was only eight – still went to school in Nairobi, but he would be following his brother and sister in a few years' time. Then they would return to take over the plantation when John in time grew old. It was a satisfying thought. Before then, he knew, there would have to be a period of grief. He anticipated it, prepared himself against it, and was yet left with a feeling of utter devastation when Adrian Barclay died in his sleep.

Adrian Barclay, the original pioneer, was buried in a simple ceremony behind the house he had built with his own hands some fifty years before. Immediately there was talk of erecting a statue to his memory as well, but John

232

vetoed the idea. His father needed no monument other than the simple fact that Kenya was a British colony, and that he and Adèle were living at Naivasha.

But predictably, Adrian Barclay's death was followed by others. Safah did not survive his master by two months. Safah was eighty-eight, and for sixty-one years he had served Adrian Barclay. He had no reason to continue living.

Joanna followed six months later. She, too, had lost her raison d'être.

The evening after her funeral, Adèle and John sat on the verandah and looked at the lake. "It seems incredible," Adèle said.

"They did appear rather indestructible," John said. "So now it's up to us."

"Yes." She glanced at him, and then away again. He knew what she was thinking. There had been no time for Cathy to come out to Kenya for either of the funerals. In the equatorial climate, even several thousand feet above sea level, interment necessarily took place within twenty-four hours of death. She had been informed, of course, of her father's death, and had written her mother a letter, presumably of condolence – Joanna had not shown it to anyone. Of all the members of the family, Joanna's feelings towards Cathy had been the most ambivalent. If she had never known the real truth, any more than her husband, she had understood that Cathy's lifestyle was unacceptable. Yet Cathy was her firstborn, and perhaps the child she had loved more than any of the others. John felt that was fair.

Now he would have to write to his sister and tell her that Mother too was gone. He did so the next morning, with an account of the funeral, and a breakdown of the wills of both Adrian and Joanna. Although the entire farm had been left to him, there were several considerable bequests to Cathy, principally personal items such as Joanna's jewellery, some pictures and one or two articles of furniture of which she had been especially fond. John told her that he would have them sent to any address she cared to designate.

There was also a clause in his father's will requiring him to support his sister as and when she required it. He informed her of this, and as he had no idea what state her finances were in, suggested that they decide on a mutually acceptable income, which could be paid to her by his lawyers without further reference to him.

After that there was nothing to do but wait for a reply. Nothing arrived for several weeks. Then Adèle brought him one of the newspapers which had just arrived on the train and been delivered to the house by the stationmaster. Her face was quite pale as she placed the tabloid in front of him, already opened at the gossip page. John read it swiftly.

Arriving in Mombasa yesterday by the *SS Ondara* was Catherine, Lady Portington. The Dowager Lady Portington will be remembered as a leading figure in Kenya society of the 1920s, and still retains a house in Nairobi. "I have come to renovate the place," she told this reporter. Accompanying Lady Portington was her steward, Mr Joseph Kinshasu.

10

Catherine Portington had actually been rather pleased to leave Kenya; the place was becoming boring. Her circle of friends had necessarily been limited; the achievement of intimacy on so vast a scale meant that newcomers to the group had to be picked very carefully – however much she had enjoyed that evening with Adèle because she had always intended to make that bitch suffer one day, as a party it was a disaster, not to be repeated.

Thus the original group had been growing too familiar, and far worse than that, they had been growing *old*. Of course there were those who would say Cathy herself had been growing old. It was not a criticism she accepted. Age was in the mind more than in the body. If she had aches and pains as much as anyone, she laughed them off. She kept her figure trim, and she dyed her hair. She had a total contempt for women who surrendered to age and could convince themselves that they were doing so gracefully.

It was, of course, humiliating to have been kicked out, and by her own brother, and even if she was sure no one else knew the exact circumstances, the bitch certainly would. She had always had every intention of getting even with both of them, but she knew that would have to wait until Pa and Ma died; she had no desire to have their deaths on her conscience, and when she got back to Kenya she intended to have such a bust-up that the reverberations would be heard all over the world – because then Johnnie would have no weapons to use against her. Ma and Pa could no longer be hurt, and after ten years or so any attempt to bring charges of assault or even rape would be laughed out of court, even supposing they could be substantiated. Oh, indeed, she was prepared to wait for a very long time to give those two a taste of what they had given her. When she was finished with them, she thought *they* might be the ones who would have to pack up and leave Kenya.

But there was another reason why she had been happy to leave, and which had made her plan her return with some caution: Murgatroyd. Murgatroyd was the most exciting experience of her sexual life. She was fascinated at once by his size, and his movements, which had an elasticity undiscoverable in any stiff-hipped white ex-guardsman. To have a black lover had been an idea from her early youth, when she was surrounded by so many stalwart Africans, nearly all habitually naked. The idea gradually became a dream, yet she had hung back, because of an innate preju- dice, perhaps, but more because of the possibility of scandal – of a half-cast child! – and because of a real fear that she might be getting into deeper waters than she knew.

But the dream had lingered, and when she found herself all alone for most of every day in that vast house outside Nairobi, surrounded by black servants, and more than anything else, in the continued presence of Murgatroyd – young, handsome, virile and utterly servile – the temptation had at last proved too much. It was heavenly, the more so because the secrecy of her private life was at such odds with the garishness of her public one. That it was a secret she shared with Murgatroyd, who could regard all her white friends with total contempt no matter how rude they were to him, had made it the more enjoyable.

But the day had come when she found herself bored even with Murgatroyd. Or perhaps if not exactly bored, beginning to wonder whether, if he was so exciting a bedmate, there might not be other Africans even more so. Never a woman to let her desires wait upon consideration, she had thus very nearly stumbled into a disaster. Murgatroyd had found her in bed with another black man, and had just about gone berserk. His rival had been beaten within an inch of his life, and she had only just escaped a beating herself. The incident had left her profoundly shocked, because although he had been abject in his apologies afterwards, and the injured man's silence had been bought easily enough, she knew that it would happen again, were she ever to stray in

236

that direction. That was unacceptable. Being dominated by a big, strong, black man had always been another dream. But not to the extent of being afraid of him.

The problem had been what to do about it. She had lived in Africa too long to feel she could merely fire him. She knew that if he did not take revenge upon her, he was quite capable of burning down her house. He had to be employed, and placated, until he could be replaced with someone who could frighten *him*. And as he was a big man, and a Kikuyu, she had had no immediate idea where such a man was to be found.

Thus she had accepted his apologies and been more loving than ever, telling him she would be away for only a few months at the outside. She had left him believing he was the only black man – indeed, the only man – for her, and given him a position of trust, until she could destroy him. But as the months stretched into years, his letters to her, so stiltedly formal at the beginning, gradually assumed a reproachful and then a threatening attitude. Of course, for all his evident feeling of betrayal, he did not give up the position she had left him in, and he collected his cheque from her bank every month. He never doubted she would eventually return, and he had decided to wait for that time, especially as he could do so in so much comfort – and because, when she returned, she would truly be his slave.

He thought.

It was a situation which had caused her anxiety. When she returned she would need to have someone with total strength and loyalty at her back. She had, indeed, given some consideration to marrying again. She did not lack for suitors, even in her middle fifties. She was rich, she was attractive, she was sexually vigorous, and she had an aura . . . even confirmed bachelors like Jimmy Wildman had followed her from Kenya in the hope of gaining her hand, although she suspected that Jimmy's ardour was not even directed so much at her money as at finding some sort of a barrier to place between himself and John Barclay, were John ever to find out about that night.

She had not told Jimmy that John already knew. She had

237

told no one why she had left Kenya, just allowed them to think she was bored. But she really had no intention of marrying any of them. That was a short road to losing her freedom even more conclusively than with Murgatroyd, however much they might claim to believe in freedom beforehand. Besides, she had no intention of giving up her title.

Seeing Ma and Pa in London had made her realize the importance of solving her problem fairly quickly; they were both now very old. She felt no deep concern about their coming deaths. They had both lived long, full lives, and she had always felt they had never given her the support she had been entitled to. Johnnie had been such an *afterthought*. By the time he was born, Kenya had become a relatively civilized place. There had of course been that trouble in 1906, but even that had had none of the connotations she remembered from her girlhood in the late eighties and early nineties, when she and Ma and Pa had been virtually alone in the midst of an entire nation of naked black men. Johnnie had no inkling of that; if he had, his entire outlook might have been different. Yet Ma and Pa had chosen to support him to the end. At least, Pa had. Ma had always been more sympathetic.

Because Johnnie had been the staid one, the obvious heir, and the man who would produce another heir, in due course. By means of his German cow.

She had been in tow, watching Cathy's every move, hovering by her children as if afraid they could catch some incurable disease. The sight of Adèle, so prosperous, so healthy, so Kenyan, had made her more than ever determined to go home. Providing she had some way of dealing with the stone she had so carelessly hung round her neck.

The problem, of how to return, with a strong man at her side, who would support her against Murgatroyd, and yet be unable to claim any of the rights Murgatroyd had supposed were his, had seemed nearly insoluble. And yet was solved only a few days after her last meeting with Ma and Pa and the German cow, when the receptionist at the hotel where she was staying called her room and said in a

238

somewhat embarrassed voice, "There is a man here asking to speak to you, my lady. A black man."

She frowned. Murgatroyd? Followed her to England? She couldn't believe it. But she certainly meant to find out. If he were to challenge her here, it would be on her own ground. "Oh, please send him up," she said, and replaced the receiver. "Stay another five minutes, Annie," she told her maid. She considered changing into something more formal – she was wearing only a dressing gown – but decided against it. The poor fool had everything coming to him that he deserved, but the very thought of him was making her randy, and she might as well enjoy him first. So she waited, facing the door with pounding heart, hand again resting on the telephone. "Come in," she called at the gentle knock, and found herself gazing at an African face she had never seen before, she was sure – and yet his face was vaguely familiar.

Joseph's decision to go to England had been a grave one, taken after much heart-searching in the company of Tom Ngolo. Because they, the two leaders of the Mau Mau cell, were the least successful on their return from prison. Kinkardu and Bolomo quickly found jobs, working for white firms, prepared to obey their instructions and be the most faithful of servants until the day arrived when they would expel all the white people from Kenya. Ngolo was unable to find work, and Joseph himself encountered that incomprehensible refusal on the part of Mr John to employ him – at the behest of that bitch-woman, the millstone round his neck. That night he had even toyed with the idea of murder, a ritual murder, the destruction of a white woman in such a fashion as would leave everybody gasping. It was nothing more than she deserved.

But the police would track him down, and beat him up, and then hang him. Joseph did not really wish to have anything to do with the police, until he was in a position to give them the orders.

The question was, what were they to do next? Ngolo said that they should immediately increase their numbers as rapidly as possible, and swiftly bring about the expulsion of the white people. Joseph knew this was impractical. The concept of Mau Mau, of a whole nation lying secretly waiting for the moment to strike, had necessarily to be a long-term one. It was essential to preserve absolute secrecy; were the police ever to find out what was being prepared in the Kikuyu villages they would not hesitate to arrest everyone they could think of. Equally, he remembered the days of the Great War. If he had been impressed by the ineptness of the British, at least in the early days, he had been even more impressed by the way they poured more and more men into Tanganyika, until they won their victory. He had a feeling that they might be prepared to do that in Kenya. He had no doubt of the righteousness of his cause, or of the eventual success of his plans . . . but that success would be greatly assisted were the British to be fully occupied elsewhere, and the white settlers left on their own. His reading of history had assured him that such a situation was bound to arise, and he was willing to await events and, in the meantime, hurry very slowly and only initiate those young Morani he could trust absolutely.

In this he had some success, and to ensure his success, he devised ever more numerous and more intricate and therefore more binding oaths – the time came when no man could join Mau Mau without swearing seven such vows, each one more terrible than the last.

Ngolo, however, called him a coward, and doubted that he ever truly intended to fight the British. There were other stars to follow, and Tom came to feel that Mau Mau had been bred of the angry despair of the Chalbi Desert, that even Joseph's heroics up there in the north were a product of despair.

Certainly he nearly despaired when he quarrelled with Ngolo, because right there in Nairobi, he had to watch the success of men like Jomo Kenyatta – born Kamau wa Ngengi, but a Christian like himself. Kenyatta, another of Thuku's lieutenants, had avoided arrest following the débâcle of the identity cards. With Thuku in eclipse, Kenyatta took control of the shattered YKA, and while they were breaking stones in the desert he became the most important man in the Kikuyu nation. And he was hardly older than himself, Joseph would think bitterly.

But Kenyatta revealed a breadth of vision – a style, an Englishman would have called it – which even Joseph had to admire. He actually went to England on his own to lay the Kikuyu case for land reform before the Colonial Office. He hadn't succeeded then, of course; that was before the Great Depression and the locusts. But who could say that the seed he had sewn had not borne fruit in the grudging apportionments made since? This was certainly the opinion of the older and wiser heads of the people.

These things were all anathema to Joseph Kinshasu. If the Kikuyu could obtain what they wanted simply by sending delegations – or worse, a single man, however talented – to England, the reason for Mau Mau went out of the window. He knew this could not be. He knew that the British would never really give up anything worthwhile: he had spent too many years observing the Barclays and their friends at first hand. He knew he was right and Kenyatta wrong, and that only with the spear and the gun, and the knife in the night, would the Kikuyu ever have what was rightfully theirs.

More important, he could not allow Kenyatta to be right, because that would prevent his revenge, and he meant to have that, over every white man and woman who had ever harmed him or his people, and he reckoned that meant every white person in Kenya. They had sent him to Chalbi, and they ruled the colony with iron hands.

But how to attain that goal? Strangely, it was Ngolo, with whom he had broken, who gave him his answer. Ngolo raised some money and went to England himself, following Kenyatta, who had returned there and was making himself a lion in English society, where the stories of the parties thrown by people like Lady Portington in the 1920s were just beginning to circulate, and the English intellectuals were beginning openly to question the right of such people to empire. A visit to England had made Kenyatta famous. Ngolo was obviously hoping it could do the same for him. Why should it not do as much for Joseph Kinshasu?

It was not easy. He did not know how Ngolo had raised his passage, but he himself had no source of income at all, apart from the itinerant jobs he was able to pick up in Nairobi and Mombasa. But he went to Mombasa, and there, with his English and his obvious breeding and education, and his still remembered reputation as the man who had accompanied John Barclay to war, he at last found himself a berth as junior steward on a ship bound for Southampton.

But England was no more welcoming than white-ruled Kenya. The newspapers might sometimes contain articles on the necessity of undertaking some reform in the political structure of the colony, the matter might even be raised in Parliament, which Joseph attended assiduously in the hope of learning what made the British great, but it was clear that they had far too much on their minds to be particularly interested in a single small portion of their vast empire.

Thus clearly the Africans would have to help themselves. This obviously was to the good. But could he make anyone else see that? He discovered where Kenyatta was living and called on the great man, and found Tom Ngolo already there, together with several other black men and a fair number of white people, men and women, all hanging on Kenyatta's every word. But Kenyatta's reaction to Mau Mau was hostile. "I have no use for secret societies. What we do must be open and above board. You speak of seizing freedom," Kenyatta told him. "Uhuru! It is a mighty word. But those who seize it must know how to use it."

That was as plain as saying he repudiated violence. And such was Kenyatta's influence and stature amongst his people, Joseph realized that what was now his whole life's project could be about to come tumbling down. Had he sat on the sand and screamed in agony for that?

Again he all but despaired. He was wasting his time in England, perpetually cold, working at a succession of menial jobs such as sweeping railway stations, watching the white people ambling their way through their lives ... if the majority of these people were not as personally arrogant as the whites he had known in Kenya, they still did not appear

242

to have any doubts as to their right to rule a third of the world.

He knew he had to get home. But with what? And to what? He was a leader without a following. If he did not doubt that his Mau Mau would rise up if he gave the signal, what would that accomplish? A dozen or so young men with knives, opposed even within their own nation, certain to be hunted implacably by the police the moment they revealed themselves . . . while people like John Barclay and his bitch-wife would grow ever richer and more powerful, and there-fore stronger and more difficult to remove. If only Mr John had taken him back, and he had had a position of respect and authority within both the white and the black communi-ties, able to lie coiled up in their midst like a gigantic snake, watching and waiting in some comfort, instead of dangling on the fringes of everything that was happening . . . how different everything would seem.

It was in this mood that, standing on the street the English so quaintly called Piccadilly, gazing aimlessly into the windows of the department store called Fortnum and Mason, mouth watering and belly rumbling, wondering if he would ever be able to afford food like that, he found himself beside Catherine, Lady Portington.

She did not, of course, notice him. Nor would he expect her to recognize him if she had; he had left the Barclay household before her arrival. But he certainly recognized her, as she emerged from the doors of the shop and waited for the doorman to summon her a taxi. And while he was still catching his breath, the taxi drew up, and she told the driver, in that clear, hard voice of hers, "The Savoy."

Then she drove off into the afternoon, leaving him aware of a growing excitement, the first he had known in years. He believed in omens, for all his Christianity. He could not forget how he had been despairing that afternoon more than twenty years ago when he had stood on the Mombasa dockside, with the emptiest of lives stretching in front of him, and seen John Barclay coming ashore. And had made up his mind to speak with the young bwana, with such immense results.

Could history possibly repeat itself? Only if he made it do so.

He knew a great deal about Lady Portington. He had kept his ears open while he worked for Mr John, and he recalled that her family had not altogether approved of her even then, before her return. In Kenya he had heard the rumours about her parties, and it had been easy to see that she and her brother did not get on, if only because he never visited her house. He knew she was very wealthy, and a widow. He also knew about Murgatroyd. Murgatroyd, with whom he had a nodding acquaintance, was wont to boast that he had had the white lady. Few of his drinking cronies believed him. Joseph had, from his more intimate if second-hand knowledge of the lady in question. But Murgatroyd was only a butler, and an ignorant man. Lady Portington had not been in Kenya for some time. It might well be that he could replace Murgatroyd, Joseph thought. Not as a lover, of course; his self-circumcision in the Chalbi Desert had left him a sexual outcast. The one time he went to an English whore, she had looked at his penis and screamed, and he had been evicted by two large white men whom she called her 'brothers'.

But Lady Portington might still be willing to employ a black Kenyan, as she still had links with the colony. She might be persuaded to pay his passage back, and give him a job there – he was even willing to work under Murgatroyd for the time being – and enable him entirely to restore his fortunes. And it would be one in the eye for Mr John.

And as on the Mombasa dock so long ago, what did he have to lose? While if he *could* secure employment with Lady Portington, and even more, charm her and impress her as he had Mr John . . . he might yet attain that central position he had always dreamed of.

He went home to the one room he shared with two other black men, and got out his suit – normally he wore a sports jacket and grey flannel trousers in the summer, with the addition of a threadbare raincoat in the winter – and bathed and dressed himself most carefully. Then he went along to the famous hotel.

And to his surprise, was sent up to her room.

They stared at one another, and Joseph got the impression that her ladyship had been expecting someone else. "I am Joseph Kinshasu," he said, before she could close the door.

She raised her eyebrows. "Joseph Kinshasu?"

"I used to work for your brother, milady," Joseph said, speaking with the greatest of care. "We fought in the war together."

"Good Lord," she commented. "Joseph Kinshasu. Of course. He spoke of you. You were sent to prison. *That's* where I saw your photograph."

"I was sent to prison for attempting to defend the rights of my people, milady," Joseph explained.

Catherine Portington had already lost interest in that. "Did my brother send you here?" she asked.

"No, milady. I have not worked for Mr Barclay for some time. May I come in?"

She looked surprised, then glanced down at herself. She wore a midnight blue dressing gown in what he would have said was velvet, and high-heeled mules. Her hair was slightly longer than when last he had seen her, and the more attractive for that – it retained its red-brown sheen although he knew she was in her mid-fifties. She was, in fact, a most attractive woman, more so than he remembered her in Kenya. But definitely déshabillé – and she had been expecting someone else. He thought he might be going to be unlucky, but after the briefest of hesitations she shrugged. "Why not?"

As she closed the door, he gazed at the elegant sitting room, the velvet upholstered settee and chairs, the vases of flowers, the little bar laden with bottles, the view out of the window of the River Thames, and caught his breath at the luxury of it all. Then he looked at the inner door of the suite, and at a white girl in maid's uniform who was staring at him, open-mouthed.

"You had better sit down," Lady Portington suggested,

ignoring the expression of disapproval on the girl's face, and instead staring at Joseph. He knew he was a good-looking man, and he was only just forty. He looked superbly fit, as he was; his body was trim and hard, mainly because he had not had a really square meal since leaving the Barclay household. His height gave him presence, and he had a firm, strong face. She would know nothing of where he was ugly.

Cautiously he lowered himself on to a straight chair, aware of a subtle excitement. Because she was excited? He had a feeling that she was.

"That will be all, Annie," she said, without looking at the girl in the doorway.

"Yes, milady," Annie said, and closed the door. Presumably there was another way out of the suite.

"So what brings you to see me," Lady Portington asked, "if you have no message from my brother?"

Joseph chose his words carefully. "I had thought that perhaps I could be of use to you, milady."

Her eyebrows arched again. "Of use?"

"I am sure there are many services I could perform for you, milady."

She gazed at him for several seconds. Then she said, "You want me to give you a job."

"Yes, milady."

"Someone who used to work for Johnnie?"

It was necessary to take a chance, but Joseph was sure he was right. "Mr Barclay and I quarrelled, milady."

"Did you, now." She gave him another of her appraising stares. "What about?"

Joseph hesitated for only a fraction of a second, but again it was necessary to play a hunch. And again he felt confident he was on the right track. "I'm afraid Mrs Barclay did not care for me, milady."

Lady Portington made a moue, and for a moment he thought he'd blown it. Then she said, "Do you drink, Mr Kinshasu? Or, if you are going to work for me, should I call you Joseph?"

He did not immediately grasp what she actually wanted

246

him to do for her, then he was at once scandalized and terrified. That a white woman, such as Lady Portington, John Barclay's sister, might wish a black lover was just possible – he had heard of other rich and titled women, right here in London, who indulged that fancy. That she had elected him was unthinkable, especially when he remembered that screaming whore. He didn't know what to do, as she dropped hint after hint, while giving him a second Scotch on the rocks; he did not like whisky – and it was having a terrible effect on his empty stomach – but it was what she was drinking. She sat opposite him and crossed her knees, so that the dressing gown flopped away from her legs and made it very obvious she was naked underneath. When he continued to tell her all the things he was good at, she at last said, "Are you a eunuch or something, Joseph?"

He stared at her in amazement, and she added, "And stupid? You gave me the impression of some intelligence. I am giving you a job, Joseph. Or at least, I am prepared to give you a trial, here and now. The job has only one requirement, that you keep me happy. Do I have to write it out for you? Or can't you read?"

Joseph licked his lips. He had come to hate that act of heroism which had made him a man in the eyes of his friends, and made all his other plans impossible to attain. "Milady," he said, "I would humour you in every way, but . . ."

"You *are* a eunuch," she pronounced triumphantly.

"No, milady, but . . ."

"Show me," she had commanded.

"Milady?"

"Show me," she repeated. "Stand up and drop your trousers." She stood up herself, took the glass from his hand and walked to the bar to refill it and pour another for herself. "Now. Or walk through that door." Her tone was suddenly harsh.

Joseph stood up, hesitated and obeyed her. He had never supposed there could be a woman like this anywhere in the world. When the time came, killing her was going to be a pleasure. He would take his time over it.

Catherine Portington turned slowly and looked at him. He stared at her face, waiting for the reaction, the horror, the disgust, because the conversation, the knowledge of what she wanted – of what she had demanded so cold-bloodedly, as if he were a male whore – had given him an erection. And instead watched a smile slowly widening those tight lips. "Well, Jesus Christ," she remarked. "Now that is what I call a prick."

Catherine had telephoned the house from Mombasa to announce her arrival, but had specifically instructed Murgatroyd not to come to the station to meet her; whatever mayhem she intended to create now she was back, she did not want it to begin with a public scene. So instead he waited on the front steps of the house, with the maids and footmen and gardeners arranged behind him, chest swelling with pride. His smile slowly changed to a scowl as he watched his mistress emerging from the taxicab, the moment he had been awaiting for more than ten years, and saw her accompanied by a black man.

A black man he recognized.

"Murgatroyd!" Cathering said, smiling at him. "How splendid to see you after all this time. And the place is looking so good. I do congratulate you."

Murgatroyd continued to stare at Joseph, and Catherine half turned. "You know Mr Kinshasu, of course."

"*Mr* Kinshasu?" Murgatroyd asked, his voice a low rumble of distant thunder.

"Mr Kinshasu," Catherine repeated firmly. "He is in charge here now. You will all take your orders from him." She walked past Murgatroyd before he could catch his breath, and began greeting the servants.

Behind her she heard Joseph's voice, "Well, fetch those bags, man. You ain't being paid to stand around here."

She went inside, and almost felt a pang of conscience. Murgatroyd had done wonders. The place was exactly as she had left it, and there was not a cobweb or a speck of

248

dirt anywhere. She went on to the verandah and looked at the lawn, cut short and crisp, and the pool, obviously Hoovered that very morning. She went upstairs to her bedroom and inspected the bed, the sheets starched and clean, every vase filled with freshly cut flowers, the room itself spotless and smelling faintly of the perfume she had worn when last she lived here – he had even thought to scatter a drop or two across the pillows.

She heard footsteps on the stairs, and turned to watch Murgatroyd bringing two of the suitcases into the room. Two of the footmen followed with the cabin trunk, and Joseph brought up the rear, also carrying two suitcases – her remaining one, and the one she had bought him for his own use, packed, as she knew, with the clothes she had bought him as well.

The bags were all placed on the floor. "Thank you, Murgatroyd," Catherine said. "That will be all."

"You hear the mistress?" Murgatroyd told the footmen, who bowed and withdrew.

Catherine gazed at Joseph. The showdown was to be immediate. But she had told Joseph what she wanted, and Joseph, she had discovered, was adept at giving her what she wanted. How she had existed for very nearly sixty years without a Joseph she simply did not know.

Joseph also waited for Murgatroyd to speak.

"What is this?" Murgatroyd demanded.

"What is what?" Catherine asked.

"This business with this convict you got here."

"Joseph is my man of affairs, Murgatroyd," Catherine explained. "He will be in charge of the house and the servants, including you, and of all finances here in Africa."

"Me?" Murgatroyd demanded. "I ain't no servant."

"Man," Joseph said, "You are being rude to the mistress."

"You shut your mouth, eh?" Murgatroyd suggested.

"Man," Joseph said, "I am going to bust your arse."

Murgatroyd glared at him. If no one knew for sure what had happened up in the Chalbi, everyone knew that Joseph Kinshasu had gone up there just a convicted criminal, and had come back a leader of men, even if he had not done any leading since his return. And everyone also knew that to survive a couple of years in the Chalbi a man had to be real tough. But that was more than ten years ago. The trouble was, Joseph still looked tough – he had a mean and hungry look about him.

"I suppose," Catherine said, "that if you do not like the new arrangement, Murgatroyd, you can always hand in your notice. Would you like to hand in your notice?"

"And leave you here with him?"

"And leave me here with whoever I choose," Catherine told him coldly.

Murgatroyd looked from one to the other, understood he was the victim of a plot and lost his temper. He lowered his head and charged at Joseph. Joseph sidestepped easily enough and stuck out his foot. Murgatroyd tripped and tumbled to the floor, and before he could recover, Joseph had kicked him three times in the groin; kicking people in the groin was an art he had learned the hard way.

"Don't kill him," Catherine said.

Murgatroyd struggled to his knees, both hands pressed to his genitals, and Joseph kicked him again, on the jaw, with the tip of his new leather shoes. Murgatroyd fell over and lay on the floor, gasping.

"You," Joseph said. "Get out of here."

Murgatroyd pushed himself up. He suddenly looked an old man. But he still gazed at his mistress, unable to believe she had let this happen.

"As Mr Kinshasu said," Catherine told him, "get out of here, Murgatroyd, and don't ever come back."

"Because if you do," Joseph told him, "I am going to break every bone in your body. You remember that, man."

Murgatroyd gazed at Catherine a last time, and a tear trickled down his cheek. Then he left the room.

Catherine smiled at Joseph. "Mr Kinshasu," she said. "I adore you."

The ancient Daimler entered the yard in a cloud of dust; the long rains were still several weeks away, and the ground was dry. Joseph watched it from the drawing room window. Then he turned and went to the foot of the stairs, and saw Catherine standing at the top. "Mr John is here," he said.

She nodded. They had both anticipated this moment, and for all their carefully laid plans, both were apprehensive. That Catherine had returned to Kenya determined to destroy her brother, Joseph found amusing. He did not think she would succeed, but it would be interesting to watch her going about it. Either way, he knew that now they were both his. When the time came. He often lay awake at night wondering how he could ever have supposed that Lord Ngai would fail him, and yet amazed that Lord Ngai should have brought him to this woman at the very time she had been looking for him – or someone very like him. Her innocent belief that she was in complete control of him gave him the most delicious feeling of power he had ever known.

The doorbell rang, and they continued to gaze at each other. "Five minutes," Catherine said.

The bell rang again, and again, and again. Joseph moved slowly across the floor, looking at his new gold watch; Catherine liked him to be exact about everything.

As the second hand reached the fifth minute, he slipped the bolt and opened the door. "For Jesus' sake," John Barclay snapped. "What do you people do, siesta in the middle of the morning?" Then he remembered who he was looking at. "Good God," he commented. "So it is you, after all."

Joesph stepped back. "How good to see you, Mr John. Won't you come in?"

John stared at the new suit, the new tie, the new shirt, the new shoes; Joseph shot his cuffs so that he could also see the new watch. Then he stepped inside and looked past Joseph at Catherine, who was just descending the stairs, looking cool and stately in a white linen dress. "Why, Johnnie," she cried. "How absolutely marvellous to see you." She ran across the room, threw both arms round his neck and kissed him on the mouth.

He disengaged himself. "You're looking well," he grudgingly acknowledged.

"I am feeling well. Did you bring Adèle with you?"

"No."

"What a shame. But you're here. I was going to drive across and surprise you, you know. I'd forgotten how fast news travels in this place. Joseph, I think we'll have champagne."

Joseph bowed. "Of course, milady."

He went towards the bar, and Catherine walked on to the verandah; John had no choice but to follow her. "Just where did you acquire him?" he asked.

"Would you believe, in London? We just bumped into each other, and he asked for a job. Well, when I discovered who he was, and that he had worked for you, I couldn't think of a better recommendation."

"And now he's your . . . steward?"

"Yes. He's proved an absolute treasure. So reliable, so honest . . . I let him handle all my affairs."

"You do realize that he spent two years in prison after leaving me?" John asked, and glanced in some embarrassment as Joseph came on to the verandah bearing a tray with two flutes.

"Of course I do. But that was a political offence. Wasn't it, Joseph?"

"Yes, milady. I would not carry a pass book. I have one now, Mr John," he added. "In my pocket."

"See? He's a reformed character." Catherine lifted a glass. "It is so good to see you again."

"Is it?" John did not take his glass. "Push off, will you, Joseph."

"Of course, Mr John." Joseph placed the tray and the remaining glass on an occasional table, bowed and left.

"You're not going to be difficult, I hope," Catherine said.

"I once said that if you ever came back here I'd break your neck."

"Is that what you meant? I seem to remember you uttering all manner of threats about taking me to court and plastering my name all over the newspapers." She sat down and crossed her knees. "Do you still intend to do that?"

He glared at her.

"Because it won't work, now, will it? Ma and Pa are dead. The only people who can be hurt by rattling the skeletons in the family closet are your own brats. And the German cow, of course. But if Adèle tried to bring charges of attempted rape against anyone who was at that party – God, thirteen years ago; how time flies – she'd be laughed out of court." Her voice suddenly hardened. "Maybe out of Kenya."

He stood above her. "I ought to break your neck right away."

"Now, that would be another exciting page in the history of Kenya, wouldn't it?" she mocked. " 'Settlers' leader hanged for murder of his sister.' Especially when the police got around to reading my diaries. I have kept one for forty years. I record everything, and it wouldn't do you any good standing up in court and claiming it was all lies, because I would be dead, and you wouldn't be able to prove it."

They stared at each other, and Joseph, watching and listening through a vent in the bar, knew that Mr John was indeed very close at least to hitting her.

But then she gave one of her sudden smiles, got up, and handed him the glass of champagne. "But I didn't come back here to quarrel, Johnnie darling. I came back here because I love Kenya, and because I wanted to see you again – and even Adèle, believe it or not – after all these years. Maybe Ma and Pa dying made me realize that we're none of us immortal, and that you are the only relative I have left, except for those in the States. Anyway, you wouldn't begrudge me placing flowers on Ma's grave?" She raised her own glass. "I would like to drink to friendship. Our friendship. And don't forget we have business to discuss."

"You mean you need money."

"Not at all, darling. I can't spend all Porty left me, no matter how hard I try. I'm only interested in Ma's bits and pieces."

253

He sipped the champagne. "If I could believe that you had turned over a new leaf . . ."

"Well," she said, "I'm trying. If you'll let me."

He sighed and sat down. "Of course I'll let you."

"I knew you would. Now, I imagine almost everybody in Kenya knows I'm back by now. So what I propose to do is contact a few of my chums, and then have a supper party."

"Cathy. . . ."

"And of course I want you and Adèle to come."

"You must be out of your mind. And if you start that nonsense again. . . ."

"Darling, there isn't going to be any nonsense," Catherine said, as if she were remonstrating with a small child. "It's going to be a supper party, that's all. To prove I'm on the up and up, I'm not even going to have it here. I'll have it at the club. Now, what can possibly be sinister about that?"

"Well. . . ."

"So you'll come? Do say you'll come. With Adèle?"

"Well. . . ."

He stayed for lunch, and left at three. Joseph showed him out, then followed Catherine upstairs. "Don't you think he went for it?" she asked.

"I think he was happy to do so," Joseph agreed. "I congratulate you." Because if he did not know what his mistress really intended, he did know that it began with a public display of the reconciliation between herself and her brother.

"Poor sod," Catherine remarked. "He never did know the time of day."

"I have never been so nervous in my life," Adèle confessed as the car drew up outside the Muthaiga Club; it was already dark, and the fireflies were gleaming in the bushes that bordered the drive, while the building itself was a blaze of light.

"Well, don't be," John told her. "I really think she's finally grown up. About time."

"But . . . suppose she's invited some of the people who were at that party?"

"So what? It was fifteen years ago, my darling. They are probably now all old and grey, while you are still the most beautiful woman in Kenya. They're the losers."

"Is Catherine old and grey?"

"As a matter of fact, no. But I suspect most of her looks come from a chemist. Just remember, you're the one in the catbird seat now. Nobody else. There is not a single soul in Kenya can harm you, my darling."

She blew him a kiss. "I know that."

They were shown into one of the private rooms, where champagne flowed and they found Catherine and her other guests. For all John's bold words they were both relieved to find that she had had the good taste not to invite any one present on that unforgettable night. Her guests were impeccably from the top drawer of Nairobi society; people who could hardly be her "chums", John surmised, although she might have met one or two of them in England. Clearly they had all heard some of the rumours surrounding their hostess, and sat there with bated breath, while Catherine scintillated in the most respectable manner, playing the role of Lady Portington to the hilt. And if they were disappointed that nothing scandalous was said or done, they could not be disappointed in the standard of food and wine served them, which was the best the Muthaiga Club had to offer.

The meal lasted for a good three hours, and then, after the ladies had rejoined the men, they continued to enjoy the lavish hospitality being thrown at them. "It is such a treat to be back," Catherine said. "Kenya is so bright, so relaxed, so . . . alive, after London. And can you imagine my feelings when I got back to my house, after thirteen years, mind you, and found it as perfect as when I left. Not a speck of dust."

"And it was in black care all of that time?" asked one of the women, unsuspectingly supplying the cue her hostess had been seeking. "I find that unbelievable."

"Why should it be? The secret, my dear, is money. Pay even an African enough and he will be honest. I left it with

255

Murgatroyd, my butler. Well, he was more than a butler, of course. Much more." She smiled at them, while they blinked at her through an alcoholic haze, uncertain what she had actually told them.

John sat up.

"But then, I had to let him go," Catherine said. "Because I had found someone so much better in England. A Kenyan, of course. Johnnie's old valet, Joseph. Now Joseph is a real treasure. Without him I'd just be a lonely old widow."

"Cathy," John said. "Shut up."

She gazed at him from beneath arched eyebrows.

"You promised me. . . ."

"What did I promise you?" she challenged. "I said I wanted us to be friends. I do. And I promised you this party would be all proper and above board. Well, it is. That doesn't mean I have to change my private life, or be ashamed of who I sleep with."

"Oh my," said one of the women, the penny at last dropping.

"You wretched woman," John shouted, getting to his feet.

"Johnnie!" Adèle uneasily held his hand, as if to restrain him from violence.

Catherine tilted her head back to laugh at him. "What are you going to do? Break my neck, in front of all these people? Think of the gossip!"

John glared at her in impotent fury, then pushed his chair back. "Adèle and I are leaving."

"So early?" Catherine asked. "It's only just midnight. I thought we'd go on to a nightclub. I've been told there's a great roadhouse just along the way."

"Go where you like," John said, and pointed at her. "I am coming to see you tomorrow morning. And you had better have Kinshasu out of there by then." He glance at the other, shocked faces. "I'll say goodnight."

Adèle ran out of the club behind him, grabbing her wrap from one of the barmen as she did so. "Johnnie. . . ."

He slammed the door and got behind the wheel. "That foul little bitch. And I actually believed her." The engine raced, and the car burst out of the yard.

"Johnnie," Adèle begged. "Don't lose your temper. She's not worth it."

"I should have strangled her there and then," he growled, as they bumped over the road out of town. "She's only come back to torment us. Well she won't get away with it, the randy whore."

Adèle bit her lip and said nothing. She had never known him so angry.

They drove in silence while he hunched over the wheel, and got back to Naivasha about two in the morning — it was roughly fifty miles from Nairobi to Naivasha, and as the road was not terribly good, the journey invariably took about two hours to drive at night. He drew up in front of the house with a squealing of brakes. "I'll see you later," he said.

Half out of the car, Adèle hesitated. "Where are you going?"

"That's my business."

"You're going back to town, Johnnie. . . ."

"My sister, and my valet," he said. "My black valet. Damn them."

"What are you going to do?"

"Throw him out of the house for a start."

"Johnnie. . . ."

"Are you going to get out of this car or not?"

She sighed. She had *never* known him in such a mood. She got out of the car. "Please be careful."

"Do you suppose I'm afraid of Joseph Kinshasu?"

"Of course not. But . . . if there's a brawl, you could get arrested. I mean it *is* Cathy's house."

"Then I'll be arrested," he said. "It'll be worth it."

She stepped back, and the car roared into the night.

"Now that the spectre at the feast has departed," Catherine said, "I suggest we all enjoy ourselves."

Her guests were happy to do so. Not only had they had too much to drink, but none of them had met quite such an exciting woman, or had quite such an exciting evening before, either. As for what she might or might not have been doing with her black steward ... that was quite in keeping with her reputation, and John Barclay had the reputation, in contrast, of being a rather strait-laced old fuddy-duddy. Besides, she was paying.

They went to the nightclub and danced for several hours, by which time they were all exhausted. "Whooee," Catherine said, fanning herself. "I'm for bed." She grinned at them. "All by myself."

They laughed uproariously, and one of the men asked daringly, "Are you sure you won't need protecting?"

"From dear brother John?" She laughed in turn. "He huffs and he puffs, but he never really does anything, does he? Now, if he could have me incarcerated and operated on, or something, to make me less randy ... that would appeal to him. Besides, I always sleep with my doors locked. So I'm off."

"I could drive you home," the man suggested, more seriously; she was swaying.

"Forget it. I've driven more miles drunk than you ever have sober."

She went down the steps, got behind the wheel of the Sunbeam roadster she had bought only three days previously, started the engine, drove out of the yard, realized she was on the wrong side of the road and hastily got the car back under control. She *was* tight. But not too tight to drive. Besides, it had been a gloriously successful evening. Not only had she reduced Johnnie to impotent fury – she wouldn't be surprised if he had a heart attack – but she had gained the wholly unexpected bonus of a new set of friends all simply dying to be as naughty as she could make them. That was going to be a whole lot of fun, while Johnnie would have to look on and squirm.

But she wasn't finished with him yet, she thought. Oh, no, not by a long way.

She drove into her yard and left the Sunbeam at the foot of the steps. Joseph could garage it in the morning; he loved driving expensive cars, even if only for short distances. Joseph! She lurched up the steps. What a happy chance that had been, bringing him into her life, in every way.

Every possible way. She felt like having him now; she was very sexually excited. But she had given him the night off. She wondered what he did with his nights off. She had made him swear never to touch another woman, as she didn't want any horrible disease. And she knew he would keep his oath, not only because he was the sort of man who kept oaths, and because he was afraid of losing his job – the best job he had ever had – but because he was ashamed of his prick. That was his big secret, and she possessed it. Therefore she possessed him.

She reached the front door, fumbling in her handbag for her key. It took her some time to get it into the lock and then she discovered the door was open anyway. Joseph had still been there when she had left, so he must have forgotten to lock it, she thought. The bastard. She'd tear a strip off him in the morning. She giggled. It was already morning. A cock was crowing, and when she looked at her watch she saw that it was just after four. Then the door had probably been unlocked by Joseph coming home. Silly bastard.

She went inside, switched on the lights and blinked at her drawing room. As usual, everything was flawless; Joseph was even more meticulous in that regard than Murgatroyd had been. In fact, it was too meticulous, she decided. She must get some more dogs and a couple of cats, and let them mess the place up, really give the servants something to do.

She climbed the stairs. If Joseph was home, then she could get him out of his bed and into hers. But suddenly she was too sleepy. She'd wait until he brought her a cup of tea in the morning. She pushed open her bedroom door, then undressed, leaving her clothes scattered across the floor. Something else for Joseph to do; he was the most perfect ladies' maid. She had left Annie behind in England because the girl's disapproval of what her mistress was doing with a black man became impossible – and she had not missed her at all.

She went into the bathroom and cleaned her teeth, then looked into the mirror and caught sight of the man standing behind her. Slowly she turned. "What the *hell* are you doing here?" she demanded.

"You be quiet," he said. "Or I will kill you."

She stared at him, aware of being more angry than frightened. She knew *he* wasn't going to kill her. "You must be out of your mind," she told him.

"All you want is sex," he said. "Sex, sex, sex. You don't care who it is with. Sex, sex, sex. Well, I am going to give you some sex."

Catherine raised her eyebrows and laughed. "You do that," she said. "And then I am going to have you gaoled for rape. Even if I enjoy it – which I am sure I will."

"You lie down," the man said.

Catherine shrugged. She certainly wasn't going to fight him. She lay on the bed, but frowned when she saw the cord he had taken from his pocket. He saw her concern and grinned. "I don't want you scratching my face, eh?"

She lay still, the first vague stirrings of alarm in her mind as he secured her wrists to the bedhead. Then he went to a little bag he had left behind the door, where he must have been standing when she entered the room, and took out a roll of thick black cloth.

"Now look here," she said.

"You going to fight me?" he asked.

Catherine drew a long breath. Brother, she thought, am I going to have you strung up by the balls tomorrow. But she knew she couldn't fight him tonight. She allowed him to push the cloth into her mouth and secure it there, made no demur when he spread her legs and tied the ankles, one to each bedpost. "There," he said, looking down on her. "Now you lie real still."

Get on with it, you crummy bastard, she thought, not at all sure she was going to enjoy this, after all.

But he was in no hurry; he went to the corner and took something else from the bag. It wasn't until he turned round and came back to the bed that Catherine saw what he had in his hand: a small, sharp-bladed knife.

Then she tried to scream, but could only make a kind of high-pitched moaning noise through the gag.

3
THE LAND OF FEARFUL HAPPINESS

11

It was just after five when John regained Nairobi. He was drunker than he had thought, and although his anger had maintained his concentration and enabled him to drive home comparatively sensibly, he fell asleep at the wheel as he began the climb back out of the valley. The car went off the road and came to rest in the ditch, and he lay there for an hour before he woke up. Then, discovering there was no damage, he went on. He was almost sober now, but no less angry. If Catherine and Joseph thought they could come back to Kenya to make his life a misery, they had another think coming. Throwing Joseph out of Catherine's house would not only be a pleasure, it would be an act supported by every right-minded member of the community, he had no doubt, and would put Catherine firmly where she belonged: beyond the pale of white society. And if either of them tried to bring charges of assault and battery, that would put even more people on his side.

He roared into the house yard, and nearly hit the Sunbeam, which had been left where visitors normally parked. He slammed his door and went up the steps. No doubt they had heard him and were hastily scrambling out of bed and getting dressed, he thought. That wasn't going to do them any good.

The front door was open. That was typical. She could have been robbed of everything she possessed while lying in the arms of her black paramour, and not know a thing about it.

Uncertain of his whereabouts, he fumbled up and down the wall for the light switch, finally located it, then blinked in the sudden glare. He knew he had made some noise, but there was no evidence anyone had heard him. He went to the foot of the stairs and looked up. "Hello!" he shouted.

Still there was no response.

He went up the stairs, reached the landing and found another light switch. The extensive gallery had a polished wooden floor submerged beneath scatter rugs, and lined with chests on which stood brass plant pots containing various specimens of African flora. On the walls hung prints of famous horses. It was so long since he had been up here he had forgotten how elegant Cathy's house was.

Five of the bedroom doors were shut; the sixth was open. He went towards it, moving slowly, his nostrils suddenly afflicted by a faint scent he could not immediately identify but knew he did not like. He stood in the doorway and gazed into the darkness. "Catherine?" he asked; now the hair on the back of his neck was prickling. But he knew she was home; the car was outside.

Another fumble found the light switch, another blink brought his eyes into focus, and he stared at his sister. And knew what the scent was, because he had smelt it during the war. It was the scent of blood.

Roused by his detective sergeant, who had received John's telephone call, Detective Inspector Curtis was at Lady Portington's house by six. Dawn was just breaking, but already there were several people gathered outside, staring at the police constables who had mysteriously appeared, and at the cars which had come racing up to the house half an hour ago. "Make sure none of those people come inside the yard," Curtis told his men, and went up the steps.

He was aware of a feeling of suppressed excitement. He had no real idea what he was going to find; his sergeant had been a trifle incoherent. But something terrible had happened involving Lady Portington and her brother, the two people in all Kenya he most disliked. And it was something seriously criminal, or the police would not have been called. It might be the dream of a lifetime coming true.

The policeman on the door saluted. The interior was a blaze of lights, and he saw John Barclay, who was wearing a decidedly dishevelled dinner suit without a tie and sitting on a settee by the empty fireplace. There was a half-consumed glass of brandy on the small table at his elbow.

John raised his head as the police officer came in. "Upstairs," he said. His voice was thick, and Curtis observed that there was a trace of vomit on his chin.

Curtis went upstairs and was saluted by another constable and then his sergeant waiting at the bedroom door. "Dr Miller still in there, sah," he announced.

Curtis nodded. "Aren't there any servants?"

"Oh, yes, sah, but they sleep in a separate building out the back. I have my men taking statements. But they don't know nothing, sah. Only Mr Barclay was in the house."

Curtis nodded again. He gazed at Dr Miller, who had left the bedside at the sound of his voice and come to the door. The doctor was a heavily built man, with a red face – normally. This morning his cheeks were quite pale. "Got a strong stomach?" he inquired.

Curtis stepped inside and then stood absolutely still. He was first of all aware of naked female flesh, for there was a lot of it on display. Then he became aware of blood, because the woman's thighs and the coverlet beneath them were soaked. Then he became aware of horror, as he looked at the nature of the wounds and then at the wide, staring eyes and the expression on the face behind the gag, and realized that Lady Portington had been alive when this was done to her.

He glanced at Miller; the doctor's hands were also bloody.

"I made a preliminary examination," Miller explained, "and took the rectum temperature. Difficult to do when the body is tied on its back. That puts the time of death at somewhere between four and five; she really was still quite warm. I'll conduct a proper post-mortem when you can let me have her. The photographer's here, by the way, but I told him to wait."

Curtis had to swallow before he could speak. "You mean someone shoved a knife into her? There? And left her to bleed to death?"

"No, no. Cause of death was asphyxiation. The gag was a little tight, and the pain must have been extreme. And of course she was not exactly a young woman. There may have

265

been premature heart failure as well, but I won't be able to tell that until I've had a look inside."

"But . . ." Curtis couldn't speak any more. He pointed at the blood between the legs.

"Oh, that. Well, old man, she's been circumcised."

Curtis stared at him with his mouth open.

"Fact," Miller said. "The Kikuyu way."

Curtis waited for the photographer to finish, then he cautiously released the cords binding Lady Portington to the bed, and allowed the body to be wrapped in a sheet and taken downstairs to the waiting ambulance. By now the sun was high and a large crowd had gathered, including several newspaper reporters. "Man, sah, they are wanting something too bad," the sergeant said.

Curtis went on to the front steps, and was besieged with questions. He held up his hand. "All I can tell you is that Lady Portington has died, rather suddenly."

"You mean she was murdered?"

Curtis turned to the questioner. "So far as can be ascertained at this moment, she died of a heart attack."

"A heart attack?" The question was one of disappointment.

"Then why all the police? Do you suspect foul play?" asked someone else.

"It is the duty of the police to establish the circumstances of any death of this nature. I can tell you no more than what I have just said, because at this moment I know nothing more. I will give a full statement at the station this afternoon. Good morning, gentlemen." He went back inside and left his sergeant to see them off. The telephone was ringing, and John Barclay was on his feet. "Don't touch it," Curtis said.

John looked at him. "It's certain to be my wife."

"She knows you're here?"

"She knew I was coming here."

Curtis picked up the phone.

"Johnnie? Is that you? What are you *doing*?"

Curtis coughed. "I'm afraid this is Detective Inspector Curtis, Mrs Barclay."

266

"Detective. . . ." There was a gulp on the other end of the line. "What's happened?"

"Ah, I'm afraid there's been an accident," Curtis said carefully.

"Oh, my God!" Adèle said. "Johnnie?"

"Your husband is unharmed, Mrs Barclay."

"Oh, my God," Adèle said again.

"Lady Portington is dead," Curtis said.

There was a moment's silence. Then Adèle said, "Johnnie did *that*?"

Curtis held the receiver away from his ear for a moment, while he looked at John Barclay. "Would you repeat that, Mrs Barclay?"

"I . . . what *happened*?"

"I think perhaps it would be a good idea for you to come into town, Mrs Barclay," Curtis said. "Can you do that? I am sure your husband would like to see you."

"Of course. I'm coming right up." The telephone went dead.

"That was rather a blunt way of putting it," John said.

He had not of course heard his wife's remark. "I'm afraid murder is rather a blunt event," Curtis observed.

"Was it murder? Miller was saying something. . . ."

"Your sister died while a criminal act was being committed upon her body, or immediately after as a result of that act. That is murder, Mr Barclay. Do you know what what was done to her?"

John sat down again. "Yes. My God, yes. I saw. When I first went in."

Curtis glanced at his sergeant to make sure he had his notebook ready. "When was that?"

"Oh, God knows. Just after five. Yes."

"You'd spent the night here?"

"Lord, no. We'd all been to dinner at the club, and I drove my wife home about midnight. Then I came back here."

"May I ask why?"

"There . . . there was something I wished to discuss with my sister."

"After having been up all night?"

"It was urgent," John said coldly.

"I see. And you walked into the house – you have a key, of course."

"No, I do not have a key," John snapped. "The front door was unlocked."

Curtis raised his eyebrows. "Wasn't that a little careless of Lady Portington?"

"Well of course it was. She was probably drunk when she came home. She was heading that way when I last saw her."

"Which was?"

"I've told you, Curtis. My wife and I left the Muthaiga Club at midnight."

"And drove home to Naivasha. What time did you reach there?"

"About two."

Curtis nodded. "And you stayed there for a while, before deciding to come back."

John frowned. "No. I drove straight back."

"But it took you three hours?" Curtis asked.

"Well. . . ." John flushed. "I fell asleep at the wheel and ran off the road. I suppose I'd had quite a lot to drink too."

"Ah. That's why you didn't arrive here until just after five. If you hadn't run off the road you could have been here about four."

"I suppose so. Is it important?"

"Very. If you had got here at four, you would have interrupted the murderer at work."

John stared at him.

"Circumcising your sister," Curtis said relentlessly. "A particularly foul and brutish crime, would you not say?"

John snapped his fingers. "Not to the Kikuyu. It is something which is done to every Kikuyu maiden immediately before marriage," John said. "You must know that, Curtis."

"Are you suggesting a Kikuyu came in here and circumcised a fifty-seven-year-old woman who certainly didn't want it to happen? Why in the name of God should anyone do that?"

268

"Don't you see?" John shouted. "The Kikuyu do it to their girls to make sure they stay at home. Because a circumcised girl is less randy. Catherine was randy as hell." He gazed at the policeman. "I assume you know *that?*"

"So you think a Kikuyu came into the house to circumcise Lady Portington in order to make her less, ah, randy. Am I permitted to ask why your sister's habits should be of the least interest to any Kikuyu?"

"Because . . . my God! Joseph!"

"Joseph?"

"Where is he? He should be here."

"If you'd tell me his name," Curtis said gently, "I might be able to find out if he *is* here."

"I can tell you that he isn't," John said. "Or he'd have been in the house. He lives here."

"This Joseph."

"Joseph Kinshasu," John shouted. "You must remember Joseph Kinshasu. He used to be my servant. You sent him up to the Chalbi in 1922, remember?"

"And now he lives here? In Lady Portington's house?"

"He did. My bet is that he's in the bush by now. But he's your man, Curtis."

"You'll have to explain that to me. Just because he's a Kikuyu?"

"Because he was my sister's lover," John said.

"Are you serious?"

"It happens to be a fact. She acquired him in London and brought him back here. As her steward. And lover. She boasted of it. And she must have gone off with some other bloke, and Joseph found out and circumcised her, just as he would one of his own women, to keep her from being promiscuous. Only she died while he was doing it. Joseph, by God! After all we did for that bugger. You just find Joseph Kinshasu, Curtis, and I hope you hang him so high they see him from Mombasa."

"Hm," Curtis remarked. But he looked at his sergeant. "I think we had better find this fellow, sergeant. Now, Mr Barclay, would you mind making a statement for me –

beginning last evening, before you said good night to your sister at the Muthaiga Club? There's a desk over there."

The statement took some time, because John couldn't concentrate. He kept seeing that tortured body upstairs. And Joseph bending over it, knife in hand. Joseph! The man with whom he had spent four years in the jungle, whom he had come to trust with his life. But that was before Joseph was sent up to the Chalbi, and learned to hate. How he must have thought he had fallen on his feet when Catherine took him on, and invited him into her bed, as well. But he had become jealous, and reacted as only a Kikuyu could. Joseph!

It was also difficult to concentrate because of the comings and goings, the policemen tramping about, and Curtis questioning the servants, not one of whom had heard anything. Catherine had clearly known her murderer, had not believed he would harm her, until it was too late; so there had not been the least sign of a struggle in the bedroom. She must even have allowed herself to be tied up, expecting only some variation in her unending quest for sexual gratification.

Easy to say she had had it coming for a long time. She was his sister. Had been his sister, he thought bitterly. Last night he had been angry enough to throttle her. Today he wanted only to avenge her.

Tyres scraped on the gravel and Adèle hurried in. "Johnnie!"

He had just about finished; he signed his name.

"Where's Cathy?"

"In the morgue, I imagine." He got up wearily; he hadn't slept and it was catching up with him.

"What happened?" Adèle asked. She was more distraught than he had ever seen her. She was wearing only slacks and a loose shirt and sandals, no make up, and he was sure she hadn't even brushed her hair or washed her face – her eyes were still heavy with drink and sleep.

"It was pretty ghastly," John said. "I'll tell you about it, when we get home."

"But. . . ." She glanced at the policemen. "Who . . . ?"

"Joseph."

"*Joseph?*"

"Can't be anyone else."

She stared at him, and then at Curtis as he came through the doorway from the kitchen.

"Mrs Barclay! This is all rather horrible, isn't it."

"Horrible," Adèle repeated, and looked at her husband again.

"Have you told her what happened?" Curtis asked.

"No," John said.

"I'd like – " Adèle began.

"I'm sure you would, Mrs Barclay," Curtis agreed. "Would you mind if I had a word with your wife, Mr Barclay? Alone."

John raised his eyebrows. "What for?"

Curtis shrugged. "She is a witness, sir. If not to the murder, to the dead woman's way of life. As you yourself said, that's where we are going to find our motive and our murderer."

John hesitated. "I suppose you're right. But for God's sake mind how you put things."

"I shall. Why don't you take some fresh air, Mr Barclay."

"Out the back," Adèle said. "There's an awful crowd in front. Ghouls."

"People are like that, Mrs Barclay. And your sister-in-law was a well-known woman. I think your wife is right, Mr Barclay." He showed Adèle to a chair, waited until John had gone down the steps to the lawn and then sat beside her. "It *is* rather horrible," he repeated, gazing at her.

"Tell me."

He did so, and watched the changing expressions on her face, from consternation to revulsion. "Did that really happen?" she asked when he had finished.

"I'm afraid so. Do you agree with your husband that the murderer is probably this fellow Kinshasu?"

"Who else can it have been? To have done something like that?"

"I agree that it was certainly someone with an intimate knowledge of Kikuyu customs and a powerful dislike for

Lady Portington, or at least for her way of life. I do not believe the man actually set out to murder her; perhaps he felt she would be too ashamed to denounce him afterwards."

"Catherine would have denounced him," Adèle said.

"What makes you so sure?"

"You obviously didn't know Cathy,' Adèle said.

"Which appears to have been my misfortune. May I ask what you meant on the phone when we spoke this morning?"

Although Adèle knew this question had to come, she was unprepared for it. "What did I say?"

"When I told you that Lady Portington had been murdered, you said, if I remember correctly, 'Johnnie did that?' "

Adèle stared at him. "I don't remember saying that. You must have misheard me."

"Mrs Barclay," Curtis said. "This is a murder investigation. In the course of it I am going to discover everything I can, everything anyone will tell me, about Lady Portington's relationships with everyone, including your brother, and including you. Now, other people, the people you were with at the Muthaiga Club last night, for example, may tell me things which you might feel are incorrect. Would it not be better for you to tell me the truth, as you see it?"

"The truth about what?" Curtis could tell she was thinking as hard as she could but not making much progress – too much had happened too quickly, and she had a hangover.

"The truth, to begin with, of your husband's relationship with Lady Portington. He was her brother. He bears a famous name, as does she. He admits she was promiscuous. Did he approve of this?"

"Of course he didn't. They quar—" She bit her lip.

"They quarrelled about it. Often?"

"John has never approved of Catherine," Adèle said coldly. "And neither have I."

"Understandably. Did they quarrel last night?"

"Well. . . ."

"A quarrel so severe your husband decided he must come back and have it out with her before dawn?"

"He wanted to talk to her about something."

"Joseph Kinshasu?"

She glared at him, suddenly realizing what he was thinking. "You must be insane."

"Do you think so, Mrs Barclay? I agree that the man who circumcised Lady Portington was probably insane, at least when he committed the crime. Insane with jealousy, or outrage . . . something. What time did your husband leave you at Naivasha?"

"Oh, just after two."

"He says he did not get here until after five."

"Three hours, to drive from Naivasha to Nairobi. Oh. . . ." She checked herself.

"He says he fell asleep at the wheel and ran off the road. Miraculously, he wasn't hurt. Nor was the car damaged."

"If that is what my husband said happened, Inspector," Adèle said, "then that is what happened. As for what you are suggesting, I have never heard anything more disgusting in my life. Catherine was John's sister. And he is John Barclay. You should be ashamed of yourself." She got up. "We will be going home now."

Curtis made no move to stop her. He was more interested in the appearance of his sergeant in the kitchen doorway making signals. He got up in turn and went towards him.

"We got Kinshasu," the sergeant said in a hoarse whisper.

Joseph had returned home at about a quarter to six. He knew Catherine was throwing a party at the Muthaiga Club, at which she was planning to implement the first step in humiliating her brother, and although he did not know what that step was going to be, he knew *her* well enough to be sure that she would get drunk and be just able to stagger home to bed. She was not going to require him until it was time for her morning cup of tea.

The night was an important one for him. Everyone knew he was back in Kenya, but he had not yet had the chance to do more than make one or two telephone calls while his mistress was in siesta. Thus he had arranged a meeting of Mau Mau for that evening. It was necessary to reassert his

273

authority, and now the old uncertainty had gone. His feet were firmly set on the path they would follow to the end.

Yet he was apprehensive about the meeting. As a Kikuyu, he never doubted that any man who had pushed his penis through the hole in the thorax of a goat, eaten of the meat which had lain against his own most private flesh, and begged it, the goat and his friends to kill him if he ever failed to answer the call, would never break such an oath. But still, in the years he was away, he could have been supplanted as leader of the sect by someone like Kinkardu or Bolomo, founder members who had been here all the time. The telephone calls to those very two had reassured him to a certain extent, but he was still overwhelmed and gratified by the reception given him this evening, and still more by the turnout. All the forty-odd initiates were there, with the exception of Johnny Mtaba, who had been hanged for murder in the interim. Johnny had been impatient at the delay in implementing their plan and had killed a white man on safari. There was no need to worry about it, Tom Ngolo had told him, because the police knew nothing of any secret society and Johnny Mtaba had not betrayed them. It had simply been the act of an African angry with a white man, and soon forgotten.

The presence of Tom Ngolo, back from England, was the most gratifying thing of all. Tom had grown weary in turn of Jomo Kenyatta's patience, and the lack of action on the part of the British Government, and had decided that, after all, Mau Mau was the hope of the Kikuyu.

Thus they stayed together until just before dawn, talking and planning, and then he returned home, once again to discover all his plans ripped apart in front of his face.

He pushed his way through the crowd, with the arrogance he had observed in the Barclays, and absorbed from them, not at first realizing that these people were gathered outside Catherine's house. Fortunately, he had been back so short a time that few of them recognized him, and equally fortunately, he caught snatches of what they were saying before he reached the gate. Then he stepped back into the crowd, and watched the policemen, and the comings and goings,

274

and the white-shrouded body being placed in the ambulance and driven away. He found it difficult to accept what was being said on every side, that Lady Portington was dead. Catherine? His own selected victim? And until then, not only the most exciting of women but also his meal ticket? And more than that. As Lady Portington's steward he was an important man. As the ex-steward of the dead Lady Portington, he was once more nothing.

He retired to the fringes of the crowd to think, while he watched and listened. He had seen Adèle Barclay arrive, and he had already recognized the old Daimler; Mr John was inside. He had no desire to confront Mr John at such a time; he decided to sidle off until the heat died down. But then he began to hear his own name being mentioned. And realized that to disappear would be the worst thing he could do.

Besides, he had to find out what had happened, even if it meant putting himself into the power of the hated Curtis and his filthy policemen. But this time they had nothing on him. So he stood straight and stared at Detective Inspector Curtis, as Curtis stared back at him.

"Joseph Kinshasu," Curtis said. "Remember me?"

"I remember you, Mr Curtis," Joseph said.

"Good," Curtis said. "Because I remember you, Joseph. Now I am told you are Lady Portington's houseboy."

"I am her steward," Joseph said. "Was her steward."

"I see. You know she is dead, then?"

"Everybody out there knows she is dead," Joseph said.

Curtis stared at him. He had not experienced such arrogance from a black man before. "And are they also saying how she died?"

"No," Joseph said.

"She was murdered, Joseph."

Joseph frowned.

"Murdered, Joseph," Curtis repeated. "By someone she knew very well. While you were out of the house. *Were* you out of the house, Joseph?"

"Yes," Joseph said, this time adding, "sir". He needed time to think.

"Where were you?" Curtis asked.

"I was with friends, sir."

"Can you prove that?"

"They will vouch for me."

"Give me their names and addresses."

Joseph gave him the names and addresses of Tom Ngolo, Rupert Bolomo, and Harry Kinkardu. He knew they would give him an alibi. But he was still intrigued, more than alarmed, to be a suspect. "You think I killed milady?"

"It is my business to suspect everybody," Curtis told him. "You will stay here while my constables find these three men and find out how long you were with them."

Joseph shrugged. He had come straight home from leaving the meeting. And he had arrived as Catherine's body was taken out. He had read enough about murder to know the doctor would be able to set the time of death within fairly narrow limits, so he also knew he could not possibly be accused of being involved. But Catherine . . . murdered? It didn't make sense. Every other living member of Mau Mau had also been at that meeting. And besides, he had given no orders.

The sergeant, having given instructions to three of the constables, was back, muttering in his chief's ear. "Oh, let them go," Curtis said. "We know where to find them. But I want you to send someone down to the Muthaiga Club and obtain the names and addresses of everyone who was there last night, especially those who attended a party thrown by Lady Portington."

Joseph listened with interest. He was obviously not the only suspect. He glanced out of the kitchen window and saw the Daimler and the Austin driving out of the yard; the Barclays both looked hot and bothered, but obviously neither of them had any idea he had returned.

"Your old boss," Curtis remarked.

"A long time ago," Joseph said.

"Isn't it odd, that you should wind up working for his sister?"

"Life is like that," Joseph remarked.

"You are a damned arrogant bastard," Curtis said.

"Would it interest you to know that Mr Barclay virtually accused you of killing Lady Portington?"

"Me? I wasn't here."

"So you say."

"And why should I kill milady?" Joseph asked. "She was good to me. She was my mistress."

"In every possible sense, eh?"

"We were fond of each other," Joseph said.

"God, I am going to ram those words down your throat," Curtis threatened.

But Joseph was a lot older and wiser now than in 1923. "You arresting me, Mr Curtis? Because if you are, you must caution me first. And if you ain't, then you have no right to threaten me."

For a moment Curtis was speechless. Then he said, "You and Lady Portington were fond of each other. You mean you were lovers?"

Joseph did not lower his gaze. He enjoyed the spectacle of the white man so outraged. "Yes," he said.

"You were in love with her."

"Yes," Joseph said. Because perhaps he had been.

"And therefore you were jealous of her."

Joseph shrugged. That had never crossed his mind.

"So suppose I told you that Lady Portington was murdered by a jealous lover?"

"He left a note?"

"Yes," Curtis said savagely. "He left a note. All but. He cut away her external sex organs. Isn't that what the Kikuyu do to keep their wives faithful?"

Joseph stared at him in utter consternation.

"So that got to you," Curtis said triumphantly, but also with some disappointment; he could tell from Joseph's reaction that he hadn't done it. "You're a Kikuyu, Joseph," he said. "And you were Lady Portington's lover. But Lady Portington had other lovers. You tell me why I shouldn't arrest you?"

"Because I wasn't here," Joseph insisted, while his brain whirred. By God, he thought, when I lay my hands on that swine. . . .

277

"So you've arranged with a couple of friends to give you an alibi," Curtis said contemptuously. "That's not going to stand up in court, Joseph, and you know it. You are going to wind up with a noose round your neck."

Joseph hardly heard what the man was saying. He wanted to get out and start his hunt for Murgatroyd. The thought of someone other than himself cutting up Catherine made him want to be sick.

"Unless, of course," Curtis went on, "you are prepared to cooperate."

Joseph's eyes flickered. What was this stupid man talking about?

"I would like to know about the relationship between Lady Portington and her brother," Curtis said.

Joseph frowned.

"You worked for them both," Curtis went on. "You must have seen them together, heard what they said to each other."

Joseph's forehead slowly cleared. The man must be out of his mind, he thought. But he was the man in authority. "I left Mr John's employ before Lady Portington came back to Kenya," he said. "And I started working for her in London. We'd only been back here ten days."

"Oh," Curtis said, plainly disappointed.

The idiot actually thought that Mr John had murdered his own sister, Joseph realized, as a Kikuyu might have done. It was a plausible theory, providing one did not know Mr John very well. Now he could use Catherine, poor dead Catherine, to destroy Mr John, and all without lifting a finger of his own. Except that he didn't want Mr John to hang. The destruction of Mr John was to be a very personal thing. He had been robbed of the destruction of Catherine. He was not going to be robbed of the destruction of her brother, and the bitch-woman. But he didn't want Murgatroyd to hang, either. Murgatroyd was another personal matter. And most of all he didn't want the police to keep on breathing down his neck. They thought they had a suspect. Well, he would give them their suspect . . . and take him away again when he was ready. After Mr John had

278

been good and scared. That will be rather amusing, he thought. I will give him his life, so that I may take it away again. When I am ready.

"So I only ever once saw them together," he went on.

"Oh?" Curtis had lost interest. "When was that?"

"That was the day after we arrived back here," Joseph said. "Mr John came to call on milady. It was then he threatened to kill her."

The two cars bumped into the yard at Naivasha and drew to a halt in a cloud of dust. Little Adrian ran down the steps to greet them; he still didn't understand why he had not gone to school today. No one on the farm did. "Mummy, Daddy," he shouted.

John swept him from the ground and held him high while he waited for Adèle to get out of the smaller car, then set him down again. "Go and catch us a fish for lunch."

"I couldn't eat a thing," Adèle said.

"But you feel like a drink, I imagine. I know I do." He looked down at his bedraggled dinner suit. "Christ, what a mess." He went into the drawing room. "Pinkers?"

"No," she said. "No, please. Not today."

"No," he agreed, and poured out two stiff brandies. "Medicinal," he said, giving her one of the balloons.

She sipped and shuddered. "You saw her."

"Yes." He sat down, his balloon held between his hands. "And brought up my dinner."

"Oh, Johnnie. Was it . . . ?"

"If I wake up screaming just give me a nudge."

Adèle sat down as well. "Do you really think Joseph Kinshasu did it?"

"Who else could it have been?"

She didn't reply, and he slowly raised his head. Then she said, "Curtis was making all sorts of insinuations about you."

"Which you accepted?"

"Johnnie! Of course I did not. But he has this thing about that hour you were asleep on the road."

279

"He was muttering about it to me as well. But he has to prove I was there rather than me having to prove I wasn't."

"Johnnie," she said, "you *were* there. The point at issue is when."

They gazed at each other. "And you really believe that I could have killed Catherine?"

"No," she said. "Not the way . . . the way she was killed. I know you didn't do that. But . . . you were so angry last night I was terrified that you might lose your temper with her . . . and hit her. As you did once before."

"As I did once before. Well, Curtis doesn't know anything about that. Or how angry I was."

"Um," she said.

His head came up again.

"I am such a fool," she said. "When he told me on the phone that Cathy was dead . . . I. . . ." Her eyes were enormous. "I said something like . . . 'Johnnie did that'?"

She waited for an outburst, but John merely drank some brandy, then grinned. "I thought his manner changed after the telephone conversation. So you did think I had killed her?"

"I didn't know what to think. I couldn't really believe she was dead. I knew you had gone back to have it out with her . . . anything might have happened. Oh, Johnnie, I am so terribly sorry."

He came across to sit beside her and put his arm round her shoulders. "So he thinks I invented that hour's delay on the road. Well, he'll just have to prove otherwise. And he can't force you to testify against your husband. Anyway, he'll have found Joseph by now."

"And you really believe Joseph killed her? Like that?"

"It's because of the way she was killed I think Joseph did it. Don't you think he's guilty?"

"I have no idea."

"But you never liked him."

"I hated him." She gave a nervous smile. "I suppose I was jealous of the friendship between you and him, while I was all alone, on the outside as it were, looking in."

"You were never alone, my darling. Not as far as I was concerned."

She squeezed his hand. "Anyway, I hated him."

"You once said you thought he was evil. Well, maybe you were right. Anyway, it all fits, don't you see? Cathy boasted he was her lover. He was. But what she didn't understand was that he could be jealous of her carrying on with other men, and that being a Kikuyu, he would be capable of taking such a terrible revenge."

"God," she said. "What she must have thought, when she realized what he was going to do – God!"

"Yes," John agreed. "As I told Curtis, I hope they hang him so high he can be seen from Mombasa."

She gave him a curious glance. "He was your friend."

"Cathy was my sister."

They finished their drinks and tried to eat lunch. Adèle telephoned the school to explain why Adrian hadn't gone in that day – she could tell from the schoolmistress's tone that word of what had happened must have spread right round Nairobi, and hastily hung up before she could get involved in a conversation.

Then they tried to rest, but both were on edge. "I should be making arrangements for the funeral," John said. "I'm not sure of the form in a murder case. I suppose there'll have to be an autopsy . . . God. I'd better ring Curtis and find out what's happening." But when he called the police station he was informed that Inspector Curtis had gone out.

"Who shall I say called, sah?" asked the sergeant on the desk.

"John Barclay. When Mr Curtis comes in, ask him to get in touch with me as soon as possible, will you?"

"Mr Barclay," the sergeant said. "Where you calling from, Mr Barclay?"

"Why, Naivasha, of course."

"Ah." The sergeant seemed relieved. "Inspector Curtis going to be in touch with you soon, Mr Barclay."

John hung up. "So we have to wait for that twerp."

"I suppose he's rushing around collecting clues or something," Adèle said.

"He'd better be rushing around collecting Joseph," John growled, and looked out of the bedroom window to see two police cars coming down the drive. "Ah, he must have been on his way here all the time. I thought that sergeant sounded a bit odd."

Hastily he dressed and went downstairs. Curtis was already out of the car, accompanied by his detective sergeant and two uniformed constables. Facing them was Ali, Safah's grandson, who had inherited the position of butler – and was equally inclined to treat all callers with suspicion.

"They say they want to see you, Mr John," he explained.

"Well, I want to see them," John said. "Come in, Curtis. Come in. What news? I've been trying to get in touch with you to find out about things like funerals."

Curtis came up the steps slowly, his sergeant immediately behind him; the constables remained at the foot. He said nothing until he reached the verandah, then he spoke in a very careful voice. "John Adrian Barclay," he said, "I have a warrant here charging you with the murder of Catherine, Dowager Lady Portington, on the morning of Sunday, 19 March last. You are not obliged to say anything in response to this charge, but I must warn you that if you do, it will be taken down and may be used in evidence against you."

12

The news that Lady Portington had died caught most evening papers in the western world, and merited a small paragraph. The news that she had been murdered reached London in time for the morning editions, and most of these had time to insert a Stop Press with the latest information – that her own brother had been charged with the crime.

Thus Catherine's last act became headlines. But by the following morning there had been the inevitable leaks, and then the headlines became banner: LADY POR-TINGTON SLAIN BY OWN BROTHER IN BIZARRE AFRICAN RITUAL! they blared. It made no difference that John was a long way from being found guilty; the possibility that he could have killed his only sister and in some unspeakable manner, was too good to be missed.

"It's horrifying," Adèle said. Appalled to see her husband being escorted off, she had hurried behind the police cars into town and insisted on being present when he was formally charged at a special session of the magistrate's court; it only took five minutes as Curtis asked for, and got, a remand of a week. But the detective raised no objection next day when Mrs Barclay wanted to visit her husband's cell. Not that she appreciated his cooperation. "Curtis is having the time of his life. And now the newspapers. . . ."

"Have you rung the children?" John asked. He had been given a cell with some creature comforts, and was even allowed to read the newspapers, but they had not reassured him at all. He felt as if he were stumbling his way through some unimaginable nightmare in which only he was sane. Because even Dela, however loyal she was being now, had thought he could have done it.

"I got hold of Lizzie and explained what a terrible mistake there's been, and she promised to contact Mal. I'm afraid

I've rather kept Adrian in the dark. When are they going to let you out of here?"

"I don't think they are. Billy Adams made a formal application for bail yesterday and was turned down. Murder trial and all that."

"Oh, God! Johnnie, are you sure Billy can handle it?"

"He knows his way around a court."

"Yes, but a murder trial? And one like this?"

"I don't honestly think there's anyone better in Kenya."

"I was thinking of going outside Kenya."

"I doubt that's necessary."

"Do you? Johnnie, they are putting you on trial for your life!"

Billy Adams, when he came in that afternoon, was inclined to agree. "Of course you have my total support," he said. "But frankly, I've seen the evidence, and with what the prosecution have stacked up against you, it is going to be sticky. The only remotely good thing about the situation, from our point of view, is that they haven't found the murder weapon yet. You know they've virtually taken the farm apart? And gone over the road between Naivasha and Nairobi with fine toothed combs, in case you threw a sharp instrument from the car windows? They've even had divers in the lake itself."

"Damned incompetent swine," John growled. "When I think what poor Dela must have gone through, with them actually in the house ... to no purpose. I just can't see what they *can* have. For God's sake, do I look like the sort of chap who would cut his own sister up?"

"Well, they think they can prove that you are, and did. I've had a chat with the Attorney-General, and he is absolutely certain not only of your guilt, but that he can prove it."

"You mean they haven't found Kinshasu, and are desperate to bring somebody to court?"

"They didn't have to find Kinshasu. He found them."

"And they didn't arrest him?"

"No, they didn't. Because he has a cast-iron alibi. Or at

284

least one to which half a dozen people are prepared to swear."

"His friends, you mean."

"Agreed. But you don't have any alibi at all. They won't accept that falling asleep at the wheel story."

"What about the scratches on the car? I drove into a bush."

"There were scratches on the car before, John. So by itself that wouldn't amount to much. But when you consider the motive. . . ."

"I have a motive for murdering Catherine?"

"I'm afraid you do, in the eyes of the police. And they reckon the jury will agree with them. They have statements from the guests at Lady Portington's party the night she was killed that you were very angry with her."

"For God's sake! Do you mean every time a brother and sister have a spat one of them is guilty of murder?"

"They also have a statement from Lady Portington's ex-butler, a man she called Murgatroyd, that you once threatened to beat her up in her own house."

"Murgatroyd? Jesus!"

"Did you?"

"Oh, perhaps I may have threatened to. One says things like that. But that was years ago, after we had had a particularly vicious row."

"Do you realize what you're saying? That may have been years ago, but they also have a statement from Joseph Kinshasu that he heard you threaten to break her neck only the day after she arrived back. Ten days before she *was* killed."

"Joseph said that?"

"Was he lying?"

"Oh, we probably had words. But Joseph – you say he has an alibi?"

"One I doubt we are going to be able to break."

"All right," John said wearily. "I may have threatened her once or twice. She really did some quite unforgivable things, you know. But you are not going to convince me any jury is going to accept that I had a motive to kill her,

285

much less that I would. And what about the way she died? Curtis himself said that he didn't think the murderer *meant* to kill her, he just tied the gag too tightly. And then, to circumcise her . . . Christ, the man would have had to be demented. I vomited when I saw it."

"Either demented, or devilishly cunning. The police have it all worked out, John. They reckon you intended to make it look like a Kikuyu killing, as if Joseph had done it. As for vomiting, well . . . you could've stuck your finger down your own throat."

"But *why?*" John asked. "Okay, we quarrelled endlessly. I threatened to break her neck. It's the way I talk. She embarrassed me. I can't see sufficient motive there for me to kill her. And I don't believe any jury will, either."

"They may well do," Adams said sombrely. "When they hear extracts from Lady Portington's diaries." He sighed as John's head came up. "They found them, locked in that huge trunk she always travelled with. Johnnie, I'm afraid this is going to be very, very nasty."

Committed for trial the following Monday, the defence having offered no evidence in rebuttal of the police charge, John Barclay finally came before the supreme court in June. By then the long rains had started and Nairobi was submerged in a sullen downpour, but that had not kept the crowds away. The black people came because a bwana, and a very famous one, was on trial for his life; they wanted to see how the white man's justice was going to deal with one of its own. The Kenya whites came because it was the biggest event in most of their lives, because quite a few of them had known Cathy Portington, and because several of them had been subpoenaed as witnesses. The local reporters came because there was no other news in Kenya which compared with this, and the foreign press came because they had been sent by their editors. In the three months since the murder, international interest in the case had been swamped by other events, such as Hitler and Czechoslovakia and the Australian touring team in England, but again there had been leaks, and word had reached

London that this could be the most sensational murder trial in history. In view of the identity of the accused, there was even an observer from the Colonial Office.

Also attending was Sir Huntley Makepeace. The appearance of England's most famous KC for the defence would alone have made the trial exciting. The rumour was that he had not wanted to take the brief, and had only been persuaded to do so after a personal appeal from Adèle Barclay, who had travelled to England especially to see him.

And John was intensely grateful for his presence, even if Sir Huntley, a small, intense man with a little moustache, had not been particularly optimistic. He reminded him of Lord Delamere, and *that* was reassuring enough.

"They seem to have a lot stacked against you," Makepeace remarked at their second meeting, after he had had a chance to sift through the evidence. "But of course most of it is hearsay and circumstantial. The hour you lost with the car is a pity, but we might even be able to get round that. I have my ideas there. The crux of the business is those diaries and what is in them. I have asked for a transcript, but I haven't got it yet. Apparently there is a great deal of material. I don't suppose you know what is in them, Mr Barclay?"

"No," John said. "Although I could make an educated guess."

"And would you guess that they might incriminate you?"

"I don't see how they can. She didn't expect to be murdered."

"Agreed. But if she recorded the various threats you are supposed to have made, they might carry some weight. Although I wouldn't have supposed that an adequate reason for the confidence the prosecution appear to have in them." He glanced from John to Adèle, who had been allowed to attend the interview – John Barclay was still being treated with the utmost courtesy and cooperation by the police. "Can you think of any reason why they should be so confident? Either of you?"

John and Adèle looked at each other, and Adèle gave a little shiver.

Which did not escape Makepeace's eye. "I'm afraid I am simply going to have to press you on this one," he said. "You see, the diaries will be introduced as evidence by the prosecution but whatever Lady Portington wrote in them is going to be rather, how shall I put it – rather cold, if it is merely submitted in book form, as it were. I am sure Mr Rawlings will do the best he can with his witnesses by relating any entries concerning them to establish the truth of what your sister recorded; but he can't relate them to any entry about you, or your wife" – he glanced at Adèle again – "because that would be hearsay."

"So what are we worrying about?"

"Simply that the police have built up a strong circumstantial case against you. It has holes in it, especially the missing weapon, but they might be able to make it stick unless we present a defence. As we have absolutely no witnesses to what happened that night from your point of view, the only good defence we have is you. If I can put you in the box and you come across as innocent, and you can stand up to whatever Rawlings throws at you in cross-examination, their case may well collapse. But" – he held up his finger as John would have spoken – "if I do that, he can quote the relevant diary entries at you, and ask you, under oath, to confirm or deny the truth of them. I would like to know how you feel about that."

"Oh, God," Adèle muttered.

"Bad as that, is it?"

"It's just that things happened, years ago, which, well, I would hate to have dragged up again now."

"Things affecting you both?"

"I'm afraid so," John said. "And God knows how Cathy recorded them."

"I mean, the children," Adèle said, and stared at the barrister, pink spots in her cheeks.

"Quite so," Makepeace agreed. "Well, you must decide, of course. I think if I can put you on the stand, Mr Barclay, I can destroy the prosecution contention. If I don't, then I cannot guarantee anything. You will have to decide whether your children will be more embarrassed to have some unfor-

tunate revelations about your youthful adventures read out
in court than they would be to see their father hanged for
murder."

"You can't be serious," Adèle protested.

"I'm afraid it could come to that, Mrs Barclay. Now, why
don't you tell me just what you suspect may have been in
those diaries, and we can decide how best to treat the
matter."

The courtroom was packed when the Attorney-General,
Herbert Rawlings, outlined the prosecution case against
John Barclay to a jury consisting of twelve white men. All
of them were at least acquaintances of the accused, but
Rawlings did not consider this necessarily a bad thing;
because of his decision to stand aloof from the mainstream
of the colony's social and political life, John Barclay had
never possessed the popularity of his father.

The prosecution case had been meticulously put together.
Makepeace had by now of course obtained his transcript,
and John had required only a brief glance at Cathy's record-
ing of that night at the Muthaiga Club in 1919 to realize
his worst fears about the diaries were true.

Now he sat in the dock, wearing a white linen suit despite
the heat – Makepeace's recommendation – and looking
across the court to where the Attorney-General and his two
assistants sat alongside Makepeace and Billy Adams, facing
the Lord Chief Justice. The robes and white wigs seemed
indicative of the inexorable precepts of British justice and
he knew he was in for an ordeal, quite apart from the fight
for his life.

The jury were told of a long love-hate relationship
between the accused and his sister, Rawlings dropping hints
which sent several reporters scurrying for the cable office
– this was going to be even better than they had hoped.
Rawlings went on to say how hate had eventually prevailed
over love, how John Barclay had eventually ordered her out
of the colony, and how, when she had returned in defiance
of his dictat, he had again threatened her, and when she had
ignored his threats, he had finally worked out his dastardly

scheme for doing away with her and causing the blame to be thrown on his sister's African servant.

While his character and reputation were thus being publicly destroyed, John, on Makepeace's instructions, sat staring straight in front of him, endeavouring to prevent any of his emotions from showing on his face. "Bowed head, twitchy hands are admissions of guilt, in the eyes of the layman," Makepeace had insisted.

In fact it was easier than he had supposed, mainly because his mind kept drifting off to irrelevancies. Or were they irrelevancies? He kept seeing the funeral, on that rainswept hill behind the farm, where Father and Mother were already buried. Cathy's was the third grave, and there had been only a small congregation: Adèle and Adams, Curtis and the Governor, the people who had been at that famous party, himself and the policemen who formed his escort.

And Joseph Kinshasu, come to pay his last respects to the woman who had been his mistress. And whom he had then brutally torn to death? They had looked across the grave at each other, and John had no doubt his eyes had been smouldering as much as Joseph's. Because Joseph was free. But *he* would be free one day. And then there would have to be a reckoning. Sometimes he felt that was all he had to look forward to.

Beside that, being castigated by a succession of witnesses was hardly important. But it was galling when he knew that not only almost everyone he knew, but also his own family, were sitting in the gallery watching and listening. Lizzie and Mal had both insisted on returning to lend moral support, and Adèle had decided that they should hear and see everything as it happened, rather than read a biased account in the newspapers.

Dela was actually revealing in this crisis far more strength than he had ever suspected her of possessing. And when he took the stand, her own character was going to come under fire, as she well knew.

First, however, there was the whole weight of the prosecution case to be endured. Rawlings completed his speech by promising to convince the jury that not only had John Barclay had the motive for murdering his sister, but that he had hated her enough to do so, had had the opportunity and had indeed been discovered literally red-handed at the scene of the crime. Then the long list of witnesses began, and continued for some two days.

Desk Sergeant Rawali told how he had received a telephone call from a very distraught John Barclay at five twenty-five on the morning of Sunday, 19 March, calling for police and an ambulance.

"Distraught?" Makepeace asked in cross-examination. "You had no doubt of this?"

"No, sir," Sergeant Rawali said.

Detective Sergeant Kinloko told how he had immediately telephoned Detective Inspector Curtis, and on Curtis's instructions had summoned two constables and a police photographer and gone to the house. He had also telephoned for the police doctor and the ambulance. He related finding John Barclay waiting for them, wearing evening dress which had bloodstains on it and with bloodstains on his hands.

"Would you say he was in a state of collapse?" Makepeace asked.

"Oh, close, sah, close," Kinloko agreed. "I give him a glass of brandy."

Dr Miller gave evidence of how the body appeared, and of his preliminary examination, and then of his post-mortem findings. "The victim was a woman of fifty-seven," he told the jury, "and had lived a full life. There was some cirrhosis of the liver and an equal amount of degeneration of the kidneys. Heart and lungs were in good condition generally. Cause of death was asphyxia. The gag was too tight, and she was subjected to an exceptional amount of pain and humiliation." He looked hopefully at Mr Rawlings, who agreed.

"I would request that the court be cleared, your honour," he suggested to the Lord Chief Justice, "while evidence as to the physical injuries suffered by Lady Portington is submitted."

291

His lordship looked at Makepeace, who grunted his assent. Reporters and spectators filed out, whispering amongst themselves, and Miller went into the details of exactly what had been done to Catherine Portington.

"Is it your opinion, doctor," Rawlings asked, "supposing she had not suffocated but had not been found for several hours, that she would have died of those injuries?"

"That would entirely depend on the length of time before she was found," Miller said. "The bleeding was considerable, but slow."

Rawlings left the rest to Makepeace, but was rather put out when the defence did not pursue the point that death then had really been accidental; Makepeace knew that was flogging a dead horse. He did, however, ask the doctor about the external condition of Lady Portington's body, apart from the knife cuts.

"Well," the doctor said, " her wrists and ankles were very badly bruised, from where she had strained on the cords binding her to the bed."

"But this would have happened when she was being cut and trying to free herself," Makepeace suggested.

"Possibly," Miller agreed cautiously.

"What I would like you to tell the jury is whether there were any marks on her body consistent with her having been manhandled on to the bed and held there forcibly while she was tied up."

"Well," Miller said.

"I need a straight answer, doctor."

"I would say not."

"In other words, she submitted to being tied up. This would suggest, would it not, that the murderer was not only someone she knew intimately, but someone with whom she was used to having intercourse, perhaps of an, ah, unusual variety. It would hardly have been someone who, however well known, or however close to Lady Portington, she knew to hate her, or who had threatened to kill her?"

Rawlings objected. "That is calling for an opinion outside the professional capability of the witness, my lord."

His lordship upheld the objection and instructed Dr

Miller not to reply. Makepeace did not pursue the matter. He was well satisfied; he knew he was accumulating small areas of doubt in the minds of the jury.

While the court was cleared, the police photographer presented his exhibits, and the truly dreadful photographs were circulated around the jury. Then the spectators were allowed back in, and if they still felt cheated of their pound of flesh, were soon fascinated by the revelations of the afternoon and the next day. Only two of Lady Portington's old crowd were still available, and they must have bitterly regretted being so. One was the American lady, who had married again and was now Mrs Whethers.

"Believe me, Mrs Whethers," Rawlings said, "it embarrasses me more than you to raise events which happened fifteen years ago, in what may be called a different era, an era when, perhaps as a result of the ending of the Great War, we were all somewhat more exuberant than we are now. Apart from being younger," he added with involuntary ungallantry. Mrs Whethers had taken the precaution of wearing a veil, so her expression was not easily observed.

"But I am afraid I must," Rawlings went on. "I would like to read to you an extract from the deceased's diary, Crown Exhibit Number One" – he picked up one of several small books from the table in front of him – "relating to a party held at Lady Portington's house on an evening in June 1923." He opened the book at a marked page and cleared his throat. "There is a list of guests and the menu for the dinner, with which I will not bore you, but then Lady Portington writes, 'What a shambles. Dela made a fool of herself refusing to go beddybyes with Jimmy W. Little B. She would have shared with OP too.' " He raised his head. "May I ask you to identify the initials OP to the best of your ability?"

"Olivia Paine," the witness said in a low voice. "Myself."

"You were at that party?"

"Yes."

Rawlings continued reading. " 'Lost T. Really wanted her buggered. No one would play. All scared of JB. So had

293

puss shaved. What a scream. Felt quite S afterward. Had 2+ with J. Then the B started threatening me, with what JB would do to me. Had to read her the RA. Will she squeal? I think I can control that.' "

The court was absolutely quiet, but heads had turned to look at Adèle, who refused to lower her gaze either and sat staring straight in front of her, her children immobile at her side.

"Would you say that is as you recall the evening, Mrs Whethers?"

"I . . . I don't know about afterward," Olivia Whethers said. "I was in bed."

· There was a rustle of laughter, and his lordship banged his gavel.

"But the earlier part you recall?"

"Yes."

"Would you say that Mrs Barclay was upset by the incident?"

"She was wild." Mrs Whethers shrugged. "It was really just a bit of fun. Like, well debagging, I guess. We all do silly things when we're young. But Adèle – Mrs Barclay – she really lost her temper. Called us a whole lot of names."

"Can you remember the names?"

"Must I?"

"I'm afraid so."

"Oh, she called us bastards, and whores, and swore she would get even with us."

"Did she say how?"

"She was going to tell her husband."

"The JB referred to in the diary. Thank you, Mrs Whethers."

"This bit of fun, as you put it, Mrs Whethers," Makepeace said, "took place after dinner, as the diary says. Lady Portington has recorded that it was a good dinner, and " – he looked down at the typewritten copy of the relevant entry he had been given – "that twenty-five bottles of champagne and sixteen bottles of claret were consumed, together with four bottles of brandy. What a meticulous housekeeper she

294

was. Between twenty people. Would you estimate that you were sober when the game began?"

"Well, I guess not. None of us were. It wasn't," she explained, "the sort of game you played when stone cold sober."

His lordship banged his gavel, and Makepeace waited for the murmur to subside.

"Therefore is your memory accurate as to what happened? You had your 'fun' with Mrs Barclay. Can you remember anything anyone said while it was happening?"

"Well, no."

"But you do remember what Mrs Barclay said."

"Well, she was shouting."

"Can you remember anything Lady Portington said?"

"Well, not exactly."

"Had she drunk as much as the rest of you?"

"Oh, yes. Cathy could drink any of us under the table."

"Therefore you would say she was drunk?"

"Objection." Rawlings was on his feet "Calls for a conclusion on the part of the witness."

"Sustained," his lordship agreed.

"But you were drunk, Mrs Whethers?"

"Well, I guess I was pretty tight."

"And yet you can remember what Mrs Barclay said, but not what anyone else said. They were speaking, I suppose?"

"Of course they were speaking," Mrs Whethers snapped, at last growing angry. "Maybe I just wasn't listening to them."

Makepeace did not react to her riposte. "Do you keep a diary?"

"Heavens no."

"But if you had done so, in view of the amount you had had to drink, do you think you would have been able to recall anything that was said after dinner that night when you filled in your diary the next morning?"

"Well, maybe if I was Cathy. She sure could hold her liquor like nobody I know."

Makepeace called it a day. He was in danger of being bruised. But worse was to follow, for the other witness of that night was Jimmy Wildman himself, brought out from England especially.

"I think we had sobered up quite a lot when Dela woke up and started threatening us," he said. "After all. . . ." He checked himself, clearly remembering the 2+, which raised another laugh.

"And can you remember the exchange between Lady Portington and Mrs Barclay?" Rawlings asked.

"Well, the beginning of it. Dela was threatening us with charges of rape and assault and heavens knows what else. I thought she meant it. I was scared, I can tell you. I mean, it was just a bit of fun. There was no need to react like that."

"And what did Lady Portington say in reply to these threats?"

"I don't know. She sent me out of the room."

"But from what you heard, was it your opinion that Mrs Barclay was threatening Lady Portington with what her husband would do to her when he found out about the evening's activities?"

"And to me," Jimmy said, and gave an even more nervous glance at the dock. "I was terrified."

"But no charges were ever brought against you?"

"Nothing was ever said of it again."

"And Mr Barclay never approached you on the matter."

"No." Jimmy wiped his brow with his handkerchief.

"So Lady Portington must have convinced Mrs Barclay, somehow, that she would be better off not going to the police, or telling her husband? Or perhaps I should say, worse off if she did do either of those things?"

"I should say so."

"Almost as if she were blackmailing her sister-in-law with some piece of information which Mrs Barclay had previously been unaware of?"

"Objection, m'lud," Makepeace said.

But Jimmy had already answered, "Almost."

"Strike question and answer from the record," his lordship ordered.

Rawlings did not look displeased. "I will now read you

another extract from the diary, written immediately following that which I have already quoted, Mr Wildman. 'Told her about JB and me, with knobs on. Poor little B. Almost felt sorry for her. Quite shattered. No more trouble there, I fancy. Might even be able to bring her round. Ha!' " He paused and raised his head, while the court was absolutely silent. "Would you have any idea to what Lady Portington was referring?"

"I could make a guess."

Makepeace was on his feet, but Rawlings beat him to it. "I do not want a guess, Mr Wildman. I wish to know if you have any knowledge of what Lady Portington was referring to."

"She never told me, if that's what you mean," Jimmy said. "I would say that was going a bit far, even for Cathy."

"Strike that remark," his lordship snapped.

But the Attorney-General had made his point. The reporters, spellbound for the previous few moments, were jostling to get through the door. John kept his head up with an effort and gazed at Adèle. She blew him a kiss, and Lizzie waved.

"I will have order in my court," his lordship said. "Any further disturbance, and I will order this room cleared. Are you finished with the witness, Mr Rawlings?"

"Yes, my lord."

His lordship looked at Makepeace, who shrugged. "I have no questions of this witness, m'lud."

"What do the children think of it?" John asked as he ate his dinner.

"I have an idea they think you're quite a hero," Adèle confessed. "You do have this rather strait-laced image, you know. And now here you are, accused of having been to bed with your sister and then bumping her off." She gave a shrug, and looked at Billy Adams, who formed the third around the little table in the cell; the two policemen stood just inside the door, watching but not interfering with the waiters from the Norfolk who were serving the meal. "What are we going to do?"

297

"God knows. Makepeace doesn't confide."

"Where the devil is he, anyway?" John asked.

"Said he had someone to meet," Adams told him. "Coming up from the coast. Old friend, or something."

"I think that's awful," Adèle said. "At a time like this. And after . . . Just how damaging do you think Wildman's testimony was, Billy?"

"What Wildman said is irrelevant. Introducing that piece of evidence is what is damaging. It adds another motive, don't you see? If Lady Portington was blackmailing both you and John . . . well. And there's the diary record of what happened at the Muthaiga Club, too." He gave Adèle a nervous glance.

"Dela knows all about that," John reassured him. "And Cathy's recounting of it, according to the transcript I have, was rather exaggerated."

Adams nodded. "But the jury don't know about it yet. And it's pretty explicit."

"I suppose swearing it's all lies isn't going to solve anything."

Billy gazed at him. "Can you do that? *All* lies?"

John flushed. "I . . . she was in my bed before I knew what was happening."

"And when he did realize what was happening, Johnnie hit her," Adèle snapped. "So hard she lost a tooth."

"Who's going to support that evidence?" Adams asked. "How long ago was that? Eighteen years? It'll be your word, a man fighting for his life, against the written evidence of the murdered person, undoubtedly written *at the time*."

"My God, my God, my God," Adèle said.

"I suppose Makepeace *is* aware of all this?" John demanded.

"Very much so. On the other hand . . ." Billy sighed. "I'm sure he's a good man, and I know I recommended bringing him out. And I also know he's costing a fortune. But . . ."

"Now you're not so sure he's worth his money?"

"Well, he certainly isn't burning any midnight oil trying to find a defence. Last night, for instance, he was out by himself. Went into the native quarter. Wouldn't say what for, but. . . ." He glanced at Adèle.

"He was looking to sample a bit of local talent," John said bitterly.

"I'm afraid it appears like it. And now, having a friend join him at a time like this, almost as if he were on holiday . . . by God, I hope he knows what he is doing."

There was no evidence of Makepeace's friend having arrived when court resumed on the third day. But the barrister himself seemed in a most urbane mood, shook John's hand and winked just before the session started.

The court was as crowded as ever, with everyone hoping that the sensational revelations of the previous day would be continued and perhaps expanded. But in the first instance they were disappointed; Rawlings knew the defence had nothing better than to place the accused on the stand, and he was saving his really heavy artillery for his cross-examination. Yet the evidence continued to be damning enough. All the guests at Cathy's last dinner party were trotted out, one after the other, to relate how John Barclay and his sister had quarrelled, how John had stormed out of the Muthaiga Club, and how, immediately before leaving, he had pointed at Lady Portington and shouted, "I am coming to see you tomorrow morning, and you had better have Kinshasu out of there by then." Rawlings did not labour any of these points; he left it to the jury to appreciate that John Barclay had done exactly what he had said he would do.

Makepeace did not cross-examine any of these witnesses. Indeed, he seemed to have lost all interest in the case, and gazed at the ceiling throughout. From time to time Billy Adams would whisper urgently in his ear, but he merely gave a quick shake of his head each time.

The last witness for the prosecution was Joseph Kinshasu. He wore a neat blue suit and a quiet tie, and was by far the most composed person in the courtroom, especially when Rawlings began exploring his relationship with the Barclays. He avoided John's gaze and in a soft voice told of his war service with the accused, and of his resignation following his master's marriage.

"Will you tell the court why you resigned?" Rawlings asked.

Joseph continued to look at the Attorney-General. "Because Mrs Barclay did not like me," he said.

He then told how he had attempted to regain his old job after his release from prison, and been rejected.

"Why do you think Mr Barclay would not take you back?" Rawlings asked.

"Because Mrs Barclay would not let him," Joseph replied.

Then he told of going to England, and finally meeting Lady Portington, who had offered him a job, and how Lady Portington had decided to return to Nairobi.

"Will you describe to the court the nature of your employment by Lady Portington?"

"I was her steward," Joseph said.

"And, ah, would you describe the exact relationship between yourself and the deceased?"

"I was her lover," Joseph said simply.

Once again, sensation, even if quite a few people in court knew it was coming.

"An, ah, unusual arrangement," Rawlings commented, when order had been restored.

"Not so unusual," Joseph observed.

"But one of which a large number of people might not approve. Especially here in Kenya."

"I wouldn't know about that," Joseph said.

"I am sure you did understand that, Kinshasu. Yet you returned here, with Lady Portington."

"It was what Catherine wanted to do," Joseph said, with studied insolence.

His lordship again had to use his gavel.

"It was what *Catherine* wanted to do," Rawlings repeated carefully. "Did you suppose Mr Barclay would approve of this relationship?"

"No," Joseph said.

"Did you in fact suppose he might be angry about it?"

"Yes."

"Very angry?"

"I thought he would be very angry."

"But this did not bother you, or Lady Portington?"

"It did not bother us."

"Was Lady Portington afraid her brother might assault her?"

"He had assaulted her before," Joseph said.

"And therefore might do so again. What was her attitude to this?"

"That I would protect her."

"Were you present when Mr Barclay called upon the deceased, immediately after her return to Nairobi?"

"I was there," Joseph agreed.

"Did Mr Barclay threaten Lady Portington?"

"Yes."

"Can you remember his exact words?"

"He said, 'I ought to break your neck.'"

"You were present when he said that?"

"No. I was in the bar, next door. But I could hear what was being said."

"And what did you do?"

"Nothing. Catherine would have called me if she needed me."

"But when she did call you, because she needed you, you weren't there."

"I had been given the night off," Joseph said.

"Do you regret not being there, Kinshasu?"

"I regret that very much," Joseph said.

"Thank you. Your witness, Sir Huntley."

"I have no questions, m'lud."

"Then that concludes the evidence for the prosecution."

The Chief Justice looked at the clock. But it was only just after three. "I think you could begin your defence immediately, Sir Huntley," he said. Like everyone else in the room he could not see exactly what sort of defence could be presented, save a blank denial of everything claimed or implied by the Crown.

"Thank you, m'lud." Sir Huntley stood up, hands

301

hanging absolutely straight at his side. "I would like to ask that you dismiss this case."

"Sir Huntley?"

"With respect, m'lud, the prosecution have *proved* nothing with respect to the murder of Lady Portington, except that she was killed in a rather unpleasant fashion, and probably by accident. They have indicated that my client may have had a reason for disliking the deceased, but on the evidence of what we have heard, so did a great number of other people. They have indicated that my client had the opportunity to kill his sister. I am prepared to refute that, but in any event, so did a large number of other people. They have produced no murder weapon. They have not even properly identified a murder weapon. 'Some kind of sharp instrument' is a trifle vague. They have indicated that Mr Barclay's fingerprints were found in several places. M'lud, Mr Barclay does not deny that he was there; it was he who called the police upon discovering his sister's mutilated body. They have endeavoured to blacken my client's reputation. My client will deny all of the allegations against him. It is therefore my contention that no case has been presented, which is why I am asking for dismissal. With costs," he added as an afterthought.

"Really, Sir Huntley," the Chief Justice said, visibly nettled. "While I am aware you have been present at far more murder trials than anyone else in this court, I am sure that there have been very few of them where the accused has not denied his guilt, or where the police have managed to cross every t and dot every i, as it were. It is my opinion that the accused has a case to answer, and I would like you to present that answer, if you would be good enough." Clearly he had nearly said, *if you can*.

Sir Huntley gave a brief bow, as if to reply, *then be it on your own head*. "Very good, m'lud. I call Billy Bsambi."

Heads turned. Rawlings ticked the name off on his sheet but did not look concerned.

The little black man entered the court, took the oath and faced Makepeace. His suit was obviously new, and ill-fitting, but he looked almost as composed as Joseph had done.

302

"Your name is Billy Bsambi?"

"Yes, sah."

"You live in Nairobi?"

"Yes, sah."

"What is your occupation?"

"Well, sah, I don't have no job right this minute."

"Then how do you make a living?"

"Well, sah, I goes around in the morning and sees what I can find from other people's dustbins. That ain't stealing," he added hastily. "They have thrown those things away." He did not look the least embarrassed.

Rawlings suddenly sat straight, frowning.

"Will you tell the court if you were doing this on the morning of Sunday, 19 March, last?"

"I do it every morning, sah."

"And what time would this have been?"

"Well, sah, it must be just before light, or I would get see."

"So you would have been about your business at what hour?"

"I left me home at half past four, sah."

"Can you tell the court if you remember anything about that morning?"

"Oh, yes, sah. I did be up in the good district, and I did be outside the house what belong to Lady Portington."

"What time was this?"

"A quarter to five, sah."

"And did you notice anything about that house?"

"There was lights on," Bsambi said. "Then they went off. Then the front door open. That scare me, and I crouch down."

"What did you see?"

"I see a man leaving the house."

"What kind of man?"

"A black man."

"How can you be sure?"

"I know a black man, sah."

Pandemonium. His lordship banged without success for

303

several minutes. When order was restored, Rawlings was on his feet. "Objection!"

Makepeace raised his eyebrows.

"On what grounds, Mr Rawlings?" his lordship asked.

"Well," Rawlings stumbled, "this witness. . . ."

"His name was given to my learned friend," Makepeace pointed out. "Along with that of my other witnesses. He did not seek to discover what I was going to ask them."

"I am afraid I must overrule your objection, Mr Rawlings," the Chief Justice said. "Continue, Sir Huntley."

"Thank you, m'lud. Now, Bsambi, you saw a black man leave the house. Did you recognize this man?"

"Well, no, sir. It did be dark."

"Will you tell us whether or not there were any motor cars in the yard of Lady Portington's house?"

"Oh, yes, sah. One."

"What sort of car?"

"I ain't knowing about that, sah. It had a soft roof."

"A tourer," Makepeace told him. "Very good. So what did you do next?"

"Well, sah, I wait until I be sure the street be empty, then I go on with what I am doing. There is always one set of rubbish in the bins outside Lady Portington house. So I fill an entire sack. So I leave it there, and I gone down the street, and the next street, and then I come back to that sack to go home."

"What time was this?"

"This was a quarter past five, sah."

"And did anything attract your attention when you went back for that sack?"

"Yes, sah. Blow me if when I am picking up the sack, a car don't come down the street."

"What did this car do?"

"It came down at one lick, sah. Then it turn into the yard of Lady Portington house. It damn near hit the other one."

"Did you recognize *this* car?"

"Oh, yes, sah, that was Mr Barclay car."

"How did you know that?"

304

"Everybody know Mr Barclay car," Bsambi declared. "He been driving it one long time."

Bang went the gavel.

"And what time was this?" Makepeace asked.

"A quarter past five, sah. Exactly."

Sir Huntley did not inquire how the witness knew the time. He left that trap for Rawlings to tumble into. "Thank you, Bsambi. I have no further questions, m'lud."

"Mr Rawlings?"

Rawlings's face was grim. "Bsambi," he said. "I would like you to tell the court who paid you, and how much, to come here today and tell this pack of lies."

"Paid me, sah? Nobody paid me. I am reading about the trial, and I say, that man is innocent. So I gone to Mr Sir Huntley."

Rawlings pointed. "You should have gone to the police. You should have gone to the police three months ago."

"I don't like the police," Bsambi confessed. "They don't like me neither."

The gavel banged.

"Bsambi," Rawlings said. "Do you know the meaning of the word perjury?"

"I ain't knowing that word, sah."

"It means lying under oath. Now, you have taken an oath to tell the truth here today. If you are discovered to be lying, you could be sent to prison for seven years. Do you understand that?"

"Why am I tell a lie, sah?"

Rawlings took a deep breath. "Very well. You claim you saw a black man leaving Lady Portington's house at a quarter to five on the morning of Sunday, 19 March."

"Yes, sah."

"A quarter to five. Exactly."

"Yes, sah."

"And half an hour later, you claim you saw Mr Barclay's Daimler enter the yard."

"Yes, sah."

"A quarter past five, was it?"

"Yes, sah."

"Exactly."

"Yes, sah."

"Bsambi, how can you be so certain of the times?"

"Because I did look at me watch, sah," Bsambi said triumphantly.

"Your watch?"

"This one." Bsambi shot his cuffs, and the gold watch blinked at the court. Now it was John Barclay's turn to sit up straight; he recognized the watch.

Rawlings could recognize its value. "Where did you get that watch, Bsambi?"

"In a dustbin, sah."

"Bsambi, you are a liar."

"I find it in a dustbin, sah," Bsambi said.

Rawlings raised his eyes to heaven, looked at the Chief Justice, who was not regarding him at all kindly in view of the way the prosecution case had been shot to pieces, and then said, "I have no further questions."

"Have you other witnesses, Sir Huntley?" His lordship's tone indicated that he did not consider them necessary.

But Sir Huntley was out for his pound of flesh. "I have, m'lud. I would like to recall Dr Miller."

The doctor had been forewarned, and was in the court.

"Dr Miller, you examined the body of Lady Portington when you arrived at her house on the morning of 19 March," Makepeace said.

"I did."

"From your examination you deduced a probable time of death. How did you do that?"

"One takes the internal body temperature," Miller explained. "A body cools at a certain rate after death. Therefore the temperature of the body indicates, within approximate limits, the time at which death occurred."

"So you were able to tell the court that death took place between four and five in the morning. That is, about an hour and a half before you examined the deceased."

"That is correct."

"Can you possibly be more exact than that?"

306

"It would be a guess. Depending on the physical state of the body, there are minor fluctuations in the cooling rate."

"Well, let me ask you this: could Lady Portington have died after five o'clock?"

Dr Miller hesitated only an instant. He was well aware of the point Sir Huntley was attempting to prove, and he also knew that the point *had* been proved. "No," he said. "If I had to give an exact opinion, remembering always that it can only be an opinion, I would say that death took place nearer four than five."

"Thank you, Dr Miller." But to the obvious dismay of the Chief Justice, Sir Huntley had still more nails to hammer into the coffin of the prosecution case; he had his client's name to clear. "I call Mr John Barclay," he said.

John took the oath. He was feeling totally confused, aware of only a few salient points, such as that Billy Bsambi had been wearing Joseph's new gold watch, and that no one else in the courtroom seemed to know that. But he was also aware that he had won, thanks to the legerdemain of Sir Huntley Makepeace – he was reluctant to consider it in any other light at this moment – and that he had only to follow his advocate's guidance to emerge with flying colours.

"Mr Barclay," Makepeace said. "I am going to read you an extract from your sister's diary, dated 27 November, 1919."

John waited.

Makepeace cleared his throat. " 'Actually had J last night, at the MC. Silly clot reacted stupidly. Do adore J. If only other men like him. Could have wanged away all night. Wish we had. Now I'm just sore.' " The court was hushed as he raised his head. "Can you explain to what Lady Portington was referring? We are assuming that you are the 'J' she is writing of?"

"Yes," John said.

"And the MC is the Muthaiga Club?"

"Yes."

"What happened there?"

"Catherine, my sister, and I had dinner there, and that night she came to my room. I was asleep when she came in, and the next thing I knew she was sitting on me. She . . . she had nothing on."

"I must ask you this, Mr Barclay: did you have sexual intercourse with your sister?"

"No," John said.

"Did you enter her vagina?"

"I did. But involuntarily, and I withdrew immediately."

"Did you do anything else?"

"Yes. I hit her."

"Hard?"

"I believe very hard. I broke one of her teeth."

"On the night of 27 November, 1919?"

"Yes."

"Was that the cause of enmity between you and your sister?"

"Partly."

"Explain that."

"She obviously resented being hit, and I did not approve of her way of life. And then, after the party where Adèle, my wife, was abused, we quarrelled seriously."

"Did you threaten her?"

"I threatened her with legal action if she did not leave Kenya."

"And she left Kenya. When she returned, many years later, did you threaten her then?"

"I was angry that she had broken her promise and come back. But she persuaded me that she had changed her mode of life. However, at dinner on the night before she died she announced that she had a black lover."

"This angered you?"

"It made me hopping mad."

"Mr Barclay, you announced that you were going to visit your sister on the morning following the dinner party, and you did so. What was your intention?"

"To throw Joseph Kinshasu out of the house."

"Mr Barclay, you are under oath. Have you ever had an incestuous relationship with Lady Portington?"

"No."

308

"Has Lady Portington ever attempted to blackmail you, or your wife?"

"She has never attempted to blackmail me. I think, in leading my wife to believe that she and I did have an incestuous relationship, she may have been guilty of at least emotional blackmail. But only for a short period."

"Because of this, did you ever plan to kill your sister?"

"Good lord, no."

"Mr Barclay, did you kill your sister, on the morning of Sunday, 19 March?"

"No," John said.

"Thank you, Mr Barclay." Makepeace looked at Rawlings, but the Attorney-General sat with his head resting on his hands.

"I must congratulate you, Sir Huntley," the Chief Justice said, signalling his surrender as well.

But Sir Huntley did believe in dotting i's and crossing t's. "I have another witness, m'lud," he said.

His lordship's expression suggested, *Oh no*.

"Your name is Humphrey Leyland?" Sir Huntley asked the somewhat elderly white man in the box. "And you practised as a dentist here in Nairobi in 1919?"

"I did."

"You are now retired, I believe, and living in Mombasa?"

"That is correct."

"But you retain your dental records?"

The smile was brief. "One never knows when they'll be needed."

"Quite so. You have brought with you one of those records, I believe. Would you be good enough to read it to the court?"

Mr Leyland read from the book he had with him. " '29 November, ten a.m., extraction, Lady Portington. Anaesthetic required. Badly broken molar, also badly bruised and contused cheek. Claimed a fall from bed but looked more like blow to me. Suggested she see doctor.' "

"May I ask what year that was?"

Mr Leyland looked at the cover of the book. "1919."

"Thank you, Mr Leyland."

"Will you address the jury now, Sir Huntley?" asked the Chief Justice. "Or, as it is rather late, would you prefer to adjourn until tomorrow."

Sir Huntley looked at Rawlings, who sighed, and got to his feet. "The prosecution wishes to withdraw. . . ."

He never finished the sentence. There was a roar of sound and the spectators surged forward, thrusting the policemen and the bailiffs aside, to surround John and Makepeace and Adams, men shaking their hands and women kissing them. The gavel banged ineffectively, and it was several minutes before order was restored. Then the Chief Justice himself congratulated John, before granting him an absolute discharge and thanking the jury. Rawlings shook his hand. "Fortune favours the brave," he observed enigmatically. "But I'm not sorry about the result."

Adèle and the children had hung back, but now they were in his arms, and the photographers were snapping away, while Sir Huntley Makepeace beamed. "There's a champagne dinner waiting for you," he said. "At the Muthaiga Club."

John was escorted to the door. He looked left and right, but there was no sign of Joseph. He wondered if he would ever know the truth of what had happened, and how it had happened. But at the moment he was too relieved even to hate. At the door, Curtis waited.

"It pays to have friends in the right places, Mr Barclay," Curtis said. "I should have understood that more clearly."

"Sour grapes," Adèle said, as they drove away.

"Oh, indeed," Makepeace agreed. "It was damned bad police work, not checking Leyland's records, and not finding Bsambi."

"I wonder," John said, "if he was ever there to be found."

It was dark, and quiet, in the forest where the meeting had been arranged. Harry Bsambi went there on his bicycle. To his surprise, Joseph Kinshasu was already there waiting for him. But this was a Joseph Kinshasu he had never seen before, for in place of the European clothes he habitually wore, Joseph was tonight dressed in an African robe, with

310

an African hat on his head. No doubt he was celebrating. Well, Bsambi was prepared to celebrate too.

"Man," Bsambi said, "I think I did well."

"You did well, Harry," Joseph agreed.

"You got the money?"

"Right here," Joseph said, patting one of the two brief-cases lying on the ground beside him.

"And I can keep the watch?"

"You can keep the watch, Harry."

"Man, I was scared," Bsambi confessed. "But they didn't see it."

"Nobody saw it," Joseph agreed. "Why don't you count the money?"

Bsambi fell to his knees and opened the case, and stared at the neat piles of notes. He took out one bundle, rifling it through his fingers. Joseph knew Bsambi couldn't count, but it was more money than he had ever held in his hands before. He was a happy man at that moment. It was the best time. Joseph stood behind him, seized his head with his left hand and cut his throat with the knife he held in his right hand.

He had never killed before, and he was surprised by the surge of exhilaration which travelled right through his system as he felt the knife cutting into the flesh and the body going limp in his grasp, and as warm liquid spurted over his hand. But there was no time to enjoy this one. There were other things to be done. . . . He took off his bloodstained robe and put it into the empty bag along with the bloodstained gloves and knife. Then he dressed in his European clothes, which had lain behind the bush, picked up the bags and walked back to town.

He got there at three in the morning, and there was still time to complete his work; he had arranged an all-night alibi with Tom Ngolo. He found the house he wanted and knocked on the door. It was several minutes before the door was opened.

"Man, you stupid or what?" Murgatroyd inquired. "Coming here this hour!"

Joseph had already ascertained that Murgatroyd lived

alone. Presumably he had enough company dreaming of the white woman he had once possessed. "I got something for you," he explained.

"For me?"

"A bequest, from Catherine," Joseph said. "She would be too angry if I did not deliver it. She would come back to haunt me."

"What is it?" Murgatroyd asked suspiciously.

"Money, man, money," Joseph told him. "In this bag. More money than you have ever seen. You going to let me in?"

Murgatroyd hesitated, then stepped away from the door and allowed Joseph into the little house.

13

Makepeace spent a week at Naivasha holidaying with the Barclays. On the third day he and John went fishing on the lake together, and John felt by now that he knew the barrister well enough to ask the question which had been gnawing at his subconscious ever since the last day of the trial. Otherwise, the reason why Joseph had murdered Cathy then engineered a perjury to save John's life was going to haunt him for the rest of that life. Apart from anything else, the case was now officially open again. It made no sense. But worse, it made no sense of the hatred he wanted to feel for the man. "What really happened with Harry Bsambi?"

"I received a note that there was a black man who wished to see me and had information vital to the defence. So I went along."

"That night you wouldn't tell Adams where you were going. We all thought you were off whore-hunting."

"Did you now? I never thought of that. I was a little scared, I can tell you that, wandering down those back alleys by myself in the dark. But it was worth it."

"I reckon we were very lucky. Who do you suppose put him up to it?"

Makepeace studied the ripples spreading across the surface of the still water. "I have a bite." After he had landed the fish, he asked, "What makes you think anyone put him up to it?"

"Maybe I don't believe in happy chances."

"You're a cynic, John," Makepeace told him. "Never look a gift horse in the mouth. And don't put it all down to luck. It was I who located Leyland." He grinned. "Although it was pure luck he was still in the colony, I'll agree."

"Would his evidence have got me off?"

"His evidence would have proved, as it did, that your sister was capable of lying to her diary, which would have been a great help. But I'll agree Bsambi's evidence was vital."

"And suppose I told you that I not only know that he was put up to it, which almost certainly means he was lying, but I also know who did it?"

Makepeace put down his rod and began to gut his catch. "I am growing remarkably deaf as I get older," he said. "Worrying, really. One should never confess, old man. It would rob all us poor codgers of a living."

Adèle threw a dinner party for Makepeace's last night. She had been hesitant, for all the congratulations showered upon John after the trial, and the letters and telegrams which still arrived in shoals every day. She had known as well as anyone that the hysteria was because a white man had been acquitted of a crime, not specifically because John Barclay had been absolved of the murder of his sister. In addition to Billy Adams and his wife she had asked two other Nairobi couples, and they had been happy to accept, and spend the evening talking about everything save the one thing they wanted to discuss more than anything else in the world. Lizzie and Mal were there as well, of course, and even Adrian was allowed to stay up. He had had to be told what was going on, once his father was arrested, even if he was spared the gory details and, like his elder brother and sister, looked upon John as a hero.

Next morning John took Makepeace to the station and said goodbye. But the train also brought the papers, and one glance at the headlines had him hurrying back to the house. Adèle was equally shocked, and they both knew what was going to happen next. Although it was not until the following morning that they saw the police car bouncing down the drive.

John led Curtis into the office. "There's no need to tell me," Curtis said, "because I already checked. Night before last you were host to a dinner party which went on most of the night."

"Yes," John said. "If I hadn't been?"

"Well, just let us suppose Bsambi had been lying when

314

he claimed to have seen you driving up to your sister's house after the murder was committed; his death would be quite a blessing for you, wouldn't it? Then he could never change his mind."

"And Murgatroyd?"

"Now, that I find even more interesting. The papers didn't report, because I wouldn't let them, that they were both ritual killings. Even nastier than Lady Portington's. Castration, other mutilations, the lot."

"You've got the murderers?"

"No. One would suppose they'd be easy to trace, because there was a considerable amount of blood. But it hasn't proved easy so far. And it was grim, I can tell you. Bsambi had his throat cut before he was mutilated. Murgatroyd was banged on the head, tied up and gagged, revived, and then cut up before his own eyes. Anything familiar about that?"

"Jesus Christ!"

"And then a panga was left on his chest. Not the knife used in killing him. But Miller says it could have been the weapon used on your sister."

"Murgatroyd," John breathed. "Of course." He had been so sure it was Joseph. But Murgatroyd was so obvious, now.

"We were coming round to that conclusion ourselves," Curtis said. "But someone beat us to it."

They stared at each other.

"Have you arrested him?" John asked.

"Went to take him into custody immediately, and there he was with his friends Tom Ngolo and Rupert Bolomo and Harry Kinkardu, playing cards. They'd been playing cards all night. 'Man,' Kinshasu said, 'when we get to playing cards, we just don't see the time passing.' So we took the place apart anyway, and everywhere else we could think of – and found nothing. Not a single drop of blood, much less a bloodstained garment – or a bloodstained knife. So we questioned them separately, and we threatened and we cajoled and we nearly went out of our heads, and they each said the same things, over and over again."

"Yet it had to have been Joseph," John said. "It's the only thing that makes sense. Murgatroyd must have killed

Cathy, because she brought Joseph back with her, and Joseph knew that. But he had no evidence, and I imagine he wanted me to sweat a little as well. Then up turned Harry Bsambi . . . my God!"

"Yes?" Curtis asked.

"You think Joseph did that one as well? Two in one night?"

"They were almost identical mutilations."

"Joseph," John said, half to himself. He almost felt admiration for the man. Far from being his sister's murderer, he was his sister's avenger. And he had certainly saved him from the gallows - if he had sent Bsambi to Makepeace. But then . . . "I find it difficult to believe that he did do them both in one night."

"What I would like to know is why he, presuming he is guilty, should have killed Bsambi at all, Mr Barclay."

John looked him in the eye. 'Have you no idea?"

"Well, I might . . . if he was still working for you."

"I can assure you he isn't."

"Then you would like to see him hanged."

"If, as you say, he is guilty of a crime. I would hardly call executing Murgatroyd for the murder of my sister a crime, although I am sure you will disagree with me. As for Bsambi, I repeat, I think it would have been very difficult for Joseph to kill him on the same night, and in such a manner. It would mean he was a bloodthirsty monster, and I can assure you he is not."

"How long is it since you have really known Kinshasu?"

"Oh, a good time. Damn near twenty years. But . . . do leopards really change their spots?"

"Tame leopards can become killers, if turned loose and forced to forage for themselves. Do you know that he accused you of murdering your sister? It was his volunteered statement that led me down that particular garden path."

"Joseph?" John frowned. Of course Joseph had given some pretty damning evidence in court, but he had supposed the police had bullied him into that. But again nothing was making sense — Bsambi had definitely been wearing Joseph's gold watch.

316

"Knowing all the time, you say," Curtis went on, "that Murgatroyd was the killer. Doesn't seem he has too much love for you."

What *was* the fellow playing at? John wondered. Yet he could not doubt that but for Joseph he would now be sitting in a cell awaiting hanging. "As you say, Inspector," he agreed. "Even tame leopards can grow savage. And perhaps bite the hand that used to feed them."

"So tell me why he killed Bsambi? We have no record of his even knowing Bsambi, and we do know most of his associates."

"I haven't the faintest idea."

Curtis gazed at him, and John realized the policeman knew he was lying. But he contented himself with asking, "That's all you have to say?"

"What more is there to say?"

"I'm afraid there may well be a lot more, one day. Don't get me wrong. I haven't made up my mind about Billy Bsambi. I'm damned sure he perjured himself. Why, I can't say, although if I didn't know you were here all that night with as many alibis as Joseph Kinshasu, I'd have you back in that cell by now. But I am not going to lose any sleep over him. And if Murgatroyd did kill your sister, then he deserved to die, and you deserve to be sitting here, and I owe you an apology. And I'll be damned glad to be able to close the file on this case and lose it deep, deep down in the cellar. But that still leaves Kinshasu. I know he killed Murgatroyd, and almost certainly Bsambi as well. And you know that too. And so do at least three other people. Yet we can't touch him as long as those other people support him. They supported him on the night of Catherine Portington's death as well. Maybe they were telling the truth then. They are certainly lying now. Yet when I ask them, or even threaten them, they just look at me and refuse to play ball. I don't like that, Mr Barclay. It gives me an uneasy gut feeling. Did you know that Ngolo and Bolomo and Kinkardu were the men he served his exile sentence with?'

"No, I didn't know that," John said, frowning.

"Well, they were. And I have come across a report from

317

the then commandant up at Chalbi that the four of them indulged in some filthy kind of ritual ceremony. You know the sort of thing."

"Yes," John said.

"No one paid any attention to it at the time. These people are always holding ritual ceremonies. But did you know that your sister refers to Kinshasu's penis in her diary?"

"That doesn't surprise me."

"Maybe not. It's how she described it. I won't go into details, but it certainly reads like some kind of ritual gone wrong. What I'm driving at is this: I have a feeling there is some kind of secret society in existence, of which Kinshasu is either the head or very high up. Of course, Africa is riddled with secret societies and most of them are just an excuse for a little bit of prick pulling. This one seems to enjoy murder, as well. That bothers me."

"It damned well should."

"So I would like you to tell me anything you can think of about Kinshasu, to give me some idea of just what this society is aiming at."

"I've told you, he hasn't worked for me for twenty years."

Curtis looked at him. "Loyalty to a man like Kinshasu could turn out to be an expensive luxury, Mr Barclay." He got up. "As I say, I have little doubt that Bsambi perjured himself on your behalf, and maybe I was hoping for a rematch, one day. Now that's impossible. The one man who could have caused a retrial is dead. Tell me, *did* you murder Lady Portington?"

"I did not," John said.

"I'm glad of that. Then did you, or anyone in your camp, bribe Bsambi to lie for you?"

"No," John said.

"I'm glad of that too." He went to the door, then looked back. "Let's keep in touch."

Adèle bade him a cold goodbye on the verandah, then hurried into the office. "You mean he didn't arrest you?"

John told her about the mutilations.

"Oh, my God!" She stared at the lake, then half turned

318

her head. "Johnnie . . . do you think Bsambi really saw the man leaving the house? And then you arrive?"

It was the first time they had spoken of the trial. Up to last night, with Makepeace in the house, she had not wanted to.

"I don't think Bsambi was anywhere near Cathy's house that Sunday morning."

"But then, if Joseph put him up to it . . ."

"And has now murdered him . . ."

"That's what I mean. Joseph knows that you haven't been proven innocent, after all."

"There's nothing he can do with that knowledge now. Curtis made that point."

"But he must know that too." She looked at him. "Johnnie.. . ."

"Do you want to pack up? No one would blame me for pulling out."

She thought for a moment. "Do you want to?"

"No. I was born right here. I would like to die right here – and know that Mal and Adrian were going to take over the farm."

"And you're not scared of Joseph Kinshasu?"

"No," he said. "I'm not scared of Joseph."

"Then we'll stay," she said. "And see the bastard off."

He grinned. He was actually feeling relieved, and happier than he had been for a long time, with the knowledge that Joseph was not only innocent of Catherine's death, but had avenged it in his own way. Even if it meant that the quiet, well spoken young man he had known and liked so much had turned into a savage? He would have to think about that. "The bastard, as you call him, undoubtedly saved my bacon, my darling girl. Maybe one day he'll ask a favour. We'll cross that bridge when we come to it. Right now . . . let's aim at another happy time."

In fact it was another happy time, even if within two years Great Britain, and the whole world, were again at war. From the Kenyan point of view the enemy was not now the Germans to the south, but the Italians to the north, in

Ethiopia and Somaliland. This was a campaign which had to be won, and quickly. Men and munitions were poured into the colony, and General Cunningham gained the first conclusive Allied victory of the war on land when the Duke of Aosta surrendered his large army in the Abyssinian mountains. It was a splendid set-off to the rather grim news coming out of Europe.

The colony enjoyed the war, even when the Japanese came rather too close for comfort at the other end of the Indian Ocean. As an old soldier, John was recommissioned with the rank of brigadier and placed in charge of mobilizing the home front – which meant that he could be very military without this time having to leave Kenya, or even his own bed for more than the odd few days at a time, which was a great relief to Adèle. She worried about the children, of course, for Mal had joined the RAF and Lizzie was a Wren, but they seemed to bear charmed lives. John worried more about Adrian, for Adèle insisted upon bringing him back from his English public school, because of the bombing, and the standard in Nairobi was not all that high. But he was a bright boy and did not seem to suffer.

There was a little awkwardness about Adèle herself, at the outbreak of the struggle. But not only had she become a nationalized British citizen, she was well known to be vehemently anti-Nazi, and also, Mrs John Barclay, which was far more important. It worried her to see many of the Kenyan and, even more, the Tanganyikan Germans marched off to internment camps, but she refused to let these things interfere with the even tenor of her life, and with Mombasa being more and more used as a staging post for British troops travelling either to North Africa or the Far East, it became quite a social whirl, as the billeting brigadier naturally had to entertain at least the most senior of the officers. They rented a house in Mombasa and spent a good deal of time there, while the farm bristled with activity as food exports grew in importance.

Of Joseph Kinshasu there was no sign. John kept his eyes and his ears open for some word of him, and found nothing. Even Curtis, now Inspector-General, had lost track of him.

"If we're lucky," he said, "he's joined the Army and will get his head shot off. Him and his pals."

John thought he would regret that. He was willing to concede that Joseph had changed a good deal since they campaigned together in Tanganyika, and he had behaved very badly in taking up with Catherine at all, while if he had indeed murdered Bsambi and Murgatroyd he had a streak of primeval brutishness which was certainly frightening. But at the crunch he had created a lie to make sure his old boss did not hang for a crime he had not committed. John knew he would always be grateful for that.

He wondered if he would ever see him again.

But he forgot all about Joseph with the coming of peace, as he and Adèle were invited to the celebratory dinner at Government House, and after the meal he was taken aside by His Excellency. "Back to civvies, eh, John?"

"For the last time. Next year I'll be fifty. They can fight the next war without me."

"I'll say amen to that for both of us. Although I'd bet you're a damn sight fitter than most men half your age. Don't you ever get ill?"

John grinned at him. "I don't believe in it."

"Well, what I wanted to say was this: I think you've done an absolutely magnificent job these past six years. But I also think you and your family have done an even more magnificent job over the past seventy years. Without you, there'd be no Kenya Colony. And people may need to remember that in the times ahead. It really bothers me that neither you nor your father ever got any recognition for it all."

"No statues," John told him. "The one of Hugh Delamere is an abomination."

"I wasn't thinking of a statue. I was thinking of recommending you for a knighthood. Would you go along with that?"

John had to swallow very hard. "Me? My dear fellow, I've been on trial for my life."

"And acquitted."

"There are still a few people around who believe I did

321

it, and then hired Bsambi. And had him bumped off to protect myself."

"Stuff and nonsense. Shall I go ahead?"

"Well," John said, "I should think Dela will be pleased."

Joseph Kinshasu got back to Nairobi in the spring of 1946. The war had seen the ending of all his hopes, and he felt an old and beaten man.

It was the event for which he had been waiting since 1924, the scenario he had drawn in his mind, over and over again, when all his plans would come to fruition: the British Empire locked in a battle to the death with a powerful and implacable foe, every man needed to fight the Nazis, the colonies left to fend for themselves. . . . He had uttered a prayer of thanks to the Lord Ngai – he had now quite given up attending church – for remembering his earlier prayers. When Italy entered the struggle on the German side, he wanted to scream for joy. Four years earlier Mussolini had conquered Ethiopia, and his troops lay like a storm cloud on the northern border of the colony. Those white men remaining in Kenya would have to fight for their lives, and it would be an even more difficult campaign, he judged, than that against Lettow-Vorbeck – and that had lasted four years.

But it did not turn out like that. Instead of no British troops being left in Kenya, the place had been filled with more soldiers than ever before. Instead of an interminable campaign against the Italians in the mountains, which would have totally occupied the settlers and left them vulnerable to a stab in the back, the Italians were beaten out of sight in a few months. And still the soldiers kept coming, and the law clamped ever tighter, and anyone who stepped out of line was enlisted into the labour battalions.

In those impossible circumstances Joseph decided to make himself scarce, and went back to England. To get a passage he had to volunteer for the Army; as he was forty he had to lie about his age, and give it as thirty-one instead, but he was so hard and fit he was accepted without question, along with a lot of much younger black men. He even did some fighting – and gained an even greater insight into the power that was Great Britain; a power he estimated it was going to take years to oppose successfully – years he no longer possessed.

Naturally, when he returned, he looked up his old comrades. Bolomo had died, but Kinkardu and Ngolo were still around, as well as the other forty odd initiates. They still held their meetings and vowed death to the white people and independence for Kenya under black rule, but none of them really believed in it any more. After a shaky start, Great Britain had emerged victorious from the greatest war in her history, and was more powerful than ever. No matter that everyone knew she would not have done it without American aid; no one doubted that the Americans would go on supplying that aid. Certainly the colonies were under firmer white control than ever before; the white determination to stay in Kenya was epitomized by the news that Joseph's old boss was now Sir John Barclay. That summed it up, Joseph thought; Mr John a knight, and him a nothing.

What made the situation the more galling was that there were now more recruits available for Mau Mau than ever before. He was only one among thousands of men who had gone off to fight. These were mostly young men, and they gained the same impressions that he had in 1914. When two men lay down alongside each other with a gun each, the men coming at them could not tell which was white and which black – their bullets killed with equal effectiveness. The same went for a knife.

These young men realized a man was a man, no matter what his colour or his antecedents, and they inevitably began to wonder what force allowed Sir John Barclay to sit up at Naivasha looking out over his thousands of acres of rich soil while each of them could not even obtain half an acre on which to tether a goat and raise a few ears of corn. And being young men, as Joseph had once been, they were no longer willing to accept that this should be so. Joseph enjoyed their adulation, and willingly admitted them to his organization, and told them what they were going to do to

323

the white men, and their women, when the time was right . . . but he no longer believed his own words.

And then Jomo Kenyatta returned. He had been away some eighteen years, and should have been a stranger. But he had kept in touch with the people he thought mattered, and was given a tumultuous welcome as a politician who would lead Kenya to independence; because he honestly thought it would happen. Unlike Joseph, who had seen only the military side of the British, Kenyatta had continued to make his way through the lower reaches of the political and social scene, and he came back with a revelation. The old imperialist spirit in England was dead. The British people were tired of the burden of empire. They were bankrupt, both financially and morally, and they wanted only peace, and if possible, prosperity. To achieve this they had got rid of the Churchill government and replaced it with a government of Socialists, well meaning men who believed that people had rights, whether they were weak or strong, and that it was the duty of a British government to see that they obtained those rights.

Kenyatta, in Joseph's opinion, was an optimist who in any event was out of touch with Africa. What he needed to do was go up to Naivasha and watch Sir John Barclay riding his fields – and try to decide then if the old imperialist spirit was dead, at least here in Kenya. But many people believed Kenyatta, and the land agitation began again. Joseph could have told them it was a waste of time. He had been through it all before. But the tribal chiefs insisted on forming delegations to go to London for talks with the Colonial Office, or to Government House in Nairobi for talks with the Governor, Sir Philip Mitchell. As the Mau Mau founder Joseph was invited to become a member of these delegations, but he declined, convinced delegations were not going to get anywhere. Nor did he take an offered seat on the council of the Kenya African Union, the political party formed by Kenyatta and pledged to reform by political means only. He suspected that Jomo was trying to muzzle him. And with sinister intent.

He couldn't quite make Jomo out. Here was a man of

approximately his own age, with an almost identical background, and therefore surely with almost identical fears and ambitions and aspirations - and hatreds. Nor was he absolutely sure that Jomo was as firmly against the precepts of Mau Mau as he pretended. He refused to join the society, but Joseph suspected that might be because it would mean acknowledging *him* as the more senior. He also suspected that, were he to step aside, Jomo might even consider taking over the group, to provide himself with a militant wing. For although he dealt with the white men as mere political opponents who could be removed by patient negotiation, on occasion he spoke as fiercely as anyone about the possible need for force.

In any event, as Joseph had predicted, the white settlers were not giving up anything. Led by Sir John Barclay, they also sent delegations to London and had meetings with the Governor. They argued that whereas goats destroyed the land, they had always improved it. They argued that on their shoulders rested the whole prosperity of the colony, that not only did they provide all the employment that was going but that they also paid all the taxes that were paid. These were cogent arguments for the bankrupt British Government. The question of land reform was shelved.

"It will never happen," Tom Ngolo said. "And we are getting old, Joseph. I am fifty-two. It is time to stop talking and act."

"And die?"

"That too, if necessary," Ngolo said.

Joseph stroked his chin. There was really not a lot left to live for, he realized. But he was not going to die until he could take John Barclay and all his family with him.

The marriage of Elizabeth Barclay to Captain Lawrence Dundas in March 1951 was the social event of the year. It took place at Naivasha, which had now grown into quite a township – albeit some distance from the farm – and if the church there was rather small, there was ample room at the house and on the lawn for a reception the likes of which

325

Kenya had never seen before. Lady Barclay had spared no expense and no trouble. This was partly relief.

Lizzie had left marriage rather late – though not from lack of suitors – and was now in fact thirty years old. She was an extraordinarily good-looking woman, with height inherited from both her mother and her father, her mother's strong face, and the splendid golden hair of her paternal grandfather, faintly tinged with Joanna's red. Lizzie had enjoyed the war years, and continued to enjoy the peace for some time. This worried Adèle, who feared they might have another Catherine on their hands. Now that fear had been laid to rest. Dundas was a handsome young man, actually two years younger than his bride but obviously madly in love with her, as she appeared to be with him. He didn't have much money, but John had set him up with a farm of his own only thirty miles further up the lake, and he was looking forward to his new career.

Adèle was looking forward to having her daughter close at hand at last. Mal was there all the time now, of course, gradually taking over the running of the farm from his father, as John had done from his; the English manager John had installed during the war years and afterwards to help until Mal was ready had retired thankfully – his wife had never liked Kenya – but the Kikuyu overseers were so experienced that the place ran like a well oiled piece of machinery. Adrian had opted out of the family business, wishing to strike out on his own rather than always being the junior son, and was operating a property business in Nairobi. Adèle knew this had been a disappointment to Johnnie, but she was perfectly happy. Adrian came home most weekends, and now she was going to have her whole family around her at last, with – she hoped – even a grandchild or two to follow. Presumably the boys did intend to get married eventually; they certainly brought home a succession of attractive girls. Maybe Lizzie's example would give them a prod.

But there was an even more personal reason than the happiness of her daughter that led Adèle to make this occasion so unforgettable. She regarded it as their own

326

coming of age, because John had at last stepped forward to take his natural position as a leader of the white community. She suspected that in the past he had been hampered by a guilty feeling that perhaps the Africans did have more right to this land than he did. This was because his father had been the first white man here, and had seen it all happen.

Then had come the trauma of Catherine, and all that had followed. She reckoned that John's attitude to the Kikuyu had changed since Cathy's murder, that he had come to see it more as a them or us situation. But of course he had been forced to keep a low profile after the trial. In that sense the war had been a godsend, and the knighthood had set the seal on his re-establishment. Not immediately: there had been considerable criticism, including a ghastly cartoon in one of the local papers of a man murdering his sister and asking the Governor, "Can I have one too?" She had had to beg John not to go into town and punch the editor on the nose.

But even that had been four years ago. Since then not only had John's political enemies realized that he was going to be Sir John for the rest of his days, but also that they needed him to oppose the excesses of the Labour Government in England. And now, today, the political triumph was being followed by the social one. As she looked out at the six hundred-odd guests who thronged the lawns and the marquees, the morning suits and uniforms of the men, the huge hats and fluttering, multi-coloured frocks of the women, as she picked out so easily the tall, commanding figure of her husband and the hardly less impressive figures of his sons, as she followed the glowing progress of the bride from guest to guest, she thought to herself: Not too bad, for a penniless refugee from the forests of Tanganyika. And she was only fifty-four. She had not yet even reached the age at which Catherine had been murdered.

But Catherine was a bad dream. She herself was here and now, socially the most important woman in Kenya. And she owed it all to the love of one man. There was happiness.

"Some party," said Inspector General Curtis, who had now

been re-ranked as Commissioner of Police Curtis. "Next year's profit?"

"Has to be spent on something," Sir John Barclay agreed. The guests were starting to leave, but Curtis had hung back. John was glad about that. Whatever their differences as young men, over the past few years they had become good friends. "The whole colony is spending next year's profit on the visit of Princess Elizabeth, so far as I can make out. I imagine that's going to be a problem for you."

"Not for me," Curtis said. "I retire at the end of this year."

"Do you?" John was incredulous.

"I'm fifty-five."

"Good God! So am I."

"But you're not retiring?"

"Not yet awhile. There's a lot to be done."

"There is. But as it isn't being done, I may as well get out. I'm not helping anybody."

John frowned at him, fetched a spare bottle of champagne from Ali and refilled their glasses. They sat at one end of the verandah and were relatively secluded. "I think you need to enlarge on that."

"Do you remember a conversation we had, oh, thirteen years ago now – a couple of days after your trial, when Billy Bsambi and that fellow Murgatroyd were cut up?"

John's frown deepened. "Vaguely."

"We were talking about Joseph Kinshasu and his friends. I thought there could be a secret society indulging in mutual protection and murder."

"Yes. I remember that. Long time ago."

"Such a society exists, John. It's called Mau Mau."

"Mau Mau?"

"God knows what it means. But one of my detectives has infiltrated it. And what he has found reads like something out of the *Boy's Own Paper*, save that this isn't kid's stuff, and it's very much for real."

"Such as?"

"I'll give you a copy of the report. I have it with me." He

328

took the envelope from his inside breast pocket. "It's very, very confidential."

John placed it in his pocket. "Sort of thing you always carry to weddings, eh?"

Curtis grinned. "I thought it'd be a good opportunity to let you have it, under the table as it were. One of the problems with Mau Mau is that no one knows who actually belongs to it or not. All your Kikuyu servants could be members."

"Well, Ali certainly isn't; he's a Somali. What is it about this lot that worries you so much?"

"Simply that it is filthy, and I mean that. Don't show that report to your wife. And it is dedicated to the death of every white person in Kenya. And your old friend Joseph Kinshasu is the boss man."

"Joseph? I thought he was dead."

"I thought so too. I certainly hoped it. But he is alive and well and living in Nairobi, and he is the centre of the most evil conspiracy I have ever known."

John started to take the envelope from his pocket, then slid it back in again. "You're quite sure of your facts?"

"Quite sure."

"Then why isn't Joseph making a noise on the political scene, like this fellow Kenyatta?"

"Maybe he's too clever. Or maybe he just doesn't believe a political settlement is possible. If anything in that report is remotely accurate, he certainly doesn't intend to stand by one. These Mau Mau swear a pretty unpleasant oath — several pretty unpleasant oaths, in fact — vowing death to all white people."

"Hm." John drank some champagne. "When is this bloodbath to begin?"

"We haven't been able to find that out."

"But it's obviously still in the future, so why don't you do something about it?"

"Don't you think I want to? A copy of that report was sent to HE several weeks ago. And he read it. He had us all in and gave us a chat. Mustn't rock the boat just now, or Princess Elizabeth might not come. It's going to be the high spot of his career, you know. He retires immediately afterwards."

"Yes," John said. "Tell me, what would you do if you had carte blanche?"

"I'd make a dawn swoop on every Kikuyu leader, and every man we've identified as a Mau Mau, and thanks to my sergeant we know quite a few. Lock the whole lot up."

"And charge them with what?"

"I'd worry about that when I had them in gaol."

"Wouldn't work," John told him. "Not with Labour in power. The stink would cost you your job."

"Doing nothing could cost a life or two. Including some close to home. I don't reckon you or yours are very dear to Kinshasu."

"Don't you reckon you're on his list? Remember 1922?"

Curtis gave a mirthless smile. "This time next year I'm going to be living in a cottage in Sussex."

John studied him for several minutes. "Is that your advice to all the white settlers?"

"Surrender? No. You won't surrender, John. And I admire you for that. I'd stay and fight with you, if I had anything to fight for. And with. But when HE tells me I can't touch them until they do something . . . that's too much for my stomach." He got up. "I should think that's one wedding sufficiently ruined." He looked across to where Captain and Mrs Dundas were bidding their guests farewell. "But I felt you should know. You have a lot to protect. And a lot that's worth protecting."

John read the report the next day, and felt physically sick, as Curtis had predicted. The thought was quite shattering that there were perhaps several thousand men – perhaps his own work force amongst them – smiling, forehead-touching faces during the day, who were bound together by an obscene oath to commit murder and mayhem at the signal of their leader, and that their leader could once have been his own servant. Even so, despite Curtis's warning, he did not feel he or his were in any danger. That would make no sense of Joseph's intervention at his trial. Indeed, he

330

considered going into Nairobi, finding him and having it out – and then reflected that the last time he had done that he had merely lost his temper, with disastrous consequences, and that now he was Sir John Barclay he simply had to behave with dignity. He filed the report in his safe and did not mention it to Adèle.

But the next time he was in town he called at Government House and brought it up with Sir Philip.

"My dear fellow," the Governor said, "I sometimes feel Curtis should have been retired years ago. You know what policemen are, always seeing burglars under the bed. When you think of the unrest in the world today, and then look at the peace and prosperity which is Kenya ... and he would have us precipitate a similar situation here by launching a programme of mass arrests on no more evidence than the obscene imagination of a detective sergeant. . . . And with the Princess due to visit us within only a few months ... really. Curtis had no business letting you see such a confidential report. I am most disappointed in him, really I am."

John promised to destroy his copy of the report, and went home with some forebodings. He wondered how Father would have dealt with the situation, and it was a long time since he had done that. The important point was, Father would have had no doubts *how* to deal with it. The difference was, in Father's day there had not been a Labour government at Whitehall anxious to accuse their own people of murdering or bullying Africans.

Yet despite his certainty that Joseph meant the Barclays no harm, he brought himself a new revolver, and a new rifle. When Adèle raised her eyebrows, he said he thought of going on a lion safari into the deep forest. He also made presents of rifles to both his sons as well as Larry Dundas, constructed a range on the lakeside, and made them practise. He also took to studying his Kikuyu servants, even asked Ali to tell him if he ever noticed any unusual behaviour, and began carrying a gun when he rode into the fields, where he might be out of sight of Mal and surrounded by Kikuyu.

"What on earth is on your mind?" Adèle asked. "You've got Lizzie all upset, and that's not good in her condition."

"It just happens to be a long time since I checked the firearms," he lied. "And I didn't like *their* condition. We have to have rifles, my love. As for carrying one in the field and practising, we're inclined to get rusty. The surest guarantee that nothing ever happens to Lizzie's baby is for Larry to prove he's a good shot."

That didn't reassure her in the least. She could tell he was worried. But her anxieties were soon submerged in the preparations for the royal visit, which was at once a triumph and a tragedy. The Princess charmed the entire colony and made even John feel he was something of a fool as he watched the cheering crowds of black Africans she attracted wherever she appeared in public. But she was forced to cut her visit short after the sudden death of her father. She had arrived a princess, and left a queen.

Kenya was shocked by its intimate connection with this enormous event, and life was muted for the rest of the year. Sir Philip Mitchell retired with a minimum of fuss, and was succeeded by Sir Evelyn Baring. The new Governor had only been in office a few days when John received a telephone call inviting him to a meeting at Government House, where he discovered to his surprise that it was to be very much a tête-à-tête.

Sir Evelyn pushed the report at him. "I'd like you to read that."

John recognized the preamble. "I already have."

The Governor raised his eyebrows.

"Curtis and I worked fairly closely together," John explained.

"And do you agree with his recommendations?"

"I told him, and I haven't changed my mind, that he needs more proof than just one report."

"Proof we may never get, until it's too late. It's not my place to criticize my predecessor, and of course I recognize that he was working in vastly different circumstances" — meaning, as John well understood, that there was now a Conservative government in office in England — "but if we continue to do nothing and there is suddenly a revolution, we'd be left with egg all over our faces."

"Curtis felt it would be blood," John said.

Baring gazed at him. "Yes," he said. "What I am about to say is in the strictest confidence, Sir John, but I intend to communicate with Her Majesty's Government immediately, requesting their permission to announce a state of emergency, and the moment I am given such permission, I intend to place every known Mau Mau leader or associate under arrest. That includes both Kenyatta and Kinshasu."

"There'll be a scream. I'm not sure they'll go for it. Even this new lot."

"I understand that. Which is why you're here. What I need, what I must have, is the support of the white settlers. Can you give me that?"

John considered. He would not have been human had he not been concerned about the report. He had immediately reacted to it strongly, despite his personal feeling of immunity. But that was two years ago, and hardly a tremor – apart from the usual political agitation – had troubled the Kenyan scene in that time. Besides, as he reflected more on both the report and the personality of the reputed Mau Mau leader, he thought that surely Joseph Kinshasu, with his background of reading and observation, would not be stupid enough to challenge the power of Great Britain. Equally, he felt that Joseph, having saved his life on more than one occasion, would be unlikely ever to pose a threat to him or his family. Over the past six months indeed, the guns had gone back into their cases.

It went against his instincts to launch such a pre-emptive strike. It was illegal, no matter what might be proved afterwards, and it would certainly involve a great deal of injustice, once non-Kikuyu policemen were loosed on their traditional enemies.

Against that was the horrifying thought that he might be wrong about Joseph, overlaid by the even more horrifying memory of Cathy tied to the bed, her eyes an eternal corridor of horror down which she had been dragged by a maniacal man. A maniacal Kikuyu!

And then he remembered that ride through the fields with his father, twenty-five years ago. Father had perhaps foreseen something like this. Certainly he had foreseen a confrontation with the Kikuyu. But there would be nothing, he had said, which could not be overcome by courage, common sense and a touch of ruthlessness. It could well be that such a touch was needed now. Certainly it was an intolerable prospect to live with the fear of such a catastrophe hanging over them for the rest of their lives.

"I cannot speak for all the white settlers," he said. "I can only speak for myself and my sons. We will support you, Sir Evelyn, one hundred per cent."

Baring nodded. "And the settlers will follow your lead." He held out his hand. "Thank you. I think you have just saved Kenya from a bloodbath."

Or precipitated one, John thought. But he didn't say so.

It began even before the Emergency Decree went into effect. The very next night a Mrs Margaret Wright was hacked to pieces on the verandah of her husband's farm not ten miles from Nairobi. The community was shocked, but still regarded it as one of those isolated outbursts of ferocious but personal violence which from time to time occurred in Africa.

However, when John heard the news, he summoned a meeting of Mal, Adrian, and Larry, and recounted to them in confidence the brief facts of his talk with the Governor.

"I shouldn't think there can be any doubt that London will agree to the proposal now," he said. "There's no need to alarm anyone, especially your mother or Lizzie, but as of this moment we must accept that we are in a critical situation." He grinned at their tense faces. "By which I mean a situation of crisis. It follows therefore that we take certain precautions. One, we will go back to being armed at all times. There is no need to start looking like John Wayne, but a pistol kept in the car is essential. It goes without saying that you will start locking your cars. Two, the women are never to be left alone on the farms. Adèle is all right,

334

because Ali is always here. It may become necessary for you and Lizzie to move down to Naivasha, Larry."

"She won't like that," Dundas objected. "Unless we tell her exactly what is going on. I'm not sure she'll like it even then."

"Well, try to make sure she and little Jo go with you whenever you have to leave the farm. If things get really serious we'll have to tell them, of course. But I'm hoping HE will be able to put his plan into effect and lock all of these scoundrels up before too long. Then the emergency will be over. Meanwhile, alertness is the key."

Joseph was scandalized by the murder of Mrs Wright. So were most of the leaders of the Kikuyu people, although for different reasons. The chiefs were merely horrified at the crime, which had been so clearly carried out by one of their people. Joseph was angry because he had given no orders, and because it was not a part of the pattern he had worked out. He had still been planning, and waiting and watching. He had determined to begin with the Barclays, not only because of the personal feelings of jealous enmity, but because the Barclays were the symbol of the white man in Kenya – destroy them and everyone would know the end was in sight for British rule. He had his plans all laid. All that was needed was the determination to begin.

Occasionally he wondered if he had the courage, although he would never have admitted it to anyone. There were times when he knew he was the man chosen by Lord Ngai and Providence itself to lead his people to freedom – and felt so elated he could have burst. And there were other times when the blood-lust also swelled within him as he thought of the bitch woman whose flesh he longed to cut. There were also times, more numerous, when he gravely reflected that once he had done so, if he failed to deal with John Barclay very quickly as well, he would be faced with an implacable and ruthless foe who would be backed up by all the resources of Great Britain. That was indeed a sobering thought.

And now, before he was ready, some crazy fools had

discovered a white woman alone and taken advantage of that situation, as if one white woman was going to have any effect on the overall situation. It was who the white woman was that mattered. Mrs Wright's death was only going to alarm the white people and cause them to take countermeasures.

"These boys are getting impatient," Tom Ngolo told him.

"Am I the leader or not?" Joseph demanded.

"I am just saying, they are getting impatient," Ngolo repeated. "You could lose control."

Joseph's anger was not lessened when he encountered Jomo Kenyatta and Jomo refused to speak to him. But two days later he discovered that Ngolo might be right, when Chief Waruhiu, one of the leading men in the Kikuyu nation, spoke out vehemently against the killing – and was himself hacked to death the following night.

Hastily he convened a meeting of the senior Mau Mau members. They assembled in the same grove where he had murdered Billy Bsambi, a place which had become sacred to them.

Joseph faced them. "You boys want to kill," he said. "I know the time is not ready yet, but if you want to kill so bad, then that is what we must do. But it must be done right. Now, I will tell you what . . ." He paused, because someone was coming, running through the bush, making a noise like an elephant. The men scrambled to their feet, and stared in dismay at Harry Kinkardu. Joseph had not even been aware that Harry wasn't at the meeting, he had had so much on his mind. "But what is the matter with you?" he asked. "You want to tell the whole world we are here?"

"The whole world knows," Harry panted. "They are coming now!"

"Who?"

"The police. They are coming to arrest every one of us. Every man who has taken the oath is going to be locked up, and beaten up, and then sent to the Chalbi."

Joseph stared at him in disbelief, even as his belly seemed to be filling with lead. "They don't work so," he protested.

"They've got to have warrants. How can they have warrants for so many without us knowing?"

"They don't need warrants," Harry Kinkardu told him. "I just got the word from Government House. Baring has the power to declare a state of emergency, and when that happens, he can do what he likes."

"Who can give him such power?" Ngolo demanded.

"The English, man. Eden. That's who. And he is sending his police to lock us all up."

They stared at one another.

"We must get away," Ngolo said.

"Man, what about me wife?" asked one of the others.

"And mine," said another. "I got to go home first and tell she what is happening."

"You do that, and you going to get locked up," Kinkardu told him.

They looked at Joseph.

"You must do what you think best," Joseph said, thanking Ngai *he* didn't have a wife to worry about. "But now we must fight. I am going to the forest. I am going north, by the mountain. That is the best. But you must follow me whenever you can. And when we are there, we will plan our fight. I will tell you how to fight. And I will tell you who to kill."

"Ah, Sir John. Come in." Sir Evelyn Baring looked pleased with himself. "All quiet out at Naivasha?"

"It is. But I'm hearing all manner of rumours."

"Probably all true. Sit down. You'll take a brandy?"

John sat down. "Are we celebrating?"

"I should say. It has worked like a charm. We have eighty-six of the blighters under arrest."

"Eight-six? Good lord. Curtis's report only listed forty-odd."

"That is two years out of date, remember. Besides, it was almost certainly incomplete. I'm sorry I couldn't inform you in advance, but it was absolutely necessary to act immediately Whitehall's go ahead came in, before the Kikuyu could learn what was going on. They have their spies everywhere,

337

as you know; all our servants are Kikuyu. So the very minute permission for the State of Emergency arrived I told the police to move."

"And now the whole colony is under martial law."

"Well, it doesn't affect you or me, old man. The important thing is that we have nipped the entire conspiracy in the bud. Whitehall took some persuading, of course, even with your endorsement of the plan; they imagine that all of you white settlers are trigger-happy gunmen just waiting for the opportunity to blow some poor Kikuyu apart. But the murder of that poor woman concentrated their minds powerfully, as the saying goes. And Chief Waruhiu's death will convince them they've done the right thing. I must say, I think the police have done a splendid job of work, bagging the lot like that."

"I would say you are right," John said. "I wonder if I might be allowed to see Joseph?"

"You mean Jomo Kenyatta? I don't see why not."

"Kenyatta?" John frowned. He had forgotten the Governor had stated his intention of arresting Kenyatta at the same time as the Mau Mau leaders. "But there was no mention in the report of him being Mau Mau."

"My dear fellow, of course he is. He's the leader of these people."

John shook his head. "Curtis was quite sure he didn't actually belong to them."

"Well, as to that, the courts will have to decide. But he has certainly associated with them. And you won't convince me he doesn't approve of them, or what they have done. In my opinion, the longer we can lock Mr Kenyatta up, the longer we are going to have peace in Kenya."

"Um," John said, realizing that the situation was more dangerous than he had supposed. He did not know Kenyatta, but he had absolute faith in Curtis's judgement. "Well, I think the real danger man is Joseph Kinshasu. He's the one I'd like to have a word with. He used to work for me, and I think I may be able to get one or two things, such as what they really want, out of him."

"My dear fellow, we know what they want: to drive the white man out of Kenya. The report says so."

"Because they can't get what they want as regards land. But they must also know, Joseph certainly does, that driving the white man out of Kenya is going to be a nearly impossible task. I think he'll be willing to negotiate."

"Negotiate? You want to negotiate with red-handed murderers? The days for negotiation are past, Sir John. They've had their opportunities. Anyway, you can't speak to Kinshasu. He's one of the few men on our list who got away."

John put down his brandy glass and sat up. "Joseph Kinshasu is not under arrest?"

"Oh, there's a special warrant out for him. But somehow the police missed him in the initial raids. They think he's run off to the bush in the north. Well, good riddance."

"Did anyone else get away?" John asked.

"Oh, well, one or two. I have the list here." He picked it up from his desk. "Let's see . . . Kinshasu, of course. And someone called Tom Ngolo. And another called Harry Kinkardu — "

"Jesus Christ!" John said.

The Governor raised his eyebrows.

"Forgive me," John said. "But while you have been locking up legitimate politicians, the hard core of Mau Mau has got away."

"Oh, come now."

"Sir Evelyn, those three men are the founder members of the sect. It was Curtis's opinion that they created Mau Mau when the three of them were in exile in the Chalbi Desert around 1924. They were sent there for refusing to carry identity cards. Those are the three men above all others we need to get."

"Oh, we'll get them."

"When?"

"My dear fellow, how should I know?"

"And what do you think they are going to be doing until you do?"

"Hiding, I should think. They certainly can't do very much with all their associates locked up."

John got up. "Sir Evelyn," he said. "I hope to God you are right."

14

And perhaps the Governor was right, John reflected, as the next weeks drifted by and the colony was quieter than it had been for some time. The state of emergency was of course the sole talking-point, but as the talking had to be done behind closed doors or in very small groups to avoid contravening the decrees, it was not very obvious. Meanwhile the Government pushed ahead the trials of the men arrested with great expedition, so that they were all in court in very short order. All were found guilty of belonging to an organization whose intent was the unlawful overthrow of the Government of Kenya. Even Kenyatta was so convicted, although on the flimsiest of evidence, in John's opinion, and sentenced to seven years' exile in the north.

And still the three leaders had not been caught. On the other hand, they had not yet revealed themselves, either. For all his pessimism John reflected that the Governor could well have sized up the situation more accurately. Joseph was certainly not a fool, and he would understand the enormous odds stacked against him. But Joseph was also the man who had calmly cut Billy Bsambi's throat, then gone along to Murgatroyd's house, talked his way in – there was no evidence of forcible entry – and then cut him to pieces before his living eyes. Joseph had saved him from the gallows, he remembered, and Joseph had once convinced the Germans he was a platoon of English soldiers, in order to save his Mr John from imprisonment. Joseph Kinshasu was a man of many parts. John wished he knew which part was dominant.

Larry and Lizzie were in the habit of bringing baby Jo over to Naivasha for Sunday lunch, and they were there as usual the weekend after the sentencing of the alleged Mau Mau leaders took place. Naturally it was the main topic of

341

conversation, with Adèle chiding her menfolk about their secrecy.

"Of course that's why you've all been wandering around armed to the teeth and looking like men about to fight a battle," she said. "Don't you suppose we guessed?"

"Well, I'm damned glad it's over," Larry Dundas said. "It has been a worry, I can tell you. And now Lizzie is on the way again . . ."

"Are you?" John cried. She had put on a little weight with Jo's birth and never lost it again, but she certainly didn't look pregnant.

"Saw the doctor last week," she said. "Baby John will be here for Christmas."

"Nobody ever tells me anything," John grumbled, looking at his wife.

She smiled sweetly. "We women are entitled to have our secrets as well, you know."

"But calling him John . . . well, that needs another bottle of champagne." Delighted, he signalled Ali. "How do you know he's going to be a boy?"

"We don't," Elizabeth said. "But it seems about right."

"By the way, how's Achmed turning out?" On his advice, they had obtained a Somali head boy.

"Oh, he's great," Larry said.

"Although his habits are so very odd," Elizabeth complained. "I'm always finding him kneeling to the east."

"Mecca," Adèle told her. "Ali does it all the time."

"And then all his food fads . . ."

"I'm sure he thinks Christian food fads are a bore too," John said. "The important thing is that Somalis can be trusted not to have too many ambitions, at least here in Kenya."

The party broke up at four, as John liked to feel the Dundases would be safely home before dark. It was in fact just after five when they drove into the yard of the smaller farm. Elizabeth carried Jo into the bedroom for her six o'clock feed, while Larry headed for the bar. Having been drinking all day, he knew there was no point in stopping now.

342

Besides, the enormous feeling of relief that it was over was only slowly spreading through his system – he could go on drinking all night. He knew that his father-in-law still felt there could be trouble, still insisted he should always be armed, but he was sure this was just the old Kenya syndrome: John Barclay had lived on a frontier for so long he could not come to terms with civilization, and policemen, and the due processes of law. Larry had no doubt at all that Mau Mau, if it had ever existed, was now a thing of the past.

Thankfully he unbuckled his revolver holster and laid it on the counter. "Achmed," he bawled. "Achmed? Where are you?"

The pantry door opened, and he gazed at Bibuyu, the Kikuyu under-butler. "Achmed is sick, bwana," Bibuyu said.

"Sick? What's the matter with him?"

"It is the bellyache, bwana," Bibuyu explained. "He sends his most humble apologies, but he cannot leave the toilet."

"Oh, for Jesus' sake. I'm sure the mistress has some medicine she can give him. All right, find me a bottle of Moët, will you."

"Of course, bwana." Bibuyu had it opened in seconds. Larry filled two flutes and carried them into the bedroom.

Jo was busily vomiting over her mother's shoulder. Elizabeth had fed her for six months, but now she was a year old and on patent baby foods – and other things besides.

"You were giving her champagne at lunch," Elizabeth said. "I'm not sure Dr Spock would say it's good for her, although it certainly makes her burp." She took a sip of her drink. "Did I hear Bibuyu saying something about Achmed being sick?"

"Seems to have diarrhoea. Don't you have something for it?"

"Kaolin and morphine. It's in the medicine cupboard, if you can persuade him to take it. It's probably against his religion or something."

"I'll make him take it." He put his champagne glass down beside hers, went to the cupboard and found the bottle.

343

"Back in a tick." He went out the back, glancing into the pantry, where Bibuyu was chopping onions for dinner. It occurred to him that cook must have a bellyache too.

He went down the back steps and into the yard; it was quite dark now. He wondered where Fritz was, and remembered that the Alsatian hadn't barked when they came home, which he normally did. Presumably Achmed would know the answer to these things.

He walked across the yard to the house occupied by the Somali and his wife and son. The other servants' houses were in darkness, but a light glowed in Achmed's bedroom. He went up the short flight of steps to the porch and knocked. "Sorya?" he called. "How's the old man?"

There was no reply, and when he tried the handle, it was open. He stepped inside, nostrils twitching at a heavy, unpleasant scent. Presumably something Somalis had for dinner, he supposed. He went past the small living room, which was empty, and reached the bedroom. Here the door stood ajar, and beyond it was the light. He pushed the door inside, stepped past it and stood absolutely still, aware only of feeling he had no control over his body or his mind and had become a thing of horror himself – and he had seen men blown to pieces during the war.

On the bed in front of him lay Achmed. He was naked, and had had his head cut off with what looked like a blunt knife. It was placed on his chest, and his genitals, which had also been severed, were pushed into his mouth. Across his legs lay the body of the dog, which had also been beheaded.

Sorya lay on the floor beside him. She was also naked and headless, and her breasts had been cut off. Their headless baby had been placed between her legs.

Larry drew a long breath and fought back the urgent desire to vomit, even as his heart pounded and blood rushed into his head. Lizzie was alone in the house, with Jo. And Bibuyu had been cutting up onions with a sharp knife. His belly rolled again, and he turned, trying to remember where he had put down the revolver when he came into the house, so full of champagne and good cheer. Then he discovered he was not alone. He was looking at Joseph Kinshasu.

Elizabeth decided Joanna had finished being sick. It was something she would have to discuss with Ma, she knew. Either she was doing all the wrong things, or little Jo had a very tender stomach. She laid the baby on the bed, looked over her shoulder in the mirror and clucked her tongue; she really should have changed before the feed.

She stripped off the soiled shirt, then changed the baby, wondering where on earth Larry had got to. Presumably Achmed and Sorya were regaling him with a blow-by-blow account of where Achmed had got his tummy bug from. She heard footsteps in the corridor and turned towards the door, idly removing her brassière as she did so – it was also pretty smelly – then hastily held it against her as instead of her husband she gazed at the black men in the corridor. There were five of them, and they carried knives.

She opened her mouth and closed it again, as a thousand thoughts drifted through her mind; idiotically, one of the thoughts was that she was a Barclay, and Barclays didn't scream. But uppermost were the twin unthinkables: the presence of Jo, lying on the bed beside her, and the absence of Larry.

The first of the men grinned at her. "This one is Barclay's daughter," he said.

Elizabeth licked her lips and backed against the bed.

"I am Joseph Kinshasu," Joseph said. "You have heard of me?"

Elizabeth's head flopped up and down.

"Then you will know I have cause to hate your father, and all of his blood," Joseph said.

"Why?" she gasped. "He thinks of you as a friend."

Joseph grinned. "That is when it is best to be an enemy."

He stepped further into the bedroom, and his men came in with him, moving to either side. Behind them came Bibuyu. Elizabeth stared at him in horror, and he looked embarrassed. "I am sorry too bad, mistress," he said. "But this is how it must be."

345

"How it must be," Joseph repeated. "You will take her after me." He stretched out his hand and caught Elizabeth's titian hair. "You going to fight me?" He glanced at the baby on the bed.

Elizabeth licked her lips. "If . . . if I do not fight you, will you not harm my child. Please."

"She does love that child," Bibuyu said. "You knowing she is pregnant?"

Elizabeth gulped.

"I am hearing them talking about it," Bibuyu said.

"Please," Elizabeth said. Barclays did not beg either, but suddenly her knees gave way and she found herself kneeling at their feet. "Please."

"Take the child outside," Joseph said.

One of the men picked Jo up by one leg, as if she were a toy, and Joanna gave a shriek of mingled pain and alarm.

"No," Elizabeth screamed, and got back to her feet, releasing the protective brassière to lunge at him. Another man caught her round the waist, and another took hold of her hair, which Joseph had released. She panted, her mind obsessed with what might be happening to Jo, for the man who had taken the baby out had not come back yet, although the child was not screaming any more. Then she was forced on to her back on the bed, and he was tearing down her skirt. She kicked involuntarily, and men caught her legs, rolling her back and forth as she fought them, breath escaping now in a high-pitched shrill.

"Woman," Joseph said. "You fighting me."

She made herself lie still, panting, glaring at him, thinking of all the strength and splendour she had left behind at Naivasha, all unable to help her now.

Joseph squeezed her naked belly, and she tried to get her knees up. "He in there, eh?" he said. "Well, when we done, we going to put him in your arms, with the other one."

Malcolm Barclay found the bodies. Lizzie had left her compact behind, and he drove over in the Jeep the next morning to return it. It was a beautiful day, with the sun not yet risen high enough to be hot and the sky above the clearest of blues. A day in which living contained a special quality. Mal was a happy man. Emma Williams had virtually said Yes, on Saturday. He had not told his mother and father anything about it yet, as he wanted to be absolutely sure. But he had an idea they had realized that Emma was the special one.

He was in fact intending to use this visit to discuss it with Liz. He and his sister were very close. He was whistling as he swung the car into the compound and stepped down, wondering where Fritz was, with his usual boisterous, noisy welcome. Then he stood absolutely still as he got out of his vehicle, because on the roof of the bungalow was perched a vulture.

Adèle heard the blaring horn and the revolver shots, and left her study to go on to the verandah. Adrian had as usual stayed the night, and again as usual, had slept in. She had only just packed him off, and then gone in to do her house-hold accounts. Now she could not imagine what had got into Mal, until the Jeep scraped to a stop in the yard, and out of the cloud of dust her son, his cheeks wet with tears, his hat gone, traces of vomit on his bush jacket, staggered like a drunk man.

"Lizzie," he gasped. "Larry. The babies . . . oh, my God, the babies. Oh, my *God*!" he screamed, and fell to the ground at the foot of the steps, on his hands and knees, his face pounding in the dust.

Amazingly, even as she knew what must have happened, Adèle felt absolutely calm. The anger and the outrage and the demoniacal fury would come later. "Get the car, Ali," she said. "Sound the bugle to call Mr John." She went into the study, took down the Colt thirty-two which hung there in its holster – a present from Johnnie she had only ever once strapped on, and then immediately taken off because she felt such a fool. Now she checked the chambers before strapping it on again. In the corner was a magazine rifle. This too she checked before slinging it on her shoulder. Then she put a slouch hat on her head and went outside.

Mal stared at her. "You can't go there, Ma. You can't."

347

"Stop me," Adèle challenged, and got behind the wheel of the Jeep. She heard the bugle blaring, but John had left the house an hour before; he would be several miles away by now, even on horseback.

"Wait." Mal ran up the stairs, grabbed his own rifle and got in beside her. "Do you think they'll come back?"

"I'm praying," she said. She stared ahead of her as they bumped over the road. "Are they all dead?"

"All. Ma. . . ."

"Is it bad?"

"Bad?" he screamed. "Jesus Christ . . . Ma!"

"All right," she said. "Shut up."

They drove into the yard. The vulture had descended from the roof and was on the verandah. It wasn't in any hurry to leave. "Mal," Adèle said, "you're a good shot. Kill that damned thing."

Mal levelled his rifle and blew the bird's head off, scattering blood and feathers across the tiles. Adèle stepped down, carrying her rifle in her hand.

"Ma," Mal begged. "Please don't go in there. Please." Adèle looked at him, then went up the steps. Behind her, John Barclay's old Daimler came hurrying.

"Oh, Jesus," Superintendent Harding said. "Oh, Jesus. I don't know what to say."

"I don't want you to say anything," John Barclay said. "I want Kinshasu. If you aren't going to go and get him, then I bloody well am."

Harding swallowed. He had only met this legendary man once or twice in the past; there had been no reason for their paths to cross professionally. He recalled him as a big, bluff personality who looked as though he had experienced most things – as the legend said he had – and taken them in his stride. "We're doing our best, Sir John," he said. "We will get the murderers eventually."

"After they've slit open a few more women and taken their unborn babes from their wombs? Raping their mothers while they do it? After they've twisted a few more year-old babies' heads back to front? After they've beheaded a few

348

more men and their servants? And their dogs and children and wives?"

Harding was frightened. John Barclay was still speaking in a calm, matter-of-fact voice, and the policeman recalled that there had always been some doubt as to whether this man was actually innocent of the murder of his sister; in which case he could well be mad. "I . . . believe me, sir, we are going to get the murderers. But right this minute, neither you nor I have any idea who they are."

"Don't be as much of a fool as you look," John Barclay said. "It was Kinshasu."

"With respect, sir," Harding said, endeavouring not to get angry, "you have no proof of that. Now, Sir John, may I suggest that you go home and try to get some rest. Is Lady Barclay . . . ?"

"Lady Barclay, like me, wants to see Joseph Kinshasu hanging, Mr Harding. She also wants something done about it *now*."

Harding gulped. "Yes, sir. But I feel that I must warn you that if you attempt to take the law into your hands. . . ."

"Are you trying to tell me that if Kinshasu appears on my front verandah with a panga in his hand I am not entitled to shoot him?"

"Oh, in that case, sir, of course. Any man is entitled to defend himself."

"Then I will get him for you," John told him. "This" – he made a despairing gesture at the farmhouse – "this was just an hors-d'oeuvre, from his point of view. It is me he wants. And he'll come to Naivasha to complete the job."

"Oh, we shall give you complete protection," Harding said. "There's no need to worry about that."

"Superintendent," John Barclay said, "I don't want your bloody protection. If I see one of your policemen on my farm I am going to shoot him as an intruder. Remember that. I want Joseph Kinshasu to come for me, and he is only going to do that if I am on my own."

"Yes, sir," Harding said unhappily. "Well, there is nothing more you can do here. My men will post a watch – "

"Your men have nothing to do here, either, Harding,"

John Barclay told him. "Have you got everything you want in the way of fingerprints and modus operandi?"

"Why, yes, sir. But – "

"Then this charnel house has been here long enough." He turned to where his sons were waiting, with Ali and some servants – Kikuyu, but swearing their faithfulness; Adèle was safe enough in her menfolk's absence, as the Naivasha farm was at this moment guarded by policemen. "Burn it."

"Burn it?" Harding cried. "But you can't just do that!"

"Why not?"

"Well, it's property, damn it."

"It happens to be my property," John told him. "I gave it to Larry and Liz Dundas as a wedding present, and now I'm taking it back because they have no further use for it."

Harding's policemen stared open-mouthed at their commander as Malcolm and Adrian Barclay and their servants carried forward cans of petrol, and Harding stared open-mouthed at John Barclay.

"Or are you," John asked him, "going to arrest us for arson?"

"Letter from Curtis," John said, placing the envelope in a neat pile with the others. Their sympathy mail was endless. "I wish he'd stayed."

"You mean he'd have done more than people like Harding." Adèle placed the next envelope on the pile. "Someone called Jennings, from Milwaukee. Claims to be a distant cousin of your mother. You know the name?"

"No." John got up and walked to the window, to look down the slope at the lake. "Mal should be home by now." It was nearly dusk, and Malcolm had been into Nairobi.

Adèle didn't reply, but he heard her move. Then she was standing beside him. "How long do we have to wait?" she asked.

He allowed himself the faintest sigh of relief. For three weeks she had not discussed the situation at all. Three weeks ago they had buried Lizzie and Larry and their two children. Their *two* children. Every time he thought of that he wanted to weep. Then he wanted to go and kill some-body. And he knew Adèle felt exactly the same way. But she had refused to break down, refused even to mention it. Her only daughter, and her two granddaughters, were dead. That had to be accepted — and avenged. Neither of them had ever questioned that. But it was three weeks, and although there had been other attacks on white people, and other murders as well, all equally horrible, the Mau Mau had left Naivasha alone. Thus she had withdrawn into that protective inner mind she must have developed when she was left an orphan in the Tanganyika forest, almost as she had done when Cathy so hurt and humiliated her. He had not known what to do about it, and was forced to wait. But now she was back. He put his arm round her shoulders. "Do you want to quit?"

"No," she said fiercely. "Not now. Never, now. I want to get Kinshasu."

"We will," he said. "He'll come, eventually."

He felt her body tense, although she knew how carefully he had prepared for such an eventuality. He had refused to put up any defences, get rid of his Kikuyu servants or alter his way of life in the least. He was willing Kinshasu to come for him. And her. And Mal. It was a challenge Joseph simply could not refuse, he felt, no matter what danger was involved.

John had of course wanted to send Adèle away, to safety; she had refused — as she felt he had expected her to. She had no life away from Naivasha, to which she had come with such innocent apprehension thirty-four years before. Nor did she wish to create a life away from her daughter. Not if it meant surrendering to Joseph.

"I wish Mal were back too," she said.

That was their only real fear, that Joseph would attempt to get at the boys. They were big strong men and capable of looking after themselves; John had hammered the need for security at all times into them. Yet young men grew careless through over-confidence. Larry Dundas had made that fatal mistake.

"There!" John pointed, and they could see the Jeep

351

bouncing down the road beside the lake, jerking from side to side, the flutter of the dress of the girl beside the driver. "Looks as if they may have had trouble."

Adèle grabbed the field-glasses and levelled them. But both the people in the Jeep were laughing, even if she now could see the cause of the erratic driving. "He has a puncture."

"And he kept on going," John said with satisfaction. It was what he had told both his sons to do.

"Thank God for that." She looked down at her shirt and slacks. "I'd better change."

John didn't demur. He knew she wanted a few minutes alone, to regain her composure after the sudden heart-rending fear that something might have happened.

It wanted half an hour of dusk. Adèle went upstairs and had a quick shower. The Jeep was in the yard now. The dogs were barking and Ali and John were greeting Mal and his fiancée. The engagement was not yet official because the family were in mourning for Lizzie, but it would be official soon. Emma would have to replace the daughter she had lost.

She dressed quickly and simply, then added a touch of lipstick. She walked to the window to look down at the lake, and saw a pelican rising with unwonted haste from one of the old tree stumps which thrust their way through the water at the end of the dry season, and which the huge, ungainly birds used as perches. But that one, close by the shore, had been disturbed. Of course that was the way they would come, because on the other side of the farm was the village, and people. Mau Mau worked where it was lonely, and when it was dark.

And the light was beginning to fade.

She went downstairs, aware of a lightness in her stomach, a dryness at the back of her throat. Had Lizzie felt those things? But Lizzie had been taken by surprise. John and the police had been able to reconstruct exactly how it happened, how Larry was lured from the house to attend a man who had already been dead for over an hour, murdered while they were enjoying a champagne lunch. John had no doubt

352

at all that Mau Mau would use the same modus operandi here, and was prepared for it; it was the oldest dodge in the world.

"Lady Barclay!" Emma hurried forward for a kiss. She was below medium height and very slender. Between Mal and his father she looked like a toy, and indeed she only came up to Adèle's chin.

"Emma," Adèle said, and kissed her on the cheek. "What kept you?"

"Had a puncture, would you believe," Mal said.

"Where?" she asked.

"Two miles out." He looked sheepish. "I did as Father said."

"Damn right too," John said.

"The wheel's buckled."

"Better than you and Emma being buckled."

"Yes," Adèle said. "Yes." Suddenly she was breathless. She glanced at the bar, where Ali was mixing cocktails. There was no one else within earshot. "They're here."

For a moment they stared at her. Even if this was the moment they had been expecting for three weeks, they were still unprepared mentally. But her words were suddenly confirmed as the dogs began to bark.

"They're coming down by the lake," she explained.

Ali stopped rattling his shaker.

"Go on with that," John told him. "Mal?"

Mal nodded, stepped into the study and brought out the pistols. Rifles were too obvious inside the house; pistols could be concealed. Mal thrust one down beside the cushions on the settee, where Adèle had sat down. "Sit beside me, Emma," she invited.

Emma almost fell down. "Gosh, I'm scared," she gasped.

"We're all scared," Adèle told her. "I'm just sorry this is happening with you here. But you're safer with us than upstairs."

Emma did not look altogether convinced. She gazed at Mal, her eyes enormous.

"Shame Adrian isn't here," Mal said. He had placed another revolver on the occasional table next to his father,

353

between two piles of magazines. A third went behind the large potted plant, resting on the earth, close to where he was standing. When Ali came forward with the tray of drinks, Mal placed the fourth gun behind the shaker. The last weapon he put in the drawer behind the bar itself.

"We could probably do with him," John agreed.

Ali's hand shook slightly as he poured the drinks; the shaker clinked against the glass.

"Easy, old fellow," John said. "Leave those, and go to your wife and children. Remember that you mustn't leave them or open your door under any circumstances, no matter who comes for you – except me."

"I would like to stay and fight with you, Mr Sir John, and Mistress Lady Adèle."

John slapped him on the shoulder. "I know you would, but you have a family to protect too. Off you go."

"Yes, sir, Mr John." Ali thrust the revolver into his waistband, beneath his white tunic.

John let him get through the door, then bellowed at the top of his voice, "Ali!"

"Yes, sir, Mr Sir John?"

"Lock those damned dogs up, will you? They're making the devil of a racket."

"Yes, sir, Mr Sir John."

Emma gazed open-mouthed at the Barclays. Like all the other settlers, she had been taught that dogs were their best protection.

Adèle knew what she was thinking. "These aren't burglars, my dear," she said. "They might not come if they see the dogs. There are too many of them."

Emma swallowed. She had not realized before that these people actually wanted to be attacked.

"I think we should have a rubber of bridge," John said. "Mal?"

"Good idea." Mal delved into the games room and brought out the folding card table, set it up and began to arrange the cards and pencils. Emma's hand stole across the cushions to touch Adèle's, and Adèle gave it a squeeze.

Mal took a very long time to arrange the cards, and had

354

not finished when the dogs started barking again, from their pen. A moment later the pantry door opened to admit Hsartu, one of the Kikuyu houseboys. "Man, Sir John, bwana," he said. "I think there is trouble."

"What kind of trouble, Hsartu?"

"Well, sir, I am hearing the dogs barking and I have gone to Ali to ask him to come and see, and he says to go away because he is not well and he cannot come out. I do not understand that, bwana."

"Does seem odd," John agreed.

"So I am afraid, bwana, and I am asking if you will come with me and see what the dogs have heard, and then speak to Ali yourself."

"I think that would be a good idea," John said, getting up and picking up his revolver at the same time, thrusting it into the waistband of his trousers; Hsartu knew he would not leave the house without a weapon. "Won't be five minutes. Let's go, Hsartu."

The Kikuyu was so tense himself that he had failed to notice the tension in the room: the way the Barclays and their guest had stared at him, the hatred which had suddenly filled their eyes as he identified himself as their enemy. He turned and led John Barclay through the pantry doorway. John kicked it shut behind him, and in the same movement drew his revolver. Hsartu heard the sound of the door closing and paused, but John had expected that and was already hitting him a savage blow across the back of the head. Hsartu collapsed to the floor without a sound.

The back door was open. John stepped to it, and the man waiting, realizing that they had been discovered, tried to get there first. John shot him through the chest, the noise enormous in the confined space. Then he pushed the door shut and shot the bolt.

From behind him there came a scream and then several shots. John thrust open the pantry door and faced five men. One was lunging at Emma with a panga; the girl had thrown herself off the settee and on to the floor, and he was tearing at her clothes while she screamed again and again. Another had been shot by Adèle but had yet closed with her, and

355

she was desperately holding off his knife as they wrestled, blood pouring down her dress – she had dropped the gun. A third Mau Mau was trying to grab her kicking legs to lift her from the ground. Mal had been hit in the first exchange and had fallen, and the other two men were bending over him.

The sight of his wife in the arms of a murderer – he did not know if any of the blood was hers – and of his son wounded, the awareness that he might yet have been over-confident, sent a wave of almost maniacal rage sweeping across John's mind. He levelled his revolver and started shooting, regardless of the danger to his family. His first bullet ripped through the skull of the man wrestling with Adèle, tearing his head apart and scattering his brains across her face as she screamed in horror. His second smashed into the thigh of the man grappling with her legs. His third blew a great hole in the back of the man trying to rape Emma. His fourth struck the shoulder of the man nearest to Mal, and swung him round as blood spurted from the wound. His last shot missed and drove into the wall, as the fifth of the attackers threw himself away from the hail of bullets.

Without checking for an instant John reached beneath the bar counter and drew the other revolver. The man who had escaped him rose to his knees, and John was face to face with Joseph. Joseph was also armed, but John was already aiming. The Kikuyu gave a howl of mingled despair and rage, and threw himself at the window. John fired, and again, but the weight of Joseph's body carried him through even the mosquito screen and he staggered across the verandah and into the darkness.

John could not follow him; two of the Mau Mau were still alive, and he had to discover how badly hurt Adèle and Mal were.

Adèle was immediately reassuring. "I'm all right," she gasped. "But Mal. . . ."

John gave her the revolver. "If either of those bastards moves, blow their heads off," he told her. He looked at Emma. "You hurt?"

356

"God," she gasped. "God! It was so quick. Mal. . . ."

John was already kneeling beside his son. Mal had been shot in the chest, but high up. There was a lot of blood, but none mixed with his breath; his eyes were open and he could almost smile. "I stood up," he muttered. "When I should have taken cover. It was so quick."

"We'll get you to a doctor," John said, stuffing his handkerchief into the wound. "You'll be okay."

"Did we beat them, Dad? Did we beat them?"

"We beat the hell out of them, boy," John said.

"You did that, Mr Sir John." Ali stood in the pantry doorway; carrying a rifle and with a revolver strapped to his waist he looked like a picture of one of the old Somali slave-traders of fifty years before, when they had been the terror of this country.

"I told you to stay with your family," John said.

"I had to come when I see the shooting. Man, Mr Sir John, you have done well."

"Not well enough," John growled. Because he would never know if he had hesitated, just for a split second, when he had had Joseph in his sights. A split second too long.

The defence of the Naivasha farm was the first real victory over Mau Mau. When John Barclay drove into Nairobi and dropped three dead Kikuyu – and two others, badly wounded and trussed hand and foot – on the pavement before the police station, it set the seal on the Barclay legend. The fact that, with the dead and wounded men in the back of his truck, he had first taken his son to the hospital to be treated for a gunshot wound, only enhanced the tale. Certain it was that his farm was never attacked again.

The Naivasha encounter heralded the beginning of the end for Mau Mau, even if the end was still a long time in coming. There were still attacks on white farms, and there were still some murders to be endured, but now people knew what to expect, and kept themselves armed and watchful. Now too the Government was getting itself organized. The King's African Rifles were called out, and soldiers

357

sent from England; the settlers themselves were organized into patrols, and these were men who not only knew the country but had a personal stake in the destruction of Mau Mau and a personal hatred for its members. Probably worst of all, from the Mau Mau point of view, the Government summoned the Masai from their reservation and put them to work hunting down their ancient enemies. The Morani felt that the gods were at last delivering a blessing as, naked except for their headdresses and their weapons, their bodies smeared with red earth, they were allowed this final opportunity to go to war. How Delamere would have loved this, John thought. Delamere would have loved the whole crisis. But then, had Delamere lived, would the crisis ever have been allowed to develop?

Perhaps most important of all, it was now that a very large section of the Kikuyu who had always opposed the extremists began to make their voices heard. In anger and frustration Mau Mau turned in their direction, and further estranged their own people.

At last the assassins overplayed their hand, and in a fit of fearful revenge descended on the settlement of Lari and murdered upward of a hundred Kikuyu – men, women and children suspected of loyalty to the Government – in a mass slaughter the likes of which had not been seen in East Africa since the days of Masai domination. That completed Mau Mau's isolation from their relatives, at the very moment when the Government forces were ready to move on to the offensive. Now whole tracts of country were cordoned off and systematically searched, and everyone the least bit suspicious was arrested; soon more than sixteen thousand Kikuyu were in detention. Several of those discovered to be leaders of the sect were hanged. Amongst them were Tom Ngolo and Harry Kinkardu. But Joseph Kinshasu was not taken, and he remained their leader. John was disturbed to read that Ngolo's last words, just before the noose was placed round his neck, had been: "You all look out for Joseph Kinshasu. He is coming, one of these days, and he will kill you all and free his people."

Yet most people felt the movement was defeated. More

and more of Joseph's erstwhile followers surrendered or were betrayed by their own relatives, until only the very hard core survived; but even they were now no longer able to exist near civilization, and had withdrawn into the thick belts of jungle that clustered on the foothills of the Aberdares and Mount Kenya.

"I congratulate you all," the Governor said, addressing an assembly of police and Army officers, and settlers he had convened in Nairobi. "I think we can safely say that we have met the most serious threat to the existence of this colony there has yet been, and we have triumphed. I am proud of you, of the way you have fought what has been a ghastly conflict. But as they say, fortune favours the brave."

"What are we going to do about those Mau Mau still in the bush, your excellency?" someone asked.

"I think we'll let them stew up there. They'll come out eventually, when they start to starve or quarrel or just get bored, and we shall be waiting for them. The point is, in the forest they can harm nobody but themselves. I do not intend to risk another man's life hunting for has-beens."

"Now we can begin to look to the future," he said to John when they got together for a private drink after the ceremony.

"Can we?" John asked.

Baring sighed. "I know how you must feel, John, believe me. And I also know it can be no consolation either that you are not the only family to have lost dear ones, or that you are one of the few families to have met Mau Mau in fair fight, as it were, and gained the day. But we cannot go through life looking over our shoulders."

"I have no intention of doing that," John told him. "I have buried my dead. But I meant that we can hardly look to the future until Mau Mau is done. I heard what you told those lads out there, and they deserved every word of it. But their work can never be done as long as there are still a good score of murderers loose in those forests."

"Twenty men, where they once numbered several thousand? You are thinking of Kinshasu."

"That's right."

"It's become a personal matter, John. I think that is a grave mistake, with respect. It would be better for everyone if none of us ever saw Joseph Kinshasu again, if he died of fever up there in the Aberdares. Who knows, he may already have done so. We haven't heard a squeak out of him in several months."

"If he has died," John said, "then we are up the creek without a paddle."

The Governor frowned. "I don't follow you."

"I won't deny that what is between Joseph and me is a very personal matter, your excellency. I won't deny that I am not going to sleep easy in my bed until I see him hanging. But believe me, there is much more to it than my personal feelings. Did you hear what Ngolo shouted just before they sprang the trap?"

"I did. Men who are about to die always shout something like that, if they are men. You have to admit that these fellows have courage."

"That's what bothers me, because they are also saying that in the detention centres and the prisons. They're not shouting, they're whispering. But that's even more effective. 'One day Joseph Kinshasu will come back.' One day."

"That day will never come."

"Which will be even more effective. Because someone will come one day, who will claim to be Joseph's reincarnation."

"Now, really, John . . ." Baring was frowning. "Just what are you trying to say?"

"That until Joseph Kinshasu is brought into Nairobi, either in chains to be hanged or dead in the back of a truck, and his body exhibited to the people, Mau Mau itself is never going to be dead. It is going to be waiting, like a poisonous weed beneath the snow, for the right conditions to spring into life again. And everyone who has died will have done so in vain."

"There are nine hundred square miles of forest in the Aberdares, John. Whitehall is clamouring for me to announce the ending of the state of emergency. There is no possibility they will allow the sort of force that would be needed to comb through that, with no guarantee of success. This rebellion has already just about bankrupted the colony."

"I will bring Joseph Kinshasu to Nairobi," John said.

"You?"

"If you will let me. I know how it can be done. I need a special warrant, and a guarantee that there will be no governmental interference."

"You?" Baring asked again. "For God's sake, John, you are a wealthy, successful man. You are a leader of the community. The colony needs you, in every possible way. And you propose to go off on a wild goose chase into the bush, where you might just get your head blown off?"

"The colony doesn't need me. There are a hundred men just waiting to step into my shoes. But the colony does need the head of Joseph Kinshasu."

Baring sighed. "John, you are fifty-seven years old, for God's sake."

John Barclay gave a brief smile. "Joseph Kinshasu is fifty-eight, your excellency."

"Are you mad?" Adèle shouted. After so many traumatic months, it was over. Even Mal's spell in hospital with his collar-bone shattered by Kinshasu's bullet was nearly finished, and he was going to be as right as rain. Emma had said Yes, and the wedding date was set. And now. . . . "For God's sake, John, you're fifty-seven years old."

"Which everyone seems to think means I'm in my dotage," John complained. "I am as fit as a horse."

"An old horse. John" – she held his hands – "I hate Joseph even more than you. But I don't hate him enough for you to be killed going after him."

"It's something I have to do, Dela," he said. She stared at him and he tried to explain. "It's not just Liz and the children, or any of the other murders Mau Mau have committed. It's not even that I feel I loosed him on the world, although God knows I did. It's a feeling. . . ." He groped for words. "He's been a sort of alter ego for too long. Saving my life, walking away from me, saving my life

361

again, almost carelessly, avenging my sister, slaughtering my daughter, and then coming for me. Like some shade out of the pit, always seeking to amuse itself with me. And then, at the house . . . I could have killed him."

"You missed your shot," she protested. "I was there. I saw what happened. You had to miss one of them."

"And the one had to be Joseph. If I don't kill him, Dela, or have him hanged, I will never sleep easy again."

"That's not a very Christian way to go hunting somebody," she said. She had no other defence.

"I don't think Joseph is a very Christian person," John said. "And I know I'm not, where he is concerned." He grinned at her. "If it'll relieve your mind, I don't propose to risk a thing."

15

John had thought very carefully about what he had to do. It was in fact a campaign he had been planning for some time, ever since it became apparent that the police and the army were never going to catch up with Joseph. His own guilt at being the only man ever to have had Joseph in his sights grew with every additional murder. So, was he seeking to expiate that guilt by killing or being killed? It was not something he cared to analyse.

His promise to Adèle had been genuine; he reckoned he was as cunning and ruthless as any Mau Mau. But he was still not sure if he intended to kill Joseph, given the chance, or if he just meant to bring him in to justice. He *should* want to kill him, he knew – for Lizzie. But killing in cold blood was not a part of his nature. That Joseph should die, should forever cease to trouble those who were endeavouring to make their way in peace upon this earth, was what truly mattered.

Having carte blanche from the Governor, he took with him six Masai Morani. They would follow the name of Barclay anywhere, and John they ranked equally with his father. At their head was Mbango, no less grizzled than John himself, and now the premier chief of his people; he was anxious to serve at Barclay's side in this last campaign. These were men who knew the forest as they knew the veins on their own hands, and could move silently and quickly through the thickest undergrowth. Upon them, he knew, his life would depend.

In support was a squad of policemen, under Superintendent Harding. Harding made it quite plain that he also thought Sir John Barclay was mad to go hunting in the forest for a two-bit murderer, when he had all of his wealth and power and prestige to enjoy. But then, Harding had never supposed him to be quite sane in any event. Nor, as

John did not immediately confide his plans to him, did he see any sense in the first manoeuvre.

John commanded his Morani to remain at the base camp they had set up just outside the trees, and then, accompanied by the heavily armed police in four noisy trucks, entered the forest. They moved slowly, following the tracks beaten by the soldiers who had briefly and futilely hunted before them. John made for the known Mau Mau assembly points, sure he would find them deserted, just as he was sure he was being watched all the time. But he was confident they would not attack him, partly because of the strength in which he was travelling, partly because he himself carried a considerable aura of invincibility, but mostly, he surmised, because they would be too short of ammunition to risk a regular gun battle.

Harding also knew this. "You won't see hide nor hair of them like this, Sir John," he protested. "We can parade around here for the rest of our lives and we won't get anywhere."

"We're getting somewhere, Mr Harding," John promised.

Before leaving Naivasha he had prepared twelve notices, written in Swahili. The first six of these, each identical to the other, he left at selected places, pinned to a tree, usually near water. Each notice read:

Why do you walk with Kinshasu in the ways of blood and hunger?

Do you not know that all your brothers have surrendered to the white men and have been pardoned, and now live at peace, with their wives and their children, and their bellies full?

The great white people are generous, and will pardon those who forsake the madness of Kinshasu and come in to surrender. But their patience is not inexhaustible. Soon they will enter this forest in their thousands and destroy everything that lives. Then you too will die.

Is this sensible? You can no longer die for your people, for Mau Mau, for your oath. You can only die for Kinshasu. Is this a man worth dying for? Have you not heard of the fight at Naivasha, when Kinshasu and the great white man, Barclay, came face to face, and Kinshasu ran away? Is this the man you would fight for now, and die for tomorrow?

That makes no sense. Your wives and mothers are crying out for you to return to them. Will you still deny those who need you? Come to Barclay, who waits for you beyond the trees. Come as a friend, without weapons, and with your hands clasped on the top of your heads. To any man, or woman, who comes thus, with the exception of Kinshasu himself, Barclay promises a fair trial and gives his word that he or she will not be executed. Barclay's word will never by broken.

"Does no harm to blow one's own trumpet now and then," Harding remarked sceptically, as he slowly read the words; Swahili was still a new language to him.

John merely grinned at him. "It's not a work of art," he agreed. "But it'll do the trick because it's couched in language the Kikuyu can appreciate, and it will drive a wedge between Kinshasu and his people."

Harding remained doubtful, and it was a slow business, but after they had waited at the police camp outside the forest for a week, a man emerged from the trees and came towards them. He was unarmed, and he walked with his hands clasped on the top of his head.

"Treat him gently," John commanded, and the man was given good food and beer.

"Now tell me of the others," John said.

"There are many would come to you, Bwana Barclay," the man said. "But they are afraid of Kinshasu. He has said he will kill any man who deserts him."

"And you believe this?" John asked. "Has he killed you?"

"I am afraid too," the man said. "But I have a wife. . . ."

"You have nothing to fear," John told him. "Not now. You spoke of many men wishing to leave the forest. Has Kinshasu then truly got many men with him?"

"There are thirty, forty men with him, and some women," the man said.

John raised his eyebrows, but he was well satisfied. He sent the man down to Nairobi, and waited a week for the newspapers to be delivered to him, then once again he and the police made a slow tour through the forest. They left the newspapers with the record of that first man being reunited with his family – although in gaol – at the watering places. All the notices had gone.

The next day two women came in. They claimed to be Kinshasu's women, but John doubted that; he knew too much about Kinshasu. Then the trickle became a flood. By the end of the month thirty-seven men and eight women had come in. "By God, Sir John, I didn't think you could do it," Harding exclaimed in admiration. "I would say you've copped the lot."

"All except Joseph," John reminded him.

"Well, if he won't come in, he won't come in. But sitting in there, all alone . . ."

"He's the one I came to get," John said. He opened his briefcase and took out the remaining six notices. These were in English.

"We should leave this place," Msano said. "Now it is no longer practical to stay. Do you not understand that Barclay has Masai with him? Only a few, but now we are so reduced in numbers, he will loose the Masai on us." He shuddered, and looked into the thick tree screen to either side, as if expecting to see the fearsome red-daubed Morani waiting there. "We should leave this place and go north, where Barclay cannot reach us."

"You are afraid of Barclay?" Joseph told them. "I am ashamed of you."

"Are you not afraid of Barclay?" Msano asked.

They were growing bold, in their fear, because they had already made their decision to leave him, Joseph knew. He had taken up the sword, after so long, and he had been defeated. By John Barclay. He recognized that now. Perhaps he had always known that would happen; perhaps that was why he had delayed for so long, perhaps he had been hoping that Mr John would die, or get ill – instead of which he seemed stronger and fitter than ever. When Joseph watched him driving through the forest with his policemen, he had nearly been tempted to shoot him there and then. He had not, because that would have given himself away and he too

366

would have died. He and his men no longer had the capability to fight a battle. Or the will, he suspected. But did he have anything left to live for?

He looked around the small encampment. Beneath this huge banyan was their favourite meeting place, but it would have to be abandoned, he knew, because one of those swine who had surrendered would certainly betray it to Mr John. Or one of these swine who were about to surrender. There were four men and one woman. Her name was Ksamba, and she loved him – or if not him, for he had never shared his blanket with her, the idea of him – she worshipped the ground on which the great leader walked.

The great leader. Once he had commanded several thousand men. Now he commanded four men and one women. Had he used them wrongly? He could not believe that. He had known he could never pit his people against the white soldiers and their black allies. He had known he would never obtain the artillery and machine guns with which to fight a pitched battle. His path had had to be one of stealth and murder, and such a path had to be strewn with terror and horror too. If he could not defeat in the open, then he must frighten in the dark.

Knowing that such a path also appealed to the dark forces in his nature had enabled him to subdue his Christianity and the conscience that had been born of it.

But now he had been defeated, even if he dared not admit it.

He got up. "Barclay will not drive me from this forest," he said. "Nor will he stay out there forever. He will go home, one day. One day soon. And then we will commence recruiting again."

He knew they did not believe him, but they followed him, five men and a woman loping through the trees, shunned even by the leopards and the hyenas, the snakes and the scorpions. That evening they approached one of the waterholes. As they watched the elephants trumpeting and blowing water over each other without a care in the world, they saw that there was a fresh notice pinned to one of the trees.

367

Msano brought it to him and held it out.

Joseph read the English words so neatly hand-printed.

Your people have abandoned you, Joseph. Those few who remain
will soon do so too, because my patience is coming to an end. Any
man who does not surrender within forty-eight hours from now
will have the amnesty from death withdrawn, and he will surely
hang. Any woman, too. As you will surely hang, Joseph. Why do
you fight me any longer, when you have been beaten? Did you not
always know you would be beaten? I am John Barclay. How can
you defeat me?

You are afraid of me, Joseph. That is why you ran away that
night at Naivasha, even though you held a gun in your hand. You
are a coward and a murdering thief in the night who can fight
only helpless women. Send out your people, Joseph, because they
can no longer help you. When you have done that, I will come to
the forest and meet you face to face. Is that not what you would
like? Or are you afraid of me still? Send out your people, Joseph,
and let us settle this matter between us.

Joseph raised his head; Msano could read English. "Why
are you waiting?" he asked.

"It is best," Msano said.

"For me to surrender, and be hanged?"

"For you to die as a hero, instead of living as a coward."

"You think I am a coward? Have I not fought in two
wars?"

"Barclay taunts you with being afraid. You must prove
to him, and to our people, that you are not. Heroes are
remembered. Cowards are forgotten."

"Do you think he will come into the forest alone?" asked
one of the other men.

"He will do that," Msana asserted. "He is John Barclay,
as he is not tired of telling us. He believes himself to be
invulnerable. If Joseph were to meet him and kill him, then
even if he himself died he would be a hero to our people,
an eternal light shining in front of us to lead us through
the ages."

Ksamba gazed at him with glowing eyes.

And Joseph knew that they were about to desert him. But

more, he knew that they were right. It needed one act of supreme courage, even if he died, and he would become immortal. If he were to kill Mr John and then make his escape, Mau Mau might yet live – in legend for a while, but then in fact, once again.

"Well, go then," he said.

He watched them file through the trees; the forest was thick and they disappeared almost immediately. Except for Ksamba. She hesitated, and then came back to him.

"Are you stupid, woman? If you do not go now, they will hang you."

"I am your woman, Joseph," she said.

"You have never been my woman."

"Then make me so, now. A great hero must have a woman. Make me your woman now, and I will stay at your side always, and die at your side, if it must be."

Joseph gazed at her. It was too long since he had had a woman. Ksamba might not smell like Catherine, or have the superb body of Elizabeth Barclay, but she was young and pretty, and so eager. Perhaps she might not scream when she saw him.

She did not scream, but stayed in his arms all night. He awoke refreshed and almost rejuvenated. He truly felt like a hero, this morning. And now he had challenged Mr John. This was to be the greatest day of his life, he did not doubt. In this mood of suddenly reawakened manhood, he knew he could defeat even Mr John. If he came alone.

They ate the last of their food and went through the forest to the water-hole. The earth around the pool was trampled and muddy, but the tracks were left by the elephants who had drunk there during the night. This morning, at this moment, the pool was deserted. "You should go now," Joseph told her.

Ksamba shook her head. "I will stay with you always."

He did not argue. "We will climb that tree," he told her, pointing to another banyan, where the huge limbs, having toppled over and reseeded themselves in the earth, made cavern-like arches. He sent her ahead of him into the branches, watched her smooth limbs moving above his head and wondered why he had waited for so long to sample the pleasures of his own women, why he had always been afraid of being ugly. Catherine had not found him ugly, and now Ksamba had not found him ugly either; they were the only two women he had ever allowed to come to him willingly.

How his life had been wasted.

He slung his rifle and climbed behind her, and they sat pressed together where the branch they had chosen joined the immense trunk. He checked his magazine. He had taken this rifle from Larry Dundas's house, along with two revolvers. The revolvers had long since run out of bullets, but he had made Msano and the others give him all the rifle cartridges that they had left; even so, he only had seven. Yet seven bullets should be enough to kill even Mr John.

The forest was still and hot as the sun climbed into the heavens. Although they could not see it, its heat reached through the tree screen to suck moisture from leaf and branch, and from their bodies, too. They listened to the rustle of the lizards and the other slithering creatures who called this home. They watched the brilliant butterflies – blue and yellow, and black and red – flitting from flower to flower. There was still enough moisture left from the rains to keep the forest floor a beautiful place in which the soft colours were dominated by the stark purple and white glow of the huge orchids. They sat still as a procession of tree ants moved slowly across their hands and proceeded on their way. And they watched a waterbuck come cautiously through the bushes, pausing every few seconds to stop and listen, before lowering its head to drink.

Joseph's hands slid up and down the rifle barrel. The sight of the buck, of the enormous amount of food the animal represented for two people, reminded him of how hungry he was, and he knew that Ksamba would be feeling the same. The antelope was so close that, if he dared not spare a bullet or risk a rifle shot, he thought he might be able to drop on it and cut its throat with his panga. Almost he had determined to do that, when the buck suddenly raised its head again, quivering for a moment, and then disappeared into the bush with a few quick bounds.

Then Joseph heard the noise too, the distant grind of a truck engine. He looked at Ksamba, and she looked back at him.

The noise grew louder, and they saw the truck bouncing up the track, its roof swept by low branches. There were six armed policemen in the back of the truck, and three men inside the cab. There was no sign of the Masai Morani who, as Msano had said, were part of the Government forces, but whom as yet John Barclay had apparently found no use for. No doubt because his people had surrendered so readily, Joseph thought bitterly. Yet he gave a sigh of relief. He could remember back all of thirty-nine years to the first time he had visited the Masai kraal, the way those high-cheekboned, smooth-faced, arrogant men had gazed at him. The memory always made him shudder.

The truck came to a halt, and John Barclay got down. Superintendent Harding did the same. Both men had revolvers on their belts, and Barclay also carried a rifle, which he slung on his shoulder as he got out.

"How do you know he will come here?" Harding asked, his voice clearly audible to the people in the tree.

"He will come to each of the water-holes," John said. "Once he is certain I am alone." He reached into the cab and pulled out a haversack and a large water bottle. "I can wait."

"And how do you know he won't seek to shoot you from cover?" Harding remonstrated.

"I don't."

"This is madness."

"I know, Harding. You've said that before. But it is the only way we are going to get Kinshasu. Anyway, I don't believe he would shoot me from cover. I believe even Kinshasu has some spark of manhood left. You heard what Msano said, that he wishes to prove himself a hero by killing me? It's not very heroic to shoot a man in the back."

"Well, I hope you're right," Harding grumbled. "Anyway, we won't be far."

"Harding," John said. "You and your men are returning to camp and staying there. No one is to move until I return,

371

or until twenty-four hours have elapsed. That is an order and, by God, if it is disobeyed I am going to have you dismissed the service. Understood?"

Harding hesitated, then shrugged. "If that's the way you really want it, Sir John. I'll be back this time tomorrow to pick up the pieces." He got into the truck, waved his hand, and the vehicle swung round and bounced back along the track.

Joseph and Ksamba stared at each other. He knew what her eyes were asking him. Could the white men be trusted? He thought they could, because that was the white man's code. That it was an absurd code was their lookout, not his.

They waited, while the noise grew fainter and fainter. He was taking no chances that the sound of a shot might bring the policemen back. He waited while a great silence once again settled over the forest, the silence of emptiness.

While he waited, he studied Mr John, watched him standing still for a few moments while the truck receded, as if getting his bearings, then watched him place the haversack and water bottle beside a tree, watched him unsling his rifle and lay it on the ground beside the haversack. Then Mr John sat down with his back against a tree, took his revolver from its holster, broke it and thumbed the chambers. As he had certainly loaded it before leaving the police camp and would have had no reason to fire it since then, that action betrayed a certain amount of nervousness, Joseph thought. The question was: How much? Certainly his other actions were deliberate as, satisfied, he replaced the revolver in its holster, laid the rifle across his knees and then took his pipe from the breast pocket of his bush jacket and began to fill it.

The sound of the truck had now entirely died, and the forest was still. Joseph knew Mr John was listening, trying to recall all his bushcraft to boost his chances in the coming encounter. And it was a considerable bushcraft, Joseph knew. But it was memory. *He* had lived in the forest for the past three months. In addition, John Barclay, for all his fine words and his pretence at ruthlessness, was not a ruthless man, in Joseph's estimate. Mr John genuinely believed that

372

he, Joseph Kinshasu, would walk up to him and say, "Let us settle this, man to man" – because that was the British way. How the poor fools had ever conquered a third of the earth Joseph would never understand.

He glanced at Ksamba, and she nodded. The time was now. John Barclay had carefully protected his back, but he had actually sat down facing the banyan tree. There was smoke rising from his pipe, half obscuring his face and certainly obscuring his vision. This man, the most famous and most powerful man in Kenya, was a total fool, Joseph realized, a man so besotted by his own code that he was like a babe in arms. And for how long had he been afraid of such a man?

Slowly he raised the rifle and sighted it at John Barclay's chest. He would have time for two shots before Mr John knew what had hit him. But one would be sufficient. He looked along the barrel and caressed the trigger, savouring this moment above any other in his life, because it was *the* moment of his life, the moment which would make him immortal to his people. Then he closed his entire hand on the trigger, as he had been taught to do in the British Army – "You squeeze the bloody thing, you black bugger; you don't pull it," the sergeant had bellowed at him.

As he did so there was a gigantic whirr. Joseph jerked his head, but the arrow had already missed him and slammed into Ksamba's throat. She gave a peculiar sigh and fell from the tree, to hit the ground with a dreadful thump.

Joseph fell beside her. He had fired the rifle, but where the shot had gone he did not know. He landed on his feet beside the already dead girl, the rifle still in his hands, panting and weeping because once again he had been outwitted, out-thought, outfought, and outgunned. He gazed at John Barclay, who was on his feet, his rifle levelled, his finger tight on the trigger – and then left and right at the six Masai warriors, three to each side of him, each with an arrow fitted to his bow.

"Not quite a fool, Joseph," John Barclay said. "As you

are not quite a hero. I am sorry about the girl. But then, perhaps I am not. Was she very dear to you?"

Joseph stared at him. He had thought to beat this man. He had thought to outwit him and outfight him. He had thought to torture him by killing his loved ones, slowly and horribly, and then he had thought to destroy him, ruthlessly and coldly, as he might have destroyed a scorpion.

And all the while he had been deluding himself. This man was representative of his people, his race, his kind. He looked like a fool. He behaved like a fool. He set up codes of conduct and pretended that they were the most important parts of life, which was a fool's philosophy. He made promises and grandiose gestures. And all were controlled by an ice cold brain which was far more ruthless, Joseph realized for the first time, than anything he could ever imagine. John Barclay had never intended to fight him face to face and man to man – any more than Joseph had ever intended to fight John Barclay face to face and man to man. But where he had trusted the white man's word, John Barclay had not trusted him; he had sent his Morani into the forest early and secretly – to have reached the water-hole so quickly on foot they must have entered the trees during the night. Why, he realized, they must have been stalking him for hours, had him in their sight for hours – as Barclay had known and planned.

So now he gazed at the man who had destroyed him, and Mau Mau, and everything he had dreamed of. He held a rifle, but it was pointing the wrong way. Long before he could direct it at his enemy he would be shot by Barclay's rifle and cut down by the arrows of the Masai.

"Throw down your gun, Joseph," John Barclay said. "Or die."

Joseph stared at him. He could not doubt the words. He had watched John Barclay fighting in a war, where he had killed when he had had to. Now there was a personal score.

But he was going to die anyway. He was going to hang by the neck until he was dead. And when he did that, he would have been proved a coward, a man who had been unable to bring himself to face the white man and the

Masai, and had surrendered. How Msano would smile, and Jomo Kenyatta. But they never would be able to do that if he died in battle. It came to Joseph that now was his only chance to gain a victory. And it could be the greatest victory of his life.

"Then die with me," he shouted, and swung his rifle. The morning sang about him as he felt great pain. Six arrows entered his body. But they were as nothing compared with the explosion in his chest. He never heard the shot, but the expanding surge of pain carried him across the threshold of eternity.

"The Colonial Office aren't going to like it," Harding grumbled, as the truck rumbled down Nairobi High Street. "Anything about it."

"Then they can lump it," John told him. Was he sorry? He couldn't be sure of that now, any more than he had known beforehand what he would do. To bring Joseph back, and have him solemnly tried and convicted, and then, no doubt, appeal and have his appeal rejected, and then have him solemnly executed by due process of law, would have been the ideal consummation of his safari. He could not, after all they had shared together, regret that it had ended differently, that Joseph had chosen to die well rather than abjectly.

Yet there was a point to be made. Thus they had entered the city slowly, and attracted attention; everyone in Nairobi knew that Sir John Barclay and Superintendent Harding had gone up to the Aberdare forest to capture Joseph Kinshasu. Now they were back. And there was no sign of Kinshasu.

The crowd grew, and there were jeers as the truck drew up in front of the police station. Most of these people had never belonged to Mau Mau, and indeed had been horrified at the sect's excesses, but they were Kikuyu and the white men with their policemen had gone hunting a Kikuyu – and failed.

The truck stopped, and men came out of the station. The crowd pressed closer, booing and catcalling. John Barclay

375

got out of the cab and walked round the back of the vehicle, where the policemen waited; the Morani had returned to their reservation, their task completed. The tailgate was dropped and the blanket-shrouded figures were rolled out on to the road. John himself pulled the blanket away from the man and the woman, and the crowd pressed closer yet, now having to be restrained by a police cordon.

John looked at them, and raised the loudspeaker Harding had handed him. "That is Joseph Kinshasu," he said into the megaphone. "And his woman. Look well upon them. Joseph Kinshasu is dead. Mau Mau is finished. Remember that, and rejoice."

The crowd was silent now, staring at the evidence of the white man's vengeance. Then it began to melt away. But from it a gigantic whisper seeped across the morning. "That wasn't Kinshasu, man. That was somebody who just looked like him. Kinshasu ain't dead, man. He is up there, by the mountain, waiting. Kinshasu ain't dead, man. Kinshasu going to come back one of these days. There ain't no white man could kill Kinshasu, man. He ain't dead."

"Now I feel we can all sleep at night," Adèle said, handing out glasses of champagne. "Oh, Johnnie, I am so proud of you, even if I was mad at you when you went off like that."

"To Dad," Adrian said, and Mal and Emma raised their glasses as well.

"I failed, you know," John told them.

"Oh, come, Dad," Mal protested. "Because of a few fanatical rumours? Kinshasu is dead. Everybody knows that."

"I wonder," John said.

But the State of Emergency was over, and life could get back to normal – supposing life was ever going to be normal again. It slowly began to dawn on the settlers that although Mau Mau had been defeated, by at last focusing all the attention of the world press, and world opinion, on Kenya, it had forced the British Government to do the same, while the steadily worsening racial situation in South Africa was leading to a hardening of attitudes, an understanding that the white man's world, which he had enjoyed for so long, was beginning to shrink.

The Conservatives, on whom the settlers had pinned their faith for so long, retained power at the next General Election. However, that did not arrest the process; rather it accelerated it. For these were a new breed of Tory leaders, who had seen the imperial vision destroyed at Suez and were in a hurry to shrink all the way back to England's green and pleasant land, which alone could now be defended and financed.

An independent country of Kenya, an idea which had often been mooted but was regarded as a dream for the distant future, suddenly became a Government plan for the here and now. To facilitate the process, a first step was the release from detention of all the Africans locked up during the Mau Mau insurrection, from Jomo Kenyatta down.

The settlers were horrified, and again delegations went to London. Sir John Barclay refused to be a member. At sixty he felt he was too old to take part in the cut and thrust of impassioned debate, and he had never felt that Kenyatta was part of Mau Mau.

But he and Adèle made a private visit, and had tea with the Colonial Secretary, and later the new Prime Minister.

"I'm afraid independence for Kenya, with one man one vote, is now an urgent necessity, and must be implemented immediately," Harold Macmillan told John. "It is also, if I may say so, a simple act of justice for the black people."

"One man, one vote means black rule," John said.

"Why, yes, it does." Macmillan looked at him. "I have never heard you charged with being a racist."

"I'm not. I think Kenya should become independent, and I feel it can become a model multi-racial state. I would be quite happy with that prospect. But I am also aware that there are outstanding questions which must be settled first. The land business is the most important of them."

"That will be a matter for the first government of the independent Kenya to determine."

"You can't be serious," John protested, "if that government is black-controlled?"

377

"I think it was Churchill who said, a long time ago, 'After all, it is their country.'"

"Granted. But the White Highlands were given to the settlers by the British Government for nine hundred and ninety-nine years."

"A quite impossible guarantee," Macmillan told him. "Think. Nine hundred and ninety-nine years ago William the Conqueror had not yet been born."

"It happens to have been less than forty, so far," John pointed out.

"Forty momentous years. Forty years in which the world has been turned upside down. There are several million black people looking for land, Sir John. Until they have their land, we are going to experience tragedies like Mau Mau over and over again. The British taxpayer can no longer be expected to bear the burden of that kind of overseas commitment, and as the only land available is what you call the White Highlands, I'm afraid there is no other solution but to surrender it to its rightful owners."

"Good God," John commented, and wondered if his father was turning in his grave. "And don't you think it is going to cost the British taxpayer far more to compensate us for all that land we are going to have to give away?"

The Prime Minister's eyes became opaque. "I'm afraid there is no possibility of compensation, Sir John."

John stared at him.

Macmillan sighed. "Presiding over the dissolution of empire is the saddest task that can fall to a politician. It must inevitably lead to charges of broken promises and downright betrayal. Yet when that empire must be dissolved, there are certain guidelines which must be followed, if one is not to bring on disaster. The first and most important rule must be the greatest good of the greatest number – of the people for whom the politician in question is responsible. My responsibility is the British nation. That nation is some fifty million strong. It is belaboured with problems, some of which may not have escaped you, Sir John. We are in a perennial state of near bankruptcy, and here in Europe we live under the shadow of an atomic holocaust which could sweep us away at any moment. We are Europeans. Here we must stay, and dig our defences, and hope to survive. We have no other course, and we have no resources to spare from that course. The British in Kenya are also my responsibility. But in Kenya there are less than a tenth of one per cent of the British people. Can you expect me to ask that huge majority to tighten their own belts to buy out so small a fraction who for too long have perhaps lived too well? Or to send their sons to defend a group of people who in the eyes of the ordinary man and woman in this country are best known for their scandalous behaviour? I do not think you can, and remain an honest man."

"Therefore you are advising us to get out."

"Or make your peace with Kenyatta, " Macmillan said.

Many settlers did indeed pack up and go. They did so with bitterness in their hearts, and against those they felt had betrayed them. In that group they placed Sir John Barclay, because when there was a mass meeting to discuss and denounce government policy, John was invited to address them, and told them the simple truth – the days of the Happy Valley were over, and they must do as the Prime Minister said: either go, or learn to live as part of a black community.

"When I think," Adèle said, "of the blood that has been spilled, the anguish that has been endured, to seize and hold this land. . . ." She stood on their verandah and looked up the slope to the cemetery, and John knew she was thinking less of his father and mother, or Catherine, than of Lizzie and the baby girls. "I don't think I can leave them, Johnnie"

"I don't intend to," he promised her. "This is my land. I know I can no longer fight for it. But I am going to live here until they throw me out."

He felt sorry for Mal and Emma and the grandchildren, who had been going to inherit all of this. Adrian and Jennie were actually luckier, because the property business continued to thrive. Yet both the boys, who had been born

379

the sons of a millionaire, had very diminished futures to look forward to.

As a man who had seen so much traumatic change, however, he could not help being interested, and even fascinated, by the processes which resulted in the declaration of independence for Kenya, with Jomo Kenyatta, predictably, as the country's first president. There were fiery speeches and frightening threats. Men positively known to be old Mau Mau fighters were free to say whatever they liked about the settlers, and how they should be treated. The guns came out again and were oiled and loaded and worn into the fields. Yet there was surprisingly little violence. It was as if the explosion of Mau Mau had acted as a safety valve, allowing white and black alike to expiate their fury.

More disturbing was the way the economy of the colony collapsed, as the whites fled and the blacks returned to subsistence farming on the once rich grasslands of the high country.

"It is, I suppose, one way of completing the job," John remarked at lunch one day. "Drive us all bankrupt through market forces first, and then take over the land."

Government inspectors, nervous black men in tight-fitting suits arrived in chauffeur-driven shiny new American automobiles, clearly unable to believe they were standing on the verandah of the Barclay residence and being offered tea by the famous Lady Barclay and addressing her even more famous husband as equals. They had walked and ridden, and driven across his fields, assessing and noting, discussing and warning that he would soon be hearing from them. But so far no actual move had been made to sequestrate any of his holding.

"*Can* they bankrupt us?" Mal asked John, while his sons looked from one to the other of the men in anxious wonderment; since birth they had been taught to believe in the permanence of their name and prosperity.

"Not us, thank God. There's money in Switzerland. But they can certainly make it not worth our while to go on living and working here, even without seqestration orders."

"Where would we go, then?" Emma asked.

380

They stared at her, and then at each other. Whatever other people had done, that was not a question the Barclays had ever permitted themselves to ask before.

Ali stood in the doorway. "People coming," he said. "I think it is the big man heself."

John pushed back his chair and went on to the verandah to watch the motorcade coming down the drive. There were police outriders and security men, then the limousine on the bonnet of which flew the black, red and green flag, with shield and crossed spears, of the new Kenya. "Holy smoke," he remarked.

Adèle sent the children upstairs and stood with him, Mal and Emma to either side, as Jomo Kenyatta climbed the steps. "Sir John, Lady Barclay."

"Your excellency." John shook the offered hand. The two men had met on several occasions, but always officially and briefly.

Kenyatta looked out at the lake. "This is a very beautiful place," he remarked.

"We have always found it so," John agreed.

"In a very beautiful country."

"We are just finishing lunch, your excellency," Adèle said. "Will you join us for dessert?"

"Thank you, Lady Barclay, but I have eaten."

"Then a coffee?"

"That would be very nice. I would like to have a word with you, Sir John, in confidence."

"Of course." John showed him into the study, where Adèle herself brought them their coffee.

Kenyatta laid his fly whisk on the desk and sipped his coffee, while John studied him. Had this man really belonged to Mau Mau? he wondered. And could he be an avenging Kikuyu out to throw all the white men out of Kenya?

"You and I must be roughly the same age, Sir John," Kenyatta remarked.

"I would say so."

"Both born here in Kenya. And we both have fought for this sacred soil."

381

John waited. Was he about to be formally expelled?

"Yet our fight has led us in opposite directions," Kenyatta mused. "There are those among my people who regard you as an enemy, for hunting down Joseph Kinshasu."

"I thought they supposed he still lives."

Kenyatta smiled. "Some do. He will be one of the nation's first martyrs. A statue is to be erected to his memory."

"I am sure Joseph would appreciate that," John said. "Wherever he now is."

"He murdered your daughter," Kenyatta observed.

"And I avenged her death. Nothing will ever make me regret that deed, your excellency."

"He was a bloodthirsty killer," Kenyatta said.

John raised his eyebrows.

Kenyatta smiled. "But so, for example, was your Edward the Black Prince, or even William the Conqueror. A nation must have its heroes, and the passage of time softens their vices and enables men to remember their virtues. Yet, you know, a dead hero is safer than a live one, for those who must govern. Sir John, Kenya is on a descending path."

Again John waited, but now his heartbeat was quickening slightly. This interview was not taking the course he had expected.

"Our economy is collapsing," Kenyatta went on, "and with it, international confidence in my government. This must be stopped. The exodus of white men who have much to offer my people must stop. We must build a multi-racial society here, where all men will have equal rights, equal opportunity."

John gazed at him. *This* was a Mau Mau leader?

"But to do this, I need help. Your help."

"To do what?"

"I wish to restore confidence in the white community. I wish to assure them that their farms, while they may have to be reduced in size, will not be taken away from them. I wish to assure you that if *you* wish, as I do, you may die here on Naivasha, and your son may inherit your farm. In return, I wish your support in convincing your compatriots that they have nothing to fear from my government. I am summoning a meeting of all the most prominent white settlers, to hear my proposals and learn my plans. Your invitation to that meeting is already in the post. I would like you to encourage as many settlers as you can to attend, and I would like you to propose a motion accepting what I have to say."

John smiled. "Whether I like it or not?"

"You will like it, because it will be what I have just outlined to you. Your father fought for this land, as you have done. And you were born here. Have you not a duty to it, in sickness and in health, you might say?"

John nodded. "Offer us a reasonable stake, assure our futures, and I will support you to the hilt, Mr President."

Kenyatta smiled and held out his hand. "I think we have just saved our country, Sir John."

That evening, as the sun was setting over the western rim of the Rift Valley, John walked out to the cemetery. He had told Adèle and Mal of the bargain he had struck with Kenyatta. But there was someone else he had also to tell, and they knew he wanted to be alone.

He stood above the graves, looking down at them. "You bargained with the Masai, Father," he said. "And became one of them. You saw your sister murdered by angry men, and avenged her, and yet remained to live with these people, and work with them; and for all the fear you and Mother must have felt, and at times the hatred too, I believe you were happy. I have done no more than follow in your footsteps, and at times have grasped at happiness through the fear and the hate. I pray to God that my sons will have the sense to do the same. And that you will understand."

He turned away, and looked down the slope at the house, now filled with light, and the lake beyond, a sheet of silver in the sunset, where once upon a time two young men had sat together and fished. That was history. But then, so was this afternoon, when he had shaken Kenyatta's hand.

It was time to think of tomorrow, and turn that into history, too.